Glory is bought with Blood

Glory is bought with Blood

N. L. Collier

Copyright © 2020 N. L. Collier
The moral right of the author has been asserted.

Apart from any fair dealing for the purposes of research or private study, or criticism or review, as permitted under the Copyright, Designs and Patents Act 1988, this publication may only be reproduced, stored or transmitted, in any form or by any means, with the prior permission in writing of the publishers, or in the case of reprographic reproduction in accordance with the terms of licences issued by the Copyright Licensing Agency. Enquiries concerning reproduction outside those terms should be sent to the publishers.

This is a work of fiction. Names, characters, businesses, places, events and incidents are either the products of the author's imagination or used in a fictitious manner. Any resemblance to actual persons, living or dead, or actual events is purely coincidental.

Matador
9 Priory Business Park,
Wistow Road, Kibworth Beauchamp,
Leicestershire. LE8 0RX
Tel: 0116 279 2299
Email: books@troubador.co.uk
Web: www.troubador.co.uk/matador
Twitter: @matadorbooks

ISBN 978 1838592 394

British Library Cataloguing in Publication Data.
A catalogue record for this book is available from the British Library.

Printed and bound in Great Britain by 4edge Limited
Typeset in 11.5pt Aldine401 BT by Troubador Publishing Ltd, Leicester, UK

Matador is an imprint of Troubador Publishing Ltd

"For all flesh is as grass, and all the glory of man is as the flowers of the grass…" (Brahms, A German Requiem)
To the fallen of the Great War

„Denn alles Fleisch es ist wie Gras, und alle Herrlichkeit des Menschen wie des Grases Blumen…" (Brahms, Ein deutsches Requiem)
Den Gefallenen des Großen Krieges

I

The nearer to home I got, the more I began to dread it.
Maybe it'll be better this time. I just wish it weren't so bloody difficult.

The first couple of hours were all right, but then Mama said, "Franz, it's such a shame you're not spending all your leave with us. We've hardly seen you since the war began. You look so tired. You need a proper holiday."

I look tired because I've just fucked myself stupid.

"I am having a proper holiday. Karl and I had a really good time, and now I'm here."

Papa looked at me. "I always wonder what sort of 'good time' the two of you have. He's a bad influence."

For God's sake, I'm twenty-bloody-two, not fourteen. All the same, I started blushing.

"And you see him all the time," he went on. "You live together, after all. I can't think why you needed to spend part of your leave with him as well."

I shrugged. "He's my best friend. We wanted to have some fun and forget about the war."

"I don't see why you shouldn't have some fun," Johanna said. "It must be grim at the Front, with men being killed all the time."

I looked at her, surprised. "It's not exactly a bed of roses."

"And I like Karl," she added. "I think he's really nice."

"Johanna, there's a great deal that you don't understand," Papa said severely.

She pulled a face but knew better than to argue.

"And you can take that look off your face, young lady," said my mother. "Karl von Leussow is not the sort of young man we have in mind for you at all."

Johanna and I exchanged looks.

"I only said I liked him," she said.

"Yes, well that's quite enough. You're not likely to see him again, anyway."

I got up and left the room. *I don't want to think about not seeing Karl again.*

After dinner, Papa took me into his study.

Oh God, what's the lecture going to be about this time? The usual bloody crap, no doubt…

"Franz, it grieves me to have to speak to you again on this subject," he said, "but I am very concerned, because you don't seem to have paid attention to me before. The consequences of intimacy with a dirty woman are absolutely dreadful. Do you want to die rotting and insane?"

I almost laughed. "Papa, you don't need to worry about that."

You should be worrying about me going down in flames. That's far more likely.

"Abstinence is the only way of staying healthy. Abstinence before marriage and fidelity within it. And if you're not afraid of disease then you should at least be afraid of eternal damnation."

How can you still believe that? And if there really is eternal damnation then fornication is the least of my worries. I don't even know how many men I've killed. Surely the Almighty would find that more important?

"I want you to promise me that you'll live a clean life, and not give in to the temptations of the flesh."

You what? "Papa, I'm not a schoolboy any more. I'm not even a student."

"So you won't give me your word?"

"Don't you trust me?"

He looked at me. "I'm not sure that I do," he said slowly.

"Thank you very much, Papa. That's a real compliment." I got up.

"Franz, I haven't finished."

"Sorry, but – you talk about marriage. I haven't even met anyone I want to marry, and I'm not likely to. And even if I did, how could I get married when I don't even know whether – I mean how long I… Look, I really don't want to talk about this. I'd just like to enjoy my time here."

And if you've got any sense, you'll shut up and not wreck it with your stupid lectures.

He looked at me. "Yes, of course you do. And we want to enjoy your company as well."

"Then let's go and rejoin Mama and Johanna."

The next day he took me to his club for lunch, and it was even worse than the previous time. Now I wasn't just a pilot, I was the town's very own ace, complete with three medals, and the old buffers wanted to hear stories about the war in the air. I gave them a few fairly bland ones.

"So tell us about your last kill," said Brinkmann.

Seuß looked at him with disgust. He was still wearing a black armband for the son he'd lost at Verdun.

"I really don't think that's appropriate," he said.

"Neither do I," I said. "They're brave men and we have a lot of respect for them – and they have families too."

There was a moment's silence, and then to my relief the conversation turned to business.

When we got home Papa said, "You've got eleven now, haven't you, Franz?"

"Well, ten and one to be confirmed," I replied, rather embarrassed.

"How many do you need for the Pour le Mérite?"

"Twenty. It used to be sixteen but they decided they were giving out too many."

"So you just need another nine."

I stared at him in disbelief. *You want me to shoot down another nine aircraft and probably kill the men in them, just so you can boast about your son with the Blue Max? Don't I have enough blood on my hands already?*

And what makes you think the enemy will let me do that? Don't you realise that I put my life on the line every time I take off, that there are plenty of Tommies and Frenchies itching to add to their own scores, that the sight of me going down in flames would make someone very happy?

"It's not as easy as you make it sound," I said, and I couldn't stop my voice from sounding hard. "They're not exactly keen on being shot down."

Use your fucking imagination, for Christ's sake!

"Anyway, I'm trying not to think about the war. Karl said that while we're on leave the war doesn't exist, and I'd really rather not talk about it."

"No, I suppose not. But it would be quite something to see you wearing one of those."

And of course I wanted the Blue Max, but I was sharply aware that other men had to die for me to get it.

Funny, isn't it? Kill a man in peacetime, and you're a murderer and they'll hang you. Kill enough men in war and you're a decorated hero.

"Who knows what will happen?" was all I said.

"Would you like to go to a dance tonight, dear?" said Mama, changing the subject. "It's a public one to raise money for the wounded. I've got tickets for all of us."

"Yes, all right."

I haven't been to a dance since Karl and I were in Villingen.

That was for the wounded as well – and there's been another year and a half of war since then...

"Oh, good," she said. "We'll be making up a party with the Hertels. You remember their daughter, Maria – she needs an escort." She sighed. "There's such a terrible shortage of young men for partners. The poor girls have to dance with their fathers and uncles and so on. It's such a shame."

We know where the young men are – and it's rather difficult to dance when you're quite rotten.

"I don't suppose the fathers and uncles mind too much," I said.

Johanna giggled. "No, they don't! Last time, I had to dance with Lotte's uncle and he—"

She giggled so hard that she couldn't get the rest of the words out, which was probably just as well.

"What did he do?" Papa demanded.

"Trod on my feet!"

Her eyes met mine and she collapsed laughing. *I wonder where he put his hands.* I burst out laughing as well.

"Well, I don't see why that's so funny," said Mama. "Sometimes I just don't understand the two of you at all."

I got dressed for the dance in a bad mood, because I didn't like being used.

And Maria's a gawky, awkward little thing, and I'm going to have to dance with her and have supper with her. How fucking boring is that? I'd rather have another evening out with Stefan Reddemann. We'd probably end up in the whorehouse again...

I asked Johanna about him as we were waiting for the Hertels.

"He's in Berlin, having surgery on his spine."

"Let's hope they get it right." *Must be tricky, that.*

She went into unnecessary detail about spinal cords, and what happened if they were damaged. I really didn't want to think about that sort of thing.

"Did you ask your friend about helping me to get into medical school?" she asked. "You know, the storm troop officer."

"Yes – he said he'd help if he can." *But first he has to survive – hang on, Alfred's at home.* "Sis – I'm pretty sure he's on convalescent leave in Berlin. I'll write tomorrow – he might be able to have a word with someone."

She flung her arms around me.

"Oh, that's *fantastic!*" I could see her mind working. "What sort of injury has he got?"

"You know, if you didn't want to be a doctor, I'd think you were just plain ghoulish. Broken upper arm."

"Humerus," she corrected.

"Probably."

"Maria's dying to meet you," she said. "All our friends are really jealous of her."

"Why, for God's sake?"

She gestured at my uniform. "Because you're a famous, decorated ace, of course!"

Oh, for fuck's sake. More bloody fawning. Thank God I haven't got the blasted Blue Max.

Just then the Hertels arrived, and I stared dumbly at the young woman with them. Three years had passed, turning an ungainly fifteen-year-old into one of the loveliest girls I'd ever seen.

Instead of her two thick plaits, a mass of auburn hair was piled on her head, revealing the curves of throat and shoulder. My eyes followed them to the low neckline of her dress, and the soft round breasts swelling gently out of it.

I looked back up to her face and saw clear, fair skin, and the sweetest little mouth, and blue eyes looking up at me.

She seemed to think I'd changed as well, and she couldn't take her eyes off my pilot's badge and my ribbons. *I knew they'd be useful for something.*

"Don't you remember me, Franz?"

"Last time I saw you, you were a schoolgirl. I hadn't realised you'd become so beautiful."

I bowed over her hand as elegantly as I could.

She smiled and her mother frowned. *To Hell with old dragons!*

The shortage of young men really was dreadful. I had Maria to myself nearly all evening.

It's a long time since I sat and talked to a girl who's interested in me and not my wallet, I thought during supper. She asked me about the war, and seemed to understand that I didn't want to talk about it.

And I actually managed to forget it as we danced yet another waltz. She was slim and soft in my arms, and her shining blue eyes gazed into mine. The music was perfect, sweet and poignant.

"What's this waltz called?" she asked. "I know it, but I can't remember the name."

"Where the Lemon-trees Bloom," I said.

"Oh – like the poem. You know, I can't remember more than that! Isn't that awful? All the poetry I tried to learn at school and I've just forgotten it."

I steered her towards the open French windows, and in a moment we were in the garden. We sat together in a secluded corner, her small delicate hand almost lost in mine.

"'Do you know the land Where the lemon-trees bloom?'" I began, and found to my surprise that I could remember the whole thing. I was never too keen on Goethe at school and I'd always thought that poem sentimental, but that evening it was just right.

"That's beautiful," she said quietly.

Dare I risk it? I leaned closer to her, and our lips met once, twice, and stayed together in a lingering kiss that tingled down my spine. We kissed again and again, her breasts pressing against my chest.

I might get her into bed if I play this right.

We parted gently. Her hands rested on my chest and she gazed into my eyes. I lifted her left hand to my mouth and kissed her palm slowly, tasting her soft skin, enjoying the hint of sweat on my tongue.

"Oh, Franz!" she whispered breathlessly.

I took her in my arms again, and as we kissed, my hand slid down her back, towards her bottom – *Stop, Franz. She's an innocent young girl, not a tart or a dancer.*

I've only got two days, but if I rush it she'll run away.

It was a huge effort to let go of her. She looked every bit as disappointed as I felt.

I shall take a leaf out of Karl's book and see what I can get away with.

"We'd better get back inside," I said. "What are you doing tomorrow?"

"Nothing much. Mama wants me to go visiting with her, but I expect I can get out of it."

"Would you like to go for a picnic? We could go for a drive in the country, if Papa will let me have the car."

"Oh, yes, that would be lovely! What time?"

"I'll pick you up at eleven."

We got back into the ballroom just as the dance was coming to an end.

I hope no one noticed we weren't here...

We all walked home together, Johanna and the parents in front, Maria and I slightly behind, her arm through mine. We stopped in the black shadow beneath a huge chestnut tree, and I kissed her again.

I took another chance, and slid my hand from her waist to her breast. She quivered and seemed about to pull away, but then she relaxed and kissed me more passionately. I could feel her nipple through the thin fabric, and it hardened under my fingers. I squeezed it and she caught her breath.

"Franz, you shouldn't!" she whispered – and then kissed me again. My hand stayed where it was. She was breathing hard, and I thought of sliding my hand up her thigh—

Not with her parents so close. Don't be stupid.

"We'd better walk on," I said. "The parents."

We emerged from the shadow and caught up with our parents. Hers looked at us and frowned.

Well, it's your own damn fault. You threw us together.

Papa was smiling benignly, as if Maria and I were enjoying a bit of innocent fun. *What would he have thought if he'd seen me in that hotel room with Karl and the dancers?*

I kissed her hand very correctly when we said 'Good night'.

Over a brandy I asked Papa if I could borrow the car.

"Normally the answer would be yes, but I can't get any petrol. Why did you want it, anyway?"

"I'm taking Maria Hertel for a picnic. We'll walk instead. It's not far."

It was only ten minutes or so to the woods – I just wanted to show off in a motor car.

"Are you, indeed? Well, be careful, son. I don't want trouble with her parents. And remember what I told you."

Am I that transparent? I wish I'd given him that promise he wanted. Then he wouldn't be suspicious… I'll have to do better. This has to be a secret. Hers and mine.

I wonder if this will work out, I thought in the morning. *I was going to wear civvies, but she seemed to like the ribbons so uniform might be better.*

The old dragon was waiting for me in the drawing room. Maria was still getting ready, and while I waited I was given a lecture on morality, and reminded how generous Frau Hertel was being in allowing her daughter out with a young man, unchaperoned.

You're wasting your breath. The day after tomorrow I have to go back to the Front. The day after that I could be dead.

Maria came into the room, wearing a summer dress in some floaty pale yellow material which set off her slim figure beautifully. *Very nice – but you'll look even better without it.*

Her face lit up when she saw me. *This is looking promising…*

Her mother saw the look and frowned. "Have a nice time, dear, but remember what I told you."

Jesus, is that all parents know how to say?

"I will, Mama. Don't worry."

"What are you supposed to remember?" I asked after we left the house.

"Oh, to be careful of young men, especially soldiers."

I shall do my damnedest to make you forget. "No car, I'm afraid. Papa can't get the petrol. Do you mind walking?"

"Oh, no. It's such a lovely day. It's nicer than being in a noisy car, anyway. We'll be able to hear the birds."

It was so peaceful in the woods. The sunlight filtered down through the trees, and all we could hear was birdsong and the occasional rustle of squirrels. I looked up through the sunlit leaves to the brilliant blue sky and felt – almost happy.

We stopped in a small clearing. I spread the rug out and unpacked the basket. Mama had made us a cake and I didn't want to think how she'd got the ingredients. There was a bottle of Riesling from Papa's cellar, and it flowed cool and golden into the glasses.

Maria's auburn hair glowed in the sunlight and her eyes sparkled. Her cheeks were flushed – with the wine or with desire?

I leaned towards her and kissed her, drew her towards me, held her tight. Her mouth was so sweet against mine, her lips so soft… I pulled her gently down onto the rug, rested my hand on her breast again, then slid it down over the curve of her hips.

She clung to me, breathing fast. I pulled her skirt up, put my hand on her leg and moved it up her thigh. Her legs parted, and she gave a little moan which set my blood on fire. I started to pull her knickers down—

"No, Franz – no, not here!"

She pushed me away.

Shit, she's going to slap me – or worse still run home and tell her mother I tried to rape her—

Then I realised what she'd said. "Not here… You mean—"

"It's too public. Someone might see us."

"You mean you will, if—"

"If it's private."

"Tomorrow – will you meet me again tomorrow? I'll arrange somewhere, somewhere private."

"Yes – yes." She was kissing me again and I was on fire.

"Two o'clock," I said. I pulled her tight against me, slid my hand under her skirt, then under the soft satin of her knickers.

After a couple of minutes I stopped. I wanted to leave her burning.

My fingers were wet, and I inhaled her perfume and licked my fingers.

"You taste lovely," I said, and she giggled and kissed me again.

We walked slowly back. Her dress was rather creased, but that could just have been from sitting on the ground, and she was still rather flushed, but of course that was the wine rather than anything I'd done – that was what I hoped her mother would think, anyway.

Fortunately the old dragon was out, and I kissed her hand for the benefit of the servants.

"Until tomorrow," I said.

Bloody hell – I'm on a promise. Hope nothing goes wrong.

"How was your picnic, dear?" asked my mother.

I didn't want to talk about it. "Very pleasant, thanks… we're meeting again tomorrow."

"Oh. So we shan't be seeing much more of you then. After all, you're going back the day after – unless you'd forgotten." Mama's voice was sharp and rather bitter.

"Forgotten? Of course I hadn't forgotten." *You try forgetting when you have to go back to the fucking Western Front.*

"I think it's rather sweet," Johanna said.

Sweet? Oh, bloody hell, give me patience! This isn't one of your stupid romantic novels.

That night I had a strange dream. Karl and I were at the station in Berlin, but this time he was seeing me off. I got onto the train, but it was an ordinary train, not a leave train, and it was full of civilians, and for some reason I was in civvies, although Karl was in uniform.

Maria was on the train as well, looking at me with her lovely blue eyes, and Karl stood on the platform, his eyes grey and very sad. The train began to move, and we waved until he was gone from sight, and then Maria smiled at me and said, 'You're all mine now, Franz.'

I woke with a jolt and a profound feeling of unease.

What the hell does that all mean? Was it Maria and me moving off into the future and leaving him behind? I hope to Christ nothing's happened to him. If it has then I won't find out till I get back.

And why did she say, 'You're all mine now'?

I couldn't get back to sleep but lay fretting, trying not to think about the war. *Think about Maria instead,* I told myself in the end, and that did the trick.

In the morning I went to the shabby side of town. A helpful barman told me where I could rent a room by the hour, and I bought a wedding ring which I hoped would fit her.

I was careful to wear a suit. People would see a young man not in uniform, rather than a Leutnant with a pilot's badge, the Iron Cross First Class, and ribbons in his buttonhole and on his chest. I'd be too conspicuous like that, and my picture was on those blasted postcards.

I collected Maria at two. Her mother looked sideways at my suit.

"Not in uniform today?" she asked.

"It's nice to wear civilian clothes sometimes. I don't want to think about the war all the time."

Her face softened slightly. "No, I don't suppose you do."

She gave Maria the same reminder as yesterday, and Maria and I daren't look at each other.

In the hotel room, I unpinned her hair and it fell to her waist, shining in the afternoon sun. I undressed her slowly, desire mounting as one garment after another fell to the floor, revealing her soft curves and her fair, clear skin.

I knew she was a virgin, and I was careful not to rush her – and I didn't want to hurry, anyway. She was giving herself to me, and it actually meant something. And I wanted her to be satisfied, to think of me after I'd gone and wait for me to come back.

She lay in my arms, her head on my shoulder, her hair glowing in the sunlight that came soft and dappled through the lace curtains.

"Oh, Franz!" she said. "I never thought it would feel like that – I was a bit scared in case it hurt – but it was – it was all just so…"

Some minutes later she raised her face and our lips met again…

She actually wanted me, I thought as we left the hotel. *That was a bloody lovely afternoon – just too bloody short. I wish we could have had all night. I'd like to wake up beside you…*

We stopped at the garden gate. She looked up at me, her blue eyes filling with tears, and I stroked her face.

"Write to me, Maria, and send me your picture. Don't cry, now. I'll come back. As soon as I can get more leave, I'll come back."

If I'm alive.

"Oh, Franz, please be careful! I'll write every day."

"I will, I promise – better make it once a week, though, or your parents will make a fuss... Goodbye, Maria. I'll think of you every day."

She was clinging to my arm.

"Come on, sweetheart," I said. "Be brave."

"You have to be, so I must too." She straightened up and dried her eyes. "Goodbye, Franz. I'll wait for you and pray for you."

I kissed her hand, in case we were being watched, and then she turned and walked away from me towards the house, the sun lighting her hair to fire. She opened the door, turned, and blew me a kiss, and I returned the gesture as discreetly as I could.

I walked home slowly. *That was really rather special – there's a freshness and an innocence about her that I've never met before, a lack of knowingness. No one but me has ever touched her...*

And now I've got a girlfriend waiting for me, and I'll get letters like some of the other fellows, and if I do come home again I can have more afternoons like that.

"Did you have a nice time?" asked Mama.

"Yes, very pleasant."

"What did you do?" asked Johanna.

"Oh, we just went for a walk and had coffee – what they call coffee, anyway. What in God's name do they make it from?"

I was trying to avoid further interrogation.

"Acorns," Johanna said, pulling a face. "I suppose you have real coffee at your squadron."

"Er, yes, we do – our technical officer has a secret source."

"Lucky so-and-sos. I don't suppose you wrote that letter?"

"Oh, shit! Sis, I'm really sorry. I'll do it now."

That's let me off the hook. By the time I've finished it, they'll have moved on to something else.

"What letter's that?" Mama asked.

"Oh, Franz is writing to one of his friends to wish him a good recovery," Johanna replied. "He asked me to remind him, because he wanted to get it done before he goes back."

Nice one, Sis. I smiled to myself.

"What happened to him?" Mama asked me.

God, it's one question after another.

"He fell off the side of a mountain in Italy," I said. "Luckily he didn't go very far and he's just got a broken arm."

I sat at the small table, writing, and barely listened to them.

"Here it is, Sis – can you post it for me tomorrow?"

"Yes – but this is his Army address. I thought he was in Berlin?"

"I don't have his home address. They'll send it on to him. It might take a while."

My family gave me the best meal they could, no doubt all on the black at hideous expense.

The next day they came to the station with me, and I wished the train would hurry up and arrive because I had no idea what to say. The odds were so heavily stacked against my ever seeing them again.

Mama had to make a real effort not to cry.

"Look, they haven't got me so far," I said. "I'll be back as soon as I can."

"We'll all pray for you," she managed to say.

Waste of breath – but if it makes you happy…

And then, to my infinite relief, the train was there. I leaned out of the window and waved until they were out of sight, just as Karl had waved to me in Berlin.

I sat back in my seat and lit a cigarette. *I hope Karl's all right, especially after that weird dream. Don't suppose it meant anything, though.*

At Cologne I was joined by an artillery Leutnant, who was rather merry and shared his bottle of schnapps with me.

"Good leave?" he asked.

"Bloody marvellous!" I replied, with a grin that said everything. *Quite an understatement – first Karl and the dancers, and now Maria...*

"Lucky bastard. I'd been home one whole day when my wife started her wrong week. I tell you, I'd been dreaming for months of what I wanted to do when I got home – and here I am, on my way back to sodding Belgium and I've had hardly any."

"Crap timing," I said sympathetically. *I hope you're not going to go on* – but fortunately he fell asleep after about twenty minutes.

It was late afternoon when I got to the airfield, and the whole squadron was up.

"Good leave?" Fellmann asked with a wicked look in his eye.

"Very."

"You look like the cat that got the cream. Going to tell me about it?"

I grinned at him. "Not fucking likely! What's happened while I've been away?"

"Oh, let's see – there've been quite a few victories, so you've got some work to do. The Chief got two, Beilke one, Johnny got two, so he's feeling a bit happier, then Pollow's on four now, and Westermann's on three. I think that's about it."

"You're right, I—"

We were interrupted by the sound of engines, and went outside to watch them land. The Chief was there, and Westermann, and Johnny—

Where is he? My heart was pounding – and then I saw the Albatros with black and white stripes round the fuselage, and it landed safely. *Thank God.*

"Franz!"

He threw his arms round me. I was so relieved to see him after that peculiar dream that I held him tighter than usual, and

I could feel the post-fight tremor running through him. And there was something about being in his arms again…

It's so good to see you again. We understand each other so well.

"Less of that now!" teased Fellmann. "Put him down!"

Karl laughed and shook his head. "Mind your own business, Fellmann! You don't have to watch, you know."

"Ooh! You selling tickets?"

That's not funny. Sometimes Fellmann doesn't know when to stop.

"You're just jealous!" I retorted.

"Going to tell us about Berlin, then?"

"Not bloody likely!" Karl said cheerfully. "Though we might if you buy us enough drinks!"

"Welcome back, Becker," said the Chief warmly. "Good leave?"

"Yes, thank you, sir."

He gathered the others round for the debrief, and I went to our room to unpack.

And then I lingered, because I knew Karl would want to take his extra sweaters off, and I wanted to be alone with him.

I heard voices and three sets of footsteps as he, Horstmann and Patschke came into the hut. And then the door of our room opened and there he was, still laughing at something one of them had said.

I got up as he closed the door. We were in each other's arms in a second, and it felt like coming home.

"I am so glad you're back," he murmured in my ear.

"Oddly enough, so am I!" I meant it. Anywhere was fine by me if Karl was there.

"So how was the rest of your leave?" he asked.

"Oh, all right."

I wasn't sure whether to talk about Maria or not. If she'd been some girl I'd picked up at a dance hall I wouldn't have hesitated, but she'd given me her virginity and I didn't want to kiss and tell.

And that strange dream came back into my mind. 'You're all mine now,' she'd said.

"Only all right?" he asked teasingly.

"Well…" I held him tighter.

"After dark, don't you think?" he said, in that almost soundless whisper you use when you think the enemy is in earshot.

I nodded, and we headed for the mess, arm in arm.

There was a party that night, of course, to welcome me back. We got to our room very late and more than a bit pissed, and both collapsed onto our beds and fell asleep.

I barely even stirred when Schiffer brought the shaving water, and I was still asleep when Karl came back.

He sat on my bed.

"That must have been an exhausting journey," he said. "Or else the rest of your leave wore you out!"

I laughed.

"Come on," he said. "What are you not telling me?"

"What makes you think that?"

I was teasing, of course. There was no way I could keep anything from him.

"Well," I said, "I've got a girlfriend."

His expression changed so rapidly that I wasn't quite sure what I'd seen. I thought I caught a glimpse of sadness, but it was gone before I could be certain.

"Congratulations," he said warmly. "That was quick!"

"I mean, it's not serious," I said, and went on to tell him the whole story.

"So let me get this straight," he said. "After two days of complete sin, you went home and lost no time seducing a virgin. Chapeau, monsieur!"

"I thought I'd take a leaf out of your book, see how far I could get!"

"A virgin… God, most of us would give our eye teeth for that. I hope you treated her properly!"

"Of course I bloody did!" I said with mock offence.

The memory of Kempinski's was suddenly strong, and I saw the same thought in his eyes.

He put a chair under the door handle. We were taking an awful chance and we knew how stupid it was—

There was a knock at the door, and Schiffer called out, "Your hot water, sir."

Shit!

Karl leapt to his feet and moved the chair. Schiffer put the jug on the table and left.

"Jesus, that was close!" I said.

"We'd better stick to darkness," he said. "I mean, if we get caught…"

"Doesn't bear thinking about."

"They'd probably hush it up."

"Do you think so?"

"Oh yes – they wouldn't want the scandal. Two aces caught in a compromising position – just think what the papers would make of that! But they'd separate us. We'd be posted to God knows where."

And never see each other again. It was too awful to contemplate.

I got up and we embraced. *Bugger flying. I'd rather like to stay here with you.*

He undressed as I shaved, and I almost cut myself when I caught sight of his naked body in the mirror.

I felt like singing as I walked to the mess, and wondered why a bit of fooling around should make me so ridiculously happy.

And what about Maria? I asked myself suddenly.

Not the same thing. She's my girlfriend and my lover, while Karl and I just share a bit of harmless fun. And God knows I need some of that while I'm here. There's no reason at all why one should interfere with the other.

"I hope you can still find the way to the Front and back!" Westermann said as I entered the mess.

"Not a chance," said Pollow. "The only thing he can find his way to now is the whorehouse!"

"You're not telling me the Front has moved?" I asked seriously.

Westermann pulled a face. "Afraid not. Victory appears just as distant as ever."

"Well then, we'd better try and bring it a bit closer!" I said.

Our efforts were in vain. *That's what I get for having ten days off – I'm just not quite as sharp.*

Karl, on the other hand, came back victorious.

"God, I'm just falling behind," I grumbled.

"Oh, it'll be our turn one day," Johnny said with a definite edge, which Karl ignored.

It's no use being like that, Johnny.

"Let's go for a walk," Johnny said to me after lunch. "I could do with stretching my legs before the next patrol."

"Me too."

After a couple of minutes he said, "So how was Brandenburg?"

"Flat!"

"Oh, bollocks! I knew you'd say that."

"Actually it was so beautiful I didn't want to leave. You're very lucky – I've never been anywhere else so peaceful."

He sighed. "Yes, it is lovely… And how was Berlin?"

I laughed. "Put it this way – I fell asleep on the train home!"

"I'll bet you did, you lucky bastard! And did you give the dancers my love?"

"No – I was too busy giving them my own!"

It was his turn to laugh. "And so my brother has led you well and truly astray."

I felt myself blushing. *Karl, you can't have told Johnny all about it, surely?*

"Does four people count as an orgy?" I didn't sound quite as casual as I'd hoped.

"I reckon so – though that might depend on who does what and with whom. Still, I've had to use my imagination on that one."

That's a relief – then I realised that Johnny's imagination probably went a lot further than Karl and I had done. *Nothing I can do about that.*

"And I suppose he got a lot of attention in the street," he said, with that edge again. "My kid brother, the famous ace."

"Johnny, thinking like that's not going to help you. It's dangerous. Forget what anyone else does and just concentrate on your job."

"That's easy for you to say – you're not in your younger brother's shadow."

"Age isn't the number on the calendar, is it? It's experience. If you want to envy Karl his score, then you'll have to envy him all the rest of it as well. Do you really want to change places?"

"No, of course I bloody don't! No one in his right mind *wants* to have been at Verdun."

"Quite." I stopped and turned to face him. "Johnny, please keep things in proportion. It's not a competition – we all just do the best we can, to try to bring this shitty business to an end."

"You don't care who outscores you?"

"No. I couldn't give a shit."

That wasn't really true – I knew I couldn't compete with Karl, but I was damned if I wanted any of the others catching me up. The difference was that I didn't think about it in the air.

"You're fuck all use dead," I said.

"Fair point."

I thought he'd listened, but later Kühn remarked on how impetuous Johnny had been on their patrol.

"Just flew straight at it, and it was one of those Bristol things. I don't know how he didn't get hit."

Karl just looked at me and raised his eyebrows. I shrugged. *There's nothing more I can say to Johnny. I just hope it doesn't end with him in a box, for Karl's sake.*

It was party time again, for Karl's latest victory, and we started with a really good sing-song around the piano.

After we'd sung all the favourite Air Service songs, Patschke said, "How about some marching songs? I haven't sung any of those for ages."

"Why not?" Karl said, and played the introduction to 'The Watch on the Rhine'. We sang that with gusto, and then he went onto 'Three Lilies', 'Annemarie'...

Wonderful how cheerfully we can sing about getting killed.

"What about 'I Stand in Darkest Midnight'?" said Horstmann.

"Soppy! Soppy!" said Patschke. "She loves me still and all that crap! You got another flower letter today, didn't you?!"

"At least it's not about death," Horstmann retorted.

"It gets my vote too," I said.

Karl winked at me. "Well, for all those lucky enough to have a sweetheart – here we go!"

Patschke's right – it is horribly sentimental. All the same, I couldn't help wondering whether Maria was thinking about me.

The Chief, Horstmann and Beilke all sang with feeling, and I noticed that Pollow had a faraway look in his eyes, as did Johnny, who presumably was thinking about Alex.

"Sleep well in your quiet little room," we sang, "And think of me in your dreams."

I hope she does. I hope I get a letter soon.

There was a moment's silence, and then Pollow said, "Play us some more marches. How about 'The Glory of Prussia'?"

Karl stiffened, and the shadow spread itself across his face.

"Come on," I said. "This may be a Royal Prussian Jasta but some of us are from other parts!"

"That's right," said Widemayer and Kühn together.

"You're outnumbered," Karl said and struck up the first chords, at parade march tempo. He had such a bleak expression that I stared out of the window rather than look at him.

You'll have another nightmare.

"Let's have something different," I said.

"Good idea," said the Chief.

Karl started to play the English dying pilot song. We laughed, and everyone who knew the words joined in, then we had great fun teaching it to those who didn't.

In the middle of all that, Bleif announced dinner. The shadow still lurked in Karl's eyes, and was only slightly dispelled when the games got under way.

Late in the night we were sitting on the floor as usual, drinking brandy and smoking. There was too much noise for us to talk, but it wasn't as if we needed to.

Johnny gave us a rather arch look across the room and I felt a flare of irritation, then blushed as I realised that I couldn't tell him to wipe it off his face.

Karl got quite thoroughly pissed, which was unusual for him. I think he just wanted to pass out when he hit his bed, in the hope that it would stop him dreaming.

It seemed to work – he didn't wake me up, and the next thing I knew, Schiffer was knocking with my shaving water.

Shit, it's dawn already – I must have been in bed all of three hours.

There's that promise I made…

"Are you awake?" I asked.

"Yes. Have been for a while."

I put the chair against the door, turned the light off and went over to his bed, and as in Kempinski's I was astonished at myself.

I wouldn't do this with any other man born.

"And now I really do have to get moving," I said.

He put his light on and I stood up.

"Turn round," he said, and I obliged, enjoying the appreciation in his eyes.

There was no more time left and I dressed quickly. I daren't be late for briefing.

This time I actually did sing as I walked to the mess. Johnny fell in beside me.

"Someone's happy," he said softly. "Leave my brother in bed, did you?"

My back hairs stood on end. There was something about Johnny that I'd never really liked, and I wasn't sure I could trust him.

"No one gets up at this time unless he has to," I said casually.

"Too right," he said, and I saw his grin in the light from the mess windows. After a moment he murmured, "Glass houses."

"What?"

"My house is made of glass, Franz. I'm not about to throw stones."

So why let me know that you know? And what do you get up to?

And then he added, "Just be careful – keeping secrets in this place is fucking near impossible. There are some with very keen antennae."

"Point taken."

Thank God he just wanted to warn me, that it isn't about having power over us – but he wouldn't want Karl disgraced. There's still a strong bond between them, in spite of his jealousy over the scores.

I moved towards the steps but he laid his hand on my arm.

"One more thing," he said, so quietly that I could hardly hear him, "if you think anyone else knows, tell me – and I'll make sure he's so bloody compromised he'll never say a word." I stared at him, astonished, and he added, "Oh, not in *that* way – but everyone has secrets and I'm pretty good at finding out what they are."

Devious, untrustworthy, and positively bloody Machiavellian – and a very good ally to have.

Something must have brought me luck, because I shot down a Sopwith.

Maybe the Devil's rewarding me for sin... I had to laugh at the idea that there really could be a figure with horns and a tail, presiding over eternal damnation. *If there is Hell then it's called war.*

If I was happy, Patschke was positively ecstatic. He'd got his first, a two-seater.

"Now no one's on zero," he said happily.

"Party time!" Johnny said gleefully.

"Not again!" I said. "I haven't recovered from last night yet."

"Tell that to the poor Tommy you just sent to Hell," he replied.

Karl was lingering over breakfast, with a pot of coffee and a full ashtray. I helped myself to rolls and ham and joined him.

"Anything left in that pot?"

"It's probably cold. Let's have another."

He looked far more relaxed and happy than the evening before, and gave me a warm smile which I returned.

We'd better be careful what sort of looks we exchange...

"Hey, well done, Becker!" said Kühn.

"Another?" Karl asked.

I nodded. "If it's confirmed."

He was still waiting for confirmation of his latest victory – not that he cared.

"Well done! That'll be another party."

"I'm not sure I can face another just yet!"

"How about Claudette's instead, then?" Karl said.

"Bloody good idea," said Horstmann.

"She loves me still!" sang Patschke.

"Oh, shut up!" Horstmann retorted. "She's not here, is she?!"

"And she'll never know what you get up to," Fellmann agreed, with a look at Johnny.

"That's right, Mr Two Fiancées!" teased Westermann.

"Honestly, haven't you sorted that out yet?" asked Widemayer.

"No, he's just being greedy," said Beilke. "Keeping them both warm until he makes his mind up."

"Lucky bastard," said Patschke.

Johnny pulled a face. "Hardly…"

Karl looked at me. "Fancy a walk before I go flying?"

"Definitely."

The morning was already very warm.

"It'll be July in a couple of days," I said as we strolled arm in arm towards the edge of the airfield.

"Hard to believe, isn't it?"

After a few minutes we were out of sight of the huts and the hangars, thanks to the slightly rolling ground. His hand slipped into mine, our fingers interlaced, his large, capable hand so different to Maria's small, delicate one.

Neither of us said anything. There was no need.

Everything else can go to Hell when I'm with you.

Even Maria?

She was how many hundred kilometres away.

All the same… "I'm not too sure about Claudette's," I said.

He looked at me in astonishment. "You mean you don't want a fuck?"

"Of course I bloody do – it's just… now I've got a girl waiting for me—"

He stopped dead. "Franz, you're off your fucking head. You can't go without a fuck until your next leave. That's just insane." *Because you might never get another leave*, he meant. "Look, it's just commercial, isn't it? It's got nothing to do with emotion. And you need it. Everyone does."

"The Chief doesn't go."

"Yes, he does," Karl said. "Just not with us. And he's actually engaged, and so are Horstmann and Johnny, and they go too. No one's going to tell her, are they?"

"No… You're right."

We stopped and sat on the grass, our hands still linked. It was a lovely, sunny little hollow, and in the hypnotic warmth I realised how tired I was.

"I know I'm bloody well right." He yawned and stretched. "God, I could do with going back to sleep, never mind flying. I barely slept at all." He looked at his watch. "One hour to go."

"Why don't you have a kip?"

"You don't mind?"

"Of course I bloody don't, you stupid bastard."

He lay on his side on the grass, facing me. "Wake me after fifteen minutes, then?"

"If I'm still awake myself!"

I sat looking down at him as his eyes closed and his face relaxed. *We could be miles away from the war. Once it's over we'll go on holiday somewhere, maybe to Italy…* My eyes started to close as well.

Better not lose track of the time. I don't want to get him into trouble.

After fifteen minutes I shook his shoulder gently. "Wake up, Sleeping Beauty!"

"Hm?" He opened his eyes and they lit suddenly with warmth as he focussed on me.

"Your fifteen minutes is up. Time to go to briefing."

"Oh, shit!" He sat up reluctantly.

"Go and shoot down a Tommy, and we can have a joint celebration!"

"Your wish is my command!"

We strolled back, hand in hand for as long as we dared.

I went back to bed and had a horrible vague dream of disaster, and lay feeling sick and sweaty. My hangover was a lot worse, and I dragged my thumping head to the mess in search of more coffee.

The heat was oppressive, and the clouds were building to massive proportions. *I hope they get back before the storms begin.*

I was on my second cup of coffee and third fag when we heard aircraft engines. Beilke, Pollow and Patschke, who were playing skat, looked towards the windows.

"Ours," said Patschke.

And hopefully all of ours, went unsaid.

Five pilots came into the mess. Karl's face was still, his eyes cold and hard, and Widemayer was white and trembling so much he could hardly get his cigarette to his lips.

Westermann was not with them.

"What happened?" Beilke asked quietly.

"Westermann went down in flames," Karl said heavily. "One of those Bristols."

Widemayer sat down, staring into space, the side of his face twitching.

"Are we going to be able to bury him?" asked Horstmann, who had followed them in with Johnny and Kühn.

Karl shook his head. "We were over Tommy-side."

He started fitting a cigarette into the holder with those slow, deliberate actions.

The heavens opened, accompanied by a deafening clap of thunder. I jumped half out of my skin. Karl dropped cigarette and holder, and swore.

"Poor bastard," said Johnny. "I just hope he was dead before the fire took hold."

Widemayer got up and rushed out.

The rain drummed on the roof with exactly the same rhythm as on the day Kurt died, and for a moment I was back in the shell-hole, his blood running into the water—

Karl had got his cigarette lit and was staring at the floor, wreathed in smoke.

Poor Westermann. What a vile way to go.

And seeing it won't have done Widemayer any good. Wonder where he went.

"I'd better go and make my report," Karl said, and headed for the office.

The rest of us sat smoking and reading, and trying not to think.

An hour later Widemayer hadn't reappeared. The trip to Claudette's was on, as it was pissing down. Losing another comrade had made us even keener to go and have some fun while we could – most of us, anyway. Horstmann went and knocked on Widemayer's door, and reported that he'd said he didn't feel like it.

Seven of us were just about to squeeze into the car when Johnny said, "Hang on a sec – there's something I want to say to Fellmann."

He came back after about five minutes to blasts on the horn from Karl and shouts of 'Get a fucking move on!' from the rest of us.

There were two men in the salon: Hans Lethen von Thingy und Whatnot and his friend. They scanned our faces as we came in.

I went straight up to them. "You won't be encountering my late friend Westermann again. He was killed today."

"I'm very sorry to hear that," said the friend, actually sounding as if he meant it.

"So am I," said Lethen. I must have given him a sharp look, because he added, "I behaved very badly that day."

"Well, he'd had a few as well," I conceded. "But it hardly matters now, so if you'll excuse me—"

"Yes, of course."

I rejoined the others.

"Is one of those the staff bastard that Westermann called out?" Beilke asked quietly.

"The smaller one is," I said. "He almost apologised just now."

"Bit fucking late," said Horstmann.

Four girls entered the room, and one of them was Christine. *Westermann does like a nice armful of flesh*, I thought, looking at her magnificent posterior. *And there was that time he was talking about having some girl's nice big arse against his groin, just as Fellmann came in to say that Buchholz was dead...*

Did like a nice armful. Poor sod won't be doing that ever again.

I hope she wasn't sweet on him, or she'll be like Marie crying her eyes out over Lensch.

Fortunately she went to join the carmine-collared. Anne and a new girl came over to us.

"I reckon Franz and Patschke should have first go," said Johnny, "being as this is their victory celebration."

"I'm not going to argue with that!" I said, just as Patschke said, "Cheers, Johnny!"

As I went upstairs I decided not to make comparisons with Maria. *This is all you can get while you're here, so enjoy it for what it is.*

Anne knew what she was doing, and I did feel a lot more relaxed afterwards – but I was more aware than ever of the functionality, of the lack of warmth.

There's no way this will ever affect Maria and me. Even if I were trying to be faithful, it wouldn't count – and she's never going to know about it.

Widemayer didn't appear in the mess before dinner, and Fellmann went and got him. He sat at table looking like a ghost, and ate hardly anything. The Chief noticed, of course, and took Johnny into his office after coffee, before the wake got under way.

We'd put one of Johnny's sketches of Westermann on the wall, and the Chief raised his glass. "Our fallen comrade, Leutnant Westermann."

As we drank I could almost hear him saying, 'Never mind that stuffy nonsense – get on with the bloody party! And I'll be seeing you again soon. There's plenty of room for you all here.'

We got on with the party, aware that the fellow with the scythe was just outside the door.

Poor old Widemayer got so pissed that he was sick out of the window, and then slumped in a heap on the floor.

"We'd better get him to bed," said Beilke. "Give me a hand, Karl?"

"Of course."

Johnny came with us.

"That's the end of my party," he said as we deposited Widemayer onto his bed.

We looked at him.

"The Chief said I'm to sleep in here until Westermann's replacement arrives, and to leave both our pistols with Fellmann overnight. Sorry, Beilke – I forgot to tell you."

"Ah," said Karl. "Probably very wise."

Johnny shrugged. "He could still go off and shoot himself while I'm asleep – no one can lock his door, can he?"

Beilke was looking rather blank, and Karl told him about Bruch on the way back to the mess.

"Shit… And that was in that room?"

"Superstitious bollocks," I said firmly.

II

We gave Westermann the send-off he would have wanted, and the eastern horizon was purple as Karl and I headed for bed.

"I thought you said you weren't up for another party," Karl said, sounding almost sober.

"Well, y'know..." I had a horrible thought. "'m I down f'dawn?"

He laughed. "Neither of us is – so shut up and get into bed."

In the morning he looked dreadful, and I realised he hadn't slept. *Because it's all going round in your head or because you're too scared of the nightmares?*

Fellmann told him his latest would remain unconfirmed and he just shrugged. He was far more pleased when I received the opposite news.

If he was afraid of going to sleep then he was right. A couple of nights later he had a shocker of a nightmare, screaming and shouting.

I woke him and held him tight until the worst of his shaking was over, and then got into his bed.

This was bound to happen – seeing Westermann burn after having to play that music for everyone...

"Sorry, Franz," he whispered in my ear.

"Don't be daft," I murmured. "This is hardly a chore!"

The sun was pouring through the thin curtains and I started awake with a real jolt. *What the fuck time is it? Shouldn't I be flying by now?*

I was still in Karl's bed, and he was lying awake staring at the ceiling.

"Morning," he said softly.

"What time is it?"

"God knows."

I reached out to pick up his watch from his bedside table, and fell onto the floor with a thump. He started laughing.

"Bastard!"

"You're the bastard, rushing out of bed like that," he replied, his eyes warm. "Come on, get back in."

"It's eight o'clock."

"So what?"

We made it to the mess in time for a hasty breakfast before briefing.

"It looks as if the Tommies are building up to something," the Chief said. "There are reports of increased traffic between the Channel ports and the Ypres area…"

"Any questions?" I asked Widemayer and Pollow after the boss had finished.

They shook their heads. Widemayer had dark rings round his eyes, but that went for most of us, and he hadn't eaten breakfast. His uniform was looser, and his face thinner.

So long as he does the job. We're all expendable.

That thought came back with a pang as we suited up. Karl exchanged a joke with Zaffke, and as his laughter rang out it hit me just how terrible it would be to lose him.

That's why you should never have got into this, I told myself – and realised at once that I was glad I had, whatever was to come.

I almost changed my mind an hour later. We were attacked by a flight of SE5s, and were just keeping them away from the two-seaters when their Sopwith friends joined the party. That made too many guests for my liking.

Then one of the two-seater observers slumped in his cockpit. The attacking Sopwith closed in tighter, and as I went after it my right gun jammed. I gave the Tommy another burst with the left one.

Come on, break off so I can clear the jam—

An SE5 was trying to turn in behind me, one of the Sopwiths smashed into another, shearing half a wing off itself and the tail off the other, and I only just missed them.

That's two less of the bastards.

I was pulling away from the SE5, and I grabbed the hammer and tried to free the gun.

Come on, you bastard! I gave it a hard whack, and the hammer flew out of my hand and over the side. *Fuck.*

Three blue Albatri were diving into the fight. One curved in behind an SE5, and in a second the two of them were in an almighty ding-dong. As they turned I saw the black and white stripes round the fuselage and my heart leapt.

The two-seater with the unconscious observer had left, and the other observer fired two white flares, the signal to head back. Somehow I had to get Widemayer and Pollow out of the fight. They were both up to their eyeballs.

I fired a white, and then another. Pollow saw, and abandoned his pursuit of an SE5.

Come on, Widemayer!

The observer waved frantically and pointed east. *Widemayer will have to go back with Karl and co.* I signalled to Pollow to join me.

The Tommies didn't want us to leave – not with those nice photographs. Twice we had to turn and meet attacks, and the second time I saw Karl in a tail chase, sandwiched between two SE5s. It took every scrap of will to turn away from him.

The photographs were vital. My best friend's life was not, and I could only hope that we would meet again.

We saw the two-seater safely back to their base. The other was already parked, the ground crew lifting the observer out of the cockpit. *Burkhardt*, I thought as we started climbing back up.

Pollow dropped abruptly behind and below, and I turned to see him gliding down, his propeller stopping and starting. He was too low to reach the two-seaters' airfield, and had no choice but to land on a piece of rutted ground.

His Albatros touched down and turned over almost immediately.

After what felt like eternity he crawled out from underneath it, got up, ran away from the wreck and waved to me.

Thank fuck for that. I flew overhead the two-seaters' base again, rocked my wings to get their attention, then headed straight for Pollow and his aircraft. I waved to him and headed home, hoping they'd got the message.

Uhlig looked at me in dismay as I taxied in alone and parked.

"Is Braun about?" I asked. "And Ziegler?"

"Yes, sir. Er—"

"So far as I know they're both in one piece," I said.

"Oh, good – sorry, sir, I'll just be a moment."

The familiar tremor set in as I waited for them. The Chief was approaching from the main hut, followed by Kühn, Johnny and Fellmann. His eyebrows almost hit his hair when he saw just me there.

"Both two-seaters got back safely, sir," I said, "but one observer was hit and seemed unconscious. We had a fight with a flight of Sopwiths and another of SE5s, then Leussow K and his Kette joined us. Widemayer's still with them, because he didn't see the signal to disengage, and Pollow had engine trouble and turned his bus over in a field near the two-seater base, but he's unhurt. With a bit of luck they've picked him up."

"I see. Did they get their pictures?"

"Yes, sir."

"Good. And did you see anything?"

"It's hard to say, sir – there did seem to be a bit more activity than usual, but not a huge amount."

Where the fuck is Karl? They should have been back by now – oh Christ, I hope that fucking Tommy didn't get him—

Get a grip, Franz. You had to disengage to escort the two-seaters home.

"Here they are now," said Fellmann.

To my infinite relief, four Albatri were approaching the field. I took a long drag on my cigarette, feeling almost sick.

Fellmann put his arm round my shoulders.

"Valhalla's full again," he said with a grin. "And now we'd better go and fetch Pollow the Wrecker. He's obviously just as bad as the rest of you!"

"Sorry I left you in the lurch," I said to Karl in our room.

"Don't be so bloody stupid! There was nothing else you could do."

All the same, I hated leaving you.

"Widemayer never saw the signal," I said. "I don't know where his eyes were."

"Oh, he came in very handy – got that Tommy off my tail and bloody nearly got one… Don't know about you, but I'm starving."

After lunch I suggested a walk. Something was bothering me.

When we were safely out of earshot of everyone, I asked, "So what did you say to Johnny about us?"

He stopped and turned to face me.

"Nothing," he said with complete sincerity. Karl was the worst liar I've ever met, and I knew he was telling the truth.

"It's just he knows." I told him about the conversation a few days earlier.

"Ah, I see… Johnny made up his mind months ago that you and I were having it off, long before Berlin – told me he knew perfectly well what I was doing. I told him we weren't but he wouldn't believe me."

"So that's what it was about," I said without thinking.

"What?"

"I didn't mean to eavesdrop – I was passing his office when he was acting CO, and I heard the two of you talking. I don't know what you meant about him, though."

"What did I say?"

"That he should keep it in his trousers and not mess people about."

He sighed. "Johnny's been fucking Fellmann ever since he got here, and it's more than a bit cruel, because he's just having fun while Fellmann's fallen for him properly – and falling for Johnny is not a good idea."

So that's what Johnny meant about glass houses. "But hasn't Johnny fallen for Alex?"

"Oh, I don't think he fancies Fellmann – he's doing it because he can, and he knows Fellmann's clean. And let's face it, we've both forgotten what a bare fuck feels like."

I didn't want to admit I'd made love to Maria without a condom.

"There's no nice way of saying this," he went on, "but Johnny's being a bastard. He knows perfectly well how Fellmann feels, and he's just taking advantage."

"So let me get this straight," I said, laughing. "Johnny's engaged officially to Elfriede, and unofficially to Alex, but while he's here he's giving it to Fellmann."

"That's it."

"But that's far too bloody complicated! How's he going to sort it all out?"

"He only has to sort out the women, doesn't he? Fellmann's never going to breathe a word – he's just going to get hurt whatever happens, the poor sod."

I was rather confused. "But don't you have to be queer to fuck another bloke?"

"Oh, no – you just have to have a hard cock and the opportunity to get away with it. Happens in prison all the time, they say. You don't have to worry, though, Johnny won't tell about us."

We strolled on. Karl's words about a bare fuck were niggling me.

"Karl – a girl can't get pregnant her first time, can she?"

He burst out laughing. "Of course she bloody can! Pigs do, and dogs, and horses – so long as the female's in her fertile days, it doesn't matter whether it's her first time or her hundredth." He paused, and then asked, with sudden seriousness, "Franz, you didn't?"

I didn't want to answer.

"You stupid fucking idiot. What the fuck did you do that for?"

"I just didn't think – I'm so used to using a condom as protection against disease, I just forgot about pregnancy. And someone did tell me once—"

"That a virgin won't get pregnant. Well, it's bollocks. You'll just have to hope she doesn't, because it'll be a real bastard for the poor girl if she has your baby and you're dead, won't it?" He laughed. "And a real bastard for you if you're alive!"

Shit. That would mean marriage – and I hardly know her. That wasn't quite true – we'd known each other since childhood, but I'd never even fancied her until that evening, and I certainly didn't know her well enough to want to marry her.

There was a very long silence, by the end of which we were almost back at the mess.

The next day the post came, and Fellmann handed me a letter addressed in a very girlish hand. *About time, too.*

"Lucky fellow!" he said with an outrageous wink.

Oh, Christ – Johnny's told him Karl and I are lovers, and there's absolutely nothing I can say.

Beilke noticed the writing as well. "Who's the lucky girl?"

"Mind your own business!" I retorted with a laugh.

"That's why you wanted to sing 'I Stand in Darkest Midnight,'" said Horstmann.

"Haven't you lot got letters of your own to read?!"

I sat alone in a corner and opened the letter.

'Dear Leutnant Becker,' it began, 'I bought a postcard yesterday with your picture on it – as I've got yours it seems only fair that you should have mine.'

And there was a small photograph of a rather lovely young woman, attached to the second page. The letter went on to say, among other things, that she would be very happy to see me if I were ever in Stettin.

I started laughing.

Karl gave me a very quizzical look, and I handed him the letter. Two minutes later he was laughing as well.

"What's so funny?" asked Johnny.

"May I?" Karl asked me.

"Go ahead!"

He read the letter out, with sentimental emphasis, to the delight of the mess.

"Let's see the picture!" demanded Kühn, and Karl gave it to him. It made the rounds, to general approval.

"Pity you've just had your leave," remarked Beilke. "You'd have been on a promise there."

"Oh, I didn't lack female company," I said nonchalantly. "And without going all that way."

"Pollow's from somewhere round there," said Fellmann. "You could pass her on to him!"

"No, no," I said, "it's me she wants – but when he gets to five I'm sure he'll be a good substitute!"

"I'm not going to get to five with no aeroplane," Pollow said mournfully.

"You shouldn't have wrecked the one you had!" replied Fellmann. "You're just going to have to wait for the replacement."

"Talking of replacements," I said, "when does Westermann's arrive?"

"Day after tomorrow, I hope – he's coming from Albatros with a new aircraft."

"Does that mean he's a novice?" asked Johnny.

"'Fraid so. We got a bit of stick for poaching the last two."

"Didn't realise my CO cared!" said Kühn.

That evening there was another batch of post, which had got stuck somewhere. And there was a letter from Maria, a lovely warm letter that started, 'My dearest Franz,' and went on to say how much she'd enjoyed our three days together and how much she missed me.

'I pray for you every night when I go to bed, and ask our Dear Lord to protect you and bring you home to me soon, and I go into the church every day and light a candle for Our Lady – so you can see I'm doing everything I can to keep you safe! I can't wait to see you again, and to have another wonderful afternoon. Please, my dearest, be as careful as you can…'

I suddenly felt horribly guilty: not only did I fuck whores at every opportunity, but there was what Karl and I got up to. I wasn't sure which was worse – but it was all just physical release, and far more pleasant than doing it myself.

Karl and I don't fuck and we're not going to. I didn't ask myself why that would make things different.

There's a bit too much religion in this letter… it makes me realise how thoroughly I've lost my own faith. I suddenly thought of Max Levy, threatened with marriage to an observant girl and a lifetime of dull Sabbaths. Being tied to a strict Catholic would be just as bad – not that I needed to worry about that.

She's doing it because she cares about me and it's all she can do. I wrote back at once, and asked her to send me her photo.

'I won't send you mine in case that gets you into trouble – it would be better to buy one of those postcards, and make sure it's got more than one pilot on it.'

I suppose I was protecting myself as much as her – I didn't want her parents thinking there was anything serious between us. That was hopelessly naïve of me. I'd taken her virginity, and if they found that out I'd be marrying her, baby or not.

The Chief put the squadron up after lunch the next day, and nine Albatri in three Kettes made a truly magnificent sight. Pollow waved us off, looking distinctly miserable.

Once again I had to watch Karl fighting for his life, but this time I had the satisfaction of getting a Sopwith off his tail. Ten minutes later he returned the favour.

That's more like it, I thought on the way home – *it was good to fight together again. All the same, I'd rather not do too much of it.*

Two new Albatri stood on the flight line, and waiting for us in the mess were our old friend Platzer and a skinny blond officer cadet with a shiny new pilot's badge.

Jesus – he looks about fifteen. I must be getting old.

They got up as we came in.

"Well," said Platzer, "there aren't many squadrons that boast two Pour le Mérites. The Albatros Works sends its compliments – which will be arriving by train tomorrow."

"That's very decent of them," said the Chief with a smile, and I wondered what Fellmann had managed to wangle for us. He turned to the skinny chap. "And you must be Brettschneider."

"That's right, sir," said the boy, with awe in his voice.

"Welcome to the squadron."

The Chief shook his hand warmly and then introduced us all. *Poor kid, he hasn't got a cat in Hell's of remembering our names.*

"Right, come to my office, and I'll brief you on the next few days."

"On his last few days, more like," muttered Beilke as the Chief's office door closed.

"Does that mean I've got a new room-mate?" asked Widemayer.

"Oh, I should think so," said Johnny.

"Well, I hope he doesn't snore like you do!"

"You'll only have him for a week or so!" Horstmann said cheerfully. "Honestly, he looks like a bloody schoolboy."

"Let's hope he doesn't fly like one," I said.

"You are such a bunch of charming optimists," said Platzer.

Pollow came in, beaming. "She's beautiful!"

"Don't tell me some girl's sent you her picture!" said Johnny.

"No chance," Kühn chipped in. "What girl would want an ugly bastard like him!"

"I think he means his lovely new aeroplane," Platzer said with pretend gravity.

"Which he'll get to fly in about half an hour," said the Chief as he came back into the mess.

"I'm sorry we're going to abandon you," he said to Platzer, and then added, "Unless you'd like to do Brettschneider's mock combat?"

Platzer's face lit up. "It would be my pleasure!"

"My usual stakes are that the new fellow stands me a glass of fizz for each time I'd have shot him down, and I buy him a bottle of brandy if he'd have got me."

Platzer grinned. "Sounds fine to me."

When we got back, Platzer was halfway through a bottle of champagne, and poor Brettschneider was looking rather stunned.

"Run rings round you, did he?" Johnny asked sympathetically.

Brettschneider just nodded.

"Did he tell you he's a test pilot for Albatros?" Karl asked him.

"No – crikey, are you really?" The boy turned to Platzer, wide-eyed.

"Yes, and he was a Fokker pilot before that," I said. "You were set up very thoroughly – but there are plenty like him on the other side."

"Don't worry," said Horstmann. "You won't be going anywhere near the lines until the boss thinks you're ready."

Because we need to be able to rely on you, no one said.

We got Platzer completely pissed, and Karl deposited him gently on the spare bed in Fellmann's room.

Everyone got back safely from the dawn flight, just in time to see a rather pale Platzer getting into the car with Fellmann.

"Just off?" the Chief asked.

"Yes – thank you all very much for your hospitality. My head will remember it for at least a week! Oh – Leutnant Fellmann should be picking up the greeting from Albatros at the station."

We waved him off with shouts of 'Come back soon!' which probably reverberated rather painfully.

"Right," the boss said to Brettschneider after breakfast. "You can fly against Leussow K this morning, and then against Becker tomorrow. If they give you a good report, you'll be against me the day after. In the meantime you can get more flying and gunnery practice."

"Yes, sir." He looked at Karl rather apprehensively, from his face to his Blue Max and back again. "May I ask what your score is now, sir?"

"Stuck on twenty-one – I'm having a run of them not being confirmed. Look, we're all very informal here. You say 'sir' or 'Squadron Commander, sir' to the Chief, but the rest of us just use names – and everyone calls me Karl, and my brother Johnny, because it's easier, and it's 'du' all round. Apart from the Chief, of course, and 'Sie' is fine by him."

"Oh, right."

"And that name of yours is a bit of a mouthful," said Johnny. "What did your classmates call you?"

"Er—"

Johnny grinned at him. "All right – you don't have to tell us!"

"How about Bretti?" suggested Patschke. "You all right with that?"

"Oh, yes – that's fine."

"Come on, then," said Karl. "Let's go to the flight line and I'll give you a few pointers before we fly."

"Yes, sir – I mean Karl."

He did look very awkward using Karl's first name, and I realised that he probably thought Karl was old enough to be his father. The lines in Karl's face seemed to get deeper every day, and the eyes that Verdun had hardened softened only when they looked at me.

I wonder what Karl feels when he has to meet his own eyes in the mirror.

When I went to our room to fetch my extra clothes before the second flight, I looked at myself and was reassured to see that I didn't look anything like as hard or as worn.

Karl's been at the Front too long, and in some of the worst places. They should send him to Döberitz for a few months, but of course they won't – they need to keep the Pour le Mérites at the Front, for the propaganda value.

Widemayer was in my Kette, and as we climbed through three thousand he started lagging behind. At three and a half he gave me a thumbs-down, and turned back.

That had better be genuine, my friend, I thought as Horstmann and I carried on over the Front. *I'll be asking for a report on that engine, for the Chief. If the two of us meet a Tommy formation we're going to have our hands full.*

That didn't stop us getting stuck in properly when we spotted four Sopwiths, trying to cross over to our side of the lines. We weren't having that.

Neither of us got one, but neither did they get us, and we sent them back west again. It was probably the wind and their fuel state that made them disengage, but we patted ourselves on the back all the same.

When we got back, Uhlig and Schiffer had the cowlings open on Widemayer's aircraft, and Fellmann had his head in the engine bay. Widemayer was looking on, smoking.

"What happened?" I asked him.

"She was fine until about two and a half, and then she just started running a bit rough and losing power. It just got worse from there."

Either you're a bloody good actor or you're telling the truth.

Fellmann emerged, with a large smear of oil on his forehead.

"Like the warpaint," I said. "What do you reckon?"

"We'll do some full power runs," he said. "My guess would be that she's down on compression. You all thrash these poor engines to bits – I know, I know, you don't have any choice, but it does shorten the life."

I clapped him on the shoulder. "You know, Fellmann, I couldn't give a shit about engine life – just my own!"

"I'll second that!" said Widemayer.

Fellmann laughed. "Fair enough – I'd say the same in your shoes!"

Karl and Bretti were sitting on the grass beneath the mess windows. Karl's hands made graceful arcs in the air as he spoke, in the manner of all pilots. The right hand was clearly attacking the left, which didn't use enough bank…

The sun lit his light brown hair red and gold, and full-blooded life brimmed from his eyes.

Bretti asked him something, and his hands flew again. He seemed more vigorously alive than the others, like an oil painting among watercolours.

"Come on, Franz, let's get some coffee." Johnny had an eyebrow raised, and I realised I'd been gazing at Karl. When we reached the steps he muttered, "For God's sake don't look at him like that in public, you stupid bastard."

Shit. I hadn't realised I was looking at him like anything. "Like what?"

"Your tongue was practically hanging out – no, worse. Bloody well soppy."

"Oh, for fuck's sake, Johnny, you do talk rot. I was just watching his hands and thinking how we all do that."

"Yes, and the King of England's coming to tea."

"Now if you'd said the Kaiser was coming for a beer—"

"Then we could give him a litre or two from the Albatros barrels!"

The Albatros Works had sent the squadron two barrels of beer, which was very much appreciated in the warm weather. Fellmann had even devised a means of keeping it cool, and the whole squadron enjoyed a refreshing half-litre at the end of the day. For the ground crew that often meant very late indeed, but they'd set up a table by Hangar Two, where it caught the sunset.

Schiffer played the mouth organ quite well, and if it was quiet in the mess we sometimes heard them singing. There was something very wistful about the sound in the late evening light, and we usually fended off melancholy with a chorus of our own.

"I suppose the Kaiser does drink beer?" I said as we entered the mess.

Beilke chortled. "If he doesn't he'll have to abdicate!"

Karl and Bretti came in.

"What you need to do now is practise your steep turns – good and high so it doesn't matter if you spin, and get some more target practice," Karl finished.

"Thank you so much," Bretti said. "You've been so helpful." He seemed to have lost most of his earlier awe of Karl. There was a pause and then he asked, "Have the Tommies got a lot like you?"

"Some – but there's no point worrying about that."

"No," agreed Patschke. "There's no point worrying about anything!"

"He's a nice kid," Karl said to me as we undressed for bed.

War is not a game for a nice kid. "What's his flying like?"

"You'll find out tomorrow."

We were both down for dawn. *I should have drunk either more or less than I did,* I thought as I stared at the ceiling. *I need to get to sleep, but it's bloody well impossible.*

Bullets flew round my head, the windscreen shattered, there was a hammer blow to my right knee and then the fire began—

"WAKE UP!" Karl was shaking me, and to my massive relief I was in my bed and not in a burning Albatros.

"Oh, Jesus!" I gasped.

I was trembling from head to foot and pouring with sweat, my heart thumping almost painfully.

His embrace had never felt more comforting.

"Sorry," I muttered.

"No need."

I was too frightened to say that I'd had the same dream twice – that was so disturbing that I didn't even want to think about it. *I hope it's not some ghastly prophecy.*

In the early light I managed to convince myself that it was a load of nonsense.

Of course you dream about burning. Everyone probably does – there are only so many ways death can happen. It's not prophecy – it's just lack of imagination.

All the same, I felt like death warmed up. *When we get back I'm going straight back to bed. Bretti can practise gunnery or something.*

The cold air and a couple of sharp fights woke me up pretty thoroughly, but the inevitable reaction left me so drained that I had to make a real effort to concentrate on the landing, and even then it was untidy.

I arranged to meet Bretti at eleven, by which time I'd had a couple of hours' sleep and felt a lot better.

As we were walking to the flight line he said, very quietly, "Becker, could I ask you something, please?"

"Yes, of course."

"Er – this is really awkward – I'm not telling tales and I don't want to cause any trouble, but…"

"Whatever you say won't go any further," I assured him. *Well, I'll tell Karl, of course – but that doesn't count.*

"It's just – does everyone have bad dreams?"

Oh, shit. Widemayer. "Yes, 'fraid we do. It rather goes with being here."

"I thought it might."

"Widemayer having a lot of them, then?"

He nodded. "It's been every night so far – shouting about burning."

I shuddered, and hoped he hadn't noticed.

"The trouble is," I said slowly, "that no one's going to want to swap with you. There's a spare bed in Fellmann's room—" poor

Bretti looked as if I'd offered him a billet with Satan himself "– but given his position, he's exempt from sharing, and you're not senior enough for the spare room in his hut. I'm afraid you're stuck."

"What about the ground crew's accommodation? I mean, technically I'm a sergeant."

"If you like I can ask the Chief for you, but I'd bet he'll say no. It's best for all the pilots to be together."

I could almost hear him thinking that I'd have to tell the Chief what he'd said about Widemayer.

"No, it's all right, thanks. I expect I'll get used to it."

No, you bloody won't, I thought after our first mock fight. *You won't be getting used to anything.*

Then it was his turn to bounce me. I saw him coming from a long way off, but pretended I hadn't and let him get really close before I broke. And then I left him for dead, and a minute after that I was on his tail and he would have been in serious trouble.

And so it went on. He improved a bit, but I reckoned I would have killed him about four times, while he'd never even made me sweat.

After we'd landed, we sat just where he'd sat with Karl the day before, and I must have said much the same things to him.

"You need to turn a lot tighter – how did your practice go this morning?"

"A lot better, but you still ran rings round me."

And so will the Tommies, only they'll be shooting.

"Keep at it – look, why not go and practise your circles after lunch, and then go and fly again and do lots of steep turns."

"Thanks a lot, Becker – I really appreciate it." He went off to change.

I suddenly felt horribly tired, and remembered with a sinking heart that I had another patrol mid-afternoon. I lit another cigarette, and the innocent little flame of my lighter suddenly became the fire licking back from the nose the day my engine caught light—

I snapped the flame off, my hand shaking.

'So, Franz,' asked a mocking voice, 'who's going to crack up first, you or Widemayer?' The voice was so vivid that for one horrible moment I thought it was real – and then I wished it had been.

"You all right, Franz?" Karl asked me after lunch.

"Yes, fine," I lied. "Bit tired, that's all."

"Why don't you go and have a kip before your flight?"

Because I'm too scared of dreaming about burning again. "Oh, I'm not sure I'd manage it."

"Better have more coffee and fags, then!" he said, and ordered another pot.

Somehow I managed to survive my encounter with the Tommies – one of their SE5 boys was shit-hot, and we chased each other round for half a century before we had to break off. *That's one to watch. Let's hope Bretti doesn't come across him for a while.*

I need an early night, without bad dreams, I thought as I taxied in, and had to laugh. My chances of that were next to nil.

And that was without Beilke's victory party.

"He did a lovely job," Johnny said. "It was one of those Bristols, and he sneaked under the tail while we distracted the escort. Got the pilot very thoroughly, and that was the end of them."

"Poor bloody observer," said Widemayer with feeling.

Yes – that must be the observer's second worst nightmare: the pilot being killed or disabled and having to wait, powerless, for the impact.

We were just about to sit down to dinner when Möller came in, and sidled up to Fellmann, whose face cracked into a wide smile.

"Beilke, you're a jammy sod," he said. "That was the confirmation from the flak gunners. Braun and co are just setting off to fetch the bodies."

Confirmation would usually have given the victory party an added kick, but now we'd have to stay reasonably sober for the guard of honour.

"Do we know how far away the aircraft is?" asked the Chief.

"About twenty kilometres," said Beilke.

The bodies were likely to arrive in the middle of the night. *That's the end of my decent night's sleep.*

What everyone had been careful not to say was that they'd burned – but it was obvious two minutes after I took my place by the coffins. There was no way of hiding that smell.

This will do Widemayer no good at all.

The dark rings under his eyes were definitely more pronounced in the morning – but he was hardly alone in that. Karl was pale and drained, his expression fixed, and Bretti looked rather queasy. *Poor kid – but then no one's introduction to war is easy, unless he's got some cushy job or other.*

The Chief gave us all the afternoon off after the funeral, and said that everyone apart from Bretti would fly in the early evening. Karl and I went to our room, closed the curtains, and put the chair under the door handle.

I fell asleep in his arms, and it was just the sort of deep, relaxing sleep I needed. The next thing I knew Schiffer was banging on the door, and Karl was rubbing his eyes.

"Thank you, Schiffer!" he called out, and we separated reluctantly and got dressed for flying.

"I could have done with at least another hour," I said.

"So could I." He smiled warmly at me and we headed for briefing.

We were not the last to arrive in the mess. Widemayer followed us up the steps, looking as if he'd far rather be somewhere else. Bretti was a couple of paces behind him, and Johnny and Beilke brought up the rear.

The Chief was already there, of course, and coffee and rolls were laid out on the table. Karl poured me a coffee and our fingers met as he handed it to me. I smiled as I thanked him, and out of the corner of my eye I saw the boss giving us a very thoughtful look.

Ice ran down my spine and settled with a jolt in my stomach.

Oh, shit, if he knows then one of us will be posted away, and I'll never see Karl again. How fucking stupid we were to even think we could get away with it.

He began the briefing, and during it his eyes rested on each of us in turn, but without any particular expression and certainly with no animosity towards Karl or me. I tried to focus on his words. *Do the job, Franz. There's never any use worrying about what might happen.*

I reminded myself of that as we suited up. *Mind on the job, or the rest of it will be academic.*

I looked at Karl and wished there were a God, so I could pray for his safe return and for us to stay together.

Everyone came back, and I shut my engine down with profound relief that the day was over.

"I think the Chief knows," I said very quietly to Karl as we put our extra clothes away.

He looked at me sharply. "What makes you think that?"

"The way he looked at us, before the briefing."

"Well, if he asks us, we'll just deny it. No one's got any proof, has he?"

Simple as that.

"And frankly, I don't think he will," he continued. "I mean, what would he say?"

I tried to imagine the Chief starting a conversation like that, and started laughing.

"You're right. It would be far too embarrassing."

"And he'd be only too happy with a denial," Karl added. "So put it right out of your head."

There were no strange looks that evening, from the boss or anyone else, and I got on with getting just pissed enough to sleep.

The Chief slaughtered Bretti the following morning. He didn't ask Karl or me how it had gone, just let the boy show him what he could do.

"Bretti's mess bill's going to be horrendous," said Pollow as the boss got on his tail yet again.

"Better a hefty mess bill than the wooden cross," Beilke countered.

"Is the Chief really going to drink all that fizz?" asked Kühn wonderingly.

"Maybe he'll ask us to help," said Patschke.

"No chance!" Johnny said. "He doesn't have to drink it all in one evening, does he?"

After they landed the Chief took Bretti to his office, and they were still in there when Karl and I took off with a Kette each.

Widemayer was with me again, with a new engine. Fellmann had said that the old one was worn out, and that he'd sent it back to Mercedes. That meant I could still have confidence in Widemayer, which was a relief.

He got stuck in properly in the three scraps we had, but after we'd landed he shook so badly that he had to lean against his aircraft. Yes, everyone trembled with reaction, but I only shook like that if I'd had a particularly narrow escape.

I went to see the Chief after lunch. He gave me a slightly curious look as I entered his office, replaced quickly by a friendly smile. I closed the door and he raised his eyebrows.

"Have a seat, Becker."

"Thank you, sir… This is rather awkward."

He looked at me expectantly.

"The thing is," I said slowly, "I'm rather worried about Widemayer."

"Ah. You think he's getting worse."

"Yes, sir, I do." I hesitated.

I didn't want to break Bretti's confidence, but at the same time I didn't want another Bruch. *There are four in that hut.*

"I've heard – please don't ask me from whom – that he's having a lot of nightmares, and he shook very badly after today's flight, even though it wasn't a bad one. And I'm sure you've noticed his eyes and face."

Being as you notice everything – but then that's your job.

"Yes. Thank you for telling me – I appreciate it wasn't easy… Was there anything else?"

"No, sir."

I left the door open, as it usually was. I knew he'd listened, in spite of his terse response.

Widemayer would do very well as an instructor at that second fighter pilot school they're setting up.

Over dinner I raised the subject as casually as I could. "Hey, Fellmann – what was that about another fighter pilot school?"

"Oh, are we having another, then?" asked Pollow. "That's a bloody good idea."

"I agree," said Horstmann. "There are nothing like enough of us."

"Indeed," said the Chief.

"Where is it?" asked Johnny.

"Valenciennes," replied Fellmann.

"Do they need instructors?" I asked.

"You thinking of leaving us?" Beilke asked with a laugh.

"Not fucking likely! I want one of those pretty blue gongs!" I said. "And besides, it wouldn't be my idea of fun."

"Not like shooting down the odd Tommy," said Kühn. "That gives a fellow a real buzz."

"They must need experienced fellows to teach there, though," Karl said.

"Just cos you've already got the Blue Max!" Johnny was laughing. "But you don't really want to leave us, do you, Bruv?!"

Now, now, Johnny, leave it there.

"Wild horses wouldn't drag me," said Widemayer. "Teaching's never appealed."

Maybe, just maybe, the idea's been planted in your head, and in the boss's head as well…

Not much more I can do about it.

Maria sent me another letter, with a photograph. It was a small head and shoulders portrait that didn't do her justice, but I looked at it and imagined her lovely auburn hair and blue eyes, and her beautiful clear skin…

"Hey – who's sent you her picture this time?" Pollow called out. "Going to let us all have a look?"

"Certainly not! This one really is for me!"

"Ah," said Patschke, "the one who loves him still!"

"Oh, shut up – you're just jealous!"

"Not likely – no ball and chain for me!"

"No," said Beilke, "it's Claudette's tarts for you and nothing else!"

I put the picture in my wallet and concentrated on reading her letter.

She was still praying for me, and she hoped I would continue to be successful. I suppressed a stab of irritation at that. *Why do civilians all want me to be so good at killing?* But that was unreasonable – I was just as keen to increase my score. And she was very much looking forward to seeing me again…

I stared out of the window, lost in imagining.

"I tell you what," said Patschke, "there's no way I want a girl waiting for me at home—"

"No chance!" Beilke interrupted. "Who'd want to look at your ugly mug!"

"– if it makes you as soppy as Becker and Horstmann."

"Who are you calling soppy?" Horstmann demanded.

"You – always going on about the lovely Susanne!" Patschke turned to the rest of us. "You only hear some of it – I can tell you when her birthday is, her favourite colour, the name of her little dog – I tell you, if we ever meet, she'll think I've been spying on her. And I have her lovely eyes gazing at me every time I get undressed!"

Horstmann laughed. "My dear Patschke, Susanne is never going to watch you undressing!"

"Come on – show everyone the picture!"

"Not bloody likely – I'm not having you lot of lecherous bastards dreaming about her!"

We all knew what he really meant. *I wouldn't want them doing that over Maria, either.*

"Fair enough," I said.

"Leave the poor fellow alone!" Karl was laughing.

"Why are you sticking up for him when you don't have a girl?!" Patschke asked.

"Maybe I do," Karl said with a smile.

"No – all you do is fuck tarts, and dancers in Berlin," retorted Pollow.

"Ah," Karl replied, "that's what I tell you about. How do you know I haven't got a fiancée somewhere?"

"Because she never writes to you!" Patschke said gleefully.

"Maybe Fellmann hands me the letters in private, so none of you can leer over them," Karl said.

Johnny just looked at him and raised an eyebrow.

"Well, Becker – does Karl have a secret love?" demanded Kühn.

"My lips are sealed!" I replied.

"Look – he's blushing!" said Patschke. "He knows something!"

"But there's no way I'm telling any of you about it," I said firmly.

"So where does she live?" asked Beilke.

Karl and I both laughed.

"What does Fellmann call it?" I asked rhetorically. "Oh, that's it – omertà!"

"Very clever," I said to Karl when we went to get our flying clothes.

He laughed. "I think you did pretty well, too!"

With a bit of luck that's thrown them all off any scent. I was slightly cross with myself for blushing, because it was such a stupid reaction. *No way am I Karl's 'secret love'.*

The Tommies are definitely up to something, I thought as we headed north towards the coast. *I've never seen so many aircraft up at one time. It's just as well the Chief put up all ten of us.*

I wish we'd got someone experienced instead of Bretti. He's a nice lad but it'll be ages before he's any good—

Patschke rocked his wings and pointed to a formation of Sopwiths that was close enough to engage, and I was jolted out of my reverie.

They saw us coming and turned to meet us. I went after their leader and in five seconds flat it was a wild free-for-all. One of his mates was after Horstmann, with Patschke after him – a Sopwith hurtled past my nose, just missing his flight leader, and his lower right wing smashed straight into Pollow's tail and took the tailplane and half the rudder clean off, debris flying everywhere.

The nose of Pollow's Albatros dropped abruptly, and it fell into a dive from which there could be no recovery, and the Tommy fell like a falling leaf.

I had no time to stare because their boss was trying to get on my tail, but he wasn't that good and slowly I managed to gain on him. I got a couple of decent bursts into him, and he broke off the fight and headed home.

Are you hit or just bluffing? If it's the former you can go – the others tried to leave as well, and we had our bit of fun trying to stop them.

There was a Tommy two-seater trying to sneak over the lines, and we let the Sopwiths go and went after them and their escort instead.

And that turned into a lively fight, because it was a Bristol accompanied by a brace of SE5s, and they all knew what they were doing. Patschke did rather better than I'd hoped, but it would have been so good to have had Westermann there instead…

As we flew home, the icy blast penetrated to my sweat-soaked shirt and underwear, and chilled me to the bone. *And it's fucking July. It's not going to get much warmer.*

Poor old Pollow. I wonder how long it took him to hit the ground. Better than lying screaming in No Man's Land, anyway.

I don't give a shit about the Tommy – he did for Pollow, after all.

"They should give us parachutes," Johnny said over lunch.

"No point talking about that," said Beilke.

"Where did he end up?" asked Kühn.

"Either No Man's Land or Tommy-side," I replied. "I was too busy to watch."

"No funeral, then," said Widemayer.

"Funeral? Just fill the bloody hole in." Patschke was looking more than a bit shocked.

"I didn't realise you saw," I said.

He hadn't said anything in the debrief, but then I'd done most of the talking.

"Yes – I was looking round to make sure no one was getting on my tail and I saw them collide."

"Surprising it doesn't happen more often," Karl said, lighting another cigarette.

"Indeed," said the Chief.

He sighed and headed for his office, no doubt to write the usual letter and to arrange for another new pilot and aircraft.

"Fancy a walk?" I asked Karl.

"Good idea."

It was a hot afternoon, and we left our tunics in the mess and rolled our shirtsleeves up. The sun blazed from a blue sky, and the larks sang high above us.

It would be wonderful to be in Brandenburg, strolling under the limes to the rose garden... I almost said it out loud, but realised just in time how tactless that would be.

Once we were out of sight of everyone, our hands linked themselves together, Karl's bare forearm like cool silk against my skin.

We sat down in a grassy hollow, then he lay back and pulled me down into his arms, and his wonderful soft lips met mine.

"We'd better stop this," I said. "It's too public."

He released me reluctantly. "You're right – though the more of us get killed—"

"The more we need to enjoy what life we have," I finished. I paused and then added, "And that's just the thing – I want to carry on enjoying what we do. The last thing I want is for them to separate us."

"No – we can leave that to the man with the scythe."

It was as if a cloud had passed in front of the sun.

It's just a matter of time. I'll die before I let them kill you – if I'm there. Which I probably won't be.

He stroked my cheek. "Why the sad face?"

I smiled. "Why indeed? We're alive and the Devil can take everything else."

The sound of Albatros engines caused us to look up. The Chief was putting Bretti through his paces again. We shaded our eyes from the sun and lay watching the 'fight'.

"Just as well we didn't start anything," Karl said with a grin. "We'd only have confirmed his worst suspicions!"

"We probably have anyway."

"Nothing wrong with lying in the sun!" He looked at his watch. "Oh, bugger it – time we headed back."

Bretti'd put up a lot more of a fight this time.

"What do you reckon?" I asked Johnny when we reached the mess.

"Dawn."

And that was what the Chief said to Bretti: "You're down for dawn tomorrow."

Bretti's face lit up with a mixture of excitement and apprehension.

"And who'll be the lucky babysitter?" I asked Karl as we got ready to fly.

"No doubt we shall find out!"

So now there are ten flying, I thought as we climbed up into the afternoon light. *Let's just hope it stays at ten until the morning.*

It did, though the Tommies were not so fortunate. The Chief came back with that look of cold elation in his face, and we had a party to celebrate his twenty-eighth and to say goodbye to Pollow. It was rather restrained as we were all bloody tired and most of us had to be up in the dawn, which was far too fucking early.

The four of us went to our hut together. Horstmann and Patschke wished us 'Good night', and then we closed our door.

I actually slept quite well, but it still felt like two minutes before Schiffer came in with the shaving water. Karl was already awake, sitting up in his bed smoking.

"You'll set fire to yourself one day," I said as I got up.

"Not likely – I'd have to fall asleep for that to happen," he said wryly.

I looked at him. "Didn't you sleep, then?"

"For about an hour, right after you went to bed – but I've been wide awake ever since. Too much shit in my head."

"How do we get the shit out of our heads?"

"God knows – if you find out then please tell me!"

"Right," said the Chief. "We'll make a four and two Kettes: Patschke and Brettschneider will be with me, with Leussow K as fourth man, Kühn and Widemayer will be with Leussow J, Horstmann and Beilke with Becker."

Bretti looked at Karl as if he couldn't quite believe his ears – he clearly hadn't expected that the squadron's second-highest ace would watch his back.

"I'll try not to let you down," he said quietly to Karl as we made our way to the flight line.

Karl put a hand on his shoulder. "It's for me to not let you down. You just do what the Chief said and try to stay out of trouble."

The sun rose rapidly as we climbed, casting long shadows across the ground below. *Hard to believe half this year's already gone*, I thought, looking across at Johnny's Red Eagle.

Let's see, who was here at its start? The Chief, Karl, Johnny, Otto, the Prof – wonder how he's getting on in his laboratory? – Bruch, Geschke, Buchholz... I stopped, because it was turning into a list of the dead and that was not what I wanted to think about.

Staying among the living proved easier said than done. We hadn't long split up when we got into a serious fight with a flight of Nieuports, and it turned thoroughly nasty when they were joined by one of the SE5s. Fortunately Johnny's Kette saw the party and joined in.

In the middle of all that, Johnny sent an SE5 spinning down, well alight.

"Hey, Bruv, you want to watch out!" he shouted to Karl as he jumped down. "I just got another – down in flames!"

Out of my eye corner I saw Widemayer shudder. Then he turned away and headed rapidly for the lavatory block.

Johnny looked at me, then at Widemayer's departing back. The Chief raised his eyebrows. *Post him away before he gets any worse. He must be near the limit.*

I shrugged, and turned my attention to the holes my poor Albatros had collected, some of them uncomfortably near the cockpit. *It's been a while since I got that many.*

The Chief frowned.

"It was pretty hot, sir," said Johnny. "Those SE5 fellows knew their stuff."

"So did the Nieuports," added Patschke.

It's not how it used to be…

"So what did you think of that?" I asked Bretti over second breakfast.

"It was really hard to know what was going on," he said, looking a bit dismayed. "I mean, there were no aircraft at all that I could see, and then suddenly they were just everywhere, and then they'd all gone again."

Johnny laughed. "That's how it is at first – it'll make sense after a few times."

"How many holes did you get?" asked Kühn. "I got stacks my first time."

"Me too," agreed Patschke.

"Quite a few," Bretti replied, "but Karl got them off my tail really quickly."

Karl noticed the hero-worship in his voice, and looked rather uncomfortable.

"Oh, you won't need anyone to look after you in a couple of days," he said.

It'll take longer than that, I thought later when I was fourth man. *The Chief's not taking any chances, giving Bretti the most experienced pilots in the squadron as backup. It'll be Johnny next* – and sure enough, it was.

The post had arrived. Johnny had a letter from each of his

fiancées and got ribbed by everyone, and I had one from Otto and another from Alfred.

Otto reported that his wrist had improved a lot.

'So I'm a flying instructor now, and it's just terrific to be back in the air – and pretty terrifying as well. I'd forgotten just how dodgy it can be, taking the new fellows for their first lessons – especially teaching them to land.

Anyway, the doc says if the wrist stands up to flying here, I'll be able to come back to the Front!! I can hardly wait! I'm so bored being stuck here. Berlin is becoming really dreary with all the food shortages, and all the widows everywhere and disabled men. Still, at least the free love club's still popular, and there are lots of lonely women!'

I laughed and passed the letter to Karl.

"Jammy bastard," he said, "all that free sex, while we have to pay."

"Yes," I said, "beats me why he wants to come back here."

"Talking of sex, how about Claudette's tomorrow?" Beilke suggested.

"Bloody good idea," Karl agreed.

"I'd be up for that," I said.

"I'll go and ask the Chief," said Horstmann. "He and Fellmann are probably doing the programme."

Bretti looked up. "Is Claudette's what I think it is?"

"Yup," said Patschke.

"Will I be allowed in?" Bretti asked doubtfully.

"I'll lend you my coat," I said. "Just keep it on while you're in there – it tends to fill up with staff officers."

A grin started to spread across the boy's face. "I'll have to make sure I don't get shot down, then!"

Either your virginity's a thing of the past, or you're a very good actor.

I opened Alfred's letter. He was out of hospital and on convalescent leave in Berlin.

'The break was a bit more complex than anyone thought at first, and I had some fascinating conversations with the surgeon about it. Anyway, I'll soon be back in Italy and in the meantime am enjoying myself as much as I can. The first thing I did when they let me out was to go to the University and ask whether it would be possible for your sister to enrol there. My old Prof was very helpful indeed, said the best thing would be for her to write to him directly.'

And there was the address.
You are a truly wonderful fellow, Alfred. A lot of men would have just forgotten. And you don't even have the intention of getting into her knickers – at least I don't think you do.

'And say hello to Karl and give him my congratulations on his Blue Max,' he finished.

I passed on Alfred's message to Karl, and then started to write to Johanna.
Fellmann was saying something about a new aircraft that Fokker were developing.
"A *triplane*?" asked Beilke incredulously.
"Christ, that would look like a flying Venetian blind!" said Kühn.
"Sopwith have done it already," Fellmann said.
"Yes, of course they have," said Johnny. "Haven't you lot seen the pictures in the *Berlin Illustrated*?"
"And it's got a rotary engine," Fellmann went on, "so it'll turn nice and tight."
"Oh, fuck!" said Patschke. "I had a go with one of those once, and no way could I keep the bloody thing straight on

take-off! I tell you, it was just one great big zigzag until we got airborne."

There was a sudden crash of breaking glass. I looked up.

Karl's beer glass was in fragments at his feet and he was staring fixedly through the wall. God knows what he was seeing, but he had never looked so disturbed.

I got up and took his arm. "Come and sit down."

For a moment he didn't respond at all, and I could feel him trembling. His eyes were full of horror, as if he were gazing into Hell.

The others were carefully looking away, and Horstmann put a record on the gramophone. *What price Bretti's hero-worship now?*

I guided Karl firmly to the small sofa. He sat down heavily and took a deep breath.

"Thanks, Franz," he said very quietly.

"Brandy?"

"Yes, please."

He got out his cigarette case and holder, and I didn't want to watch his attempt to put the demons back in their box. They had escaped very thoroughly, and we had all seen them.

'It's something someone says that sets it off,' he'd told me. So what was the last thing I'd heard? Triplanes? No – Patschke talking about a zigzagging take-off. What in God's name does that have to do with anything?

Johnny joined us and put his arm round Karl's shoulders. "You all right, Bruv?"

What a fucking stupid question. Of course he isn't.

"Fine, thanks."

A few minutes later he got up, went to the piano, and began to play the Liesl song.

By the third time through, Bretti had learned most of the words. Everyone was laughing, but there was something brittle about Karl's laughter that I didn't like at all.

He played for us until dinner, when he didn't eat much. Once or twice the shadow crept out of his eyes and across his face, and he stared at nothing. Each time I nudged his foot under the table, and he started and then smiled at me.

The party for Johnny's victory was rather tame. *We're becoming a non-drinking squadron – which is probably just as well, given the Tommies' behaviour.*

"I could do with being a bit more pissed than this," I said as we headed for our room. "I'm not sure I'm going to sleep."

He gave that brittle laugh again. "I don't think I want to."

"Karl—" I stopped because there was no point asking him what it was about. *Probably Verdun.*

As I drifted off to sleep it occurred to me that Zaffke might know something. *I'll ask him in the morning…*

III

I almost didn't ask him anything. The dawn flight was a series of very hot fights that left me shaking.

Judging by the others' faces I wasn't alone. Widemayer had collected a lot of holes and looked dreadful. We went in for second breakfast, and he took one look at the table and left the mess.

Karl didn't look much better than he had in the evening – his eyes weren't quite as haunted, but they had dark rings under them and his face was lined with fatigue.

He started on his second pot of coffee, and I made an excuse about wanting to talk to Ziegler about my guns and headed for the hangars.

"Morning, Zaffke." *How on earth do I start this without him guessing what it's about?*

"Morning, sir."

"This – er – this is probably going to sound really strange – does zigzag mean anything to you?"

His face changed.

"It was a trench at Verdun, sir," he said slowly. "The Zig-Zag Trench. Very exposed it was, running across a forward slope, and the Frenchies shelled and machine gunned it all the time. Two good mates of mine got killed there, just before the company attacked the village."

And I can guess what happened then.

"Yes, I see. Thank you." I could see his mind working. "It was just something someone said."

And then I did go to talk to Ziegler. I thought my right-hand gun needed zeroing in, probably because I'd whacked the crap out of it again.

"We'll get onto that right away, sir – we want you to keep shooting down the Tommies as well!"

"I'll stand you all a bottle of schnapps after my next one!" *Not that you need an incentive.*

"Thank you, sir – we'll look forward to that!"

That must have been fucking horrible, being on a platter for the Frenchies, I thought as I headed back to the mess. *I wonder how long they had to stick it.*

I always hated being shelled. It was the vilest feeling of utter powerlessness, of complete insignificance. When you're face to face with the enemy, you can fight, but you can't do anything against high explosive. And being blown apart might be quick, but getting hit by a chunk of hot, jagged steel was no joke. I'd seen too many men get horribly mutilated and die slowly in agony.

"Did you get it sorted out?" Karl asked me.

"Ziegler's dealing with it… God, I could do with some more sleep."

He laughed. "What's that?"

"Come on – we've got an hour or two. We can try at least."

I know how to send you to sleep, even if only briefly.

He fell asleep in my arms – and then I had the fucking burning dream and woke screaming.

"See, Franz – sleep's vastly overrated!" he murmured in my ear.

I was shaking too much to think of a reply. *And soon I'm flying again, and that ghastly dream could very well come true—*

I stopped myself. There was absolutely no point thinking like that.

"I wonder what Bretti makes of us all," he said as we got dressed. "Widemayer looking like a spectre and not eating, me making an exhibition of myself last night – he must think he's come to a complete madhouse."

"If he makes it through the first few months he'll understand," I answered. "And if he doesn't, then I don't care what he thinks."

"Let's hope Pollow's replacement's got a bit more experience."

"Quite."

With all the holes that needed patching, we could only send up two Kettes plus Bretti in the late morning. Ziegler was sorting out my gun while the patches cured, and I lay in the sun outside the mess with Patschke and Kühn, glad of the time off.

We stripped and let ourselves brown.

"Don't let me fall asleep," Kühn said. "I burn really easily and putting the straps on will be hell."

"That's what you get for being blond," teased Patschke. "I bet the girls all love those golden curls!"

"They won't if I'm lobster red!"

Oh, of course, it's Claudette's this evening. At least I hope it is. I could do with a fuck.

That used to be so simple – pay the money and fuck the tart. Now I've got Maria waiting for me there's always a hint of guilt, plus it doesn't feel anything like as good as it did with her – though that does let me off any remorse. It's not as if I'm having an affair.

And what Karl and I get up to doesn't count at all. It's just a bloody sight better than the alternative.

It was easier to disregard our walking hand in hand, to ignore how I felt in his company.

He came back in a flying colander, and I couldn't ignore the cold that ran down my spine when I looked at the bullet holes. It was only partly banished by his grim smile.

"What was it?"

"One of those Bristols – got the observer and then the pilot."

"Bloody well done – let's hope this one gets confirmed."

Johnny was all smiles without the grimness. "That's another to the Red Eagle!"

"You're a fucking lunatic," said Horstmann.

Karl looked at them both. "Another frontal attack, Johnny?"

"Best sort!"

Karl just shook his head. "Forget about your blasted score, all right? You'll be bugger all use dead."

"You're just worried I'll catch you up!"

"I don't give a shit about that. I just don't want to have to tell Pa that you're dead because you were being a fucking idiot."

The Chief's voice cut into the argument. "Leussow J, my office, please."

Johnny pulled a face behind the boss's back, like a naughty schoolboy going to see the headmaster.

Horstmann, Bretti, Karl and I went to smarten ourselves up for Claudette's and the others headed for the mess.

"How do I get that stupid brother of mine to listen to reason?" Karl demanded as we changed.

"You won't," I answered reluctantly. "We'll just have to hope the boss can."

"The trouble is, he keeps scoring that way. And every time he gets away with it convinces him he's invincible."

And makes it harder for the Chief to do anything about it, I didn't say. Karl knew that as well as I did.

"Let's be off," I said.

"Don't forget your coat."

"What on earth for? It's bloody July!"

"Bretti – you don't want the poor kid to miss out on his last fuck, now do you?"

"Oh, Christ – I'm glad you remembered!"

Bretti's eyes lit up when he saw Christine.

"Becker, I want the amazon!" he whispered in my ear.

"Then you shall have her," I replied, and moved so she could sit next to him.

Two minutes later they headed for the stairs.

"That was quick," Horstmann commented.

The place was quiet, and he had Anne on one side of him and Jeannette on the other, and looked as if he couldn't make his mind up.

"You can have us both if you like," Jeannette said, her hand on the top of his thigh. "We start off with a nice show for you."

My eyes met Karl's, and I could see that he too was thinking of the 'nice show' Helena and Marion had put on for us in Kempinski's...

Françoise sat astride me, my face practically between her tits.

"Come on, then," I said rather hoarsely, and we got up.

"Or your friend could join us," Anne said to Horstmann.

I felt a quite absurd stab at the thought of Karl in bed with Horstmann and two tarts. To my relief Karl laughed and said, "Thanks – but I'm quite happy with Louise!" just as Horstmann said, "Not my idea of fun!"

Françoise gave me a very pleasant hour, but as always I felt grubby afterwards. *It could have been the last time,* I reminded myself on the way home. *And it helps me sleep, which should help me stay alive.*

Bretti gave a happy sigh. *Oh well, if you do get killed then at least you've had a good time.*

"She was lovely," he said. "Plenty to get hold of."

"It's a funny thing," Karl said, "but the fellow you replaced liked her as well."

"What happened to him?"

"Got shot down in flames... So, Horstmann, did you have one or both?"

"Well, I was very tempted – especially after what you two got up to in Berlin—" I nearly drove off the road "– and then I thought it'll cost double, and then I thought, oh, what the hell, and went for it. And I'm bloody glad I did – I've never had a live show like that before – oh, I've seen films, but that's not the same thing."

Then he turned to Karl, who was in the back with Bretti, and added, "I was bloody glad you didn't want to come along, though – I mean, watching the show and then having one each in private like you did would be all right, but not all in one room and especially not in one bed."

As soon as we got to our room, I whispered, "Karl, what the fuck did you tell him about Berlin?"

"Just that we spent a couple of days with two girls in a suite in Kempinski's – I had to say that much because Johnny'd already told them all we'd be meeting them. I made a point of saying there were two bedrooms."

"Can we trust Johnny to keep his mouth shut about us?"

"One hundred per cent."

"Even with his problem about your score?"

"Yes – look, he may be getting that right out of proportion, but there's no way he'd want the scandal, not after Great-Uncle, and besides, I know far too much about him. If I go in the shit, he goes in deeper."

He took me in his arms, his embrace solid and reassuring as it always was.

"There's nothing to worry about, Franz," he murmured into my ear.

I laughed. "No – there never is! Let's go and have a drink – it must be almost time for dinner."

"And our victory parties!"

"How could I forget?"

Johnny's glee at his two victories was short-lived. Only one was confirmed, and as Karl also got confirmation, the gap between them remained the same.

"I don't fucking well believe it," he said disgustedly.

"Well, you're in line for another gong, anyway," Fellmann said consolingly. "You and Becker. You've both been put forward for the Hohenzollern House Order."

"Oh," I said, "that'll be nice."

"Well, I suppose it's something," said Johnny.

"Don't be so bloody ungrateful!" said Horstmann. "I'd just be happy to have more than one victory to my name."

"Me too," agreed Patschke.

Kühn was looking out of the window. "Oh – I think that must be Pollow's replacement."

We'd heard a solitary Albatros engine, but no one had paid any attention as the Chief had sent Bretti to do more steep turns.

"Ah, good," said Fellmann. He finished his coffee and stubbed out his cigar. "I'd better get to the office."

"Fellmann's such a bloody dark horse," Johnny complained. "He never tells anyone what's going on."

Karl just looked at him and raised an eyebrow. "Just as well, really – or we'd be eating the same crap as the infantry."

"And we wouldn't have these cigars," said Horstmann.

"Let's hope the new fellow has a bit more experience," said Patschke. "Bretti's good company but he's nowhere near passing his probation."

The new man, Eichner, was off two-seaters. There was an almost audible sigh of relief when the Chief introduced him.

He flew against me in the afternoon, which gave me another nice break from the Front.

It's ridiculous to be so bloody tired – I've only just had leave. What I need is a proper break – it's nearly three years now, and I must have used up most of my lives.

Eichner was pretty good, apart from not turning tight enough, but then no one did at first. And he was a fair shot. *Promising – if he survives the first few weeks.*

"You can fly against me tomorrow," said the Chief, and told him the usual stakes.

"Just don't get too pissed tonight!" Patschke added cheerfully. Beilke had shot down an SE5 over No Man's Land, so of course we would be celebrating.

It became a double celebration: during the evening flight I got on the tail of a Nieuport and gave him a couple of good bursts before I had to break off. I was pretty sure I'd hit him, but he kept flying and I didn't think he was going to go down. Then he started to trail oily smoke, and went into a dive.

I lost sight of him for a few seconds, but when I looked down, his blazing aircraft was only too visible.

I wish you hadn't burned, I thought as we flew home. *I hope you were dead or unconscious when the fire took hold.* I shivered violently, and told myself that it was cold because the sun was going down.

Sending another down in flames does not make it more likely that the same will happen to me. That's just superstitious crap.

Live by the sword and die by the sword, or by fire… Crap. Complete crap.

I didn't want to talk about it in front of Widemayer, but of course the details came out. The result was that he ate almost nothing but got quite well pissed, and I saw Bretti looking at him with dismay.

That's probably the end of your night's sleep.

The Chief put everyone except Eichner up at dawn. Karl and I struggled to the mess in the twilight, both feeling very second-hand. I'd spent most of the short night staring at the ceiling, aware that Karl was probably doing the same.

Whatever the Tommies are up to, I wish they'd do it somewhere else. It feels as if I've barely landed from yesterday evening.

Kühn said as much as we made our way to the flight line.

"Yes, it is getting wearing," said Beilke. "Rain would be lovely."

Being their patrol leader I didn't answer, much as I shared their opinion. It wouldn't have done to encourage it.

Ten Albatri climbing into the morning sky were a glorious sight, especially when the sun crept above the horizon, lighting the sky-blue fuselages and the multi-coloured lozenge patterns on the wings. *Nothing beats this – well, almost nothing...*

The Tommies were determined to have their photographs, and two two-seaters were heading for the lines, each with its escort. Plus there was a flight of Sopwiths trying to get above us. That made ten of them in total.

The Chief signalled to me to attack one of the two-seaters, and to Karl and his Kette to go for the others. He and his four, Widemayer, Johnny and Bretti, would engage the Sopwiths.

Getting into position took forever and my nerves wound themselves up, my right foot vibrating on the rudder bar, but there was no point starting the attack too soon.

Beilke can have this one. I pointed to him and raised two fingers, and he peeled off and we followed him down.

We were on them before they knew we were there. I got behind one of the Nieuport escort and gave him a good burst, the smell of castor oil strong, my Albatros shaking with the double recoil, the tracer going into his fuselage. He reared up and fell into a spin.

His colleague was more alert, and turned to meet Kühn. The two-seater was thoroughly spooked and Beilke's chance of getting under its tail evaporated. It was the more important target, so I left Kühn to deal with the fighter and joined Beilke's attack.

Some way off, Karl was sneaking under the tail of the other two-seater – Johnny's Albatros plummeted past me, flames pouring back from the nose. The fuselage was well alight, past the cockpit to the Red Eagle. Johnny climbed out and jumped, but his clothes were already on fire, and he fell blazing like some ghastly meteorite.

Surely the wind will put it out—

A hail of bullets flew past my ears, and as I threw my aircraft onto her left wingtips I heard the rattle behind me. There was a Sopwith right on my tail.

Stupid, stupid fucking bastard, gawking instead of watching your tail. It'll serve you fucking well right if you end up the same.

I was pulling away from him, and then he broke off because another Albatros was turning in behind him. A plain blue fuselage – it was little Bretti, of all men. And then I had to help him out, because of course he'd forgotten to look behind him. Not that I could criticise.

The sky was suddenly empty.

That's at least one to us, but Johnny – oh, shit, Johnny. I hope Karl didn't see – but he'll soon see that his brother isn't with us.

We had another very scrappy fight, and then nine Albatri headed home.

No one knew what to say, and there was silence until the Chief gathered us together.

He asked me for my report first, being as I was senior to Karl in the squadron. I stated that I'd sent a Nieuport down out of control, and that we'd stopped the two-seater getting its photographs.

Do I say that I saw Johnny going down, or do I wait until I'm asked? The Chief can mention it first. Johnny was in his formation.

"Leussow?"

There was no longer any need to add the 'K'.

"I sent one two-seater down out of control, sir." Karl's voice was perfectly level but his eyes were like ice, his face still. "No other result."

"Well done... You will all be aware that Leutnant Johann von Leussow isn't here. He was shot down by one of the Sopwiths, while making a frontal attack on it." He paused and turned to Karl. "My sincerest condolences – he was a tremendous asset to the Jasta."

"Thank you, sir."

There was a chorus of expressions of sympathy, and then we headed towards the huts in silence.

It's hard to imagine the squadron without Johnny. It's going to be very quiet. And he was here before me—

That's nothing to Karl's situation. Both his brothers are dead now.

When we got to our room I put my arms round him.

"Karl, I am so sorry."

For a while he didn't answer, then he said quietly but with real anger, "It was bound to happen. The stupid bastard wouldn't listen."

I held him tighter. "We're all on borrowed time. He'd been here longer than either of us."

"True… Let's go and join the others."

When we reached the main hut the Chief came out of his office.

"Er, Leussow," he said rather awkwardly, "shall I telephone the Major, or would you prefer to do it?"

"I'll do it, thank you, sir."

"Use my office, then." He squeezed Karl's shoulder as he passed him.

I just don't want to have to tell Pa that you're dead…

Second breakfast was on the table. The last thing I felt like doing was eating – the image of Johnny falling on fire through the sky was hideously vivid, and I knew I would never be rid of it.

You have to eat, Franz. You'll be fighting again later.

Fellmann was sitting at the table, his breakfast untouched in front of him, staring at the tablecloth.

Fellmann's going to get hurt whatever happens, Karl said – and now his heart must be properly broken, and there's nothing the poor fellow can say to anyone.

I sat beside him. There was nothing I could say, either.

"At least we should be able to bury him, being as it was over our side," said Beilke.

"Yes," Horstmann agreed, "give him a proper send-off."

"Thanks," I said to Bretti. "Nice job – but do remember to watch your tail."

"I suppose the Major will come to the funeral," said Patschke.

"Yes, I expect so," I said.

We all fell silent as Karl entered the mess, helped himself to rolls and ham and sat down.

"I'll see what I can find out," said Fellmann, and went to his office.

"Well done, Franz," Karl said to me.

"And you," I replied. *Though I know what outcome you would have preferred.*

Widemayer hadn't come to the mess, but there was nothing unusual in that. *He'll waste away, the way he's going.*

The Chief flew against Eichner right after breakfast, and we all went outside to watch. It was far better than sitting doing nothing.

Eichner made a reasonable attempt at staving off the boss. Karl had taken Bretti on one side, and judging from his gestures was giving him a running commentary. *That's useful – and it gives you something else to think about.*

I just hope you don't get shot down yourself.

The 'fight' had just finished when Fellmann came out, went up to Karl and said something. Karl just nodded.

We weren't sure how the day's programme would work. Several of the aircraft were holed, and we all knew Karl would want to fly again but probably shouldn't. And someone was going to have to fetch Johnny's body.

The boss took Eichner into his office, and came into the mess about fifteen minutes later.

"Gentlemen, the situation is as follows: we have six serviceable aircraft. Becker, you take Widemayer and Horstmann. Kühn and Patschke will fly with me. We'll take off one hour from now." There was a pause and then he added, "We had a telephone call – apparently the wreckage of our comrade's aircraft has been found. Leussow, I assume you'd like to go with Fellmann and Braun after lunch?"

"Yes, sir – thank you."

"And Becker, I suggest you go as well."

"Yes, sir."

"Brettschneider, Eichner – work on your circles and think through what I said."

He left us, and as he passed the Ops Office we heard him say, "Fellmann, have you got a few minutes?"

Poor Fellmann – now he's got to make the funeral arrangements.

Karl lit another cigarette and stood looking out of the window. Then he turned to me. "Franz, would you give me a hand with Johnny's things?"

"Yes, of course. Horstmann, will you come and get me?"

"Yes – half an hour to go?"

"That'll be fine."

As with all of us, Johnny's possessions were minimal. He did have some very nice silk shirts, though.

"Pity those won't fit you," I said to Karl.

"Will they fit you?"

"No – bit small. Thanks anyway."

"Fellmann might like them," he said. "And his best boots – they're in pretty good nick. Too small for you?"

I nodded.

"Oh well, they'll fit someone."

He opened another drawer.

"I suppose it's all mine now," he said with a very distracted air. There was a sudden look of deep distress in his eyes, and then he recovered himself. "Let's just pack it all up and send it home. Pa or I can sort it out properly some time – apart from the letters, of course."

There were two bundles of letters. Karl opened one with evident reluctance.

"This is from Elfriede, so presumably the other pile are Alex's… I really don't want to have to go through them all."

"No – Johnny wouldn't have mixed them up, would he?"

"God knows."

"How did your father take it?"

He gave a short laugh. "Just as you'd expect. I could have been anyone. 'Thank you for telling me'. That was all he said. Oh, and then, 'Please let me know when the funeral will be'. I had to explain that there might not be one."

I shook my head, remembering the letter he'd written Karl after Friedrich's death. That too had been completely devoid of emotion.

Another son gone, another hero's death for Kaiser and Fatherland. And now there's only one left.

This means you'll inherit. You'll get the prime Brandenburg sand, whether you want it or not.

Karl sat heavily on Johnny's bed. There was a framed photograph of Alex on the bedside table, and he picked it up and looked at it.

"Oh, shit, I'm going to have to write to her. And I suppose to Elfriede as well, though I doubt she had any feelings for him. Probably be relieved."

"Will you have to marry her?"

"Not fucking likely. I'm not going to live that long, anyway."

"Don't say that." I sat beside him and put my arm round his shoulders. "I don't want to have to bury you."

"Nor I you," he said with a touch of warmth in his voice.

There was a knock at the door and Horstmann put his head round. "Becker, it's half an hour to go."

"Thanks." I turned to Karl. "See you later."

"Yes, right."

I left him sitting there among his brother's possessions, wishing there were something I could do. *I've never lost anyone really close to me. I can't imagine how it must be to lose an older brother, who was there before you were born.*

"Oh, Becker," said the Chief, "don't forget to put in your victory claim, and would you remind Leussow to make his?"

"Yes, of course, sir."

I'd completely forgotten about both of them.

On the way to the flight line I reminded Widemayer and Horstmann that we should forget we'd just lost a good friend and not get distracted by trying to avenge him. And then I remembered Johnny saying that after Geschke was killed, and I was suddenly filled with sorrow.

I put it aside. There would be time for that later.

Widemayer didn't look good as we suited up. He was chalk white and sweating, and fumbled with his gloves and dropped them both. *You need to stop, but if we send you away we'll have three new men.*

He fought well and hard, but shook from head to foot again afterwards, and I wondered how much of his reserves of courage remained.

This is surely one of the worst aspects of the war – everyone stays at the Front until he's dead, or maimed, or completely used up. We are all expendable.

"Becker, would you come to my office, please?" the Chief said.

"Of course, sir."

He ushered me in. "Have a seat – I'll be with you in a moment."

It was more like five minutes. When he came back he closed the door behind him, and sat next to me rather than behind his desk.

"The situation is," he said, so softly that I could hardly hear him, "that I delayed your going to fetch the body, because it took them a while to find him – and I've asked them to make sure he's well wrapped and in a coffin before you get there. I told them the deceased's brother would be in the recovery party."

"Yes, sir, I understand – I saw what happened."

"Did Leussow see?"

"I don't think so. He hasn't said anything – but then that doesn't mean anything."

"No, quite… I appreciate that Verdun was – well, that he's seen it all, but this is his brother and I'd rather spare him the truth if possible."

"So would I."

"If you set off right after lunch then it should work out."

"Yes, sir… At least Braun gets spared the nasty work this time."

The Chief sighed. "Indeed he does… This was really not the time to lose an experienced man."

"No. I had a letter from Kramer the other day. He's flying again so it might be possible to get him passed fit early. He's mad keen to come back."

"Thanks for that, Becker – I'll get a cable off to Döberitz."

Karl was sitting in the mess talking to Horstmann and Beilke as if nothing had happened. Then he turned towards me, and I saw his eyes – and all I wanted to do was hold him and give him what comfort I could.

Widemayer didn't appear for lunch and the Chief sent Bretti to fetch him. He forced down a few mouthfuls, looking as if he were about to be sick. The line of his jawbone was noticeably more prominent.

I wonder if he'll be killed before he cracks up, I thought with necessary detachment.

Karl ate normally, and I was reminded of the evening after Langemarck, when he'd made himself eat even after seeing Anton's intestines spilling out onto the ground.

That's a fucking stupid thing to think about over lunch. Even though it's nearly three years ago, it's still enough to put me off my food.

"Well, let's get going," I said as soon as Bleif had cleared the table, and Karl, Fellmann and I went to the hangars.

Braun and Zaffke were waiting by the truck, with Schiffer and Ziegler.

"I think we only need two of you," Fellmann said. He turned to Karl. "Zaffke for preference, I think?"

Karl nodded. "Yes."

"Sir, if I may," said Braun, "I'd like to express all our condolences."

"Thank you."

It took us two hours to get to the crash site. All that remained of Johnny's Albatros was a small spread of blackened debris. It must have gone in vertically, and it must have burnt to almost nothing before the impact.

"So where is he?" Karl asked, looking round.

An infantry Hauptmann was making his way towards us, accompanied by two of his men.

"Ah – are you gentlemen from the fighter squadron?" he asked.

Karl turned towards him, and the Hauptmann's jaw dropped when he saw the Pour le Mérite.

"Yes, sir, we are," Karl replied. "We've come to collect—" he gathered himself briefly "– the body."

"Yes, of course. The coffin's this way."

He looked horribly embarrassed, and two minutes later I understood why. They hadn't got the lid on. Two soldiers were shovelling earth into it, and of course they stopped when we approached.

Part of the pine coffin was occupied by a pitifully small bundle, wrapped very thoroughly in a tent quarter.

Jesus fucking Christ. That's all that's left after you've burned to a crisp and then slammed into the ground at God knows how many kilometres per hour.

Karl gazed at it, his face ashen.

Shit. You were not supposed to see this.

Fellmann turned away, making a huge effort not to be sick. *You didn't need to see it, either. That's not how anyone wants to remember his lover.*

Karl looked at the Hauptmann, who couldn't meet his eyes.

"I'm very sorry," he said quietly. "We had hoped to finish before you got here."

There was an uneasy silence, and then the Hauptmann said awkwardly, "Can I offer you gentlemen a drink while my chaps and yours – um – complete their work?"

"Thank you, sir," Karl said. Then he added, "I wouldn't bother with more earth – it's too late."

"Quite," agreed the Hauptmann, and told the men to put the lid on.

The Company office was in a little room in one of the farm buildings. A slightly-built Leutnant got up as we entered.

"I do apologise," said the Hauptmann. "Quite forgot my manners. Name's Unruh, and this is Steffen."

We introduced ourselves and Steffen disappeared for a moment.

"Tea and rum's on its way," he said when he returned.

Karl fitted a cigarette carefully into the holder and lit it. He took a very deep drag, and then said slowly, "What I don't understand is how there's anything left at all."

Unruh and Steffen looked at each other uncomfortably. They must have seen the whole thing.

"He was my brother," Karl said. "I would appreciate the truth."

"Karl—" I began, and then stopped, because his eyes had turned to me and I had never seen them so hard.

It's not that he suddenly hates me. It's the effort he has to make.

"Go on," he said, his tone far gentler than his expression.

"He jumped, just as we've said we'll do. His aircraft was on fire."

"I see."

I hope I can get away without saying any more. I hope the smell stays in the coffin. If only they'd had time to fill it up with earth.

I think we would all have preferred rum without tea. Fellmann drained his mug and then said to Unruh, "If you'll excuse me, sir, I'll just see how they're getting on."

"I suppose you must lose a lot of chaps," Unruh said.

"Yes, sir, we do," I answered, "but those of us who've been in the trenches far prefer the air."

"Yes," Karl agreed. "Death usually comes far more quickly."

"Well, there is that—" Unruh began rather doubtfully. He was interrupted by Fellmann returning to say that the coffin was in the truck.

We thanked Unruh for his hospitality and joined Johnny, to take him back to the airfield for the last time.

It was hot in the back of the truck, and it wasn't long before the stink of charred flesh began to creep out of the coffin. We all pretended it wasn't there. Fortunately I was sitting next to Karl, so I didn't have to meet his eyes.

Fellmann was quite green by the time we got to the airfield, and obviously glad to get out into the fresh air.

"I'll just make sure everything's ready in Hangar One," he said, and headed rapidly in that direction.

Braun and Zaffke had got out of the cab.

"We'll wait until Fellmann comes back," Karl said. He was still perfectly, almost unnaturally, calm.

It hasn't really sunk in yet, in spite of what you've seen and smelt.

Fellmann came back almost at once. "Can the four of you manage?"

"Easily, I should think," Karl said. He laid a hand on Fellmann's shoulder. "Why don't you get yourself a stiff drink, and I'll come and talk to you about the funeral."

"Yes, I think I will."

The four of us shouldered the coffin and carried Johnny's remains to the hangar. I could almost have carried him by myself.

The Chief appeared with Beilke, Horstmann and Widemayer, all in their best uniforms.

"The roster for the guard of honour's in the Ops Office," said the boss. "The first hour is ours – I thought you'd like some time to get changed."

"Thank you, sir," Karl said.

We were both doing the second hour, which meant that neither of us was flying again that day. *Very sensible of the Chief, that – keeps Karl on the ground.*

He said nothing to me until we reached our room. Then he closed the door behind us and said, "Franz, I want the whole truth."

I stared at my hands. The words wouldn't come out. All I could see was Johnny falling blazing through the sky.

He took my shoulders in a grip of steel.

"For Christ's sake! We were lied to about Friedrich and now you're bloody well lying to me!"

"No – I didn't lie—"

"As good as. I'm not some bloody woman who can't be told what happened to her son."

"I know – look, Karl – I didn't want to tell you. God, no one wants to – you wouldn't, in my place." I took a deep breath. "He jumped, like I said, but – but it was too late—"

"You saw it all?"

I nodded. "His clothes were already – already burning—"

"Shit." His distress was evident and he turned half away, too late to hide it. "So that's why…"

"Karl, I'm so sorry. I wish you hadn't found out. They were supposed to have the coffin closed before we got there."

He shook his head and put his arms round me. "At least this time I know what happened."

I held him tight, wishing I could reverse time and stop it happening.

"We'd better get changed," he said, "and I've got to talk to poor old Fellmann."

"I didn't want him to know, either."

"No, quite… And I've got to get the cushion ready. Poor Johnny won't get the Hohenzollern House Order now."

"No – it's a real shame. After all, he'd earned it."

But that's the Prussian custom – no posthumous awards. Logical, if a bit cold-bloodedly practical.

I had a drink with Kühn and Patschke while Karl was in the Ops Office.

"He's going to be very hard to replace," said Kühn, "with all that experience. And we're a patrol leader down now."

"Is the Major coming to the funeral?" asked Patschke.

"I expect so," I said.

"I'm surprised we're having one," said Kühn. "I mean, you'd think they'd have a family vault."

"We do," Karl said as he came into the mess. "But it's only for those who die at home. The men who died in battle are scattered across Europe."

Which is rather a lot of your family.

Karl left to put Johnny's awards onto the black velvet cushion, and I went into the Ops Office to check the next day's programme. It was all fitted around the funeral, which was at two in the afternoon, presumably to allow the Major time to get to us.

I am not looking forward to any of this – not standing in the hangar in the small hours beside what's left of a good friend, or trying to support Karl, or any part of tomorrow.

Why can't the fucking idiot politicians make peace while there are still some young men left?

There were two bags in the Ops Office, addressed to the Major at the Leussow house, and two thick envelopes lay on Möller's desk. Both were addressed in Karl's writing, one to Fräulein Elfriede von Görike-Menz and the other to Fräulein Alexandra von Warnitz.

Johnny didn't have to sort out his fiancées after all. I couldn't help smiling. *Larger than life, weren't you, leaving behind three lovers, selling cartoons to papers in both Berlin and Munich, and God knows what else.*

I could suddenly see his much-scarred face and almost hear his laughter. *I hope there is life after death, because the idea of Johnny being simply extinguished is just grotesque. And there'd better be a Valhalla, because I can't imagine either God or Satan knowing what to do with him.*

There was a third letter, addressed to Elisabeth, Lady Bartlett. *Very English apart from the spelling. I wonder how long it'll take to reach her via the Red Cross. And she'll have to keep her grief private, living in the enemy's land.*

Karl and I were immaculate when we joined Kühn and Patschke in the hangar. Karl placed the cushion with Johnny's pilot's badge and both Iron Crosses at the foot of the coffin, and then the four of us took over from the Chief and the other three.

Widemayer was trembling visibly, and I understood why – the odour was powerful in the warmth of the July evening. I tried to ignore it, tried not to think that I could be just the same tomorrow.

I hope I don't have that fucking horrible dream again…

Towards the end of our hour we heard six Albatri taking off.

"I really would have liked to fly this evening," Karl said after we were relieved.

Fucking stupid idea.

"We're all flying tomorrow," I said. *Though you shouldn't be.* "Let's just hope everyone comes back."

"Indeed…"

Karl played for us all before dinner, and we sang our favourite songs. He smoked constantly and drank a fair amount, as did we all. No one wanted to stand in that hangar completely sober.

Late in the evening, Karl and I were sitting on the small sofa, not talking because there was nothing either of us wanted to say.

Bretti came and sat on the other side of Karl, as Johnny had done so often.

"My brother was killed last year," he said rather diffidently.

"Where was that?" Karl asked.

"In the east, during that big Russian offensive… That is, he died in the hospital train."

Poor sod, I thought, remembering waiting for the train to Berlin, and the wounded waiting opposite and the shocking state some of them had been in. *On balance, I think I'd rather end up like Johnny than expire wretchedly after suffering God knows what.*

"I'm sorry," Karl said.

"He was a career officer," said Bretti, "so I suppose it was what you expect. The thing is, though, he was eight years older than me and he was a proper big brother, you know, taught me lots of things and—" He broke off abruptly.

Karl put an arm round his shoulders.

"We just have to be glad we knew them," he said gently, "and try to honour their memory."

"Yes – that's what I think too."

For a moment I was annoyed with Bretti for bothering Karl, then I realised he was trying to offer sympathy.

"The thing is," Bretti said again, and then stopped.

"What?" Karl prompted.

"Well, I hope I can do that, but – I – I get so scared." It was little more than a whisper.

"We're all scared," I said.

"Really?" He looked at us. "Even you, Karl?"

Karl laughed. "Oh, God, yes." There was a pause and then he added, "Being scared's not a bad thing if it makes you use your brain, instead of getting killed doing something stupid."

"You'd have to be a fucking idiot not to be afraid," I said. "Courage is doing the job in spite of the fear. It goes once you get stuck in, anyway."

Bretti smiled with relief. "Yes. It's strange, that, isn't it?"

"It's like stage fright," Karl said. "Once the performance begins you just think about what you're doing." He looked at his watch. "Franz, we're due in the hangar."

As we got up I said to Bretti, "Don't worry – you're doing very well. You'll be fine."

"Thanks," he said with a lovely warm smile that lit his eyes.

"Optimist," Karl said as we walked out into the night.

"What?"

"Telling the boy he'll be fine."

"Well, he will!" I replied. "One way or the other."

We stood by Johnny's coffin again as the sun rose. On that occasion we were accompanied by Fellmann and Braun, as the other pilots were all flying.

I'll be glad to get today over with, I thought as we emerged into the bright sunshine.

Everyone except Eichner flew after breakfast. I was unhappy about Karl being up and wanted to fly on his right wing, but of course I had my own Kette to lead.

I knew he hadn't slept, and it would have been obvious anyway from the dark rings under his eyes and the lines in his face. He was perfectly composed, though, and a stranger wouldn't have guessed what had happened.

"Be good to get blood in return for Johnny," Beilke said.

Your room must feel very empty now Johnny's things have gone.

Karl shook his head. "He was a soldier and he died as one. Thinking like that's not appropriate, and it's a distraction."

"Leussow's right," said the Chief. "We can honour our comrade best by fighting as well as we can."

And we did, but without result.

I was very relieved indeed to see Karl back. *If I'd been the Chief you wouldn't have flown* – but that was nonsense. The Tommies were up in such strength that leaving him on the ground wasn't an option. Even Bretti had flown as a full member of the Jasta, his probation curtailed.

After lunch we got ready for Johnny's funeral. I shaved again, just to be sure I wouldn't have a shadow, and then it was time for the best uniform and the gongs.

The Major had arrived and was in the mess, talking to the Chief and drinking a brandy. *The last time we met was in the salon at Claudette's,* I thought, with a ridiculous desire to laugh at the memory of him going upstairs with Jeanette.

He turned towards us, and I was shocked by the bleak emptiness in his eyes. He was greyer than I'd remembered and slightly stooped. *Losing another son has put years onto you – you look like an old man.*

"Hello, Pa. Not the best way to meet again," Karl said quietly.

The Major looked at him with barely concealed dislike. 'Why couldn't it have been you?' his eyes said.

"No. It isn't," he said flatly.

Jesus, that's a bit much. Karl didn't react at all, so it was obviously what he'd expected.

"Congratulations on your Pour le Mérite," the Major added stiffly.

"Thank you... You remember Franz Becker, who came to stay in summer '14?"

That's a whole world away.

The Major's pale, hard eyes seemed to look right into me, with more than a hint of distaste.

"Yes, of course I do."

My back hairs prickled. *Shit – he must think Karl and I are lovers. Is that why he doesn't like Karl – because he knows his son enjoys men as well as women? Doesn't he know about Johnny, then?*

I was starting to feel very uncomfortable. *This is the first time I've met a man who actually dislikes his own son.*

There was a definite air of embarrassment, which the Chief did his best to dispel. The Major didn't help – he was polite to everyone, but distant.

"Well, sir," said the Chief, "it's time we set out."

Fellmann had organised everything beautifully, of course. The coffin was on a gun carriage pulled by black horses, and the band was there, their instruments gleaming in the sun. The whole squadron was immaculate.

The Kaiser himself could inspect us. This is quite a show.

Karl took his place at the head of the procession, carrying the cushion. The band struck up Chopin's Funeral March and we made our way through the gate and out into the lane.

The sombre words of the Lutheran funeral service rang through our corner of the small cemetery. *They've got a point saying it all in German – better than having to remember what the words mean. My Latin's never been that good...*

I dragged myself back to the present as we started to sing 'Now thank we all our God'. Someone near me was singing counterpoint in a beautiful baritone voice, the notes perfectly pitched. *I never knew any of our fellows could sing like that – good God, it's the Major. Bugger me.*

But why in Heaven's name are we singing a hymn of thanksgiving?

Karl and his father behaved with iron self-control. Neither of them faltered for half a second, not even when we sang 'I had a Comrade'. Poor Fellmann looked as if the world were ending, and had to make a huge effort to keep his composure.

Only when I looked closely at Karl and the Major, and saw two pairs of steel-grey eyes, did I realise that the effort was just as great for them.

The ground crew fired the volley over the open grave, and we turned and left Johnny lying there beneath the cross that Zaffke had carved.

The Major came into the mess with us and had a glass of schnapps.

I hope he's not going to stay long – we were all uncomfortable having someone so senior with us, and his being bereaved made it even worse, never mind the tension between him and Karl.

"Sir, I'm very sorry," said the Chief, "but we've got another patrol to make. You're welcome to stay as long as you like."

"No, no. I should be getting back to work as well. Gentlemen, thank you all for your hospitality and for the very appropriate manner in which you buried my son. I appreciate that very much... Karl, would you accompany me to my car?"

There was an almost audible release of pressure as they left the room, as if everyone had breathed out at the same time. We all exchanged looks.

"Flippin' 'eck, he's a bit severe," muttered Beilke.

"What's up between him and Karl?" asked Patschke.

"Gentlemen, the windows are open," said the Chief.

"I'd better get to the office," said Fellmann.

"It's time I changed," I said. "Never do to get oil on this."

As we left the mess, the Major's car was already leaving the airfield. *Thank God he's gone.*

Karl joined me in our room. "Better get out of the finery."

"You did very well," I said, hoping he wouldn't mind my commenting.

He sighed. "At least I won't have to do that again… Be good to get in the air."

"Yes, it will…"

I wanted to ask him what the problem was between him and his father, but there would never be a right time for that. *He'll tell me if he wants to.*

An hour later that was the last thing on my mind. We had one hell of a fight with some SE5 boys, and one of them was the frighteningly good fellow. He got onto Bretti's tail, and I got him off it again almost at once, but then I had to work like fuck to keep him from getting behind me. The bastard could fly, all right.

I shook so badly on the way home that I nearly messed up the landing. *You're tired, Franz,* I told myself as I taxied in. *You'd feel much better if you'd had some sleep.*

I wish it would rain…

"Thank you," Bretti said. "I thought I'd be joining Johnny."

"Knew his stuff, that one," I replied, trying to sound nonchalant but struggling to get my cigarette lit.

Oh, what the hell. He'll feel better if he sees my hands trembling.

Karl looked even more tired than I felt. *It's going to be bad when it really hits you...*

Johnny's wake began after dinner. The Chief made a very nice short speech, saying what a valued member of the squadron he'd been and what a good comrade. Karl listened impassively, his eyes and face carved from marble.

That's the only way you can do it, isn't it?

We drank to Johnny's memory, then Karl sat at the piano and we sang all the Air Service songs. And then he played the opening bars of the English dying pilot song.

"A young aviator lay dying At the end of a bright summer day," he sang with the rest of us, with no apparent difficulty.

You'll pay later, surely.

We sang a few more songs and then got on with the proper drinking. A couple of hours later Fellmann joined Karl and me on the small sofa, obviously very pissed.

"Oh, God," he said suddenly, and collapsed in on himself in misery, his face crumpling.

Karl and I exchanged glances.

"Come on," Karl said, "let's get you to your room."

He didn't resist as we helped him to his feet and out of the door. Fortunately he managed to keep control of himself until he was in his bedroom.

I shut the door behind us as Karl sat him on his bed.

"I loved him," he said. "I really loved him."

Tears filled his eyes and ran down his face. Karl put an arm round his shoulders.

"Yes, I know you did."

We all know he didn't love you – but does that matter now? You can remember him however you like, and he'll always be young, and in your head he'll love you back.

Some minutes later Fellmann stopped crying and wiped his face.

"Will you be all right now?" Karl asked quietly.

"Yes. Thanks," Fellmann answered, and we wished him 'Good night' and left.

Why does Karl have to comfort everyone else? First Bretti, now Fellmann, when he's the one who's just lost his last brother.

"Poor Fellmann," he said after we closed our door. "It was never going to end well for him."

"No."

And how will it end for us? But then our feelings don't go beyond friendship. All the same—

I put my arms round him, pulled him tight against me. *Better enjoy what we have before it's too late.* After a couple of minutes he put the chair under the door handle.

Schiffer brought the shaving water the second my head hit my pillow. Karl was sitting up in bed smoking.

"Didn't you sleep?" I asked him.

He just laughed.

This can't go on. You need leave, or posting away. It's all piling up on top of you.

There was no way anyone could have leave. The aerial activity was the most intense I'd ever known. Somehow during the next day, Karl, the Chief and I all managed to fly against Eichner, and the Chief put him down for dawn the day after.

In the morning, the western horizon was a thousand times brighter than the eastern, and the ground shook and the air trembled as the Tommies launched a massive bombardment.

So that's what they were building up to – a colossal offensive.

"Poor bastards," Karl remarked as we headed for the mess, and there was a distinct tremor in his voice.

"I always hated being shelled," I said.

"Show me anyone insane enough to enjoy it!"

"Well, it's started," said Horstmann. "And I'm fucking glad I'm here and not there."

"I'll second that," Patschke agreed.

The atmosphere in the mess was electric.

"Gentlemen, now we know what the English were planning," said the Chief. "They're going to want aerial superiority over the battlefield, and it's up to us to deny it to them."

"Amen to that," Karl said as he handed me a coffee. "That was half the problem at Verdun – the fucking Frenchies had the upper hand in the air, and they saw everything we did and made sure the artillery gave us plenty of attention."

"It's going to be a hot few weeks," said Kühn.

Karl and Horstmann looked at him.

"Months, more like," Horstmann said.

Hot's about the size of it, I thought as we crossed the lines, all ten of us together. There were at least five two-seaters that I could see, with fighter escorts. Artillery spotting, from the way they were flying.

Time to help the poor bastards in the trenches.

And they were having a bloody awful time of it. Our front line was hidden by huge clouds of smoke and earth, lit incessantly from within. *Thank God I'm up here and not down there.*

I didn't have time to stare at it. Kühn and Bretti watched my back as I set up an attack on one of the two-seaters, straight out of the morning sun. The observer was intent on where the shells were bursting, and I got the bastard. I was near enough to see him slump in his cockpit as I broke away. I turned in behind them again and the pilot tried to get away, but he didn't turn tight enough and I was so close I couldn't miss.

Got you. He fell into a spin and I hurried to join the fray, because one of the escort was going after Eichner – who did far better than I expected but still needed helping out.

We didn't seem to stop – it was one engagement after another, and I was very glad when it was time to go home. And that meant breaking off from the scrap we were having with some Sopwiths, and they didn't want to let us go.

Once again the friendly west wind helped us out.

"Is that what it's going to be like?" asked Eichner after the debrief.

"I reckon so," said Patschke. "But just think – a week of that's worth a month anywhere else!"

Horstmann laughed. "That's probably what they said about the Somme."

Widemayer was shaking, and he headed for the lavatory. Beilke watched him go and shook his head slightly, then looked at me and raised his eyebrows.

Yes I know – but what can we do about it?

"Well done, Franz," Karl said. "Don't forget to put your claim in."

"Oh, Christ, I'd almost forgotten."

Fellmann was sitting in the Ops Office with his back to the window, clearly with a dreadful hangover. He looked pale and miserable.

"You won't be shouting to Bleif for coffee this morning," I said as I did my paperwork.

"Too bloody right I won't! I've got the head from Hell."

"Self-inflicted, no sympathy!" Karl said with a grin.

Fellmann gave him a ghost of a smile. "How about you?" he asked quietly.

Karl shrugged. "Was to be expected, wasn't it?"

Which surely doesn't make it any easier. He didn't eat much breakfast and a couple of times I noticed him staring into space. The Chief noticed as well, judging from his expression.

"Fancy a walk, Franz?" Karl asked.

"Good idea."

We left the huts arm in arm, and as soon as it was safe I slipped my hand into his. *It was only a couple of days ago that we last walked like this, and Johnny was alive then. Now your life has changed for good.*

Karl sighed heavily.

"Let's sit down for a bit," I said.

We lay on the grass in each other's arms. It would have been peaceful but for the rumble of the bombardment.

"I wish they'd done it somewhere else," I said. "That patrol was bloody knackering."

"Yes… you do wonder how much longer it can go on. And if it doesn't end soon then it won't end well for us."

I'd been thinking that for months but hadn't wanted to say it. *The Allies have access to men and material from all over the world, while we're boxed in. When we run out of troops and supplies that'll be that – which will mean they all died in vain.*

That's unbearable. I held him tighter, felt desire build in spite of – or perhaps because of – the situation.

The next flight could easily be the last…

"Shall we go back to our room?" I asked.

His eyes looked into mine, warmer than they'd been all day. "Yes, why not?"

As we neared the huts Karl said, "That's the car Pa came in, isn't it?"

A staff car was parked by the main hut. There was no sign of its occupants.

"I don't know – it's very similar."

Shit, I really don't want to meet the Major again – and I don't suppose Karl's too bothered, either.

The Chief was standing on the steps.

"Ah, Leussow, there you are—" He broke off, obviously very uncomfortable. "I – er – I've got General von Grimnitz in my office. He's come to see you – it's – er – a personal matter."

The colour drained from Karl's face. "Can you give me a few minutes to smarten up, sir?"

"Yes, of course. I said you were resting between flights."

"He hasn't been waiting long?"

"No, no – only about five minutes."

We went to our room in silence. *This was not what I'd imagined,* I thought as Karl took off his worn, oil-stained tunic and old shirt. *What in God's name has happened?*

"I think I'll stay as I am," I said as casually as I could. "It's not an inspection, after all."

"No, quite."

Karl put on his best uniform and brushed his hair. There were still traces of oil around his eyes, but then we never could get rid of those.

He did look bloody good, especially with the Blue Max gleaming at his collar.

"Very smart," I said. "Every inch a Prussian officer!"

He threw a pillow at me. "Oh, shut up! Come on, then – let's find out what His Excellency has to say. I expect Pa's got himself in some scandal with someone else's wife again."

We both knew it wouldn't be anything as trivial as that.

He entered the main hut ahead of me and went into the Chief's office. As I turned towards the mess, I heard the click of Karl's heels and the Chief saying, "Leutnant von Leussow, Your Excellency."

An older, deeper voice said kindly, "Please sit down—" as the door closed.

IV

That's the closest I've ever been to a general – and the only other time I've heard one speak was at that parade, years ago, and I could only make out one word in three.

The mess was so quiet you could hear the guns clearly. Bretti, Kühn and Patschke were sitting there like mice.

Horstmann came clumping up the stairs and into the room. "Bloody hell, you lot are quiet—"

"Shut up!" hissed Patschke. "Grimnitz is in the Chief's office."

"Yes, and I'm the Queen of fucking Sheba!"

"No – he really is," I whispered. "He's come to see Karl."

"Shit – what about?" Horstmann whispered back.

I shrugged. "I doubt it's good news."

I tried to concentrate on the *Berlin Illustrated*, but it was one I'd read before. I had a very bad feeling.

I hope the post comes soon, I thought, trying to distract myself. *It would be good to hear from Maria again—*

The Chief's office door opened and we all looked up. Karl came out, his face white, his eyes shocked.

The Chief followed him into the mess. "Leussow, I'm most dreadfully sorry, especially… You can help Fellmann in the office today – there are a few outstanding matters that need chasing up, and of course you'll be free of all duties tomorrow."

"Sir – I'd like to fly later today."

The boss looked at him doubtfully. "Well, we'll see."

He went back into his office, where the General was still sitting.

"I think I'll go and change," Karl said. "Franz?"

I got up at once and we left the mess.

Neither of us spoke until we got to our room.

"What's happened?" I asked quietly.

For a moment he didn't answer. Then he sat on his bed and stared at his hands. "Pa's dead."

I sat beside him and put my arm round him. "Karl, I'm so sorry."

"It – I never thought I'd – it's just so soon after Johnny—"

"How did it happen?" I hardly liked to ask.

"He – they're quartered in a chateau. It has a marble staircase. He was up late drinking – he was pretty well pissed, apparently – and he fell down the stairs. There were a couple of officers still in the mess, and they heard the crash and rushed out, but it was too late – his skull was – they think he must have slipped near the top… The funeral's tomorrow. The General's sending his car for me."

"That's very kind of him."

And good of him to take the trouble to come himself today. Very unusual for a general to go in person to tell a mere Leutnant that his father's dead.

"He and Pa go back a long way."

"Would you like me to come with you?"

"If possible, yes, please…"

There was a knock at the door and Horstmann's voice called out, "Becker – briefing's in ten minutes."

"Thanks!"

"You'd better go," Karl said.

I nearly said 'Will you be all right?' but it was pointless. I had to go flying, however he was.

"I'll ask the Chief about tomorrow," I said. "And shall I tell the others?"

"Yes, please."

"Ah, Becker," said the Chief as I passed his office door. "Come in and shut the door… Have a seat."

He got up and sat next to me.

"Am I right in thinking that Leussow is the last of his family now?" he asked quietly.

"Yes, sir. I mean, there's a sister."

But of course she doesn't count, not as far as the name is concerned.

He looked very thoughtful. "Please don't tell him I asked."

"No, sir… Would it be possible for me to go to the funeral with him, please?"

"Yes. That's a very good idea." He paused. "On a completely different matter, I've decided to appoint a formal second-in-command. It would make things a little clearer when I'm on leave, and so on. You'd be most suitable, if you'd like the position."

I nearly fell off my chair. "Well, yes, sir, I'd like that very much. Thank you."

"Good. Keep it to yourself until I make the appointment."

"Of course, sir."

Strange day this is turning out to be, I thought as I went into the mess. The others were all there and they looked at me expectantly.

"Karl's father's dead," I said. "He fell down the stairs."

There was a stunned silence.

"Jesus," said Horstmann. "What shit timing."

"How's he taking it?" asked Beilke.

"As you'd expect," I replied. "He won't be on this patrol – the Chief's got some paperwork that needs doing."

"Good," said Patschke. "He's got far too much to deal with."

"What a horrible coincidence," Kühn said.

"It wasn't," I replied.

"Jesus," said Horstmann, "you don't mean it was deliberate?"

I hadn't even thought of that. "No – it was very late and he was drunk. Upset about Johnny, I expect."

"Oh, I see."

"Was he upset?" asked Kühn. "I mean, he didn't seem to be, and death in battle's just what that lot want, isn't it? It's that Junker attitude to war that's got us into this mess."

"Oh, come on," said Horstmann. "That's crap!"

"Whether it's crap is immaterial," said the Chief. "We have a job to do."

Kühn went scarlet. "Er – sorry, sir," he mumbled.

"Everyone's entitled to his opinion," the boss said with a smile. "Now, Leussow won't be with us on this patrol, so we'll fly as a six and a Kette – I'll lead the former and Becker the latter, but we'll stick pretty close together and be ready to offer support…"

The patrol was just like the last one, except that the Chief got a Nieuport. Beilke got a couple of good bursts into a two-seater, which headed west trailing smoke, and we all collected more hits than we wanted. Fortunately none of them caused any real damage.

Karl joined us for lunch. There was a quiet chorus of condolence, and then Eichner really put his foot in it.

"How's your mother coping?"

Karl gave him a blank stare. "My *mother*?" Then he sighed and said, "Oh, she died before the war."

"Oh, shit," said Eichner. "I'm really sorry – I didn't know."

"Of course you didn't. Don't worry about it."

I was starving but still full of adrenaline, and it was an unpleasant combination – as soon as I began eating I started feeling sick, and had to force the food down.

Neither Fellmann nor Karl ate much. As soon as the table was cleared, Karl approached the boss.

"Do you have a minute, sir?"

"Yes, of course."

They went to the Chief's office.

"So who's Karl got left?" Eichner asked quietly.

"A sister in England," I replied, "and assorted uncles and so on, I think."

"In England?" asked Bretti.

"Yes – married a Tommy lord before the war."

"Bet she's having fun," said Patschke.

"Bit awkward having your brother-in-law on the other side," Horstmann reflected. "But there must be quite a few in that position."

"Yes," agreed Fellmann. "I don't understand how we've fallen out with the English when they were our allies for years."

"And the Kaiser's mother was English," added Bretti.

We all shut up as Karl came back into the mess.

The boss put his head round the door and said, "Fellmann, come and give me a hand with the programme."

Half an hour later we assembled again for briefing, and this time Karl was with us.

"Leussow will be leading Widemayer and Patschke," said the Chief.

That is not a good idea. As we made our way to the flight line I asked Karl, "Why the change of plan?"

"We need everyone flying – it's as simple as that."

I shut up, because he didn't need me querying whether he was in the right frame of mind, and because he was right. And he knew perfectly well that he was expendable – after Verdun he could hardly have doubted that.

When you get killed I shall just have to carry on until I follow you.

I tumbled into bed that night, exhausted and yet still so strung out that I was wide awake. I'd drunk a fair quantity of wine and brandy, but it had almost no effect and I lay staring at the ceiling, listening to the bombardment and wishing I could sleep.

At least I'll get part of tomorrow off - though how I wish it were for a different reason...

Bullets flew round my head, the windscreen shattered, there was a hammer blow to my right knee and then the fire started—

And then I was clinging to Karl in terror, because the dream had been *exactly the fucking same.* Again.

"Oh, Jesus," I heard myself gasp - and wished I hadn't, because I sounded like a man on the edge of insanity.

"It's all right, Franz," he said gently into my ear. "Whatever it was, it can't get you now."

No - it's waiting for me in the clouds. I'm going to end up like Johnny and Westermann—

"Sorry."

"Whatever for?"

"Waking you up."

"You didn't... Move over and I'll get in."

"You seem to be helping everyone else," I said, "when it's you that—"

"Oh, I'm all right."

I started to say something else, but his lips landed softly on mine and his strong arms pulled my body tight against his, and there was nothing to say and no need to think.

The dawn flight was as insane as those the day before. *I don't know how much of this I can do,* I thought as I parked. I slid down the fuselage, my knees trembling.

"You've been busy, sir," Uhlig remarked, pointing at a line of holes along the right lower wing and another in the fuselage.

God, those are close. That was that SE5 fellow again. Still, he missed me and that's the main thing.

Everyone had made it back, but we were all pale and shaken. Poor Widemayer looked terrible and didn't come to the mess.

The post came as we were having second breakfast. There was a package for me from Berlin.

"What's this?" I asked.

"What do you think it is?" Fellmann replied.

I'd completely forgotten about the Hohenzollern House Order. "Oh. This is rather handsome."

Another black and white ribbon for my buttonhole, this time with crossed swords on it, and another gong for special occasions like – ah. Funerals.

"Congratulations, Becker," said the Chief with a warm smile.

"We've got the same number each now," Karl said, and his eyes thawed as he looked at me.

"Party tonight!" said Beilke. "Ow!"

He glared at Kühn who was opposite him, and then blushed as he remembered that Karl had to go to his father's funeral.

"That's a bloody good idea," Karl said. "We'll start with a good sing-song."

Give your Pa a decent send-off – probably better than the one those bloody staff officers will give him.

"Time to get ready," he said, and we went to change.

"I suppose this goes ahead of my Blue Fritz as well," I said with mock grumpiness.

"Certainly does! But after your Iron Cross Second Class."

"Why the fuck does it have to be so complicated?!"

"You've got a bit of fluff on your shoulder," he said, and removed it with a caress. There was a pause, and then he added, "Thank you for coming with me today."

"Don't be daft – what else could I do?"

The General's car collected us at eleven. The roads were so busy that we got stuck for about half an hour, and I thought we were going to be late. Karl sat relaxed and unconcerned beside me, and I had the feeling he wouldn't mind if we missed the funeral altogether.

I tried to imagine burying Johanna and Mama within a week, but couldn't manage it. *And that would be different, anyway – they're civilians.*

The General received us both very courteously, and there was just time for a brandy on the terrace before the procession began. His staff were polished and shining – none of them ever got dirty – and very posh.

For the second time in less than a week, I listened to the Lutheran funeral service and sang that beautiful chorale 'Now thank we all our God'. *It must be family tradition. I must ask Karl why, some time when it won't be inappropriate.*

He behaved just as he had at Johnny's funeral, with complete self-control, and I wondered whether I could have done it.

After the burial we went back to the chateau. Karl stopped in the hall. In front of us was the marble staircase, its treads worn smooth down the decades. He looked at the foot of it, where the Major's body had been found, and then lifted his gaze and followed its sweep slowly up to the first floor and along the gallery, his eyes very cold.

There was an uneasy silence.

"Leussow, the late Major's effects are all in his room," said the General. "I'll show you up."

"Thank you, Your Excellency."

"Oh, Herbold – would you take Leutnant Becker into the mess?"

"Of course, Your Excellency."

The mess was very grand, and everyone was very formal compared to the front line, and especially to the Air Service. *Doesn't matter how upper-class you are, you're all base-hogs and so I, the most junior officer in the room, can look down my nose at all of you.*

Which was just as well, because they all looked down their noses at me and my bourgeois, unornamented name. They treated Karl rather differently – but then he was a nobleman, and a holder of the Pour le Mérite, and the son of their late colleague.

I almost laughed as I remembered Johnny saying 'du' to the Chief of Staff at Christmas. *He wouldn't have liked that one bit.*

There was an excellent buffet laid out in the dining room. *Bloody hell, I thought we ate well, but this is on another level.* I felt a surge of contempt for the men who enjoyed such luxury and slept in safe, comfortable beds, while others were dying and being mutilated under the English bombardment.

Karl's eye caught mine and I could see him thinking much the same.

"Thank you for today, Your Excellency," Karl said. "I appreciate it very much… We should be getting back now."

"Yes, of course. Herbold, would you order the car for our guests, please?"

"Of course, Your Excellency."

Lucky Herbold. Who'd be a general's office boy? I wonder what his official title is.

Grimnitz came to the car to see us off.

"Leussow, do please let me know if there's anything at all that I can do."

"Thank you, Your Excellency."

Thank God we're out of there. That was all just too artificial.

Karl was silent for quite a while, and then he said quietly, "Makes you sick, doesn't it? I could almost wish for a fucking great shell to land on the place. Bit ungracious of me after Grimnitz was so kind, but it sticks in my throat."

"Mine too."

"You know, the Fifth Army HQ was forty kilometres back at Verdun. Hardly surprising they never knew what the fuck was going on."

"And when you think that our fellows in the trenches are having the crap shelled out of them…"

"Quite. I suppose we should remember they're not all like that – we had an artillery general in the Brandenburg Corps who was always right up with his guns, until the bastards got him – but there are far too many who are... Smoke?"

"Thanks – I'll stick to mine!"

There was a sudden flash of gold from his left hand as he lit both our cigarettes. For a moment I wondered what it was, because Karl had never worn a ring in all the time I'd known him. Then he rested his hands on his legs, and I got a good look at it and recognised it as his father's.

You're not the youngest son any more. You're the head of the family. It's all yours now, whether you like it or not.

The roads were appalling and we arrived back too late to fly. *Good thing too. It's the last thing Karl should do, however much he might want to.*

Beilke returned a happy man, having sent a two-seater down out of control.

"Double reason for a party," he said cheerfully.

"Sounds good to me," Karl said. "I could do with a bit of fun."

I'll bet.

"Ah, Leussow," said the Chief. "Come to my office for a moment."

I went to change, and left the gongs on my best uniform. *There'll be another funeral before long, and if it's mine then Karl – or someone – will put them on the cushion, before sending them to my family with the rest of my things.*

It's only a matter of time.

Karl came into the room and started changing. The late sun slanted in through the window, and I watched with appreciation as it lit the muscles moving under his skin.

"What did the boss want?"

"I've got six days' leave, to go to Berlin and see the lawyer."

"Good."

He smiled. "Nice to know you want to be rid of me! Do I snore that badly?"

"Horribly. Pity you haven't got longer."

"Even greater pity you can't come with me."

"Now that would be bloody good… Are you going home?"

He shook his head. "No. Möller's booking me a room at the Adlon."

"Very nice too!"

"I'm not sure it will be, with all the shortages."

"Oh, the Adlon won't be suffering from those."

He pulled a face. "No – any more than Grimnitz's staff. Honestly, the contrast between that buffet and infantrymen's fodder, let alone iron rations! And it's the same at home – you can have what you like if you can afford it."

"You always could – though you're right, it's far worse now… What time do you leave?"

"Straight after second breakfast. Let's get to the party."

Late in the night we were sitting on the floor. The others were either singing along to the gramophone, or playing some silly game or other.

"Well, that's the end of the old bastard," Karl said softly.

So it's mutual. "What – er – what was…?"

He sighed. "You know, Franz, I've never been able to answer that. The animosity was always there… and then when I was ten he told me I'd be going to cadet school, like Friedrich. That was the last thing I wanted – all I wanted to do was play the piano, and cadet school would have ruined that. I told him I wasn't going, and he took his belt off and laid into me. I should have expected it – there was no way Pa was going to allow one of his sons to defy him."

"What made him change his mind?"

"He didn't. Uncle took my side, said I was going to the same school as Johnny. Pa was furious, but Uncle was the boss. And Pa took it out on me. Every now and then I'd do something that set him off, and I'd get beaten. Not often, but unpredictably and pretty thoroughly. It went on until I was fourteen – I was quite big by then, and I decided that next time I'd hit him back, and bugger the consequences. For some reason he never did."

I struggled to make sense of it. Papa had hit me twice, when I'd done something really stupid, but he'd never beaten me.

"I never realised."

He smiled. "Of course not."

"I thought maybe he disapproved of your being – as you are," I said very quietly. *What's the right word? You're not queer, not like Fellmann.*

"Oh, he did. Just before he left the other day, he said he knew all about my 'proclivities', as he put it, that the family'd had enough scandal because of that sort of thing. I reminded him that we'd last met in a whorehouse, and he said, 'Exactly. You're one of those wretched perverts who can't make his mind up.' And then he made a remark about you, and that really pissed me off."

"Jesus – I thought that was what he was thinking."

"I told him straight out that I'm not fucking you, and that you're not fucking me, either. He didn't like the choice of words, but that was his problem... I also said that his sexual activities had caused a bit of a fuss as well – and he didn't like that, either. I told him he could disown me if he liked, but of course he wasn't going to do that, because then the land would pass out of the family."

He paused and added, "I never thought I'd give a shit when he died – it's just with it being so soon after Johnny..."

I squeezed his shoulder.

"Let's go to bed," I said into his ear. "Indulge your 'proclivities' and no doubt mine as well!"

He fell asleep in my arms, and I detached myself very carefully and went to my own bed. A couple of hours later he woke screaming, and it was my turn to hold him and try to banish the terror.

"At least you'll have a few quiet nights," he said.

"And no one to wake me when I have a bad dream!"

The next morning Fellmann drove him to the station. I walked to the car with him, and as we embraced he said, "Please be here when I get back."

"I'll do my best," I said. "I'm in no hurry for Valhalla or wherever!"

"Stoking the fires in your case," said Fellmann. "With every serviceman that's ever lived and died!"

"Speak for yourself!" I retorted.

I stood waving as the car left the airfield. There was nothing to say that we would meet again.

Johnny's 'replacement' arrived the following day, a Dragoon Leutnant called Steyer with both classes of the Iron Cross and a battered pilot's badge.

"Where are you from?" asked Horstmann.

"Prenzlau."

That provoked a cheer from Horstmann, Beilke and Patschke, and a loud groan from Kühn and Widemayer.

Bretti grinned at me. "More quality!"

Kühn threw a magazine at him.

"We remain outnumbered," Widemayer said. "Fighting beside Prussians in Prussia's war – eh, Becker?"

"Don't drag me into it," I replied, laughing.

"No," said Patschke. "Becker's an honorary Prussian."

Oh shit – what's he mean by that?

To my relief he added, "Look how many black and white ribbons he's got!"

"And what were you flying before your transfer?" Beilke asked.

Steyer grinned. "Same as you."

There was a collective lifting of mood.

"I heard through the grapevine that you needed another pilot," he continued, "and being as you've got two ranking aces and a bit of a reputation, I applied. I don't think my CO was best pleased – he was a bit sour when I left."

"Who cares?" said Horstmann. "We're very happy to see you – the chap you're replacing was very experienced."

"Oh, I can't claim that," Steyer said. "I've only done a couple of months."

"That's two months more than I'd done," said Bretti.

Steyer flew against the Chief that afternoon, and only had to stand him three glasses of champagne, which was a record. He was down for dawn the next day, with the rest of us.

"Be good when Karl gets back," Fellmann said to me in the evening. "It doesn't seem right having no Leussows in the squadron."

"No, I know what you mean."

I missed Karl terribly – his voice, his laugh, the way he often looked at me, and most of all the physical contact. I tried not to count the days until his return – I had no idea if I would survive them, and part of me didn't want him to come back.

He's done more than his share of fighting. Surely it's time he had a desk job in Berlin or a posting to Döberitz. Trouble is, he'd hate it and wouldn't rest until he was back here.

Our room was horribly quiet without him, as was the mess. We had to sing unaccompanied or to records, and it wasn't the same thing at all.

Somehow I did survive, though several times I thought I wouldn't. The worst scrape was complete engine failure in the middle of a very hot fight. Some bastard Sopwith pilot decided that made me fair game, but Horstmann came to my rescue and sent the fellow down in flames.

It's the only time I've been happy to see someone burn.

"Thanks and well done," I said to Horstmann later, and bought him a bottle of fizz.

"We're better off without someone like that," he said.

The Tommies continued shelling at the same horrific rate. All we could see below was a wasteland of shell-holes full of water.

Poor fucking bastards.

The Chief got a two-seater, putting him on a nice round thirty. We garlanded his aircraft and Beilke took his picture standing in front of it. Fellmann smiled, no doubt thinking of the exchange value of the image.

Later that day he came out of the boss's office with a small stack of signed prints, and got on the phone in the Ops Office.

"One of those should keep us in cigars for a month," said Horstmann.

"Optimist!" Patschke said.

"Come on," argued Horstmann. "It's easily worth that."

"Not what I meant!" Patschke retorted cheerfully.

"No," replied Horstmann firmly. "I intend to be here a month from now, even if you don't!"

"We need Karl to tell your fortune," said Beilke.

"Not fucking likely," Horstmann said. "I don't want to know!"

"When's he due back?" Kühn asked me. "I really miss his playing."

Steyer looked a bit baffled, and Kühn pointed to the piano.

"Oh, I see. I wondered why no one played, but I didn't like to ask."

"Tomorrow," I said, and sure enough, when we walked into second breakfast the next morning there he was, smoking and talking to Fellmann.

My heart lifted instantly, in the most stupid manner.

He lifted me off my feet and swung me round. "So, you bastard! Valhalla has no place for you!"

"Apparently not! How was Berlin?"

He shrugged and raised an eyebrow. "Depends where you look. The Adlon was as luxurious as ever – well, almost."

Karl welcomed Steyer warmly, in spite of his being Johnny's replacement.

"Where are you from?" he asked, and when Steyer replied, he said, "from the town itself?"

"Yes – we've got a place near the lake."

"It is beautiful there," Karl said. "Our – my – place is in the country some way to the south-south-west."

I'd thought he looked slightly better, but when he corrected that slip his face was suddenly shadowed again. *I don't think you should be here, but what can we do?*

When I went to change, he came to our room with me, closed the door and took me in his arms.

"I've missed you," I said.

"Franz, I – I can't tell you how glad I am to see you."

A while later he asked, "I take it things have been just the same?"

"That's for sure. They're still shelling – God knows when they're actually going to start the assault."

"That's two weeks they've been going."

"Yes – doesn't bear thinking about… so how was Berlin really?"

He sighed. "Rather depressing, quite apart from the reason I was there. Let's see, here are some highlights: I signed the papers to transfer the prime sand into my name for however long my life might last – that gave me a really good feeling, as I'm sure you'll appreciate. And I had to see some old buffer in the Wilhelmstraße."

"What about?"

He snorted. "Apparently they don't want the old names to die out, so being as I'm the last Leussow, he wanted me to take a job in Berlin."

Thank God.

"And what did you say?" I asked, with a horrible feeling that I knew the answer.

"That my 'fine old name' would be worth absolutely nothing if I abandoned my duty. I'm afraid I was rather rude."

I almost said, 'Don't you think you should consider it?' but realised I'd be wasting my breath.

"And I knocked the Elfriede business on the head. I rang her up and suggested we meet for coffee. She's a nurse, so I was lucky she had time."

"I'll bet."

"Anyway, I told her as far as I'm concerned the arrangement was between her and Friedrich, and his death put an end to it. I also said I thought it was ridiculous that she and I should be expected to contract an arranged marriage in 1917 – and she agreed one hundred per cent. Said she was sick of being passed round our family like some sort of parcel, and that she'd marry whom she pleased."

"Good for her."

"Quite. The irony is I rather liked her, though I certainly don't want to marry her. So I called on her mother the next morning and told her the good news – good from my point of view, that is. She wasn't best pleased, but that's her problem… And then I went to see poor Alex."

"How was she?"

"Livid. Johnny'd mixed the letters up, the stupid bastard. There was one to Elfriede in the packet I'd sent to Alex, and she was so angry she almost refused to see me. Then when I explained, she just burst into tears… Berlin's full of orphans and women with black armbands, not to mention the poverty. If this carries on much longer there'll be a revolution – the gap between rich and poor is far too big."

"Revolution in Prussia?! Whatever next?"

"I sometimes wonder just how Prussian Berlin really is – it's a hotbed of socialism these days... anyway, I bumped into Alfred."

"You did? How is he?"

"Very well. Be back in Italy next week – he said the Austrians are fucking useless as usual, but our mountain troops are good blokes and they've been having great fun kicking the shit out of the Italians, so he's looking forward to more of it. And he said to say hello to you."

"So he's just as belligerent as ever?"

"Every bit! And, while I didn't meet any virgins, I did have an excellent evening at the free love club. Fucked myself completely stupid."

"So it wasn't a waste of a trip, after all!"

There was a loud knock at the door and Horstmann called out, "Wake up, you lazy bastards! Briefing's in fifteen minutes!"

"Coming!" we called out together, and dressed hastily and headed for the mess.

The day after he got back he sent an SE5 down in flames. Widemayer was in his Kette, and judging from his haunted expression afterwards he'd seen the Tommy burning.

Bretti sought out Karl and me at the party that evening.

"I'm really worried about Widemayer," he said.

You've come to the right two men. Not far behind him in the fruitcake handicap...

"Nightmares getting worse?" I asked.

"Yes – but – sometimes he talks to himself. Out loud, I mean. Just as if someone's there."

Karl and I looked at each other, and I could almost hear him thinking that neither of us had got to that stage yet.

"Bretti, you've got to tell the Chief," Karl said.

Bretti looked horribly uncomfortable.

"I could do it if you like," I said. "After all, I'm his deputy now."

"Would you?"

"Yes, of course. But I'll have to say it was you who told me."

"I don't know – it really feels like snitching."

"Not at all," Karl said. "It's not as if you've caught him cheating at cards. He's ill and he needs help."

"Yes, do, then. Thanks."

"That's all right," I said. "You were right to tell me."

Karl had another terrible night and looked awful in the dawn. *I'll have to talk to the Chief about you as well. God knows I don't want to do that, but I want even less for you to get killed.*

He came back with his aircraft badly holed. The Chief frowned and summoned him to the office, and judging from Karl's face afterwards he must have had quite a bollocking.

As soon as we'd finished breakfast, I went to see the boss.

"Ah, Becker, come in."

I closed the door behind me. "Sir, this is rather awkward."

"Go on."

"Last night I heard that Widemayer, er – Brettschneider says he's started talking to himself out loud."

"Ah… It really is time he was posted away somewhere quiet, but I'm not sure we can manage without him at present."

"We'll be without him if he cracks up."

"Yes, indeed. I'll get Fellmann to see how quickly we can get someone else." He paused. "I thought you'd come to talk about Leussow."

I looked at my hands. I'd realised very quickly that Karl was worse. It wasn't only the bad nights – during the intervals between flights he often stared into space, with that disturbed look in his eyes.

"I'm not asking you to break his confidence," he said, "but between you and me, I'm very concerned about him. He's had far too much happen at all once."

"Maybe he should be ordered to take that job in Berlin."

"What job's that?"

I told him, and he looked very thoughtful.

"But please don't let on that I told you," I added. "He'd kill me."

The Chief smiled. "I doubt that, but don't worry – any orders will come from Berlin."

We both knew that replacing Karl would be impossible. *If he gets shot down we'll have to replace him,* I thought – and immediately wished I hadn't, because I was afraid the thought would bring bad luck.

"What did the Chief say?" Karl asked me as we fetched our extra sweaters for the next flight.

"He's going to ask Fellmann to look for a replacement for Widemayer. As soon as that's sorted out he'll post him away."

"Good. Let's hope it doesn't take too long."

We assembled in the mess for briefing, but there was no sign of Widemayer. The Chief looked at his watch.

"Brettschneider, would you go and fetch Widemayer?"

"Yes, sir."

Bretti came back a couple of minutes later, looking worried.

"Sir, I can't get into our room," he said. "I could hear him talking and I banged on the door and shouted, but he didn't open it. And he's blocked it shut."

We all looked at each other and followed the Chief to their door.

Just as Bretti had said, we could hear Widemayer talking, or rather muttering to himself.

The boss banged on the door. "Widemayer! Open the door!"

No response.

He banged again, harder. "We take off in thirty minutes!"

No footsteps, just more muttering.

The Chief turned to Karl. "Break the door down, would you, Leussow?"

"Yes, sir."

Karl's shoulder slammed into the door with such force that it gave way instantly, and he almost fell into the room. Widemayer had put a chair under the handle and we picked our way over its remains.

At first we didn't see him – then Bretti gasped, "Oh, Jesus!"

Widemayer was cowering in the corner between the end of his bed and the wall, staring wide-eyed into nothing and raving, his arms wrapped round himself.

"Widemayer," Karl said quietly, and reached out a hand.

Widemayer screamed in terror and shrank back against the wall. Karl turned and left the room, his face ashen. I followed.

He was leaning against the railing at the top of the steps. I put my arm round him and felt him shaking.

"Let's go back to the mess," I said, a noticeable tremor in my voice.

Is that what happens? And how long before it's my turn?

The atmosphere was very sombre as we reassembled. None of us had needed to see that. The Chief called into the Ops Office briefly, said something to Fellmann about getting Widemayer taken to hospital, and then joined us.

"Gentlemen," he began, and paused before continuing slowly, "no one should judge our comrade – he's given more than he could, and is just as much a casualty as if he'd been shot down."

Well said, I thought, and wondered what on earth the doctors could do for him.

"We have a job to do…"

And we did it to the best of our ability, and it was another series of fights that left me drained and shaking.

By the time we got back, Widemayer had been taken away. Beilke helped Bretti to sort his things out.

It was rather difficult to recover our sense of humour.

That was worse than watching someone bleed to death. If you're dead it's all over, but Widemayer's in some private hell and might never escape.

Karl was very quiet and ate hardly any lunch.

"Let's go for a walk," I said after coffee.

The feeling of his hand in mine had never been so reassuring.

"The poor bastard," he said. "I wonder if he'll ever recover."

"God knows… Let's try to forget everything, just for a few minutes."

He smiled. "Good idea."

We lay side by side on the grass.

"Close your eyes," he said. "Now pretend you're somewhere really peaceful and beautiful, and tell me all about it."

I shut my eyes and the image that came was of Brandenburg.

"Sitting on the terrace of your house," I said, "just the two of us, with the sun going down across the lake. The war's over, and we're both fine, and there's no need to go anywhere…"

He looked up at me, his eyes actually warm. "And we can spend all day in bed."

Lovely thought.

"How long have we got?" I asked.

He looked at his watch, and the answer was obvious.

"Oh, well," I said.

"Later, then. We can leave the others boozing in the mess."

"Good idea." I sat up and stretched. "I suppose we'd better get back."

"You know," he said as we headed towards the mess, "it's far too lovely a day for killing."

"Tell that to the Tommies."

The loveliness of the weather only intensified the fighting in the air. As we crossed the lines, we saw machines from another

Jasta in a spot of bother with some SE5s, and the Chief indicated to Karl and his Kette to help them out. The rest of us found our own trouble five minutes later: a pair of two-seaters with their fighter escorts.

And so it went on, until the fuel state forced us to go home.

My lives are being used up far too quickly, I thought as I inspected the holes in my Albatros.

All the aircraft were holed, and I was relieved that Karl had no more than the rest of us.

"Pity we can't get to Claudette's," Horstmann sighed.

"It would be lovely," agreed Bretti.

"We'll just have to get pissed and sing songs instead," Karl said with a grin.

"It's all right for you," said Patschke, "you've just been to Berlin and I'll bet you got plenty there."

"Of course. Berlin remains Berlin, after all!"

"Ah, yes – the Capital of Sin!" commented Fellmann with a wink. "I'll just have to wait for my next leave – whenever those blasted Tommies allow me to have any."

"I hope we get a replacement for Widemayer soon," said Beilke. "It's not good being a man down."

"I do have some feelers out," Fellmann said. "There are a couple of fellows just finishing at Valenciennes and one of them's off two-seaters so I've asked for him, but these things don't always work out."

"You'll have to get the boss to sign some more photos," said Kühn.

"I have to keep the supply scarce," Fellmann pointed out, "or the currency will lose its value!"

That evening we had a bloody good sing-song around the piano. Patschke asked for marching songs again.

"Anyone would think you actually *missed* marching!" Horstmann teased him.

"Christ, no!" Patschke retorted. "I swore when I left the infantry that I'd never walk anywhere again as long as I live. I did always like the singing, though, and they are good songs."

Even if most of them are about death. Well, at least that's realistic. Might as well face up to it.

The drinking was fairly subdued – by our standards, that is. Everyone was dog-tired and we were all shocked by Widemayer's breakdown.

It was still lively enough for Karl and me to slip away. At some point they'd notice we'd gone, but now I was second-in-command no one really expected me to piss it up.

We closed our door, and I had the simple joy of Karl's naked body against mine.

I woke in his arms and was wondering how to get into my own bed without waking him, when he started shouting in his sleep.

"Machine-gun! Here!" He sat bolt upright, sweat running down him. "*Quick, damn it!*"

I grabbed his shoulders and had to shake him hard.

"Jesus—"

"It's all right…"

I'm seeing the Chief again after second breakfast. I know you want to do your duty until the bitter end, but you'll fight much better if you have a break.

It was another fine, brutally early dawn. *I wish it would rain. I could sleep for a week – provided I don't dream.*

Karl looked as if he'd been awake the rest of the night, and his face was heavily shadowed. God knows what awful episode at Verdun was haunting him.

Everyone looked half-awake in the lights of the mess. I felt as if I'd died, and been dragged out of my coffin to go flying.

I only hope the Tommies are feeling the same, I thought as we climbed into the limitless blue of the summer sky. *This would be so beautiful if only we didn't have to fight.* For a second I cherished a stupid hope that we wouldn't meet the enemy.

We were still climbing when we met their first patrol – they had the advantage of height, but we were ten to their four so they didn't want to engage us. They were over our side, so we went for them as soon as we were at the same altitude.

As the distance closed, I noticed a two-seater and its escort some way beneath us. I rocked my wings but Karl had already seen it, and the Chief was signalling him to attack.

At the same time I saw four black specks approaching from the west and above us. There was something odd about them – they didn't look like anything I'd seen before, and I didn't like the way they were manoeuvring. They were getting steadily closer, and holding onto their height advantage.

Karl was passing through the two-seater's level, curving round to get into position under its tail.

The four Nieuports scattered, turning to meet us, and half a minute later the four strange aircraft joined the fight in the most unfriendly manner – and one dived straight past us and turned in behind Karl.

"KARL, LOOK OUT!!" I shouted uselessly into the slipstream.

He'll break off, he'll have to – oh, shit, he hasn't seen it! – His aircraft reared up, wallowed, the right wing dropped—

Bullets pinged off my struts and exhaust and I threw my Albatros onto her left wingtips. My pursuer shot better than he flew and I got away from him easily – and I glanced down but couldn't see Karl.

And then I had no more time to look because a Nieuport was trying to get on my tail, and another of those strange aircraft was going after Eichner and he made the mistake of turning right. It was behind him in a flash, and I couldn't get anywhere near it.

I've never seen anything turn like that.

It was a peculiar-looking thing with a stubby nose and a long tail, quite out of proportion. Another spun down past me, missing me by twenty metres or so. I found myself on the tail of a Nieuport and gave it a good burst but without result, Kühn flashed past my nose chasing a Nieuport which was chasing Horstmann, the Chief was attacking the two-seater with Beilke protecting his back—

And the sky emptied in that strange way that I never did understand, and nine Albatri regrouped, and the missing aircraft was the one with black and white stripes round the fuselage.

He was bluffing, playing dead to get away – but I knew that was crap. I'd seen his Albatros rear up and I knew he'd been hit. I just had to hope that he wasn't badly injured and that he'd been able to land… and that he hadn't – burned.

That last thought was just too horrible. That Karl was injured or dead was sickening, and I had to make a massive effort to concentrate on the rest of the flight. Gawping had nearly cost me my life once already.

Oh, Jesus, Karl… If only I'd been nearer I could have saved him.

If he's dead I—

There's no point thinking like that. If he were in my place he'd put me out of his mind and focus on the job, and that's what I have to do. I can't help him now.

We had a fight with a group of Sopwiths, but didn't see any more of those new aircraft, whatever they were.

I flew home with a feeling of sick dread that grew and grew. *He's dead and I'll never see him again, never hear his voice or his laughter, never feel his arms around me. It's over.*

No – I won't believe it until I see his body. We were over our side when it happened.

I parked and shut the engine down, my ears ringing. My legs would hardly bear my weight.

None of the others wanted to look at me. Zaffke came out of the hangar and his face creased in dismay.

"He's been shot down," I said, "but I didn't see him crash. There's still hope."

The words sounded hollow. I was trying to convince myself as much as him.

We gathered round for the debrief. The Chief looked at me very sympathetically, and after he'd finished speaking he fell in beside me as we walked to the mess.

"I'll get Fellmann phoning round at once," he said. "Let's just hope."

We went into the Ops Office together.

"Ah, Fellmann," said the Chief. "Leussow was shot down early on in the patrol. Could you get on the phone and see what you can find out?" He pointed at the map. "It was about here."

Fellmann went pale and looked at me.

"I'm sure he's fine," I said, and once again I knew that I was saying what I needed to hear.

No one said much over breakfast. I couldn't eat, but smoked and stared out of the window and chewed my nails.

I'd better go and put my extra clothes away – but I couldn't face the emptiness of our room.

Horstmann came and sat next to me, in silence. Too much time was passing.

If he were alive he'd have phoned in by now.

I was trying not to listen to Fellmann, because every conversation ended, "No. Thank you anyway."

Bretti sat on the other side of me.

"I wish I'd been closer," he said. "He's helped me out so many times and I was just too far away."

"Don't worry about it—"

The phone rang and I jumped half out of my skin. We all strained our ears.

"Yes, that's right," said Fellmann. "We've got blue fuselages."

Shit.

"Yes, I see… Where did you say? … Thank you very much indeed." His voice was heavy and yet it had risen slightly on the last phrase.

He came into the mess and we all looked at him. He took a deep breath, his face serious.

"He's alive."

"Thank Christ for that!" The sun was suddenly brighter again, and I found myself trembling with relief.

There was a babble of voices. Fellmann held up a hand, and we fell silent again.

"Becker – I'm sorry, but they said he's in a bad way. He landed near one of our heavy batteries, and they took him to – look, come into the office and I'll show you on the map."

The Chief joined us. "Becker, Fellmann, take the car and find out how he is."

We ran to the car.

"You drive, I'll navigate," said Fellmann.

"What exactly did they say?"

I knew what 'in a bad way' meant, and I felt cold and sick.

He sighed. "It was the battery second-in-command who called. He said an Albatros landed near them early this morning. The pilot was badly wounded, and their medics said the best thing was to get him to the field hospital about ten kilometres away – they had wagons going back for shells so they put him in one of those."

"And that's it?"

"Yes. He didn't see any of it himself – they're pretty busy trying to put the Tommies' batteries out of action."

The roads were clogged with traffic. *We'll be too late. He's going to die and I'll be too late. I want to be with him when it happens.*

Don't think like that, Franz.

Eventually we found the hospital, in some official building in a village. A small procession of ambulances waited to unload, while others drove away empty. I didn't want to look at any of the casualties. I'd seen more than enough of the cost of war.

There was a desk in the hall, manned by a harassed sergeant.

"Where can we find Leutnant von Leussow?" I asked him.

"When was he brought in, sir?"

"This morning."

"He'll be outside, then, sir – round the back."

The field behind the hospital was covered in stretcher cases.

"Jesus Christ," said Fellmann, and I realised again how sheltered his war had been.

"You start at this end of the first row," I said, "and I'll start at the other end. When we meet in the middle we'll move to the next row and work outwards again."

"All right."

I looked into one shocked, white face after another, but none of them was Karl's. Most of them were silent, and some were so still I thought they must be dead. They were nearly all casualties of the English bombardment, many obviously mutilated.

I'd forgotten how truly sickening this is.

We were on the third row, and I was beginning to wonder if we would ever find him.

It'll be too late—

"Becker! *Quick! Over here!*"

V

The urgency in Fellmann's voice made me run. He was folding back the blanket from a man slumped against the raised head of his stretcher.

"*Oh, Jesus!*" I heard myself gasp. The ground seemed to crumble, as if I were falling into a bottomless void.

So much blood. The front of his flying jacket was sodden, and more was splashed down his arms and legs. Bright red blood covered his mouth and chin, starting to dull in the July heat. He was gasping for air and it gurgled horribly in his throat, bubbled between his lips.

There was a ragged hole in the right breast of his flying jacket. *Oh, shit. The Tommy was behind him.*

And the jacket's still done up. No one's even done anything!

I unfastened it. His tunic and shirt had been ripped open, and congealing blood was sticking them together and to his skin.

Your silk shirt's ruined, I thought stupidly, and then, more sensibly, *must keep you warm.* I buttoned the jacket with shaking hands, and put the blanket back over him.

"Karl," I managed to croak. I crouched beside him, took his hand in both of mine. It was ice cold and lifeless.

Karl's hands are always so warm...

"Karl – can you hear me? Just squeeze my hand – *please*."

He didn't respond. Fellmann called his name as well, but he just stared through us with dazed, distressed eyes. I could hardly bear to look at them.

Fellmann shook my shoulder. "Becker – there aren't any medics nearby. Look – they're all working over there."

Several orderlies were busy with the men at the other side of the field. I looked at those lying around Karl, and realised how wrecked they all were. *They've left him – them – here to die.*

"We'll have to get them to see to him now," Fellmann said.

"Yes."

As I got up, something gleamed in the open collar of Karl's flying jacket, and I realised he was still wearing his Blue Max.

"I'd better take that before someone nicks it," I said, and eased the ribbon carefully over his head.

There was blood on the cross, clotting on the bright blue enamel. *Bought with blood, bought with blood...* I put it in my pocket, then took the ring from his left hand and put that in my pocket as well.

Fellmann's fingers dug into my shoulder.

"*Stop fart-arsing about!*" he barked, in a tone of such stern command that I obeyed instantly. "Take the front end and we'll get him to the doctor. NOW."

I'd never realised how heavy Karl was. *I hope we're not hurting him,* I thought as I stumbled slightly – but there were no sounds of pain from behind me, just that dreadful gurgling, bubbling sound.

It means he's breathing, Franz.

We reached the open back door of the building and followed the signs to the operating room. Fortunately it was on the ground floor.

The door opened, and a doctor came out and lit a cigarette. His hands and apron were bloody, like a butcher's.

"What the devil are you doing?" he demanded.

We put Karl down at his feet.

"Sir, this – this is our friend," I stammered. "Please can you do something?"

He glanced at Karl and shook his head.

"There's no point. He'll die anyway." His voice was flat and matter-of-fact.

"He can hear you!" I burst out.

Fellmann put a hand on my arm.

"This is Leutnant Karl von Leussow," he said. "He's one of our top fighter aces, and a holder of the Pour le Mérite."

The doctor looked very sceptical.

"Becker," said Fellmann, and I pulled Karl's Blue Max and signet ring from my pocket.

The doctor's face changed for a moment, then he shook his head again and said in the same flat tone, "We're operating day and night. I can't spend time on hopeless cases."

"And our CO is Oberleutnant Adalbert von Kralewski-Zentzytzki," Fellmann added.

"What the hell difference – oh, all right, since you've brought him here." He put his head through the door. "Schmidt! Klein! Bring this one in and get his clothes off!"

Two orderlies came out, picked Karl up, and took him through the door. *Thank Christ.*

"Thank you, sir," I said.

"Thank me if he lives," said the doctor, and disappeared back into the operating room.

I sagged against the wall.

"Come on, let's get back," Fellmann said. "I'll drive... And – er – your hands."

I looked at my hands and the world spun.

Fellmann took my arm. "Come on. There has to be a gents' somewhere."

The water ran red from my hands. *It's hardly the first time, Franz* – but Karl's blood was different.

I sat in the car, staring blankly ahead and smoking, trying not to think what must be happening at the hospital. *Karl will* be on the table – the thought of him lying there naked like some pagan sacrifice, bleeding from that hole through his chest, filled me with a deep, desperate ache.

I would give anything for him to be at the airfield in one piece. Absolutely anything, even my own life.

And what can they do for him? How much blood can you lose and not die? And I've seen more men die from that sort of wound than survive it…

Fellmann had kept his head far better than I had.

You might not have commanded in the front line, but you're still a Regular officer.

"Thanks," I said. "I was fuck all use."

"Nonsense," he said firmly. "It was a horrible shock, seeing him like that – and it must have been twice as bad for you."

There was no point trying to deny anything, not to Fellmann.

"We'll just have to hope he makes it," he said quietly.

When we got back to the airfield he said, "Look, why don't you have a brandy while I tell the Chief the situation?"

I thought for a moment. "Thanks, but I'd rather you told the others while I tell the boss."

"Yes, I see what you mean."

The Chief's office door was open, and he got up and came towards me.

"Come and sit down," he said, closed the door, and sat beside me. "How is he?"

I took a deep breath.

"Shot through the chest, sir," I managed to say. "His right lung."

The whole day had begun to feel like a bad dream, but saying that out loud crystallised it back into reality.

"Oh… I see." His face said far more than his words.

"They weren't going to do anything for him," I said, "but we – Fellmann, that is – persuaded one of the doctors to change his mind, and they took him into the operating room."

I could hear the strain in my voice.

"I'll give them a call in the morning," he said quietly. "They might have an idea by then how he's doing."

"What time are we flying?"

He looked at me doubtfully.

"We're down to nine, sir."

"Yes… All right, then – but no ideas about vengeance."

"No, sir – we promised each other we'd never do that."

"Good." He paused, as if searching for words, then added with a smile, "I don't want you getting shot down as well."

That wasn't what you wanted to say.

"Have we heard any more about a replacement for Widemayer, sir?"

"Yes – he should be here tomorrow. We did get the chap from two-seaters."

"Oh, good."

He looked at his watch. "Briefing's in thirty minutes, so I'll see you in the mess then."

"Thank you, sir."

Once again I had the feeling that he wanted to say something more personal, but didn't quite know how.

I went to our room. It was quiet and empty. I looked at Karl's rumpled bed and at the shirt thrown carelessly onto a chair, and despair almost overwhelmed me.

If only I could believe that there were a God.

I picked up the shirt. It smelled of Karl, and I breathed in the scent and hoped with all my heart that he would live, because the thought of burying him and never seeing him again was more than I could stand.

I'll have to pack his things up, because he won't be back for a long time. A small hope started to germinate. *If he survives then they'll send him home, and he'll be safe because there's no way he'll be fit to come back, not after an injury like that…*

Under his sweaters was a letter addressed to me, with 'Open only in the event of my death' under my name. 'Only' was heavily underlined, and I put the letter in my drawer.

His Iron Crosses and Hohenzollern House Order were in their cases, and suddenly I remembered that his Pour le Mérite and ring were in my pocket.

His blood had dried on the cross and its gold eagles, and the white stripes in the ribbon were stained with it.

I'll have to wash that, next time I've got hot water in here. It won't come out of the ribbon, but that hardly matters.

There was a knock at the door.

"May I come in?" asked Horstmann.

"Yes, of course."

"Fellmann told us," he said, his face sombre. "He did bloody well to land the thing."

The small shoot of hope shrank again. *He won't make it,* I thought, remembering how bad he'd looked and sounded.

Horstmann looked at Karl's Blue Max lying beside the shaving bowl, and I saw his expression change at the sight of the blood.

"Let's get to briefing," I said.

"You're flying?"

"Yes – better than sitting on the ground."

He nodded and we headed for the mess.

At the end of the briefing the Chief said, "Gentlemen, it is more important than ever that we all concentrate on the job and avoid getting distracted. Becker told me earlier that he and Leussow promised each other not to seek vengeance, and that has to be good enough for us all."

No, I'm not looking for vengeance, but if Karl is dying then I want to honour him as best I can.

Most of the patrol was so hot that I completely forgot about him. As we flew home it all came back, and I was almost dreading landing in case there was a message from the hospital to say that he was dead.

Zaffke came up to me as I got out of my jacket and overalls. "Sir – may I ask how he is?"

"Of course… You know what happened?"

"Yes, sir."

I sighed. "He's – as you'd expect."

"He's a Brandenburger, sir – we're a tough lot."

I couldn't help smiling. "Yes, so I've heard. I'll let you know as soon as I hear anything."

"Thank you, sir."

I hope I don't have to tell you he's died. I'm not sure I could actually say it.

There was no message, and I felt I could breathe again.

The late flight was just as bad – and yet I was glad to have my mind totally occupied.

I was suddenly starving hungry, and realised I'd missed lunch and hadn't even noticed. Dinner barely touched the sides, and part of me wondered how I could eat like that when my best friend was on the edge of the grave.

He would do the same. I have to be fit for the job.

The piano stood silent, and while we drank a fair amount no one wanted to play silly games. If Karl had been dead we would have had a wake, but in the limbo of suspense we could neither mourn him nor celebrate his recovery.

I drank what I hoped would be enough to send me to sleep, and went alone to our room.

Karl's shirt was lying on my bed where I'd dropped it, and I undressed and put it on and got into bed. The smell of his sweat was immensely comforting, and suddenly it was as if he were in the room with me.

'Don't be upset, Franz,' he said, quite clearly.

"Karl—" But he'd gone.

Oh, Jesus. Does that mean he's dead? I lay awake staring at the ceiling. The conversations we'd had about haunting came back, all too vividly. *I'd know if he were dead – but was that him telling me exactly that?*

Sleep was impossible. I put the light on and tried not to think, but I kept seeing Karl lying on the stretcher, covered in blood and trying to breathe. The feeling of his cold, limp hand in mine wouldn't leave me.

I must have fallen asleep because Schiffer was banging on the door. I shaved and dressed quickly, and then left Karl's Pour le Mérite to soak.

The dawn flight was just as we expected. Fortunately we all got back, and Fellmann came out of his office as we headed for the mess.

Oh, shit – the hospital must have phoned. Karl's dead and they want us to collect his body—

"He's still with us," Fellmann said. "They said he's weak but holding on."

Thank God.

"At least we didn't meet any of those new Tommy aircraft this morning," said Beilke.

"No, quite," Patschke agreed. "And I don't mind if I never do again."

"Me neither," said Kühn. "It's not natural the way they turn."

"Rotaries," said Horstmann, "and that's what we'll need as well if they deploy many more of those."

The old rotary versus inline debate started up. I lit another cigarette and stared out of the window, dog-tired from emotion and lack of sleep.

I wonder if I'll be able to visit Karl.

Widemayer's replacement seemed pleasant enough, though he looked appallingly young. His name was Schaff and he was from Königsberg.

"I'm so glad to be here," he said. "I couldn't believe my luck."

"Things have changed a bit," said Horstmann quietly.

"Yes, er—"

I could see him wondering where our other big ace was.

"Leussow was shot down yesterday and he's in hospital," Horstmann explained. "It's – well, he's been badly hit."

"Oh – I'm really sorry. I hope he'll be all right."

"So do we," I said.

"What were you doing before flying?" asked Beilke.

"Oh, nothing – I was at school. I volunteered for pilot training as soon as I could. We left, you see, when the Russians invaded, and the victory at Tannenberg meant we could go home, and—"

"'No aviation, no Tannenberg,'" quoted Patschke.

"Yes, that's it. And I read everything I could about Immelmann and Boelcke and Richthofen – and the Chief, of course. I can't believe I'm really here."

I didn't want to look at him. *You don't even look old enough to shave, and in a few days you'll come up against the Tommies' finest.*

We were airborne again in no time, and once again I flew home soaked and shaking. The weather was pitilessly fine, and all I wanted was rain for at least a week.

"Becker," said the Chief, "I'd like you to fly against Schaff this afternoon – and I want a more detailed report on Leussow's condition as well. What I suggest is that you fly straight after lunch, then go to the hospital. If you're back in time then you can join us on the evening flight."

My heart lifted. "Thank you, sir. Thank you very much indeed."

"Not at all."

Schaff flew quite well, but I would have killed him with no difficulty.

"That's four beers you owe me," I said, and went over the flight with him. All I really wanted was to get to the hospital as fast as I could, but I made a huge effort to give the boy the time he needed.

"Thank you," he said sincerely. "That was so helpful."

"Just sit down somewhere quiet and go over it all – and practise your circles."

He looked blank and I said, "Ask Fellmann to show you – no, I've got to go to the Ops Room, so I'll ask him."

"Come with me," Fellmann said to Schaff. "I'll show you what that's about…"

Möller gave me the starting handle and I got the car going. *I hope the journey's better than yesterday, or I'll get there in time to head back. They need me on the evening flight.*

It wasn't. I sat stationary while they cleared a broken-down lorry off the road, chewing my nails and smoking.

I hope he doesn't die while I'm sitting here—

I've never visited anyone in a field hospital. I'd never even been inside one until yesterday.

The traffic outside the hospital was just as heavy. The same Sergeant was on the desk, and he looked as if he'd been there all night.

"Could you tell me where Leutnant von Leussow is, please? He was brought in yesterday."

"One moment, sir." He consulted a large book, and his face seemed to change. "First floor, sir – up the stairs and turn left, third door on the left."

Nurses and orderlies bustled along the corridors and up and down the stairs. The place smelled strongly of ether and disinfectant, and I had a sudden longing for fresh air.

Third door on the left…

There were six beds in the ward. They were all bad cases, and the air was thick and full of groans and muttering.

Jesus, what a place! If I get badly hit then I want to crash and have it over with.

Karl's bed was near the door, on the right. A nurse was sitting beside him, and as I got closer I heard him talking agitatedly, his voice barely more than a whisper, the words in bursts between gasping breaths.

"Hello, Karl," I said.

He didn't hear me. The nurse turned to me with relief.

"Oh, good. Perhaps you'll be able to settle him down." She turned back to him. "Your friend's here. I'll leave the two of you to talk."

She got up, and I sat carefully on the edge of his bed, afraid of hurting him. He stared through me, his eyes bright and unfocussed. His face was ashen, and sweat was beading on his forehead and trickling into the lines of pain.

My heart turned over. All I wanted was to hold him and somehow make him better.

"Hello, Karl," I said again, trying to keep my voice steady.

His eyes settled on my face, but with a strange distance in them.

"Franz – thank God – give me – give me – my rifle—"

Oh, Jesus. He doesn't know where he is.

"It's best to go along with it," the nurse said quietly. "Try to calm him down."

I took hold of his hand. It was hot and clammy.

"You don't need your rifle now, Karl," I said gently. "You've been hit."

He moved his head impatiently. "I know… but my sight – in – in the case—"

"It's all right. Taschner's done that for you. He's looking after your gear."

His other hand clawed at the blanket.

"But it's – still there – look—" He gazed past me into space.

"That's not your rifle," I improvised. "It's Taschner's."

He relaxed a little. "Where is – he then?"

"Having a break. Probably gone for a – to the latrine."

I realised that the nurse had left us, that I could have said 'gone for a piss'.

"Oh."

The tension left him abruptly, and his hand went limp in mine. I thought he'd passed out, but then he whispered, so faintly that I could hardly hear him, "He got me, Franz… the Englishman – too fast—"

He must mean the English sniper that he had the duel with in '15.

"No, Karl, he didn't. You got him. You're a pilot now, like me, do you remember? You were shot down and now you're in hospital. They never got you when you were a sniper."

He looked at me without understanding. *Never mind. It really doesn't matter – but Jesus, you look bad.*

His eyes were sunk deep into their sockets and ringed with dark shadows, and his lips were tinged with blue.

"Try to sleep now, Karl," I said softly, trying to ignore what I could see so clearly.

"When are – they coming?"

"Who?"

The medics, of course, you stupid bastard. Who else can he mean? Who else do you wait for when you're lying wounded in the bottom of the trench?

"They're very busy. I expect they'll be here soon."

"Tell them – hurry… don't feel good… can't breathe—"

Oh, Christ. I've never heard Karl say he felt ill.

"I'll fetch them now," I said, a tremor in my voice.

I stood up unsteadily and looked round. There was an orderly a short distance away.

"My friend says he's feeling bad," I said, and as he looked at Karl I could see what he was thinking.

He made his way to Karl's bed with almost feminine grace. I'd never seen anyone quite so camp in my life, and my mind clung desperately to the distraction.

"Your friend says you're not feeling well," he said as he bent down and laid his hand on Karl's. "I'll just have a look at your dressings, make sure you're not bleeding, then we'll see what we can do for you."

His voice went with his walk, but there was something very reassuring in it, something that would have made me feel safe and comforted if he'd been looking after me.

Karl's in good hands, however girly the fellow might be.

I caught sight of the clock and exclaimed, "Shit!" before I could stop myself. *I should have left by now, I'm going to be late and I mustn't miss the patrol.*

"Karl, I've got to go. I'm on duty in a couple of minutes."

I've got to go. I've got to leave you here and I'll never see you again, because you're going to die.

"I'll try to come tomorrow, but it depends how busy we are. I can't promise."

I can't promise anything. I might be dead myself – and if you die then how can I live?

What on earth are you thinking, Franz? You've got Maria waiting for you.

Karl didn't answer. His eyes were closed, and he was frighteningly still.

"It's all right, sir," said the orderly. "Don't you worry. I'll look after him."

He looked at me with very sympathetic eyes. 'I understand,' they said.

What has Karl said in his delirium?

"He – er – he was talking nonsense about the trenches," I said.

"Oh, they say all sorts of things, sir. No one takes any notice, especially if—" He stopped himself abruptly and turned back to Karl.

Especially if they're dying.

I walked slowly out of the ward. It was as if the light had gone from the day, as if there would never be light again. I found my way to the car, and sat wondering where I was going to find the strength to drive back to the airfield, to fly and fight.

I made it just in time for briefing. It was a relief to fly, to have something else to think about. I bloody nearly got a Sopwith but the bugger didn't go down.

That would have been good – then I reminded myself of my promise to Karl. *'He was a soldier and he died as one,'* he said about Johnny. *Karl always knew the stakes he was playing for.*

"How is he?" the Chief asked me as we walked to the mess, and it all flooded back in.

"Pretty bad, sir." *Of course, you wanted a more detailed report.* "I – he, er, he thought we were in the trenches… He looked, well—"

"But he was conscious and knew who you were?"

"Yes. Yes, he did… He just looked so bad…" My voice trailed off.

"I'll come with you tomorrow."

I almost asked if he was sure he could spare the time – but that was stupid. The Chief always visited anyone who was in hospital.

"Beilke's coming on well as a patrol leader," he said, "and I'm going to give Horstmann a trial."

"Yes, I think he'd do well."

We've lost three experienced men in the space of a couple of weeks.

"Come to my office a minute, would you?"

"Of course, sir."

He closed the door behind us.

"You'll appreciate I've had to request another pilot – we can expect Leussow to be off the strength indefinitely – and I wondered whether you'd prefer to share with someone you know."

"Yes, thank you, sir, I would."

That was very thoughtful of you, and you're spot on. The last thing I want is a strange room-mate.

"Have a think who you'd like – obviously it's subject to the other pilot being happy with the arrangement."

"Yes, of course."

Asking could be really awkward. Maybe I should just share with the new man.

I'd better finish packing Karl's things.

The room was unbearably quiet. I had a sudden, stupid longing to be lying in his arms, and for one horrible moment I thought I was actually going to cry.

Pull yourself together, you pathetic idiot. You always knew this was likely to happen – and he's not dead yet, is he?

Karl's Pour le Mérite lay on the washstand next to the bowl. The medal was clean but the ribbon was heavily bloodstained. *It won't show when it's under his collar, and he wouldn't care anyway.*

I put his shirt under my pillow and started packing. His cigarette case and lighter were on his bedside table, with his black holder. *The holder's not worth anything, but these are solid silver and engraved with his coat of arms. Even if he doesn't make it, someone in the family should have them.*

He's the last one.

Maybe they're right about keeping the names alive, especially when they're so bound up with Prussia's history…

Too valuable for the post, anyway.

I fastened the bag and took it to the Ops Office.

"Möller, send this to Leutnant von Leussow at his home address," I said, and somehow the words seemed to make his survival more likely.

"Yes, sir."

"How is he?" Fellmann asked.

"Holding on," I said. "He was able to talk to me." I didn't want to go into detail.

"Oh, good."

"Look, I've got his medals here, and his cigarette case and lighter. Is there any secure way of getting them home?"

Fellmann thought for a moment. "Leave it with me – I've got an idea. It might take a day or two."

Fortunately the Chief had told the others how Karl was, so I was spared too much questioning. I wasn't sure if I could talk about him without becoming emotional.

The post had come, and there was a letter from Maria which I read with mounting irritation, because of course she had no idea what life was like at the Front. I knew I was being unreasonable, but the chasm between home and the war was too wide to bridge. *We live in parallel worlds, which never meet.*

"Horstmann's got another flower letter!" Patschke said gleefully, and sang, "She loves me still—" with his hand on his heart.

"Oh, shut up!" Horstmann retorted.

Patschke carried on singing, and Horstmann threw a magazine at him and missed. Patschke sauntered over to him, hand still on heart.

"My heart beats warm in the cold night—" he sang, and picked up a dried violet from the floor.

"Give that back!"

"When I think of my true love—"

Horstmann leapt to his feet, and Patschke dodged nimbly out of his way and headed for the mess door, where he collided with Fellmann who was just coming in. Both of them ended up in a heap on the floor.

"God did that," said Horstmann, retrieving his flower.

"But what had *I* done?" Fellmann asked in mock bemusement.

"Now that would be telling!" I said, laughing.

Fellmann looked at me and raised an eyebrow, and sadness flooded over me. *Here I am, laughing while Karl is dy – in hospital.* His face changed as well, and I knew he was thinking of Johnny.

Horstmann put the violet carefully back in Susanne's letter.

"Hey, Horstmann," I said, "how do you fancy sharing with me instead of that piss-taking bastard?"

"You serious?"

"Certainly am."

"You're on. You hear that, Patschke? I'm going to live with someone who actually has higher feelings."

Patschke pulled a face. "You mean Susanne won't watch me undressing any more?"

"No," I said. "She won't – and I'll be careful to turn my back!"

I turned to Horstmann. "I'll tell the Chief in the morning."

"Thanks, Becker."

Good – but he'll wonder why I wear a shirt in bed.

I'll sleep in it tonight and then wear it for flying. It's a bit big, but that won't matter.

The Chief and I didn't get to the hospital the next day or the day after that. The Tommies were giving it everything they had – directing their artillery, taking photographs, trying to shoot us down – and we were so busy that we barely had time to eat and gulp down some coffee while the engineers and armourers did their work, and then we were off again.

Schaff got thrown into it earlier than anyone would have liked, and had a couple of very narrow scrapes with those new Tommy fighters. His Albatros had so many holes that none of us could understand how nothing vital had been hit, and he was stuck on the ground for the rest of the day.

We'll be after two replacement pilots soon.

Horstmann moved into my room, into Karl's bed but not into mine. The only man whose body interested me was clinging to life just a few kilometres away, and I couldn't even go and see him.

Fellmann called the hospital each morning, and the report was always the same: no change. I didn't know whether to hope or not, and I was trying not to think or feel anything.

I was glad of Horstmann's company, and the lovely Susanne was exactly that. Her photograph stood on his bedside table in a silver frame, her beautiful serene eyes gazing towards his bed.

I can guess what you think of when you go to sleep…

After a second day of hard flying, Karl's shirt smelled of my sweat as well, and the mixture of the two reminded me powerfully of lying in each other's arms.

I'll have to send this to the laundry, I thought reluctantly as I undressed. *It's getting a bit strong now.*

Once again I woke thinking Karl was in his bed, and then dark reality hit me. *I wish I could see him before it's too late…*

For some reason the Tommies weren't out in quite such force that morning. Maybe they'd got all the photographs they wanted for the time being – there was no doubt that their guns were impeccably ranged.

"Right," said the Chief after lunch. "Becker, I reckon we can go and visit Leussow."

"Thank you, sir. I really appreciate it."

"I want to see him as well – it's been rather weighing on me that I haven't been able to get away."

I hope Karl doesn't say something indiscreet in front of the boss – but it would only confirm what he thinks, anyway, and he's being so kind to me that I don't think he's worried about it.

As we entered Karl's ward the Chief paused briefly, then gathered himself.

The stifling July heat beat into the room, and the open windows let in only the slightest breeze. It did nothing to dispel the choking odour of sweat and shit, overlaid with disinfectant.

Karl's breathing was tortured, and the air rasped horribly in his chest.

You're worse, I thought with dismay. *I'd hoped so much that you might have improved, just a little.*

He seemed at first to recognise us, but his disjointed words were about a village they couldn't take and, shockingly, that his company was down to forty men.

Verdun.

His glittering eyes looked straight through the Chief, and I flinched because he said 'du' quite clearly.

The Chief laid his hand on Karl's.

"Don't talk so much, Karl. Save your breath," he said gently, also in the familiar.

I've always thought of you as a hard, practical man. I'd never imagined you could be so kind.

"He's burning," the Chief said to me. "No wonder he's delirious."

I wished I didn't have to listen to him. I could almost see the savage hand-to-hand fighting in the ruined village, continuing relentlessly until the dead far outnumbered the living.

He was increasingly agitated and distressed, the pain clearly getting worse. I looked round several times but couldn't see any staff.

His next words died in a cry that went right through me. *You lay in the trench with a broken leg for hours and never complained. You must be in agony. Oh Jesus, what are they doing, leaving you like this?*

The Chief got up, his face like thunder. "I'm going to find a doctor."

I sat on Karl's bed and took his hand. It was trembling, and his face twisted as he fought to breathe. I could hardly bear to look at him.

"The Chief's gone to get the doctor." My voice shook. "He'll sort you out. It won't be long now."

He cried out again and my stomach turned over. It was the sort of sound you heard from someone lying in No Man's Land. *I thought once they got you to hospital you'd be all right.*

Where the hell's the Chief got to? Surely it can't take that long to find a doctor?

"I don't know what you're all doing!" The Chief's face was as black as thunder, and the nurse following him was glowering at his back. *He must have given her both barrels, and with good reason.*

I got up to make room for her, but Karl's hand was locked around mine and I had to prise his fingers loose. I felt a sudden flicker of hope. *You're not as weak as I thought. Perhaps you'll make it…*

I watched, fascinated, as she prepared the syringe. When the needle went in he looked at her with such gratitude that I felt sick.

"Thank you," I said for him.

She didn't reply. *Nice manners.*

The Chief looked at me and raised his eyebrows.

"God, it's hot in here," he muttered.

I knew we were both thinking the same: *I'd rather be dead than lying in pain, hoping someone will do something about it.*

"I hope she's given him enough," he said, almost to himself. "You can never be sure in these places."

She had given him enough. I watched the pain leave his face, relieved that we'd been able to do something for him.

The Chief sat on the edge of the bed again, and I had the feeling that he didn't quite know what to say.

"You're one of the best in the squadron, Karl," he said, rather awkwardly. "One of the very best. You get well, and we'll see you back before long."

Karl's eyelids flickered, and he whispered something neither of us heard.

"'Ere, mate, where's the dyin' officers?" said a voice outside. "I've got these 'ere blankets for 'em."

"In there. Put them on the table – and keep your bloody voice down. One of the poor bastards has visitors."

An orderly came into the room, put a pile of blankets on the table, looked round and left.

Dying officers. The Chief's eyes met mine.

"Never thought I'd feel sorry for officers," said the orderly's voice. "Right bloody mess that lot are in."

"I told you, keep it down," the other man said. "No one wants to hear what you think."

"Karl, can you hear me?" the Chief asked.

No response.

"I hope to Christ he didn't hear all that," the Chief said to me. He paused. "Look, why don't you sit with him for a bit? There's someone I want to have a word with."

He got up and left. A moment later I heard the orderly who'd brought the blankets say, "Bloody 'ell – did you see all those ribbons? And a bloody Blue Max round 'is neck! And that was one 'ell of a look 'e gave us."

"That's why I told you to shut up – we don't want trouble from someone like that."

I went to the doorway.

"The *poor bastard* we're visiting has a *bloody Blue Max* as well," I said. "I just hope he didn't hear anything you said – and I hope none of the others heard, either."

They both fell over themselves apologising. I almost felt guilty, because I couldn't have done their job in a thousand years.

No, Franz, killing's easy, isn't it? Looking after people would be quite another matter.

Karl was sleeping peacefully. I sat on his bed and held his hand, keeping very quiet, not wanting to disturb him. The orderly's words wouldn't leave my mind, but went round and round.

This is the dying room. Karl is in the dying room...

The Chief came back after about twenty minutes, and as we left I turned in the doorway and looked back at Karl. I didn't want to leave him.

I'll never see you again. Never.

We walked down the stairs in silence and out into the bright sunlight.

"He must have thought you were with him at Verdun when he said 'du' to you, sir," I said, feeling the need to explain.

"Yes, indeed." There was a long pause, and then he said quietly, "It's always bad seeing your friends like that. You want so much to help them, and there's nothing you can do."

"Yes, I know."

Don't I just, I thought, remembering Kurt in the rain. *At least Karl's in a warm bed – but does it really make any difference? You die just the same.*

"That was Verdun he was talking about, wasn't it?" I asked.

"Sounded like it. Bad business."

"Did he really say there were only forty men left in the company?"

The Chief sighed. "That would be about right. I had a friend in the same regiment. He was killed in late May, and by that time only a handful of the original men were left."

No wonder Karl couldn't talk about it before.

"And my cousin was in the 24th – they were in the line beside Leussow's lot – and he got hit very badly near Fort Douaumont. Fortunately he's behind a desk in the War Ministry now."

I shook my head. *And all for nothing.*

"It wouldn't be so bad if we'd taken the bloody place," the Chief said, echoing my thoughts. "As it is, you do start to wonder..."

No, you won't finish that sentence. Not to me.

There was a long pause and then he asked, "Do you think Leussow understands how bad he is?"

"I don't know. I hope not."

"No. I hope he didn't hear what that orderly said... Becker, what on earth happened to your hand?"

"Why? What – oh."

There were four curved red marks on the back of my hand. For a moment I couldn't work out how they'd got there – and then I didn't want to explain.

"Er – Leussow's fingernails, sir."

"Jesus... I went and found one of the doctors, asked if he could be moved to one of the base hospitals. I thought it might be a bit less crowded there, that he might get better care."

"Thank you, sir."

"No, don't... You'll understand, when you have your own squadron. It was nothing doing, I'm afraid. The doctor said he's too ill to be moved."

"He's probably right," I said heavily.

When we got back I said, "I promised Zaffke I'd keep him informed."

"Yes, of course."

Zaffke wasn't in the hangar. Braun said he'd been summoned to the Ops Office, and that was where he was, with Fellmann and Möller.

"And if you could take this package to the Leussow house on your way home," Fellmann said, handing Zaffke what I guessed were Karl's medals and other valuables.

"Yes, sir. To whom should I give them, sir?"

"To Herr Henning," I said. "He's the butler. Tell him you were in Leutnant von Leussow's platoon at Verdun – you'll get a warm reception. He fought in 1870."

"Thank you, sir... May I ask how he is?"

"Still alive. He – er – he was much the same, really. In rather a lot of pain, but then it is a nasty injury."

Zaffke hesitated. "Would you wish him a good recovery from me, sir?"

"Yes, of course I will. He'll appreciate it." *If he actually understands...*

That night I dreamed that Karl had died and we were burying him, and I woke to a feeling of black dread.

"You all right?" Horstmann asked as we shaved before the dawn.

"Yes – just a bad dream."

"We could all do with a rest."

That's for sure, I thought as I looked at the bleary eyes in the mess. *But when in God's name are we going to get one?*

The next couple of days were frantic – the aerial activity got even heavier, and the squadron was struggling. In less than a month we'd lost three experienced pilots, and those new Tommy fighters were far better than our Albatri. Our days of air superiority were over.

The intervals between flights were mercifully short. While I was fighting for my life I couldn't think about Karl. The rest of the time I fretted and fretted. Every time Fellmann called the hospital they said the same thing. No change. I was desperate to see him, but it was impossible.

"The main thing is he's still alive," Horstmann said. "The longer he hangs on, the better his chances."

Kühn opened his mouth and then closed it again. I never found out what he'd been thinking, because he was shot down that afternoon over Tommy-side. We had a wake for him, which released some of the tension.

Karl's replacement arrived, another horrifyingly young man. He turned up in formation with Platzer, both of them flying a new variety of Albatros. This one had an elegantly rounded rudder, in contrast to the slightly squared-off one on the D.III, and the top wing was a little lower, giving us a better view.

Having regard to the number of Tommies up that was definitely a good thing.

What wasn't such a good thing was Platzer's stern warning.

"You really do have to be careful not to dive the D.V too fast," he said, his single eye looking at us very seriously. "I had to jump a couple of weeks back – got vibration which got suddenly a lot worse, then one of the lower wings failed."

We looked at him and at each other.

"When are they going to give us parachutes?" asked Bretti.

"Good question," said the Chief. "Several of us are arguing for them very strongly – the problem's the size. They're just a bit big for our cockpits."

"So make the cockpit bigger," I said to Platzer.

"That's easier said than done," he replied. "They're trying to make the parachutes smaller."

"Well, I wish they'd get a bloody move on," said Horstmann.

"The older Leussow brother went down in flames a couple of weeks back," said Beilke. "He'd still be alive if he'd had one."

"I'm sorry," Platzer said simply.

"And the younger one's in hospital," said Horstmann. "Shot through the chest. And he had to land the bloody thing. God knows how he did it."

Platzer winced. "Nasty… Do wish him a good recovery from me."

"Thanks," I said.

"And now I really must be off," said Platzer. "I'm to take one of your D.IIIs to Valenciennes."

"You'd better take mine," said the Chief. "It's the oldest, isn't it, Fellmann?"

"Yes, sir, it is. You'd need a new engine before long."

"Well, then – I'll have a nice new aircraft instead!"

"You can't take it at once," Fellmann said to Platzer. "We'll have to paint over the Chief's lightning first."

The Chief's personal marking was an eagle's talon clutching a trio of thunderbolts, from the colours of his old regiment.

"You'd be best staying here overnight," Fellmann finished.

Platzer grinned. "Does that mean more Air Service hospitality?"

"We're a bit muted these days," I said.

He grinned again. "Good – my hangover won't be quite as appalling!"

The new pilot was called Neidhart, and like Schaff he was as green as the leaves. Beilke did his first mock combat, and the poor boy looked stunned.

"But I thought I did well on my course," he said.

"I felt the same," said Schaff. "Believe me, it's better to be 'shot down' by these chaps than by the Tommies!"

"You can fly against me tomorrow," the Chief said.

The phone rang and I jumped half out of my skin. Neidhart gave me a strange look, and I didn't feel like explaining.

I strained my ears, and to my relief I heard Fellmann talking about spares.

There was a pile of spares under a tarpaulin at the back of Hangar Two. The tip of a left aileron protruded from it, and I'd turned my back and walked away because I didn't want to see anything that had been part of Karl's Albatros. He'd wrecked it, of course, and had been bloody lucky to escape without further injury.

Fellmann put his head round the door. "Becker, would you come and have a look at the spares request, see if there's anything else you think we need?"

That was a job the boss had delegated to me, no doubt with relief.

"Yes, of course."

There was a letter in the Ops Room addressed to Elisabeth, Lady Bartlett, this time in the Chief's writing. *That's taken him a while to write*, I thought, and realised that he'd been waiting in case Karl died. My heart lifted slightly. *He must think Karl's got a chance of pulling through.*

Stupid bastard, Franz. There's no way he knows any better than you do. He's had to write to Elisabeth – Karl must have been quite a scalp for the Tommy pilot, and no doubt his shooting-down and probable demise made the English newspapers.

Poor Elisabeth. Karl's the only one of her own family that she's got left. I hoped for her sake that Lord Bartlett was still alive, and had to smile at myself for wanting a Tommy to survive.

I looked at the spares form. "I think we could do with more ammunition. I don't see any sign of the Tommies slackening off."

"No, indeed – especially as they finally sent their infantry in this morning."

"And we always seem to be a man light."

"Yes… the Chief's trying to get our strength increased by one more."

"Let's hope the next two fellows have some experience," I said quietly. "It's beginning to feel like a kindergarten."

Fellmann grinned. "With rather dangerous toys!"

"Becker, it's time for briefing," said Horstmann, and we were off again.

We had two more patrols that day and both of them were very lively. *If Schaff survives this he'll be quite useful. If only we could have more like Steyer.*

I was so dog-tired that I almost fell asleep in my chair after dinner, and spilled my brandy on my trousers, which was a shocking waste. The piano stood silent, but Bretti and Schaff put on one record after another.

I should go to bed – but I couldn't face it. I wanted Karl's arms round me and his voice in my ear. I didn't even know how he was, and it was half killing me.

Go and lie down, Franz. You have to fight again tomorrow.

Horstmann screamed in the early hours, something about Tommies. I got up to wake him, but he gave a final loud yell and fell silent.

"Sorry, Becker."

"Don't worry." *You'll hear my burning dream before long.*

"What's that noise?"

Something was rattling on the roof of the hut. *No, it can't be—*

"I think it's rain," I said cautiously.

He went to the window. "It is absolutely pissing down."

"It'll stop before dawn."

"I don't know where you get your optimism!"

I lay listening to the rain, and I must have fallen asleep again because when I woke it was broad daylight. Schiffer hadn't brought the shaving water, and the wonderful noise was continuing.

Horstmann was still asleep. I peeked through the curtains and saw the most glorious deluge soaking the airfield and bouncing off the puddles. *That is the most beautiful weather I've seen for weeks. I can go back to sleep now, and later I'll be able to visit Karl.*

Going back to sleep was a very bad idea. I had the fucking burning dream and woke screaming. *Why does it always have to be the same – and oh, Karl, how I wish you were here!*

"Sorry," I said to Horstmann.

"Look," he said, "everyone has those dreams, doesn't he, so let's forget the apologies."

"Good idea."

We sloshed over to the mess an hour or so later. There was an ill-disguised feeling of relief among those who'd got out of bed. Bretti, Schaff and Neidhart were nowhere to be seen, and I dimly remembered what it was like to be seventeen and able to sleep for hours on end.

Beilke was watching the rain with obvious appreciation.

"That's the best weather I've seen for a long time."

"The Chief's in his office and the door's open," Patschke said quietly.

"Yes, and he's bloody well knackered, same as we are," Beilke replied – though he did drop the volume.

Fellmann came in for his coffee and cigar, and I realised how late it was – and also that I hadn't been in the mess at that time of day for quite a while.

Jesus, I need a rest. Maybe if I don't fly for a couple of days I'll be able to sleep.

"Any news?" I asked him.

"No change, they said."

I went to see the boss. "Could I borrow the car after lunch, sir?"

He smiled. "Yes, of course. Let me know how he is."

"Thank you, sir."

The roads were even worse – the Flanders mud had returned, and the traffic clotted as wheels and vehicles slid on it. There was an endless procession of lorries, artillery wagons and ambulances heading in both directions, and I had to pull into the side of the road several times.

The Tommies really mean it. Let's hope our boys can hold them off.

The hospital was horrifyingly crowded. Men lay on the floor in the corridors, on stretchers or on paillasses. *They must be recent arrivals, they can't leave them outside in this weather* – but then I noticed that some were freshly bandaged and I realised there was nowhere else to put them. The wards were all overflowing.

A nurse hurried past me, her face worn with fatigue. All the staff looked like that. *This is impossible. They could work all the hours God made and still not be able to look after this lot.*

The place stank of shit and sweat, blood and piss and vomit, and the air fairly vibrated with pain. Someone was screaming – or rather, trying to scream, someone who was in agony but who couldn't get enough air into his lungs. It was a horrible noise, a series of shrill, sobbing cries that made my hair stand on end.

Poor bugger's got it in the chest. Nasty, that—

Franz, what are you thinking? I was suddenly sick with apprehension. *That can't be Karl, it just can't. He wouldn't be making a racket like that. You know how tough he is—*

Oh, Jesus Christ. I stopped in the doorway, unable to take another step. Two orderlies were holding him down so the nurse could get the needle into his arm. The terrible agony had lent him strength, and he writhed and struggled.

My knees went from under me and I was almost sick. I leaned against the doorframe, fighting for self-control.

Oh Jesus, it's not working, she hasn't given him enough. Why did they let him get into a state like that? For Christ's sake, why didn't they do something sooner?

I looked away. I couldn't bear to watch any longer. *That could be me, tomorrow or the day after – don't think like that. You can't afford it.*

My eyes wandered round the walls. *This was the village school. There's a mark on the wall where the blackboard used to hang, and a line of hooks for the children's coats.* I imagined them sitting neatly at their desks, chanting their tables and writing on their slates…

And now it's full of broken, dying bodies, the lisping young voices replaced by groans and half-choked words and the quiet, firm speech of the nurses.

Have we no better way to resolve our differences?

"Excuse me, please, sir." It was the very camp orderly.

"You said you'd look after him," I managed to croak.

"We're doing all we can, sir," he said quietly.

I nodded and moved shakily out of his way.

What do you expect them to do, Franz? There are hundreds of men here, and they're all in pain.

Karl had fallen silent. I stopped the nurse in the doorway.

"How—" I had to clear my throat and even then the words would hardly come out. "How long has he been like this?"

"About two days. One of his ribs is shattered and the wound's infected."

Her eyes were sympathetic. I must have looked as shaken as I felt.

"What – I mean – is he—?"

"I'm sorry, it's not good. The bullet went through his right lung and he's lost a lot of blood. He was doing quite well but he's in no condition to cope with the infection."

"I see. Thank you."

No change, you told Fellmann.

I took a deep breath and walked unsteadily to his bed. He was lying quite still, his eyes half open, his face peaceful and suddenly so young. Something inside me contracted to a point so sharp that I could neither move nor breathe.

Do something, Franz. Don't just stand there staring.

The blanket was dark with sweat and his skin was wet. *They should bring you a fresh blanket, but I bet they won't.*

I got out my handkerchief and sat carefully on the edge of his bed, the straw mattress rustling. I dried his face as gently as I could, trying not to catch his stubble.

His eyes seemed to rest on mine.

"Karl, it's Franz."

His fingers moved slightly, and I took his hand in mine.

"Let's... sit... here... " A whisper, barely audible.

"Yes, all right."

"... sun..." The rest of it was too faint to hear.

"Don't talk. Just rest now," I said softly.

"Stay…"

"It's all right, I'm still here."

I pushed the damp hair back from his forehead. He sighed and I went cold. After a terrifying pause his breathing continued, laboured and noisy. I realised that I'd stopped breathing myself, and that my hand lay motionless on his hair. I stroked his forehead again.

"Franz… I…" The words faded away, inaudible, as he sank into sleep.

I realised to my horror that he was completely silent. Then I heard a rasping breath, and after a pause, another, frighteningly slow.

I leapt to my feet. "Sister! *Sister!*"

"Yes, what is it?" It was the nurse who'd given him the injection.

"My friend – he's hardly breathing! Look!"

She looked at me and sighed. "There's nothing we can – it's the morphine, I'm afraid…" She paused, then continued reluctantly, "The amount he needs to relieve the pain is – well, it's dangerous, but—"

"You mean you're giving him so much it could kill him?"

Jesus – either you don't bother or you give him a bloody overdose!

"You saw how bad he was."

"Yes… Yes, I did."

"I have to get on," she said, and left the ward.

The head of the bed was raised slightly and he'd sagged down it, his head rolled to one side. *Being crumpled up like that won't help you breathe, but how do I move you without doing any damage?*

I put my hand under his head, lifted it carefully and straightened his neck.

"Let me do that, sir," said one of the orderlies.

He leaned over Karl and said, "I'll just move you a bit, sir, make you more comfortable," and I was astonished by the ease with which he did it, being as he was a small, wiry fellow.

"Thank you," I said. "I was a bit worried about his breathing, but I didn't want to hurt him."

"Don't worry. You wouldn't have done."

He tucked the blanket gently round Karl, and then rested his hand briefly on the side of his face. The kindness of the gesture went right through me, because there was only one reason for it.

I sat on his bed again and took hold of his hand, wishing I had the power to heal him.

Please live, Karl. Please survive this and go home, and then after the war I can come and stay with you and we can be together...

How ironic, that I can hold your hand and stroke your hair in public, because you're – as you are. The last time I put my hand behind your head was to kiss you, and I never imagined how the next time would be.

His cheekbones and jaw stood out sharply, and I could see his collarbones. I was telling myself fairy stories about a future.

The rain battered on the window, and the cold flat light shone on his grey face. *Is this how I'll end – lying shattered in some overcrowded ward while my life drains away?*

I didn't want to leave him, but in the end I couldn't stand it any longer. He didn't know I was there, and the smell and constant sounds of pain were getting too much. I disengaged my hands carefully from his, and he didn't stir.

"I'll come back tomorrow, if I can," I said quietly.

Tomorrow. Will you still be here?

I picked my way between the men on the floor, stopped in the doorway and turned to look at him again.

It's enough to break my heart.

I hurried through the hospital and out into the fresh air.

It was still pissing down, and it took me four increasingly desperate attempts to light my cigarette. The rain pounded on the car roof with exactly the same rhythm as the day Kurt died, and helpless despair almost overwhelmed me.

I lit a second cigarette and managed to calm myself a little. *I should be getting back* – but I felt too shaky to drive.

Get a grip, Franz. Finish this fag and then get going. The engine noise might shut out the sound of the rain...

I parked the car in one of the hangars, hoping the Chief wouldn't be cross about its being so wet, changed into dry clothes and went to the mess, where I had a couple of very stiff brandies.

I wish I'd arrived at the hospital ten minutes later. I didn't need to hear him screaming. That could be me tomorrow.

My hands shook.

The Chief came and sat next to me. "How is he?"

I shook my head. I couldn't find the words, and I really didn't want to talk about it.

"Becker, I'm most awfully sorry—"

I shook my head again. "No, he's alive, it's just – when I got there he – he was in so much pain..."

And they said he's going to die... I couldn't bring myself to say it.

"Worse than when I went with you?"

I nodded. "He was screaming," I managed to say. "It's infected."

"Oh, Christ. What the hell are they doing? Aren't they giving him morphine?"

"Yes, but that's a problem too – I thought he was going to stop breathing... and it's even more crowded than when you went. There are men lying everywhere. They can't look after them all. They don't have time. And the nurse told me he's not strong enough to fight the infection."

It hit me hard that Karl really was going to die, that he wasn't going to pull through after all.

He squeezed my shoulder. "She might be wrong, Becker. Leussow's a tough chap, or he wouldn't have hung on this far."

He got up, and came back a minute later with a very large brandy.

"You could probably do with this," he said, and I realised that I must look as miserable as I felt.

I wanted to pretend it hadn't happened, but everyone asked about him. By the time I'd finished answering, it was all burned even deeper into me and I felt even worse.

"How about Claudette's?" suggested Horstmann.

"Count me out," I said.

"Come on, Becker, it'll do you good," Beilke said. "You can give them one for Leussow as well."

"For God's sake, that's not funny."

Fellmann shot me a sympathetic look.

"He'd tell you to go if he knew," he said. He took me to one side. "Look, I know what a shit time it is, but you'll feel better if you go. It'll take your mind off it. You can't make him better."

"I know…"

"Go on, then. Be off with you."

He was right. The tart stopped me thinking for a while, and at the party that followed I got so blind drunk that I couldn't remember going back to the hut. I obviously did, because I woke to the sight of Horstmann lying in Karl's bed, and I almost burst into tears.

The appalling hangover made me feel wretched. The thought of sitting in that ghastly hospital watching Karl die was almost too much, but I couldn't leave him alone.

"Take as long as you like," the Chief said kindly.

I didn't ask if anyone wanted to go with me. I knew they didn't, and I didn't blame them. No one wanted to see what could happen to him.

The roads were frightful and I thought I would never get there. *I wouldn't do this for anyone else*, I thought as I went up the stairs, trying to close my nose and my ears.

There was someone else in his bed.

My heart stopped, and the floor seemed to crumble beneath my feet. *No. Oh, God, no. They would have told us, surely, told us to come and fetch the body. Not Karl any more, just 'the body'.*

The nurses and orderlies bustled about. *What can the death of one man mean to them, when men are dying all around them?*

"Can I help you, sir?" asked one of the orderlies.

I could hardly find my voice. "I came to see Leutnant von Leussow. He was in that bed, but—"

"We had to clear the hospital last night. They're all on their way home."

"What?"

"He'll be in the hospital train, on his way to sunny Germany. No more Belgian rain."

I left, trembling with relief. *He's alive. Thank God – but they told the Chief he was too ill to be moved. He won't survive the journey. What if he starts bleeding again in the train?*

I'll never see you again. You're going to die far away from me, among strangers. I should have been there, holding you for the last time.

I must have looked exactly as I felt, because no one wanted to ask me how Karl was. The Chief called Fellmann and me into his office, to talk about the state of the airfield.

"Er – how is Leussow?" the boss asked rather awkwardly.

I sighed. "God knows."

They both looked at me in astonishment.

"They said he's in the hospital train, on the way home."

Fellmann and the Chief exchanged glances.

"Well, at least he's out of that hospital," said the Chief. "He should get better care back home."

If he gets there.

I did manage to tell Horstmann and Beilke, both of whom expressed the same cautious optimism as the Chief.

I can only hope. The thought of Karl being jolted about when he was in such a precarious state was just too horrible.

The rain continued, and the days felt like months. There was nothing to do but read the newspapers and magazines that I'd already read twenty times, listen to the same old records and get drunk. All I could think about was Karl. I couldn't stand being in our room, so I practically lived in the mess until I couldn't stand the sight of that, either.

None of us could. Everyone's nerves were beginning to fray. What had begun as a glorious holiday was turning into trial by rain and boredom. It was enough to make you *want* to be on patrol. And at least when I was fighting I couldn't think about Karl.

I had no idea how he was. Fellmann managed to establish that he'd been taken to a hospital in Brussels. They gave us the same reports as the field hospital: 'no change'. I didn't believe them – it just meant they didn't have time to check. Fellmann extracted a promise from them to notify us if he died or was moved, and all I could do was wait and hope.

VI

The Chief had run out of paperwork, and he'd taken to pacing up and down, looking up at the sky each time he passed the window. It drove us all mad.

"When are we going to fly?" asked Fiedler.

He'd replaced Kühn, and like Schaff and Neidhart he had fluff on his face and reminded me of a lively puppy.

I smiled to myself. *You don't appreciate knowing you're not going to die today. Not yet.*

"Soon enough," said Patschke with a smile.

The rain was drumming on the roof, and I wound up the gramophone and put on the first record that came to hand.

It was the Liesl song and we all joined in loudly. *Karl should be here playing for us… I hope he makes it home. Maybe one day I'll be able to stay with him in Brandenburg.*

Germany's a mirage, or a land in an old legend.

Patschke, Bretti and Beilke sat down for another game of skat. The sums they apparently won and lost had become quite horrifying, but Bretti assured me that he was on a small net gain.

"It nearly all cancels out," he said.

"Well, it's not my problem!" I replied.

"Anyone for Claudette's?" asked Horstmann.

Fiedler looked at him rather sideways. Apparently he had religion, which reminded me of that observer we'd had out East who couldn't shoot anyone, and who'd ended up assisting the chaplain at the field hospital. I couldn't for the life of me remember the fellow's name.

I hope Fiedler's scruples are confined to prudery.

"Yes, count me in," I said.

"And me," said Bretti.

"Why don't we see if we can borrow a truck?" said Patschke. "Then we can all go – and we won't mess up the car."

Otto drove off the road and tipped us all into the ditch, and that corporal thought Karl was a major...

And when we walked into the salon at Claudette's I saw Karl sitting there, and Johnny, and Westermann, and Karl's father.

'I sometimes think I know more dead men than living ones,' Karl said clearly. *Oh, shit' – now I'm hearing things. Is that how Widemayer started? And is Karl dead?*

"Becker."

"What?"

"I asked if you'd like more champagne," Beilke said.

"Oh, sorry – yes, thanks."

I went upstairs with Anne. I felt a lot better immediately afterwards, but as I got dressed I longed to be lying in Karl's arms. Fucking tarts was just physical release, and what I really needed was warmth and comfort.

After dinner I got slowly and determinedly drunk. There was no way we'd be flying the next day – the field was completely waterlogged – and I didn't care how bad the hangover was. I just wanted to stop thinking or feeling anything.

And I succeeded, until three in the morning when I found myself lying wide awake, staring at the ceiling with a mouth that felt as if something had died in it.

The rain was still drumming on the roof, and I pulled the covers over my head and waited for the dawn.

I crept to the mess with a head from Hell. For the first time in days the clouds parted, and there was a brief ray of sunshine.

I turned my back to the window and ordered another pot of coffee.

In the afternoon the sun was pouring through the mess windows.

"Does this mean we can fly?" asked Fiedler.

"No chance," said Beilke. "The field's far too wet. It'll take days to dry out."

"Bit much, having weather like that in August," said Eichner.

"I'm just bloody glad I'm not in the trenches," Horstmann said.

"Too fucking right," agreed Patschke.

"Were either of you in the Ypres sector?" I asked them.

They both shook their heads.

"The Somme got pretty fucking wet," said Horstmann.

"War and mud are inseparable," Patschke said.

"Let's go and look at the aircraft," I suggested. "At least we can get some fresh air without getting soaked."

"I think my Albatros has forgotten what I look like," said Bretti as we sloshed our way across the field.

"So long as she hasn't forgotten how to fly!" Beilke said.

"No – it's Bretti who's done that!" said Horstmann.

"Speak for yourself!" Bretti retorted, and tried to push Horstmann over.

He'd picked the wrong man – Horstmann's reactions were lightning quick, and Bretti landed in the mud with a splash that got us all.

"That'll teach you to take on an old trench fighter!" I said as Bretti clambered to his feet.

He grabbed two handfuls of mud and threw them at Horstmann, who dodged with perfect timing. Perfect for him, that is – Beilke was behind him and caught the full impact.

"Right, you little bastard!" He lunged at Bretti, who tried to scarper but slipped and ended up in the mud again.

We all stood there laughing. He tried to get up, but Patschke planted a foot firmly in his back and he went sprawling again.

"You need to learn some respect or you'll never get those nice shiny epaulettes!" Horstmann said with a grin.

"No, sir – I mean, yes, sir!" He looked up at us. "Any chance of a hand up?"

"Not fucking likely!" I said. "We're not that stupid!"

"Bloody cadets," said Beilke. "I'm almost as filthy as he is."

Bretti managed to get to his feet and followed us to Hangar One. Braun looked at him very sideways.

"It's all right, Braun," said Horstmann. "He won't touch anything. Will you?"

"No, sir," Bretti said, his innocent manner contrasting with the mischief in his eyes.

I suddenly felt immeasurably old. *I will never be young again. Even if I survive the war, it's taken my youth.*

"Thank you for the tip about Herr Henning, sir," Zaffke said to me. "He was very welcoming – he and his wife gave me a lovely lunch in the kitchen. Quite set me up for the journey home. And then he took me to the station in the trap. Most kind, he was – and very concerned about Leutnant von Leussow."

"Yes, I can imagine… He must have watched all three of them grow up."

"That's exactly what he said, sir… Is there any news?"

"They still say 'no change'."

"We can but hope, sir."

"Indeed… How's your family?"

His face lit up. "Growing fast, sir – my older boy's twelve now and even my little daughter's at school."

It must have been a wrench to leave, I thought but of course couldn't say.

My Albatros was looking out of the hangar at the sky, as if she were longing to fly. I stood by her nose, looking out with her, and breathed in the scent of oil, wood and doped fabric. *Not long now, girl – then we'll be after the Tommies again, and let's see if we can't get a few more.*

After lunch a lorry turned up with a load of duckboards.

"Right," said Fellmann, "some of these are for paths between the huts and to the hangars – the old ones are completely rotten – and then there are some for a seating area for us, on the sunny side of the mess hut, and the rest are for similar for the ground crew, wherever Braun decides to put them."

"Well done, Fellmann," said the Chief, obviously as surprised as the rest of us.

"This was a bloody good idea," said Horstmann as we sat enjoying the evening sun. We'd each taken a dining chair outside, and Schaff and Neidhart had brought the gramophone.

"Yes," agreed Patschke. He looked round and then added quietly, "I reckon we should get Fellmann some sort of present."

"How about an hour at Claudette's?" suggested Schaff.

Everyone except him and Fiedler burst out laughing.

"What's so funny?" he asked, bemused.

"Tell you later, you stupid sod," said Neidhart. "You must be fucking well blind. Any sensible suggestions?"

"Needs a bit of thought," Patschke said. "Why don't we all give Becker our suggestions, and then we can have a vote on them?"

"I know what he'd really like," said Beilke.

Bretti looked at him and raised an eyebrow. "Isn't procurement a criminal offence – especially with his – er – tastes?"

"You'll be in the mud again in a moment," warned Horstmann. "Go on, Beilke."

"Some really good cigars."

"Now that is a good idea," I said. "But where on earth are we going to get them? I mean, Fellmann gets his hands on just about everything, so if it were possible surely he'd have done it."

Beilke shook his head. "That's just the point. Fellmann gets everything for everyone else."

The gramophone wound down and he stopped talking.

"Hey, Schaff, put something else on, would you?" Horstmann called out.

"And he never uses his contacts for himself," Beilke finished, once the next song had started.

"Does anyone have leave coming up?" asked Eichner.

"Would it matter if they did?" I said.

"Well, there is the black market."

Something struck me.

"They have pretty well everything at my father's club," I said. "I was there in June and they had bloody good cigars. I'll write and see if he can get some."

The gramophone had wound down. Bleif came out and announced dinner, and after the meal we sat watching the sun set.

Fellmann came and sat beside me, with half a bottle of brandy and two glasses. There was no need for either of us to speak, and we sat in friendly silence.

The ground crew had finished work and were sitting outside Hangar One. Schaff was about to wind up the gramophone when we heard Schiffer's mouth organ drifting across to us, and the sound of them singing, poignant beyond bearing in the twilight.

"In the homeland, in the homeland, there we will meet again…"

We listened in silence, all our thoughts far away. I realised with a stab of guilt that I'd hardly thought about Maria, or my family, or anyone except Karl.

Will I ever see any of you again?

I thought of the thousands who would never go home: Anton, Kurt, Burkhardt, Geschke, Johnny… all the men I'd known who were dead. My chances of making it home were next to nil.

Horstmann and the Chief were both staring into space. Steyer gazed fixedly at the duckboards, withdrawn into himself, twisting his wedding ring on his finger.

The song ended but no one spoke.

After several minutes the Chief said quietly, "Well, I'm off to bed. Becker, Fellmann, I suggest we inspect the field at ten, provided there's no more rain."

Steyer got up a minute later and left without a word, his face set.

The field was practically a swamp, in spite of the warm sunshine. Fellmann prodded the mud with his cane, slipped and almost fell over.

"Well, if it doesn't rain for a week, we might be all right," he said.

That was not what either the boss or I wanted to hear, and we exchanged glum looks.

We slithered back to the main hut, and the Chief went into his office and closed the door.

"Well?" asked Horstmann.

I shook my head. "You can hardly stand up on it."

"As we can see from your boots," Patschke commented.

I'd wiped my feet but a few clumps of mud had fallen onto the floor. *Bleif won't be pleased – but then it's been a while since he's had to clean up after a real mess-wrecker.*

The post had come. I had three letters: from Maria, Johanna, and another addressed in a strange hand. My heart turned over and I ripped it open – but it wasn't news of Karl. It was another letter from some daft girl who liked my picture.

They haven't told Fellmann he's dead, so he must be alive. I wish I could get leave and go to Brussels…

"Becker, do you have a moment?" the Chief's voice cut through my thoughts.

"Of course, sir."

I got up and we went to his office, where he closed the door.

"I don't know if you're aware that I'm engaged to be married," he said rather awkwardly.

"Yes, sir, I did know." *What has that got to do with me?*

"I was hoping for leave next month, but having regard to the state of the airfield, I asked for it to be brought forward, and we've been able to arrange the ceremony for four days from now."

"Congratulations, sir."

He smiled. "Thank you. I'll be leaving first thing in the morning, so you'll be in charge, of course, and I'll be back ten days after that."

That's the end of any chance of getting to Brussels and seeing Karl.

I did have another thought.

"Sir," I said very quietly, "we were all thinking it would be nice to get a present for Fellmann, being as he does so much for all of us."

"Yes. I agree. What do you suggest?"

"Beilke suggested a box of good cigars – really special ones. I don't suppose you'd be able to get some?"

He thought for a moment. "Actually yes, I think I can… Better make a note so I don't forget." He scribbled something on a scrap of paper and put it in his wallet, then said, "Well, we might as well get the handover done."

"What did the boss want?" asked Bretti.

"Oh, he'd better tell you that," I replied, and opened Maria's letter.

She chattered about this and that, hoped I was well and being careful. She'd seen in the papers that we'd had losses, and was scared to look at the casualty lists.

That's understandable. I don't like looking at them, either – though maybe because my imagination always puts flesh on the bare words 'fallen', 'missing', and so on. I remembered how I'd always felt when I was on leave and Karl was fighting, and felt real sympathy for her.

I'll write back this evening, reassure her that there's nothing to worry about for the next few days.

The next sentence had me rather worried.

'I do hope you can get leave again before long,' she wrote, 'because it would be so wonderful to get married.'

Married? That's for men like Horstmann and the Chief, who love the girl and know her well. We had three days together and one afternoon in bed. And while the boss's private life is obviously his business, I do think it's a bit irresponsible to get married when you're probably going to get killed.

'After the war' we can take time to get to know each other, and then we can decide if we want to marry. Better be diplomatic for now, and say that I won't have leave for the foreseeable future.

Be careful what you write, Franz – remember how Johnny found himself engaged to Alex after a casual mention of marriage?

And of course she was praying for me.

It was a relief to open Johanna's letter – until I actually started reading it.

'The Professor in Berlin wrote me a really nice letter. He said he'll be happy to have me if I get good enough grades, and in the meantime I should get some nursing experience, which I really want to do, but Mama won't have it unless it's in a maternity ward!!! Honestly! How boring! Just because I'm a woman doesn't mean that all I want to do is help women have babies!

I said I want to work in the surgical ward but she said that washing strange men wasn't appropriate for a young lady! You should have seen her face when she said it – she just couldn't bring herself to say what she meant! As if I care about that!'

I shook my head. *Poor Sis.*

There was a lot more of the same, ending with a plea to try to make Mama change her mind.

More diplomacy. But at the same time she's got no idea what state some of the poor fellows are in…

She'd scribbled a hasty PS.

'I'm so sorry about Karl – I saw in the casualty lists that he's been badly wounded and I really hope he's recovering. Please give him my best wishes.'

I sighed. She would want all the details, and I didn't want to write about any of it. Putting it in black and white would make it so much worse.

"Bad news?" Eichner asked.

"No – just my sister having trouble with our parents."

"Oh, God – yours as well! I've got two, and they're nothing but trouble. Both got stupid ideas about becoming lawyers or whatever."

"What's stupid about that?" asked Patschke.

"Women don't have the brains for it," Eichner replied dismissively.

Patschke burst out laughing. "Tell you what, my sister's a bloody sight cleverer than I am!"

"That is not difficult," Bretti said.

"Cheeky bastard!" said Steyer.

I left them to it and wrote back to her.

'Why not start off in the maternity ward and then get yourself transferred? If it comes from the hospital authorities then it's harder for the parents to argue.'

I had a thought. "Hey, Horstmann – isn't Susanne a nurse?"
"Yes, in a military hospital in Potsdam. One of her brothers is a patient there – poor fellow's paralysed."
"Thanks."
I picked up my pen again.

'One of the pilots here is engaged to a nurse, and she's a noblewoman. If it's good enough for her, you can tell them.'

I was careful not to mention that the lady in question was a Junker, because that would give them a get-out. I thanked her for her good wishes about Karl and managed, just, to write what had happened to him, but I shied away from reading the words on the page.

And now I'd better write to Maria. It was far harder than I'd imagined. I was having difficulty remembering her face without looking at her picture.

Horstmann had a letter addressed in very familiar writing, and he'd opened it very carefully and put the dried flower in his wallet before Patschke could say a word. He would paste it into his diary later, in our room, along with the others. He'd kept a diary since the start of the war in numbered books, and sent each one home once it was full. I was under strict instructions to send the current volume home if anything happened to him.

We gave the Chief a good send-off – well, we had a good party, anyway. He did have a bit more to drink than usual, but left us to it once things started to get silly.

It was a real mess-wrecker, of the good old-fashioned sort. *The last time we had one of these, Johnny was alive, and Karl and*

Widemayer were here... I had no enthusiasm for the games, and just got quietly pissed and went to bed.

Fiedler didn't appear the next morning. Bretti and Schaff both surfaced at about eleven, and claimed to be amazed at the state of the mess. Neidhart walked in carefully, looking rather green.

Horstmann, Beilke and I were eating breakfast off our laps – the table was broken again.

"How can you eat anything?" asked Neidhart.

"Easily," replied Horstmann. "You just haven't had enough drinking practice."

Patschke came in and helped himself to rolls and ham. "God, I'm ravenous."

Neidhart looked at him as if he had two heads.

"Your problem is that you weren't in the trenches," Horstmann said to Neidhart.

"Too right," Patschke agreed. "It was always best with a bit of booze inside."

"That's for sure," I said. "Especially on cold winter nights."

"Or when all Hell was breaking loose," said Patschke.

"It always amazed me the sheer quantity that blokes carried," Horstmann said.

Patschke grinned. "We had an acting officer who was a temperance nutter. Maintained that drink was the work of the Devil."

"Maybe he had a point," said Neidhart ruefully.

"No," Horstmann said. "Patschke's right – nutter."

The field dried out slowly. Fellmann and I inspected it every day, and we reckoned that a few more fine days would see the higher strip useable.

"It'll be good to get in the air again," I said as we walked carefully along it. *And it would be even better to actually hear from Karl – though he won't be capable of writing for some time.*

"Yes, you must be going crazy."

I sighed. "I just wish I knew how he actually is."

"Look, why don't we try to get one of the doctors on the phone?"

"Won't they be too busy?"

Fellmann smiled. "I might be able to persuade them."

We went into the Ops Office.

"Möller, get the hospital in Brussels on the phone, would you?"

"Certainly, sir."

Bloody hell, I thought when Fellmann took the phone – *so that's how you manage to get so much for us all. I hadn't realised you were quite such a silver-tongued bastard.* He had one of the senior doctors on the phone in two minutes flat.

"Good morning, sir… Oh, I'm so glad you like the pictures. Oberleutnant von Kralewski-Zentzytzki appreciates very much what you're doing for Leutnant von Leussow – I'm only sorry he can't be here to thank you personally…

"Oh, no, no, nothing like that, no, he's on leave, getting married…" Fellmann laughed. "You're not wrong there, sir! I do have our second-in-command with me, Leutnant Becker, and he'd very much like to speak to you on the Chief's behalf… One moment, please."

He put his hand over the mouthpiece and turned to me.

"It's Staff Doctor Silbermann, Becker."

"Thank you very much indeed," I said, and took the telephone from him.

"Sir, may I thank you all on behalf of the squadron," I said. "Leutnant von Leussow is our top ace after the Chief, and we've all been very concerned about him."

"Yes, I can believe." The doctor's voice was friendly but somewhat guarded. "I don't know how much you know about his wound?"

"Bullet through the right lung, smashed rib, blood loss, infection," I managed to say, the words all running together.

"Yes, that's about right… Well, he's doing as well as can be hoped."

"Is he out of danger?"

He paused and I felt cold run down my back. Then he said, "I really shouldn't discuss his condition with you… Can I call you back in a few minutes? I'll just go and see if he's awake."

"Yes, of course. Thank you."

"What did he say?" asked Fellmann.

I told him.

"I was afraid he might say something like that," he said.

"You're a cunning bastard, aren't you?" I said, trying to lighten the mood. "You had this all fixed up."

He grinned. "Well, I thought if I sent him signed photos of both of them he might agree to speak to us, busy though he must be."

"You got Karl to sign his pictures as well?"

"Oh, yes – I've got quite a stock of both him and the Chief."

A few minutes later the phone rang. Fellmann gestured to me and I answered.

"Ah, Becker – I've just spoken to Leussow and he said to tell you everything. So: we operated to cut out the infection, and it's not completely clear but it's more under control, and the fever's gone down and he's lucid. The blood loss is a big concern, and we just have to hope he doesn't have another haemorrhage. Overall he's holding on but as you'll appreciate he's very weak."

"Thank you very much indeed, sir." I didn't know whether to be relieved or not. "Please give him my very best wishes."

"Yes, I will – and he said he hopes to see you again soon. You can write, you know."

"Thank you – that makes a real difference."

He dictated the address to me and ended the call before I could say any more.

"Fellmann, I owe you a bottle of brandy," I said.

"No, you don't," he answered quietly.

"Well, I'm buying you one anyway."

I wrote to Karl at once, and it was surprisingly difficult. I read and reread my words, and they seemed far from what I really wanted to say – and yet I didn't know what that actually was.

'Next time I get leave I'll come and visit you in Brandenburg,' I put. I wanted to write something about how the squadron wasn't the same without him, but I was aware that someone would probably read the letter to him and that I had to be careful – and I knew he'd want to come back, and I certainly didn't want to encourage that idea.

Writing made me even more aware how much I missed him. *We still can't fly – I could get to Brussels and back in a couple of days...* but I was in command and couldn't leave.

I bought Fellmann the brandy and we sat side by side on the decking, watching the sun go down as Bretti and Neidhart kept the gramophone going.

"If that strip's a bit drier tomorrow I'll give it a go," I said. "This is getting far too tedious."

It was drier, and fortunately the wind was light and in the right direction. We slid a bit but that was all.

"Well, my girl – things could be worse!" I said as we climbed into the wide blue expanse.

I daren't go far alone – the guns were loaded, but I really didn't want to fend off a flight of Tommies all by myself – so I contented myself with climbing to about a thousand metres overhead the airfield. And there I played for twenty very happy minutes, looping and rolling.

That was bloody good, I thought as I throttled back and half-rolled into the descent. *Just what I needed – now I'd better get the landing right. The useable strip's not very wide and only just long enough, and it'll be very embarrassing if I fuck it up...*

It went off without drama, but I did have to work at it.

"Well?" asked Fellmann.

"Experienced men only for the next day or two," I said. "Come on, let's get a programme together."

An hour later I was leading Schaff, Bretti and Eichner, while Beilke made up another four with Horstmann, Patschke and Steyer. I reckoned that was a fair distribution of experience, but that I had to think so hard about it brought home how diluted we'd become.

Neidhart and Fiedler had waved us off with very wistful expressions. *It's better to be here wishing you were over the Front than the other way round, but I really need to get you on patrol as soon as possible...*

Half an hour later I was very glad we'd left them behind. We encountered two flights of those new Tommy fighters, and looking after a novice would have been impossible.

In all the mad twisting and turning I found myself on the tail of one. He was turning towards Bretti, and made the mistake of not looking behind. I closed in until my propeller seemed about to chew his elevator, and my Albatros shook as the twin Spandaus fired and—

Jesus Christ! His aircraft reared up as he was hit, and for one horrifying second my windscreen filled with olive wings.

I braced myself for the crunch of collision, but by some miracle it never came. *That was far too close, you stupid bastard. Be bugger all use to get taken out yourself.* I glanced down and he was spinning.

That's one for Karl, I thought before I could stop myself.

No vengeance, Franz.

Steyer was under attack from another, with Horstmann hot on the Tommy's tail... I got stuck in again, and had a merry dance with one of the leaders. He knew what he was doing, and it was all I could do to stop him turning the tables on me.

They all buggered off abruptly, and we let them go and looked for more trouble. It wasn't slow in coming…

As we set off home I had the feeling of a job well done. *I hope that gets confirmed. It's been a while.*

The sun glinted off the land below. I couldn't believe the state of the battlefield – it was a huge swamp of overlapping shell-holes, all filled with water. The soldiers were invisible from our altitude.

Poor bastards – the only cover will be in those shell-holes, and they look like they're all full to the brim. And even in summer it'll be bloody cold being up to your neck in water.

I shivered, remembering the misery of getting soaked and being unable to dry out for days.

The wind had changed direction and picked up slightly. *This could be interesting. That strip's none too wide, and now the wind's slightly across it.*

I let all the others land first. If anyone cocked up and blocked the strip, I would be the one with the difficult landing.

Bretti was down safely, and Steyer… Schaff touched down all right, but as he slowed, the wind caught the tail and pulled it round, and he went off the side of the dry patch onto the mud.

It grabbed the wheels, and his Albatros was left standing on her nose. She was only just clear of the strip, which made it bloody awkward for the rest of us. We didn't have the fuel to wait for the ground crew to pull her away.

To my intense relief everyone else landed without difficulty.

Poor Schaff was very crestfallen. "I'm really sorry, sir – I just don't know what happened."

"Don't worry," I said, "that was a very difficult landing and you don't have much experience yet."

"Well done!" Horstmann said to me, and I gathered everyone round for the debrief, surprised I could remember so much of the fights.

I used to wonder how the Chief did it...

The next day was business as normal. I took Neidhart over the Front for the first time, and he kept his wits about him and even had a bit of a pop at a Nieuport.

You'll be very useful if you survive the first few weeks.

Beilke came back with a grin right across his face.

"What was it?" I asked him.

"Sopwith. Christ, I thought some of our blokes were green, but the Tommies must be putting up schoolboys. Poor bugger never even knew I was there."

"Fingers crossed for confirmation, then!"

Not a bad couple of days' work. Two victories for one slightly damaged Albatros. Schaff's needed an engine change and repairs to the nose, but that was all.

"Bloody hell," said Horstmann, "you ever seen a cloud like that before?"

The western sky was filled with a huge mass, pitch-black below and dazzling white at its several cauliflower tops, God knows how many thousand metres up. Above them a sharply defined anvil protruded eastwards.

I'd seen all that many times – but never the huge rounded globs that hung off its underside like a bunch of monstrous grey grapes.

"Look at the tits on that!" Bretti exclaimed.

"Tits?" retorted Steyer. "More like bollocks if you ask me!"

"What in God's name has that number of either?" demanded Horstmann.

Admitting I'd thought of grapes would sound horribly prim.

"Ever seen that before?" I asked Fellmann.

"No – it's weird."

The day Buchholz crashed into the hedge and burned there was a thunderhead with a strange cloud beneath it...

I turned to Braun. "Better get the aircraft in the hangars before that gets here."

"Yes, sir."

"Lend a hand, everyone," I said, and we began to drag the Albatri through the thick gloop into the relative safety of the canvas hangars.

Three of them were still outside when the storm hit. I'd noticed the wind picking up from the east, and that vast cloud blotting out the sun. I was lifting the tail of Horstmann's aircraft when a massive gust hit from the opposite direction.

I should have had the wit to let go, but my hands clung on. Uhlig, on the leading edge of the right lower wing, made the same mistake. My stomach lurched as the aircraft rose into the sky and began to turn over, taking us both with it.

Jesus fucking Christ – this is no way to fly!

Uhlig looked at me. *Hold on or let go?* We were about ten metres off the ground and I knew how soft it was. I didn't know how far the Albatros would go, or how high or how fast.

Let go. It's up to Uhlig what he does – I can't give him an order when I've no idea if I'm getting it right myself.

I hit the ground hard, and my right ankle seemed to explode. And then the heavens opened and I was sitting in the mud, rain battering onto my bare head, Kurt's blood running red into the water—

"Becker! BECKER!" Horstmann had hold of my shoulders and was shaking me hard. "Jesus, man, are you all right?"

"Er – yes, yes, I'm fine. Just a bit shaken."

"I'll bet – we thought we'd lost you both there!"

I tried to get up, but my right ankle wouldn't take my weight. Horstmann helped me to my feet, and I found I could stand with his support.

"Where's Uhlig?"

He pointed to the crumpled wreckage of his Albatros, about a hundred metres away. Uhlig was lying beside it, with Braun and Schiffer bending over him.

"Shit!" I exclaimed. "Come on."

Fellmann joined us, and we crossed the field as fast as I could hobble. Just as we got there Uhlig sat up, to my immense relief.

"How are you?" I asked.

"I think my leg's broken, sir, and my arm... Maybe I should have let go when you did, but I couldn't."

"Maybe I should have told you to – but I didn't know whether I should be letting go myself."

"I don't think I could've let go, sir, no matter what you'd said! And I did think maybe she knew more about flying than I do."

"Well, you're alive, anyway," said Fellmann, "and you can go home and have a nice holiday."

He surveyed the wreck. "That's three aircraft damaged – luckily the others aren't too bad."

"Fellmann," I said, "can you organise getting Uhlig to hospital, and then come and give me a full damage report?"

"Yes, of course. Can you get to the mess?"

I tried my ankle out again. *Not broken, just a bad sprain. Very lucky, really.*

"Yes, with Horstmann's help."

"Put it in a bucket of cold water," Fellmann advised, "and I'll send Schiffer to strap it up for you."

"You didn't get off unscathed, then, sir?" Uhlig asked.

"Oh, it's just sprained. Give all our love to the homeland, won't you?"

He grinned. "Will do, sir!"

You won't be quite as cheerful once the pain sets in.

An hour later I was feeling less cheerful myself. My ankle was throbbing and I could only hobble with a stick. Fellmann consoled me with the news that the other two aircraft had only minor damage and would be airworthy in a couple of days, and that both my and Beilke's victories had been confirmed.

The downpour made the field unusable again, until the day before the Chief was due back.

There was no way I could fly. I managed to get into the cockpit with a bit of help from Schiffer, but the stab of pain when I tried to operate the rudder made me wonder whether my ankle wasn't broken.

I climbed out with difficulty and went back down the steps, which raised a few eyebrows. Steps were only used for getting into aircraft.

"Can you strap it tighter for me?" I asked Schiffer.

He shook his head. "Not without cutting off the circulation, sir."

"Bugger it… Beilke, you lead. Fiedler, go and practise spinning and then your circles."

"Yes, sir."

"Fellmann, can you drive me to the hospital? I'd like to see Uhlig."

"Yes, of course."

On the way there he said, "You know, you really should get that X-rayed."

"What for? It can't be a bad break, and I can't leave the squadron until the boss gets back."

"Just get it X-rayed, in case it needs surgery."

I laughed. "You want some army doctor operating on me?"

"Have it your own way!"

"And I don't want six weeks in plaster."

"You know, Becker, I never had you down as stupid. Most blokes would jump at six weeks out of action."

"Six weeks bored out of my skull?" *Sitting on the ground worrying about Karl…*

"Bloody bonkers."

The hospital was just as appallingly crammed as the one Karl had been in. *I'd feel a right fraud asking for an X-ray, and*

I'd have to wait hours, and hanging around here is not my idea of fun.

Uhlig was sitting up in bed with his left arm and leg in plaster, looking quite perky.

"They say I'm down for the hospital train tomorrow, sir," he said cheerfully. "It'll be good to see my old lady and the kids."

"Where's home again?"

"Oh, it's a small village near Heidelberg."

Once upon a time there was a university full of carefree young men, with bright hopes for the future. Now most of them are dead or mutilated.

"I was studying there before the war," I said. "Along with Leutnant von Leussow – Karl, that is – and Sergeant Kramer. Feels like a long time ago, now."

"Yes, sir, it does – everything's changed, hasn't it?"

"How's your family?"

"Doing all right, but it's hard for them."

"Well, you make sure you take it easy and have a good holiday," I said, "and we'll see you back as soon as you're well."

"Thank you, sir."

As we walked out of the entrance Fellmann asked, "Did the hospital Karl was in get as bad as that?"

"Yes… possibly a bit worse. He was in the – with the bad cases."

I couldn't say 'the dying room'.

He shook his head. "When I think of the pre-war Army, how professional it was – that's all gone now, all the good, solid officers and NCOs, all the experienced men. I had some good friends at Lichterfelde, and one by one, all of them… The last of them fell last week, and now I'm the only one left…"

I put my arm round his shoulders.

"Let's get back," I said quietly.

We got into the car without another word. Neither of us wanted to face the obvious question – how much longer can we last, after three years of a war that had to be won quickly?

The Chief came back the next day, looking happy and relaxed.

The first thing he said to me was, "Becker, what happened to you?"

"Sir, I'm sorry to report that we lost Horstmann's aircraft, and Aircraftman Uhlig should be in the hospital train." I told him what had happened. "And I've requested a replacement aircraft, but I asked Albatros not to send it until today because of the mud."

"Yes, I see. Well, from the sound of things we were lucky to lose only one aircraft. When do you think you'll be able to fly again?"

"Hard to say, sir – I tried yesterday but I couldn't operate the rudder. It should be all right in a couple of weeks."

We completed the handover and I hobbled back into the mess.

"Just as well Patschke's got such big feet, or I'd be barefoot," I said. My ankle was too swollen to get my boot on, and he'd lent me a spare.

"You know what they say about big feet," Beilke said with a wink. "Patschke must be hung like a donkey!"

Horstmann started laughing. Fiedler looked most uncomfortable.

"Well, is he?" asked Bretti.

"Certainly is! Quite alarming when he gets out of bed in the morning, isn't it, Fiedler?"

Fiedler went scarlet. "I don't look," he said rather primly.

"Don't blame you!" said Horstmann.

We all burst out laughing.

"Haven't you noticed – one or two of Claudette's girls avoid Patschke like the plague?" Horstmann managed to say.

"I wondered why that was," said Eichner. "I thought maybe he liked something odd."

Poor Fiedler didn't know where to put himself.

"Well, that may be," Horstmann conceded, "but my money's on discomfort!"

Patschke came into the mess and we all shut up.

"Talking about me, were you?!" he asked.

"Just commenting on the size of your feet," I said, "for which I'm truly grateful!"

"Oh, right."

None of us dared look at each other. I couldn't look at Patschke, either – I kept picturing him with an erection like a field marshal's baton.

I'll have to ask the girl, next time we go to Claudette's...

The Chief lost no time getting airborne. I could only watch with Fiedler as our comrades took off and headed west, Horstmann in my Albatros.

"Oh, well," I said to Fiedler, "at least you've got your target practice to do."

"Would you watch and give me some tips, please?"

"Yes, of course."

He was making quite a reasonable job of it, but not getting close enough before opening fire. He climbed up for a third pass and, just as he was rolling into the dive, a D.V turned in behind him. It got into a perfect firing position before breaking off.

Platzer. Poor Fiedler doesn't know it, but he's dead.

The D.V descended overhead the field and landed neatly. Platzer joined me outside the mess just as Fiedler landed.

"New boy?"

I laughed. "How did you guess?"

When Fiedler joined us I said, "Not sure I should be talking to you."

"Why's that, then?" he asked, puzzled.

"I'd have to hold a séance."

His expression changed to complete bafflement.

"Platzer here shot you down just as you started your third run."

"But I wasn't expecting – oh."

"Exactly. Never, never forget to check your tail – even here."

I debriefed him on the rest of it, and the three of us sat talking in the sun, waiting for the others to return.

"How's Leussow?" Platzer asked.

"In hospital in Brussels, a bit better, I think."

"Good. Fingers crossed, then."

We heard the squadron before we saw them. Fellmann came out and scanned the sky with us.

Schaff landed, Bretti, Beilke… and the Chief flew a very cautious circuit with wide, shallow turns, not at all in his usual positive style.

Unusual for the boss to get bullets in his aircraft. He's normally far too slippery for that.

He landed safely, and we all breathed out.

"Wonder what the problem was," Fellmann said.

We found out a few minutes later. The Chief came up to us and said, "Ah, Platzer – just the fellow! You can take that new D.V straight back to Albatros and tell them I want two more D.IIIs. If they can't supply them then I'll be getting Berlin to send us Pfalzes instead."

Platzer frowned. "I take it you had trouble, sir?"

"Come and look at the right lower wing."

Jesus fucking Christ – no wonder you were flying so carefully. Several ribs had broken, leaving a sagging, misshapen surface. *How the fuck did that stay together?*

"I am most sincerely sorry," Platzer said slowly. I could see him thinking that it would have been a real disaster to lose a top ace to structural failure. "When did it happen?"

"During a fight with those new English aircraft – the ones with the stubby noses."

"The Sopwith Camel," said Platzer.

"Camel?" asked the boss. *Whoever heard of a flying camel?*

"Yes," Platzer replied. "Apparently the Tommies think the fairing over the guns looks like a camel's hump."

"They want to take more water with their gin!" Horstmann said, laughing.

"I'm surprised they didn't think of tits," Platzer said. "You know, there was a trench near Fort Douaumont that got called the Bosom Trench, just because it had two small round projections. You had to be really desperate to see those as tits, believe me, even from the air."

Everyone except Fiedler laughed. *That boy needs to stop being so bloody serious.*

"And then there was the French position that everyone – even the staff – called the Crab Louse, because that was exactly what it looked like."

We laughed harder. Fiedler looked horrified.

"All well and good," said the Chief, "but I shan't be flying one of these again, and nor will any of my men – and I doubt anyone else will want them after Fellmann's finished phoning round."

"No, quite… How much warning did you get?"

"Very little. I was being careful with the airspeed, in view of your earlier warning – the problem came when I had to turn in the dive. There was a loud crack and she gave a bit of a jolt, and when I looked at the wing I realised a rib had broken. The others went one by one over the next few minutes."

Jesus, I thought, impressed by how calmly he was telling the story. I didn't want to imagine sitting there in the middle of a fight with one rib failing after another, wondering when the wing would break or when I'd be shot because I couldn't manoeuvre…

"So it wasn't the best patrol I've been on," the Chief finished.

There's a fine piece of Prussian understatement.

"No, indeed," Platzer replied. "How many had you done in her?"

"That was the first," the boss said with a smile. "It's such a shame – the D.III was such a wonderful aircraft."

"Yes… pity they're being outclassed now. Look, I'll take the new one straight back, and we'll send a lorry for this one – the factory will want to see what's happened. Could you write an account for me, please, as detailed as possible?"

"Of course. Give me ten minutes – unless you'd like to stay overnight?"

"Thank you, sir, but I'd rather get going. This business needs sorting out before someone else gets killed."

We all raised our eyebrows at that.

"Indeed," the Chief said drily.

Half an hour later Platzer was on his way with the Chief's account in his pocket, accompanied no doubt by a stinking letter to the board of Albatros.

We had a party to welcome the Chief back, and to celebrate his marriage and – more importantly – his survival.

After dinner I caught Fellmann's eye. He left the mess, and returned with Braun and the ground crew, all smartly turned out. Then he disappeared into the kitchen and came back with Bleif and the stewards.

Fellmann turned to the Chief. "Sir, we would all like to congratulate you on your marriage, and to wish you and Frau von Kralewski-Zentzytzki every happiness."

The Chief started to blush. "Thank you, everyone."

"And we wanted to get you a wedding present," Fellmann continued, "but there wasn't time before you left. So now you're back," Braun stepped forward and handed Fellmann a box, "this is from all of us."

The Chief stood up, his face completely red. "Well, I don't know – this is most kind of you—"

He put the box on the table and opened it.

"Oh, I say – that's rather special."

'That', as we all knew, was a table lamp made from a Mercedes cylinder, with a very pretty glass shade that Fellmann had managed to get from somewhere.

"Thank you all so much," the Chief said. "It's really beautiful. My wife will love it."

Bleif brought in the champagne and we all drank his health.

Then the boss said, "Well, this is where I have a presentation to make… Now, where on earth have I…"

He made a show of looking under the table and then nipped to his office. He returned with his hands behind his back.

"Fellmann, we're all aware how much you do for the squadron, so here's a small token of our thanks."

He handed Fellmann what looked like a very expensive box of cigars. It was Fellmann's turn to blush.

"Well, I – I – oh, Lord, I wasn't expecting – I mean, you didn't have to—"

"Of course we didn't," said the boss. "That's the whole point."

We drank Fellmann's health as well, and after another glass the party got going.

The Chief was obviously rather tired and went to bed early.

"That was a bloody narrow escape he had today," said Horstmann.

"Would have been rotten luck to get killed on the first day back from his honeymoon," said Eichner.

"Yes… Mrs Chief must be half expecting it, but even so…" Patschke added.

"He was so calm about it," Neidhart said with a note of wonder.

"Especially when he saw Platzer sitting there," said Schaff. "You'd have thought he'd have just let rip at him."

"Not his style," Fellmann commented. "I've never seen him lose his rag."

"Neither have I," I said.

"I don't know how he can just go to bed," said Fiedler, "not after something like that."

Eichner chuckled. "I don't suppose he got much sleep after his wedding, the lucky bastard!"

"Christ, no!" Horstmann agreed. "You wouldn't want to waste time sleeping, would you?!"

"Not likely!" said Bretti. "I wouldn't even get out of bed!"

"Oh, I don't know," Schaff said. "You'd have to refuel."

"Yes, but how long does that take?" said Beilke. "I mean, I'd just want to get in and stay in…"

Steyer was staring at the floor.

"Must be bloody wonderful, knowing she really wants you and she's all yours," Neidhart said, rather wistfully.

"No – bloody ball and chain!" objected Patschke. "Best to be footloose and fancy-free!"

"But then you've got the hassle of trying to get someone into bed," said Eichner. "Whereas if you're married then you know she'll be waiting when you get home, and you can just get into bed and stay there."

"Especially with a lovely creature like yours, Steyer," Bretti said.

Steyer didn't answer for a moment, then he started and said, "Sorry – what was that?"

"We were just saying how good it must be to have a lovely wife like yours waiting at home."

Steyer's face clouded. "It was," he said quietly.

Bretti looked confused. "Sorry, I didn't mean to – er – it's just that – that is your wife's picture in our room?"

"Yes," Steyer said in the same soft, flat tone, twisting his wedding ring round his finger. "And it was lovely."

She can't have left him, or he wouldn't have her picture on display.

"I'm really sorry," Bretti said. "I've really put my foot in it."

"I should have told you," Steyer said. "It's just it's rather hard to find the words... It was last October. We'd been so happy that she was pregnant... It was a little girl. She didn't make it either."

"Shit," said Bretti awkwardly, and the rest of us mumbled words that were totally inadequate.

"You don't think of that happening," Steyer went on. "I mean, you expect men to be killed, but not that your wife... She was just twenty."

No wonder you're always so quiet.

"I've cast a bit of a cloud over the evening," said Steyer. "Sorry, chaps."

"Don't be daft," I said. "You've got nothing to apologise for."

"Well, anyway... Shall we have some music?"

"Good idea," said Neidhart with obvious relief.

As he headed towards the gramophone, Fiedler said, "You can think of them in Heaven, looking out for you."

Oh, for fuck's sake – why did you have to come out with sentimental tosh like that?

To my surprise Steyer's face lit with a warm smile. "I do like to think that."

What would I think if Maria died? I wondered – and realised that my feelings for her were nothing like that strong. *I'd be sad at the death of a lovely young woman, of course, but not grief-stricken. The child would be another matter, but then there isn't one.*

"No one I know would be looking down from Heaven," Patschke said. "My mates will all be in the other place!"

"Mine too!" said Horstmann with a laugh.

Neidhart put on a popular song, and the mood began to lighten.

"Poor old Steyer," Horstmann said to me as we undressed. "Bit bloody rough, that."

"That's for sure."

When he left for the dawn flight I lay in bed half-awake, wondering how Karl was and wishing he were with me.

Eventually I got up, and arrived in the mess just as the others got back. The Chief had pinched Fiedler's aircraft and returned with that familiar look of grim satisfaction.

"That rather makes up for yesterday," he said. "Fellmann, is there any news from Albatros?"

"They're sending us two new D.IIIs," he replied, "and an apology."

"Good – let's hope they get here soon."

"Amen to that," said Horstmann.

"Agreed," I said, "then I shan't have to worry about you getting mine shot full of holes!"

"I love the way you care about me!"

The post came, and I had another letter addressed in a strange hand. *It's probably another one of those stupid women, having fantasies about someone she's never met.* I almost forgot to open it.

"Aren't you going to open your letter?" Bretti asked.

"Oh, I suppose so."

I opened the envelope with a complete lack of interest, which was suddenly reversed.

'My dear Franz,' said the unfamiliar writing, 'thank you so much for your letter. I was so pleased to get it. And especially for your visits. I hope you're well and enjoying success. This is rather different to my last Brussels trip, as you'll realise. Please burn the letter I left you. I don't plan to kick the bucket just yet. Write soon. Ever yours, Karl.'

Ridiculously – and quite unexpectedly – I had to stare hard at the floor to compose myself. *For fuck's sake, Franz – get a grip!*

"Who's that from?" asked Horstmann.

I handed him the letter without a word, and lit a cigarette while he read it.

"Thank God for that," he said.

I nodded. "He must be a lot better."

Though clearly a long way from his usual self.

"Is that news of Karl?" Bretti asked.

"Yes," I said.

"Why don't you read it out to everyone?" suggested Horstmann, and I did, just as the Chief came into the room.

"Oh, that *is* good news," he said, smiling warmly at me. "It really was a bit of a worry, their having to move him… I'll tell Fellmann."

"That's all right, sir, I heard," Fellmann said as he entered the mess. "Bloody good news."

"I'll go and tell Zaffke," I said. "He'd like to know."

"Oh, that is such a relief, sir," he said with a smile. "As I said, we're a tough bunch!"

"You did indeed – and you were right."

On the way back to the mess, I went to our room and got Karl's letter out of the drawer. I set light to one corner, and envelope and letter curled and blackened, and dropped into the ashtray.

I wonder what it said.

The doctor's words suddenly came into my mind. 'We just have to hope he doesn't have another haemorrhage.' *Suppose he does? Maybe I shouldn't have burned it just yet…*

I wrote back, passing on everyone's good wishes and giving a light-hearted account of my 'flight' with Horstmann's Albatros. 'And so here I am, stuck on the ground and bored out of my skull…'

It was another three weeks before my ankle allowed me to fly, three weeks in which I had to sit on the ground and do the boss's paperwork, while other men came back with victory claims. I was climbing the walls with boredom and frustration.

The Chief added another, as did Horstmann and Beilke, and Steyer got his first, which was the occasion for a proper piss-up. I got so drunk that Horstmann had to half carry me to our room, and I didn't even notice when he left the next morning.

I couldn't even go to see Karl. Fellmann told me that the Chief had tried to find a reason to send me to Brussels on squadron business, but without success.

Neidhart got shot down in flames, the poor little sod, and we buried him with all due ceremony. I just managed to hobble along in the procession – the Chief had said I could sit it out, but that didn't seem right.

It was the usual depressing affair, and I didn't want to look at the cross, because he'd been born in 1900. It seemed obscene that the war was sucking in boys who'd first seen light in the new century.

Fiedler followed him the next day, but ended up in No Man's Land.

Two dead children.

"Poor Fiedler," Bretti said at the wake. "He was still a virgin, you know."

"Maybe that means he'll go to Heaven," I said, "not like the rest of us!"

The next day Bretti got a two-seater and I could have screamed with envy. And then I realised that I was jealous because he'd killed someone and I hadn't, and for the umpteenth time I wondered what I'd become.

A soldier, Franz...

Later that day Horstmann came back white and visibly trembling.

"Jesus, that was – those Camel things are bloody bad news." His hands shook as he lit his cigarette, and there was a twitch at the corner of his right eye. "Bastard knew what he was doing, as well."

"It's not like the spring," Steyer agreed.

"When are Albatros going to sort out those bloody wings?" Patschke demanded. "It's getting beyond a joke."

"They must be losing a fortune," said Beilke. "No one wants to fly them."

"I heard Richthofen's complained as well," said Horstmann, his voice a fraction steadier.

"How in God's name do you know that?" asked Patschke.

"Friend in Berlin," Horstmann replied.

"Who's that, then?" Bretti asked.

Horstmann just grinned at him.

"Should have known better than to ask," Bretti said.

"You're learning!"

"So what else does this contact say?" asked Steyer. "If I can ask, that is?"

"Apparently there've been a few crashes," Horstmann said. "Fatal ones."

"That's pretty well what Platzer said," said Beilke.

Eichner sighed. "It really is the last thing we need, having to wonder whether the wings will stay on."

"Hopefully they'll sort it out before long," Horstmann said.

"Or give us parachutes," said Beilke.

"Ask Santa!" Eichner said. "If you make it to Christmas!"

In place of Neidhart and Fiedler we acquired Ewald, who was about as young as the two of them and straight out of Valenciennes, and, to our great joy, the lanky figure of Leutnant Friedrich von Lentzke, who already had six.

"You've got quite a reputation," he said. "I've been trying to join you for about a month."

I expected someone to make a sarcastic remark about another bloody Junker, but no one did. *It was Widemayer and Kühn who used to say things like that. Now everyone's just happy that he's an ace.*

Ace or not, he nearly got killed on his second day with us. Those bloody Camels again.

Finally the wonderful day came when I managed to move the rudder bar without a teeth-gritting stab of pain. Yes, it hurt a bit, but I didn't care.

I won't feel it once the adrenaline's flowing. Best painkiller in the world, that stuff.

I didn't score that day – it would have been too much to hope for – but I gave a Nieuport pilot a decent fright, and it was bloody great to be off the ground again.

Back in business.

The days were noticeably shorter, and the evenings were becoming cool. No one minded – the long days of summer had been exhausting, and it was easier to sleep without the heat.

It'll soon be the equinox. I daren't think any further ahead than that.

In the middle of September the Chief and I were in his office, discussing whether we could move base before the autumn rain set in, when Fellmann came in looking like a small boy in possession of a secret.

"Come on, don't keep it to yourself!" said the boss.

"Well, sir – I think you'll like this…"

We looked at him expectantly.

"Spit it out!" the Chief said, playing Fellmann's game. It would have been unkind not to.

"We're getting three Fokker Triplanes!" Fellmann said gleefully.

"Is that right?"

"Really?" I copied the Chief's mock solemnity.

"When?" asked the boss.

"Ah, now that's the thing—"

"There had to be a 'but,'" the Chief said, laughing.

"Isn't there always?" Fellmann agreed. "In about two weeks' time. Richthofen gave a very positive report and wants more for his lot, and of course we're below them on the waiting list."

"Fair enough," the boss said. "So the question is, who's to have them?"

"Well, you, of course, sir," I said. "That goes without saying."

"And you," he replied.

"What about the third one?" asked Fellmann.

Part of me felt slightly uncomfortable about having one of the new aircraft. I knew it made sense to give them to the highest-ranking pilots, but at the same time it was virtually saying that the others were more disposable.

"On the basis of victories it should be Beilke," I said. "But who should it be on seniority?"

Fellmann consulted a note he'd made. "Just sticking to Air Service seniority and ignoring date of commission, it would be Horstmann, but on commission date—"

"Not relevant," said the Chief. "It's between Horstmann and Beilke, then."

"Has either of them flown with a rotary before?" I asked.

"I'll ask them," said Fellmann.

He came back a couple of minutes later. "Neither."

"Becker?" asked the Chief.

"My vote's for Beilke," I said. "Stick to number of victories."

The boss nodded. "My thoughts exactly. The new aircraft have to go to the men who can make best use of them. If the Triplane's satisfactory then we can request more."

"What are you going to tell everyone?" Fellmann asked him.

"Nothing as yet. There's no point saying anything until they actually arrive."

Because what's to say any of us will be here? he didn't need to add.

"Beilke and Horstmann will have realised something's up," I said. "It would probably be best to tell them, or they'll talk about it."

"Good idea, Becker – I'll leave that to you."

"Thank fuck for that," said Horstmann. "At last we'll be able to match their rate of turn. I just hope I last till mine arrives!"

Me too...

That thought returned with force in the afternoon – we had a very hot fight, and I was lucky to escape alive.

Schiffer looked at the holes and shook his head. "I don't know, sir – we do our best to fix them, and you bring them back like this."

Aircraftman Bauer, who was new, gazed at Schiffer as if he couldn't believe anyone could get away with speaking to an officer like that.

"You wouldn't want to be bored, now, would you?" I managed to say. My knees and hands were shaking and all I wanted was a fag and a large brandy. "How long before she can fly?"

"Oh, she'll be all set for dawn, sir."

You know just what to say to cheer me up – but I changed my mind in the morning when I sent a Camel down in flames.

That's one less of those bloody things – but the Tommies are probably building them faster than we can shoot them down...

The post came, and there was still nothing from Karl. He'd been sending me dictated letters twice a week, but I hadn't received one for ten days. Staff Doctor Silbermann had telephoned to say that he'd been put in the hospital train, and we'd heard nothing more.

I couldn't help fretting. *Bretti's brother died in one of those trains.*

There was a letter from Maria, though, which referred again to marriage. A nasty little thought crept into my brain. *What if she's pregnant?*

Don't jump to conclusions. She wants to get married because she'd rather be a war widow than a bereaved girlfriend, and she's hardly alone in that. If she were pregnant then she'd tell you, wouldn't she?

Or would she? What does a nice young lady do in those circumstances?

Shit – if she's pregnant I'll have to marry her—

The sound of a rotary engine cut through my thoughts.

"Shit!" exclaimed Horstmann, and we all rushed outside – to see a flying Venetian blind making a low pass.

VII

"I hope Braun's boys have seen the black crosses," said Beilke, "or that fellow's in for a nasty shock!"

The ground crew didn't open fire, and we all watched as the Triplane made a neat touchdown and taxied in, the engine cutting out repeatedly. We reached the flight line at the same time as it did.

"Not natural, a rotating engine," Patschke shouted in my ear, and it did look most strange with the cylinders a blur behind the propeller.

"Not to mention all that stopping and starting," added Eichner.

"Can't do the crankshaft any good," added Steyer.

The engine stopped in a cloud of oil and the pilot slid down, landing rather awkwardly.

"Good God!" I exclaimed as he took off his helmet and goggles. "Otto!"

"Well, bugger me!" he replied. "Satan doesn't want you, then?!"

I threw my arms round him. "You've escaped from Döberitz?"

"Well, I reckoned you lot wouldn't manage without me!"

"Welcome back!" said Braun.

"Crikey, you still here as well?"

"Of course," Braun replied solemnly.

"Ah, Kramer!" said the Chief, joining us. "Welcome back! And I see you've brought us a gift."

"That's right, sir. Brand new and all yours!"

"Thank you very much!"

Fellmann added his welcome, and the boss introduced Otto to the others.

We linked arms and followed them to the mess.

"It's bloody good to have you back," I said to him.

"You and the Chief are the only ones I recognise – of the pilots, that is."

"Yes…"

"How's Karl?"

I sighed. "The last I heard he was in the hospital train. We don't know where he is now."

He shook his head. "When I read your letter I just couldn't believe it. I really hope he's out of it for good, now – I mean, after an injury like that he's never going to be fit to fight again."

I saw Karl as he'd looked the last time I'd seen him. Whether he'd return to the Front was a long way second to whether he'd survive.

"No."

"He's done more than enough, after all," Otto went on. "I mean, Verdun – God knows how he managed not to get killed."

I didn't want to talk about Karl. I just wanted to hear that he was safe in Germany and recovering.

"Tell me about the Triplane," I said.

"Oh, you'll love it!" he said, and rattled on in typical Otto fashion about its virtues. I couldn't really give a shit as I'd have to wait for the next one, and who knew when that would arrive – but it was bloody brilliant to have an old friend at the squadron again.

He moved into the empty room in Fellmann's hut, which caused a bit of murmuring among the young fellows until I pointed out that Otto was second only to the boss in squadron seniority.

The Chief wasted no time test-flying his new machine, and treated us to a beautiful display of aerobatics before blasting the targets.

He had a wide grin on his face as he jumped down. "Becker, I'll see you overhead the field in fifteen minutes!"

"Yes, sir!"

This will be interesting – I haven't flown against the Chief since I joined the Jasta. But I have flown against enough rotary engined aircraft…

I was still impressed. The Triplane was slower than my Albatros, but had a terrific rate of climb and was very, very manoeuvrable.

"What did you reckon to that?" he asked me afterwards.

"I'm bloody glad Fokker came to us and not the Tommies!" I replied, laughing.

"Oh, he did go to the Tommies," said Fellmann, "but they told him to go away."

"Bet they've regretted that," Horstmann said, "what with the monoplane and now this."

"Right," said the boss. "Becker, Beilke, Horstmann – you can lead after lunch. Ziegler, we need to get these guns zeroed, and Patschke, you're flying against me afterwards. I want to get to know this a bit better before I meet the Tommies."

So after lunch I led Steyer and Otto, and it looked very strange because Otto had borrowed the Chief's Albatros and it was rather difficult to remember that it wasn't the boss.

Until we met the Tommies – Otto possessed neither the Chief's flying skill nor his marksmanship. He was perfectly competent and a good wingman, but that's not the same as a thirty-victory ace – and of course he was rusty. A refresher course isn't the same thing.

Steyer fought in his usual bold manner. *He probably doesn't care about surviving, after losing his wife and daughter.* I'd thought he was just a death or glory merchant until he told us about that.

I don't know why people say 'death or glory' as if they're mutually exclusive – I reckon they go together most of the bloody time.

"Bloody hell, that Triplane can turn on a fucking sixpence," said Patschke. "The boss is going to be fucking lethal in that."

"Shoot you down, did he?" asked Lentzke with a grin.

"I lost count after the fifth time or so."

"And how many times did you get him?"

"Oh, piss off!"

"That'll be none, then!"

Patschke pulled a face. "What do you expect?! Does my score stand at thirty-two?"

We had quite a piss-up to celebrate Otto's return, which ended with the cavalry game.

It's a while since we played this, I thought as Lentzke hoisted me onto his shoulders. We lasted all of half a minute, but fortunately the ground was still soft.

I had a horrible head the next dawn and for some reason was covered in bruises, including an almost black one on my arm from Bretti's 'sabre'.

The Chief's Triplane looked quite odd beside the Albatri, and for a moment I wondered what it was doing there. *Wake up, Franz, for fuck's sake!*

I did, and in spite of my massive hangover I managed to knock one of those Bristol two-seaters out of the sky. The Tommies didn't like that one bit, and we were joined by a flight of SE5s. Two of them were far too good for comfort and we were really struggling to hold them off – and then the boss turned up with his Kette, and their leader was spinning down in flames before you could blink.

The Chief's Triplane was practically dancing. *I want one, as soon as fucking possible.*

Half an hour later I didn't think I was going to live that long. We met a flight of those fucking Camels. One of the bastards flew straight at me, and I felt a tug at my left sleeve and another at my flying boot before he chickened out and broke off. I threw my Albatros on her wingtips to go after him, but he was leaving the fight as fast as he could.

I reckon you came off worst. Close call, though…

"You know what we used to say to Johnny about frontal attacks," Horstmann said as we walked to the mess.

"Oh, bollocks!" I retorted. "He started it."

"Yes, but you kept it up, you stupid bastard."

Maybe you've got a point…

"When's my Triplane coming?" I asked Fellmann, after yet another week.

"Oh, let's see – I did get a cable from Fokker… Now where is it?" He made a show of rummaging around on his desk. "Ah, here it is." He pretended to read it slowly.

"Get on with it, you bastard!"

"That's no way to talk! Tomorrow, it says here. Weather permitting, of course."

"Thank fuck for that."

"In the meantime, you've got a couple of letters."

One was addressed in an unfamiliar, very feminine hand and I opened it first, just in case it was news of Karl.

It contained a single sheet of paper, with a few lines scrawled uncertainly in pencil, the writing unrecognisable. *Who the hell—?*

At the bottom it said, 'Ever yours, Karl'. My heart leapt and I went to the window to decipher the rest of it.

"Another fancy woman?" Beilke asked.

"No – it's from Karl."

There was an immediate chorus of "What does it say?"

"Hang on…"

The writing was spidery and very faint in places, as if he hadn't been able to use enough pressure, and some of the words were illegible. *He's still dreadfully weak, but he survived the journey and he can write himself now. Oh, thank God.*

"'My dear Franz, many congratulations on your latest victories. You'll soon have the Blue Max. I'm in Baden-Baden – the hospital is very comfortable and they say I'm getting better. Write soon," I read out, guessing the words I couldn't read.

"That's bloody brilliant," said Otto. "Give me the address."

"Here." I passed it to him.

The other letter was from Johanna, and as I started reading I said, "Shit!" before I could stop myself.

"Woman trouble?" asked Lentzke with a wink.

"Sister trouble," I said.

"You want to tell her to behave herself," said Eichner. "Women are getting well above themselves these days."

"Oh, I don't know," Lentzke said. "They're far more interesting now – but then I like talking to them."

"Women should stick to kitchen and family," Eichner said firmly.

"Bollocks!" Bretti retorted.

"That's just it – they don't have any."

I left them to their argument and read on.

'Do you know anyone I could stay with in Berlin? I've had enough of Mama telling me that all I need to learn is how to be a good housewife. If I could go to Berlin then I could get the experience I need, and see the Professor about enrolling in the University once I've passed my exams.'

I knew Johanna well enough to realise she meant it. *She's probably packed her case already. She could even be on the train.*

So who do I know? Max Levy – but he's a prisoner in Wales and I've never met his family. Alfred – but he's fighting in Italy and the same applies. And given the food shortages, no one's going to want a lodger, even with her own ration card.

'Sis, going to Berlin is not a good idea,' I wrote. 'There's no one I can think of, and you can't go there by yourself, not with no job and nowhere to live. You'll end up in some ghastly tenement with nothing to eat. For God's sake start working in the maternity ward and try not to argue with Mama. The world's changing and you'll get what you want – you just have to be patient for now.

You'll be pleased to hear Karl is on the mend and is in Germany – and no, he doesn't have a house in Berlin!'

I hope she listens…

My Triplane turned up, flown by yet another smashed-up former fighter pilot. This one was called Wendt, and his face looked as if it had half-melted and resolidified. It was not an illusion. His left hand was similar and frozen into a claw, the bone visible in a couple of places.

None of us wanted to look too closely and no one asked what had happened. I concentrated instead on the briefing he gave me, and fifteen minutes later I was heading skywards with the altimeter winding up faster than I'd ever seen before.

And five minutes after that I was turning tighter than I could have believed. *Thank you, Herr Fokker,* I thought as she pivoted on her wingtips. *A very nice piece of work indeed.*

The view from the cockpit could be better, though, with all those wings…

I had twenty minutes of glorious fun and then had a go at the targets, which showed that Ziegler's boys had a job to do.

"Well, what do you think?" Wendt asked.

"Bloody fantastic!"

The Chief grinned at me. "Overhead as soon as she's refuelled, then!"

"Yes, sir!"

The 'fight' was much more balanced this time, and by the time we'd finished I was confident that I could deal with the Tommies.

I'll have a bit more of a play this afternoon, have a go against Beilke.

After lunch we lounged on the grass, enjoying the late September sunshine. It was almost warm enough to strip off, and Bretti started doing just that—

"GET IN THE AIR! *NOW!!!*" Fellmann's parade ground bellow carried easily to the hangars, and some of the ground crew actually jumped.

So did we. Bretti grabbed his tunic from the grass and put it on as we ran to the flight line.

My Albatros was in the hangar, its wings removed. My Triplane was sitting outside.

"Fuel? Guns loaded?"

"Both, sir!"

Kessler put the steps in position and I fairly leapt into the cockpit, the urgency in Fellmann's voice ringing in my ears.

We hadn't had time to zero the guns. *Too bad. I'll just have to get in closer.*

Kessler swung the propeller but the engine was still warm. *Start, damn you!*

The Chief was already taxying out, so were Horstmann, Steyer, Schaff…

The engine coughed and caught, Kessler pulled the chocks out and I taxied just far enough to not point my tail at anything.

Flat calm. I gave her full power and we were airborne in no time and climbing up.

Not a second too soon. Two flights of SE5s were diving down towards the field, already at about a hundred metres.

I glanced down as I turned towards them.

Bretti was just getting airborne, and Eichner. Lentzke was taxying out, Patschke took off and tried to climb far too steeply.

Get the bloody nose down!

I had no more time to look. I got on the tail of one of the bastards as he started his pass across the airfield. He was too busy shooting up everything he could see to notice me closing in.

I got him with the first burst and had to pull up sharply as his aircraft reared up – and then I broke hard right as I came under fire myself.

How odd – there's no one near me.

It turned into a proper scrap. After a few minutes the Tommies tried to get away, and we weren't having that.

You wanted to visit. We didn't invite you.

We had fuel and they didn't, and we chased them all the way to the Front, forcing them to turn again and again to defend themselves.

My agile little Triplane out-turned them easily and I was bloody sure I hit another, but he didn't go down.

That was a bloody rude interruption to our afternoon, I thought as we flew home. *I wonder how much damage they did.*

There were two wrecks on the field. One was my victim, and the other was Patschke's Albatros, which had obviously spun in.

Schiffer and Bauer were carrying his broken, crumpled body to Hangar One. Both legs were horribly mangled, and his face was covered in blood.

You won't be scaring Claudette's girls any more.

"Any other casualties?" I asked them.

"Ziegler's dead, sir," said Schiffer. "And Kessler got hit in the legs. Leutnant Fellmann's looking after him."

I'll leave him to it. I went to the SE5.

No difficulty getting this confirmed, right on the airfield with Wendt here.

The cockpit had folded around the pilot, and Zaffke and Braun were cutting him out.

He looked at me and tried to say something, but couldn't speak for the blood bubbling from his mouth, vivid red against his white face.

Just like Karl. I'd aimed between his shoulders, just as that Camel pilot must have done.

"We bring you in hospital," I said, and realised I'd got my English wrong.

"Should be able to get him out now, sir," said Braun, and I unfastened his straps and got my arms under his and round his chest.

This is going to hurt, but it has to be done. He gave a gurgling cry as I lifted him and then went limp in my arms, the sudden dead weight unbalancing me. The other two helped me to get him out, and we put him on the ground.

His eyes stared blankly at the sky and he'd stopped breathing. *I don't give a shit. Patschke and Ziegler are dead because of you and your mates.*

I'd rather you hadn't died in my arms, though, and you've made a bit of a mess. There was blood on my hands, and on my sleeves and the front of my tunic.

At least it's not mine.

"Good work, Becker," said the Chief.

"Thank you, sir."

"Yes, well done," added Wendt. "Nice to see you putting my delivery to good use – as far as I'm concerned, you can kill as many of the bastards as you like!"

"How's Kessler, sir?" I asked the boss.

"He'll be all right – Fellmann's given him a shot of morphine and he'll be on his way to hospital as soon as possible. We were very lucky we didn't lose more."

"What about the aircraft?"

"Three are damaged, one badly – still, with a bit of luck that means we can have another new Triplane!"

I looked again at the dead Englishman, and suddenly saw how young he was. *You look as if you should still be at school. What was it someone said about Spots? That's what happens when a boy plays a man's game...*

Zaffke stood beside me. "I – er, I must apologise, sir," he said very awkwardly.

"Whatever for?"

"Nearly hitting you, sir."

For a moment he'd lost me.

"Oh – you were manning our machine gun!" *So that's who shot at me.*

"Yes, sir – we didn't see you until the Tommy pulled up, being as you were right behind him, and it took us a moment to stop firing."

"Don't worry – you missed!"

He looked quite discomfited, and I wondered whether it was worse to have fired at me or to have had such poor aim. *Well, it wasn't his usual weapon, and moving aircraft are bloody hard to hit.*

"That was a bit bloody much," said Horstmann, "right after lunch like that—" His face creased in sudden concern. "Bloody hell, Becker, that's a lot of blood."

"Oh, it's not mine."

That's what I said after Langemarck, when my face was covered in someone else's blood... The memory was so vivid that my vision blurred, and for one nasty moment I thought I was going to find myself back there.

"You sure?"

I gestured to my victim.

"Well done. Serves the bugger right."

"Well," said Lentzke. "Do you get visitors like that often?"

"No – only the second time."

I went to clean myself up. *So that's a triple funeral tomorrow, and we'll have the guard of honour tonight for Patschke – and as far as I'm concerned we can put Ziegler next to him. And we'll have to put the Tommy there as well. I sometimes feel we've got more in common with them than we have with the people back home.*

The Chief must have had similar thoughts, because all three coffins were in Hangar One. Braun had somehow managed to make Patschke and our late enemy presentable. Ziegler's coffin was closed, and Schiffer told me he'd been hit in the head.

"Ricochet from the look of it, sir."

I tried not to use my imagination.

Horstmann was subdued over dinner. He'd just finished helping Lentzke sort out Patschke's things.

"I'll write to his parents later," he said to me. "Yes, I used to get pissed off with him taking the piss all the time and pinching my flowers, but he was a good bloke and a good pilot."

"Yes, he was."

Wendt accepted our hospitality, and offered to participate in the guard of honour and attend the funerals.

"The only thing is, sir," he said to the Chief, "that – at the risk of sounding like my former girlfriend – I've got nothing to wear!"

We all laughed. He was perfectly dressed for flying, in old trousers and shirt and a tatty sweater. All were oil-stained in spite of his flying suit and jacket.

"No, quite," said the Chief. "I take it you're not still serving?"

Wendt shook his head. "Medical discharge – fit for bugger all. I was a Leutnant, if that helps."

Fellmann looked at him. "You're about the same size as me, I think. I don't get quite as mucky as the others, so you're welcome to borrow my everyday uniform, if it fits."

"Thanks."

Fellmann's tunic was a bit big for Wendt, but he looked quite passable.

"You can try the trousers on when we get undressed," Fellmann said.

Johnny would have raised an eyebrow at that.

So many of the men I knew are dead.

Otto caught my eye across the table, and I knew he was thinking something similar.

Wendt put away a quite amazing quantity of booze – even by our standards – and remained apparently stone-cold sober.

"Fucking hell, I thought *we* could drink," Horstmann said to me in our room. "I've never seen anyone put it away like that!"

"Maybe he uses it as anaesthetic – I mean, his body's probably just like his face."

"Probably."

He seemed hangover-free the following morning as well – he was just coming out of the hangar as we made our way to the flight line, and was far perkier than I was. I'd had the usual depressing night, standing in the hangar and trying to grab a bit of sleep in between, and I missed Karl almost unbearably.

Sending a two-seater down into No Man's Land improved my mood no end. *I like this aircraft. I've had her less than twenty-four hours, and I've scored twice.*

If that gets confirmed I'll be on eighteen – shame about the last but one.

"Nice job, Becker," said Steyer.

"Yes," added Eichner. "Gives us a *good* reason for a party tonight."

Yet again we made the journey to the cemetery, and once more we sang 'I had a Comrade'. *If I survive the war I'll never want to hear this again.* Patschke's death was inevitable at some point, as he'd been a Regular officer, but for Ziegler to get shot like a rabbit when he wasn't even fighting seemed wrong.

I said as much to Otto.

"Franz, that's complete bollocks! Ziegler and his chaps set up the guns for us, don't they? And that's as good as firing them. Look, don't you remember? If you provide the murder weapon you're an accessory, aren't you?"

I laughed. "Did you keep up your studies in your spare time, then?"

"What, between being scared shitless by student pilots and going to the free love club? Of course I bloody did! I mean, I've got to have something to do after the war."

Horstmann and Bretti both burst out laughing.

"'After the war?'" Horstmann said. "What the fuck are you talking about?"

"Fairyland," Lentzke said.

"Hey, Beilke!" said Bretti. "You ever heard of somewhere called 'after the war'?"

Beilke pretended to think. "Er, yes – but it's only for staff officers!"

"Unless of course you end up like me," Wendt said. "Anyway, I'd better be off. Thank you all so much for your hospitality – with a bit of luck I'll be back before long with another of Fokker's finest for you."

"I'll take you to the station," said Fellmann, "unless you want to take Becker's old Albatros."

Wendt laughed. "It would be a lot quicker, but…" He thought for a moment. "Yes, why not? Where does it have to go?"

"Come to the Ops Office and I'll check."

"See, Kramer?" said Bretti once they'd left the building, "the only way to get to 'after the war' is to get fried like that. How much luck would you have at the free love club looking like that?"

"About the same as he does now," I replied. "They always make him do it from behind!"

By the end of the month my score stood at nineteen, one tantalising victory away from the Blue Max. That didn't escape Papa, who wrote me a letter so full of nauseating patriotic drivel that I couldn't read it.

Maria, on the other hand, hadn't written for a fortnight. It was a bit odd, given her previous references to marriage.

I really don't mind if she's gone off me, or found someone else. Our afternoon together was a vague but pleasant memory – so much had happened since that it felt quite unreal.

Karl's letters were longer and more clearly written, and he was starting to sound like himself again, which made me very happy. He'd made it, so he'd survive the war. I couldn't imagine any man being fit for the front line after an injury like that, and especially not a fighter pilot. Not at high altitude with a fucked lung.

Whether I'd ever see him again was quite another matter. *Just be glad he's alive,* I thought as we got ready to fly again.

We had yet another new boy, and I had the joy of flying with him that afternoon.

The trees were gold and brown beneath us as we gained height before setting course for the Front.

That was probably my last summer – unless of course the war ends this winter, which it had better do because the Americans will be here soon, and then we'll be completely fucked – oh, come on, Schulte, do try to hold formation a bit better than that…

Steyer rocked his wings urgently and pointed. A flight of Camels – no problem for me in my lovely Triplane, but not so funny for most of the squadron, who were still in Albatri.

In the melee Schulte 'forgot' what I'd told him and joined in the fight, and of course he had a Camel on his tail in five seconds flat. Bretti was closer than I was, and fortunately for Schulte he had his eyes open.

Half a minute later I found myself behind and below a Camel. I pulled up and poured lead into him, the Triplane seeming almost to hover – and I broke away as he fell into a spin. *Got you, you bastard.*

We had a very hot fight after that one – Schulte had redeemed himself somewhat by spotting a two-seater, but Steyer had barely started setting up his attack when we were attacked ourselves by a flight of Nieuports. Then a Kette of Pfalzes joined in, and a flight of SE5s, and the sky was so full of aircraft that I thought we would all meet in the middle.

Every other minute there was a fucking Tommy trying to get on my tail, and as I got away from one I was immediately attacked by another. After what felt like forever the sky emptied, and for a moment I didn't dare believe it. Then I realised that it really was over, and that somehow I was still alive and unharmed, and I sagged in my seat, sweating and shaking.

It was only on the way home that I realised I'd just reached the magical twenty – subject, of course, to its being confirmed.

"Well?" asked Schiffer as I jumped down.

"One Camel." My knees were trembling, and I hoped no one would notice.

His face cracked into a wide grin. "Well done, sir!"

It took all of two minutes for the entire squadron to get the news.

"Hey," said Beilke, "that's going to be a proper party!"

"Well done, Becker!" said the Chief. "Fellmann's already phoning round for confirmation."

It came after lunch. *My turn for the big party. The last time we had one of those was for Karl.*

And so in the evening I stood in front of my Triplane, with a garland on her nose bearing a large '20'. Beilke took my picture and everyone drank my health, and then we headed to the mess for a proper piss-up.

I just have to stay alive now until they give me the Blue Max...

Steyer got shot down the next morning, blazing out of the sky like a comet, and in the afternoon Schaff crashed, spinning off his final turn. The mood that evening was very subdued, and once again we kept vigil in Hangar One.

"It's hard to be sorry about Steyer," Horstmann said.

It was very late and he, Bretti, Lentzke and I were sitting in the mess with a bottle of brandy. We'd just left the hangar and none of us felt like going to bed. The odour of charred flesh was still in my nostrils and I was afraid of the burning dream, and the others all had their demons.

"No, quite," said Bretti. "I felt so bad that day – I just didn't realise."

"You're not a bloody mind reader," Horstmann said. "I take it his things go back to his parents."

Bretti nodded. "I don't know who they've got left now."

"No point thinking about it," I said.

Lentzke was staring into his glass.

"It's all shit," he said quietly, without looking up.

"I think I'll try to get some sleep," I said.

I don't know why I bothered. I lay staring at the ceiling in the darkness, trying to find something nice to think about – and all that came to mind was how lovely it would be if Karl and I were in his house, lying in bed together with no reason to get up. And then I felt even worse, because that was never likely to happen.

All I can hope is that I have a quick end. It truly is all shit.

It pissed down for the double funeral, and we were all soaked before we were out of the airfield gates. The lane to the cemetery was muddy and puddled, and the gun carriage got stuck. The horses pulled and strained, but it wouldn't budge and we had to push. Eichner slipped, and fell in the mud in his best uniform.

"I thought I was finished with getting soaked after I left the infantry," Horstmann said on the way back.

"At least you're just wet," grumbled Eichner. "I don't think this will ever be clean again."

"Oh, it'll brush out," said Beilke. "Frankly, all I want now is a very large schnapps."

"You and me both," I said.

"It's not like it was," Otto said in my ear a few days later. We were sitting on the small sofa and Bretti had the gramophone going, while Beilke, Eichner and Lentzke were playing a noisy game of skat at the dining table. "The Tommies have really got the upper hand now."

"We need more Triplanes," I replied. We were up to four, with Beilke and Horstmann flying the other two. "The Chief's pushing hard for more."

"Well, I bloody well hope they get here soon – and can't we have some blokes off two-seaters instead of these children out of Döberitz and Valenciennes?"

Reinhard, who had arrived to replace Steyer, was another with fluff on his face. He was listening intently as Schulte was telling him some flying story, his hands chasing each other. *The one-eyed man in the kingdom of the blind.*

"They have to start somewhere."

"Hey, anyone fancy Claudette's?" asked Horstmann as the gramophone wound down.

"Yes," I said, "but Otto's not driving!"

"Oh, for fuck's sake!" Otto exclaimed. "That was bloody months ago!"

"Yes, and it was raining then," I said. "Besides, we'll need to take a lorry – the car will just get messy, even if we stay on the road."

"If we go now we might beat the staff officers to it," Beilke said.

And we did, and I had a pleasant hour with Eugénie, who was new and who was very – well, never mind about that.

The lane and the airfield were both sodden.

"Proper wake, then," said Beilke to general agreement.

I fell onto my bed fully clothed and passed out, but was woken by Horstmann yelling something about Tommies.

Back at the Somme. I shook him, and dodged too late as he lashed out, catching me in the face.

"SHIT!" I yelled.

"What the hell – where—?" His voice was shaking.

"You just whacked me in the face, you stupid bastard!"

"Oh, Jesus – sorry, Becker. I thought – well, you know – there were three Tommies with bayonets, they'd got into the trench—"

"Oh, don't worry about it. There's no damage."

Except that I developed a real shiner.

The Chief gave me a very quizzical look.

"Walked into something in the dark, sir."

Eichner grinned. "That's what my aunt used to say when my uncle had been thumping her. I reckon you and Horstmann fell out!"

"Damn, you guessed!" I said, laughing. "It was over that tart in Claudette's!"

The Chief just shook his head and went to his office.

Fellmann came in for his coffee and cigar, looked at me and raised an eyebrow.

"Lovers' tiff?" he asked in his campest voice.

"Mind your own business!" Horstmann retorted.

The autumn sun poured through the mess windows, and I turned my back on it. My head was throbbing and I blamed Horstmann's whack. It made a good excuse, anyway.

The sun might have been bright, but it wasn't warm enough to dry the field out. A beautifully clear night was followed by fog in the morning, so thick you couldn't see the hangars from the mess.

We could hear the guns, though – the battle was still raging. The Tommies were intent on pushing our fellows off the Passchendaele ridge, and they were resisting desperately. How anyone could even move in that swamp was beyond me. I was just fucking glad I wasn't there.

The fog was succeeded by more rain, and more fog, and the Flanders mud reasserted its claim on our airfield. Once again we began the search for an alternative base, but everywhere we looked at had a problem of some sort.

The boredom was relieved only by trips to Claudette's and copious quantities of alcohol, and, of course, the post. Karl was starting to sound quite lively.

'They let me out of bed now!' he wrote jubilantly, 'and I'm sitting in the dayroom with a load of other crocked-up wrecks and a crashing hangover. Some of the fellows who can go into town brought back schnapps and champagne yesterday, and we all got splendidly pissed. The head doctor gave us all a rocket – God alone knows what effect he thought that would have.'

No – none of you gives a shit, after all.

'It was bloody difficult not to laugh, but the miscreants are all confined to barracks. Christ, I can get pissed cheaply these days! One glass and I was half comatose. I'll have to watch out next time we meet – you'll have me under the table in no time.'

I drifted off into a very pleasant daydream. *I don't need to get Karl drunk to have my way with him, and I'm the one who puts the brakes on what we do...*

My reverie was broken by the sound of several lorries passing the mess windows.

"What the hell is that about?" Horstmann asked, and we all looked out.

A Pioneer officer jumped down from the cab of the first lorry, and almost went arse over tit.

"And a very warm – or clammy – welcome from the Flanders mud," said Bretti.

Fellmann went up to him and the two of them began an animated conversation, with a lot of gesturing towards the middle of the airfield, and then they set off in that direction.

"Come on," said Otto. "I'm dying of curiosity."

"One of the better things to die of these days," said Beilke, and we followed Otto out of the mess.

"So I reckon if you put it down running roughly north-east to south-west, that should give us the best chance," Fellmann was saying. "And it is fine grade, isn't it?"

"Certainly is," replied the Pioneer Leutnant. "Have a look."

A couple of the Pioneers pulled him and Fellmann up into the back of the lorry.

"Oh, yes – that'll do very nicely."

"Fellmann," I asked, "what is going on?"

"Ah," he said. "I thought you might all like a surprise."

"You're certainly giving us that," Horstmann remarked.

"God, Fellmann, you do like your drama," said Lentzke. "You should have been on the bloody stage."

"In drag!" Bretti said cheekily.

Horstmann gave him a warning look, and he moved apparently casually, putting me between the two of them. *Wrong move, Bretti.*

The Chief appeared. "What's all this?"

Fellmann grinned. "A little surprise, sir!"

The boss and I exchanged baffled looks. *So you're as much in the dark as I am.*

"Come on, then," said the Chief. "Whose birthday is it?"

Ewald looked furtive, which did not escape Bretti's notice. *That'll be a party later, then...*

Fellmann looked almost disappointed at having to reveal his scheme.

"Leutnant Schäfer and his fellows have brought us some – I don't know what the technical term is, but it's fine rubble, and they're going to lay it across the field so we'll have a useable strip."

There was a babble of voices as we all spoke at once.

"Gentlemen, please," said the Chief. "Fellmann, that's a bloody good idea – there are just a couple of things that come to mind... first, won't it just sink straight into the mud, second, will it be smooth enough, and third, how big is this strip going to be, and in what direction?"

Fellmann looked at Schäfer, who was gazing at the Chief with something like awe and who had to gather himself before he could reply.

"Well, sir, we use it on the roads and yes, it does sink under load, but your aircraft are very light and they won't be spending much time on it so it should last quite well. The stuff we've brought is pretty fine so it shouldn't be any rougher than a grass surface, and finally, I'd be grateful for your instructions on the dimensions and orientation of the strip, sir."

"Yes, of course... I think the three of us had better go to my office, and Becker, you come as well. Braun, look after Leutnant Schäfer's chaps, would you?"

"Yes, sir."

After quite a bit of coffee- and tobacco-fuelled discussion we had a plan, and we went out to help Schäfer and his Sergeant mark out the area. And then everyone mucked in to spread the stuff, which was rather like gravel.

"Christ, I haven't worked like this since I left the trenches," said Horstmann, stretching his back.

"Probably do us good," said Lentzke. "We all spend too much time on our arses."

"Do they bring a steamroller or something to flatten it?" asked Reinhard.

"No idea," said Beilke. "But the more we shovel, the sooner we'll be finished."

"And the sooner we'll be able to fly," added Ewald.

I envied his keenness, but at the same time I was sick of sitting on the ground. It felt wrong being safe, when the poor bastards in the trenches were up to their ears in the shit.

I don't know how the staff do it. They can't have anything resembling a conscience – or maybe they're just convinced of their own importance.

The sun was close to the horizon, and the job was less than half done.

"Let's hope it doesn't rain overnight," Otto said.

"Quite," agreed Schäfer.

Bretti turned to Ewald. "So how old are you today, then?"

"Twenty – you *bastard!* I was trying not to let on."

Nice one, Bretti. Straight out of the sun.

"At least the ground's soft," said Beilke with a glint in his eye.

"Oh, no," groaned Ewald. "I really wanted to avoid this."

"No chance," said Horstmann. "Fellmann's put everyone's birthdays in the squadron diary. No one escapes. Just get pissed, then you won't feel it."

It was a magnificent piss-up. We all forgot the hard work waiting for us in the morning, and Schiffer's arrival with the shaving water had Horstmann and me cursing.

"Bloody hell, what was I doing last night?" Horstmann asked as he struggled out of bed. "Did you bastards give me Ewald's bumps or something?"

I laughed – until I tried to get up myself. I ached from head to foot, and even sitting up was a major effort.

"No, you stupid sod," I said. "We were spreading all that gravel, weren't we? And we've got to finish it today."

"Oh, fuck! I'm not sure I can move!"

"Not optional, is it?!"

Everyone was in the same state apart from Schäfer, who was far more used to hard labour than we were.

His pain was in a different place.

"Bloody hell, you bastards can drink!" he said. "The last time I had a head like this was on the Somme – I got 'entertained' by some bastard Brandenburgers with hollow legs and concrete stomachs!"

Lentzke laughed. "You probably met my brother, then, or someone like him!"

"Or my cousin," Horstmann added.

"Or my best mate!" I said.

The Chief just smiled.

"I joined the Air Service to *not* do this sort of thing," grumbled Schulte as we got down to work. "My older brother told me about it, and I thought fuck that for a joke."

"Just be thankful no one's shooting at you," Lentzke said cheerfully. "Though it does help you work – amazing how fast sandbags get filled under fire."

"And how fast a trench gets dug," added Horstmann.

The sky was beginning to cloud over. We went into the mess to snatch a quick lunch.

Fellmann nipped into the Ops Office and then joined us with his 'I can keep a secret – no, really, I can!' face.

He went up to the Chief and handed him a piece of paper.

The Chief stood up and rapped on the table, trying to look solemn and failing dismally.

"Gentlemen, I have here a telegram from Berlin." His face cracked into a wide smile in spite of his best efforts. "'His Majesty the King of Prussia and German Emperor is graciously pleased to bestow on Leutnant der Reserve Franz Becker for his valuable service in destroying twenty enemy aircraft the Order Pour le Mérite.' Becker, many congratulations!"

For a moment I couldn't speak. Yes, I knew the award was really a matter of time – but now I'd actually got it: the highest military decoration of the Kingdom of Prussia and thus of the Empire.

In a moment I'll wake up and find that none of it has actually happened, that I'm sitting in a dugout with the rain pissing down...

The Chief was standing beside me, taking off his own Blue Max. I stood up, and to thunderous applause he hung it round my neck and shook my hand.

Everyone crowded round to congratulate me.

"Bloody well done!" Horstmann said.

"I'll second that!" said Beilke. "Bloody good excuse for a party!"

"Best get back to work," said the boss.

"I'd better not get this messed up," I said, and laid my tunic on the sofa with his medal on top of it. I looked at it for a moment and had a very unwelcome thought: *I hope I don't get killed before my own arrives.*

But we can't fly until the gravel strip is finished...

A couple of hours later it started raining, which was pleasant at first as we were all very warm. It soon got heavier and colder.

"Oh, shit!" grumbled Reinhard. "I'm soaked through!"

"Me too," said Ewald.

"This is normal in the infantry," I said. "Except you'd be infested with lice."

"Cheers, Becker," said Horstmann. "I'd almost forgotten those fucking creatures."

"Can't we have a rest now?" asked Ewald. "My back's killing me."

"And my hands," said Reinhard.

"The Chief's still working," Lentzke said, "and so's Becker, and so am I. And Fellmann's working like a Trojan as well. Just get on with it."

The boys exchanged looks and carried on shovelling.

Darkness was a relief. My back and hands were sore as well, though I wasn't about to admit it.

"Good work, everyone," said the Chief. "Tomorrow should finish it."

Half an hour later we were dry and changed. I scurried to the mess in my shirt sleeves, retrieved my tunic from the sofa and put the boss's Blue Max round my neck.

"Have a look in the mirror," said Beilke.

I feigned disinterest. *Bloody hell – that does look good. Like all fighter pilots I dreamed of wearing one of these, but I never imagined it would actually happen.*

Now I really am an ace… Yes, Franz, and if you start thinking like that you'll be a dead ace. Everyone's going to want to kill you now, personally. They won't just want to shoot down a Hun. They'll want Franz Becker, with the Blue Max and the white knight on his fuselage.

"Very smart!" said Lentzke, cutting across my thoughts.

The interruption was welcome, and I turned away from the mirror.

"I reckon a fellow's entitled to preen a bit when he gets one of those," said Horstmann.

"I'll need a picture," Beilke said.

"Signed," added Fellmann with a wink.

Oh, shit – I'm going to be legal tender! How fucking absurd is that?

We had another glorious party. I gave the boss his gong back before the mayhem got going, which was just as well because it all got rather physical.

Schäfer introduced us to a wild game that involved one team trying to overcome the other to get a cushion across the mess. There were no rules, and the game only ended when all the cushions had been destroyed. By that time the mess was ankle deep in feathers, sticky and soggy with spilled booze.

It was still raining the next morning, and we were pleased to see that the gravel hadn't been washed away. We set to in fine style, to keep warm as much as anything, and were finished by lunchtime.

"Now all we need is for the rain to stop, so we can test it out," Beilke said.

We gave Schäfer a good lunch in a somewhat scarred mess.

"Gentlemen, thank you all for your hospitality," he said as he left. "I shan't forget you in a hurry!"

Towards evening the sky cleared, too late for us to fly.

"But not too late for me to take your portrait!" Beilke said gleefully.

And so I had to get togged up in my best uniform, with my own gongs on my tunic and the boss's Pour le Mérite round my neck, and sit looking resolute and warlike by the mess window.

"That'll do very nicely," Beilke said eventually. "I'll do some prints later, and you can sign a few for Fellmann's stock – and I take it you'd like one to send home?"

Oh, shit. Yes, of course my parents will want a picture like that to display.

"Yes, please."

"And one for your girlfriend?"

I hesitated. I hadn't heard from Maria for weeks, and I was rather hoping the whole thing was over. Maybe if she hadn't mentioned marriage I'd have been keener.

"Oh, just let me know," Beilke said.

We had a relatively early and sober night, and in the dawn I found I was trembling as we walked to the flight line. *That's what a break does to you – or is it the feeling that they'll really be out to get me now?*

What we were going off to do suddenly hit me full force and I was almost sick. *Stupid bastard – it's nothing you haven't done hundreds of times before. Get a fucking grip and get on with it.*

"Becker, let's inspect the surface," the Chief said, and the two of us walked out to the strip and along part of it. *With a bit of luck it'll be too slippery.* I pushed that idea firmly out of my mind.

It was slightly greasy on the top from the rain but quite solid underfoot, and the wind was very light and blowing right along it.

"What do you reckon?" he asked.

I nodded. "Should be all right, sir. The new boys might slide a bit."

"Yes, I agree."

We're really going to have to do it. Another day of rain would have been so nice...

"When I got mine," the Chief said quietly, "I felt as if I suddenly had a large target painted on my back. But really nothing changed."

I nodded again. There was no need to reply.

Just concentrate on what you're doing.

And I did have to concentrate on take-off, because the surface was greasier than I'd realised, and some of the gravel was loose in spite of Schäfer's boys going over it with a heavy roller.

As we flew up and down the Front the sick apprehension returned, and my right foot vibrated on the rudder bar as we looked for the enemy.

Eichner rocked his wings and pointed, and my stomach lurched as I saw a flight of Camels. It didn't help that I had Reinhard along on his first patrol.

They'd seen us and were already diving down. As we scattered and turned to meet them I was suddenly completely calm, my mind working with its usual cold clarity.

Their leader went straight for Reinhard, and I went straight after him. He saw me coming, of course, and the two of us had a merry dance until one of his comrades decided to join in. Otto was on his tail in a flash, and then I saw Beilke and his Kette coming to the party.

That tipped the balance in our favour until a flight of SE5s arrived.

Thank God I'm in a Triplane – but poor Ewald was in an Albatros, and before I could close the distance he was spinning.

I got behind the Tommy who'd got him, my Triplane pivoting on her wingtips, my cheeks sagging in the turn – and I know I hit the bastard. He buggered off westwards, trailing smoke.

We had another lively fight after that one, and I flew home soaked through with sweat and shaking from cold and adrenaline.

I hope Ewald pulled out of the spin…

I'd be perfectly happy if the war ended tomorrow, or better still today. I could go to Baden-Baden on my way home and see Karl, and then when he goes home from hospital…

Keep your fucking mind on the job, or you'll get jumped and your next award will be the wooden cross.

Landing was trickier than I'd expected and I was very pleased that Reinhard got it right. *He'll turn into a good pilot if he lives long enough.*

I clapped Otto on the shoulder as we walked to the mess.

"How, my dear friend, can you still manage to miss from that range?"

He looked offended. "I didn't miss. My tracer was going right into his cockpit – I just didn't hit him."

"Exactly! Look, why don't you go and practise your circles? Karl was always practising, and you know what a good shot he is."

"Yes, you're right… I'll see if the new boys want to join in."

The Chief arrived back shortly after us – they must have been running on fumes – and the first thing he noticed was the absence of Ewald's Albatros.

"Went down out of control, sir. I'm sorry but I didn't see any more."

He nodded. "We'll just have to hope."

There was no news, so he hadn't landed and phoned in. *That is not good.*

I could see the others thinking the same. Eichner looked more shocked than I'd expected – they must have lost plenty in his two-seater squadron – but then he and Ewald had become good friends.

It doesn't get easier.

The post was a welcome distraction for us all, and there was a package for me.

That'll be my Blue Max – that was quick.

The package did contain a box about the right size, but it wasn't from the Kaiser. It was from His Majesty the King of Württemberg, who was graciously pleased to award me the Friedrich Order, First Class with swords, and it was accompanied by a very flattering letter signed by the King himself.

Wow. That's really special. That letter will have to go home at once.

I opened the box and thought *wow* again. It contained a beautiful white enamel cross with golden rays between its arms, and crossed swords above it.

"Beilke," I said, "you know that portrait you took? Well, I'm afraid it's obsolete."

He gave me a quizzical look and I handed him the box.

"Crikey," he said, "that's lovely. Who's it from?"

I handed him the certificate.

"Oh. Well, I suppose he didn't want to be outdone by the King of Prussia!"

Fellmann came into the mess followed by the Chief, both looking very grim.

"Gentlemen," said the Chief, "I'm sorry to have to tell you that Unteroffizier Ewald never pulled out of the spin. Braun and Zaffke are setting out to retrieve his body."

Eichner looked at his hands.

"At least it was quick," I said to him quietly, thinking of Anton and Kurt.

He nodded.

"Would you like a hand with his things?" asked Bretti. "It's always easier with two."

"Thanks."

This is the second time I've got a gong just in time for a bloody funeral, I thought, remembering that my Hohenzollern House Order had arrived just after Johnny died. *And I really don't want to think about Johnny, falling blazing like a meteorite...*

I opened Johanna's letter instead.

'The strangest thing has happened. The Hertels have gone away, quite suddenly, without telling anyone where to. No one can talk about anything else. Even Liese doesn't know where they are. Maria just told her that things were getting too much for her mother – her health's "delicate" and the food shortages were making her ill! As if they're not making everyone ill – and everyone doesn't have the money to just run away, and where would any of us go even if that were right?

So we're all guessing that they've gone to Switzerland somehow. Papa said that would be close to treason…'

I could think of only one reason why Maria's parents would take her away.

She must be pregnant.

Shit.

I'll have to marry her.

"What's up?" Horstmann asked.

"Oh, nothing," I said as casually as I could.

He looked at me, completely undeceived, and went back to Susanne's latest letter. I knew he wouldn't pry.

It's academic, anyway. They won't want her going down the aisle pregnant, so the wedding can't be until – let's see, we went to bed in June, so nine months would be March at the earliest. I almost laughed. *Fat chance.*

But it would be really something to be a father, to create life instead of taking it. If it's a boy I can teach him all the things I know... like killing, Franz? That's what you do best, isn't it? But no doubt the poor little kid will grow up either to fight and die, or to mourn her son or husband.

And then I had a really nasty thought. *What's to say it's mine? She fairly leapt into bed with me. Yes, she was a virgin, but there could easily have been someone else afterwards...*

"Crikey, you're looking thoughtful," said Beilke.

"Girlfriend trouble," I said.

He grinned. "Just find another – or stick to fucking tarts!"

"Next time it rains that's exactly what I have in mind!"

The sky was clouding over again. We managed one more patrol before the low cloud and rain set in, and the lorry carrying Ewald's coffin arrived just after we'd all landed.

It was quite unreasonably heavy for a slightly built fellow. *They've put too much earth in this, or too much Albatros.*

So much for Claudette's next time it rains.

Another night in the hangar, another funeral.

The autumn was advancing, and a sharp wind blew brown and yellow leaves across the cemetery and snatched the padre's words away.

I fell in beside Eichner on the way back.

"It was a good way to go," I said.

"Yes. Yes, it was. Better than burning."

The rain set in again in the afternoon, and we did indeed go to Claudette's and had a fair wake afterwards. Horstmann and I staggered back to our hut, somehow keeping our balance on the slippery duckboards.

"Wha's tha'?" he asked, pointing at something shiny in a puddle.

I peered at it and then looked up at the sky, almost falling over as I did so.

"'s the moon," I managed to say.

"You do tal' crap."

"No, really, is."

"Shi'!"

Who cares? Won't be the first time I've flown half-pissed and it won't be the last.

The Chief was stone-cold sober.

Maybe I should follow his example – but the Front without large quantities of booze is unthinkable. I'll set an example when I'm a squadron commander, I thought with a chuckle to myself.

The sick fear was just as bad as the last time, but once again it left me as the first fight began. *I hope that's not going to carry on, because feeling like that every time won't be funny.*

Over the next couple of weeks things went slowly back to normal. Yes, I was apprehensive before every patrol – you'd be insane not to be – but that awful deep dread ebbed away.

There was just one problem. I hadn't had the burning dream for a while, but the young Englishman kept coming back. Each time he looked at me accusingly from the seat of his wrecked aircraft and tried to gurgle something through the blood, and each time I woke sweating and shaking.

For fuck's sake, why can't you stay bloody dead? I asked into the darkness.

'Why should I?'

I shivered and wished it would get light.

My Blue Max arrived, and so did Ewald's replacement. Otto's prayers had been answered, and Teuffel was an experienced Albatros pilot with two victories.

To my astonishment, he looked at me with respect when we were introduced and said, "Yes, I've heard of you."

Bloody hell. I laughed. "I doubt any of it was true!"

I got an even bigger shock a few days later. The boss and I were sitting in his office, sorting out a leave roster, when Fellmann came in.

"Have a seat," said the Chief. "You can help us with this."

Fellmann grinned. "Of course, sir – but that wasn't why I came in."

"Go on, then," the boss said with a slight smile.

"We're going to be in a film."

The two of us burst out laughing.

The Chief looked at me. "Is it the first of April already?"

"Must be."

"No, really – we are," Fellmann said. "I've just had a letter from Berlin, from HQ. They're making a film about the aces, to be shown in cinemas all over Germany. They're starting with Richthofen's mob, of course, but then they're coming here, and they want footage of you, sir, and Becker, and squadron life. Well, some of it, anyway!"

I laughed even harder at the thought of the German public seeing one of our parties.

"That means we'll get even more of those stupid letters," the Chief said with resignation.

The amount of mail the two of us got from perfect strangers was ridiculous. I always answered letters from children and sent them a signed photograph, and so did he, but those from adults were either filled with patriotic drivel and went straight into the stove, or were from dizzy women who wanted anything from marriage to a quickie in the afternoon. The Chief being married didn't deter them at all.

We held a weekly beauty contest, lining their photos up on the dining table. The winner was pinned up on the wall until the next one took her place, whereupon she was claimed by whoever was feeling especially lonely.

Horstmann never took a picture. Why would he, when none of them could compare with the lovely Susanne?

I realised that Fellmann was talking, and that I'd missed most of it.

"Sorry – what was that last part?"

He gave a theatrical sigh. "They'll be here in two weeks' time. So please would you both still be here, and Beilke, Lentzke and Horstmann."

"I'm sure we can manage that," the Chief said.

"Just as well we hadn't told Beilke he'd be having leave," I added.

"Indeed… What a load of nonsense," said the boss. "But what can we do?"

I suppose someone thinks it'll improve morale, but I can't see it myself. Oh, well… Orders is orders.

Alfred wrote, saying he was in hospital in Vienna.

'Frankly I'd prefer Berlin, but I'll be able to see the sights once they let me out. I don't quite know how I got out of that last one alive – quite a lot of our fellows didn't. There's bugger all to choose between our allies and the Italians – left to themselves they'd both get nowhere.

I saw in the paper about Karl before I got your letter – please give him my best wishes. I'm not too bad – shell splinter in my thigh – but it'll be a month or two before I get back.'

Good old Alfred. How many times is that? It really is time he had a safe job – but the idea of Alfred in some general's office was just absurd.

The day before the film-makers were due to arrive I knocked a Bristol two-seater out of the sky. It was only my second victory since my Pour le Mérite had arrived, and I never liked those breaks in scoring. They always made me wonder if I was losing my touch.

And when I thought about that, I didn't want to look in the mirror. *Is it better to be as I am or like Taschner? I'll bet he never lost sleep over shooting Tommies.*

VIII

The film was the most embarrassing experience of my life.

The director was a tall, thin fellow a few years older than my father. He was almost obsequious to the Chief, and nearly as bad to me.

I'll never live this down, not in a million years.

"Sir, if you would lead your pilots out as if you were going on patrol, please," he asked the boss.

"Yes, of course."

We trooped after him towards the flight line.

"Er – perhaps you could walk in twos and threes, talking and laughing?"

"Why?" Beilke said to me.

The director heard him. "So the audience can see how joyfully you set out to destroy the enemy," came the perfectly serious reply.

Horstmann's eyes met mine and they said, 'We're talking about killing,' as clearly as if he'd spoken.

"We do our job to the best of our ability," the Chief replied. "And it's a rather dirty one. I wouldn't say there's much joy in it."

"We don't want people at home to see that. They want to see heroes, going cheerfully into battle."

Fucking hell.

"All right," said the Chief. "If it'll help to keep morale up, then we'd better do it."

We had to do it five times before the fellow said he was happy.

"Look," the boss said, "it's rare to have such a fine day at this time of year, so we're going to have to get going now. Why don't you film us suiting up and taking off – and then in a couple of hours you can get us coming back."

"Yes, sir, that's exactly what we want."

"But we can't keep repeating things," the Chief said firmly.

"No, sir, I can see that."

"So if you could set up over there, and – without wishing to be rude – please be unobtrusive."

"Yes, sir, of course."

Nicely done.

We headed to the mess for briefing, and at the end of it Lentzke said, "Do we have our usual pre-flight schnapps or miss it out?"

Beilke pulled a face. "Come on – who fights stone-cold sober?"

"Buggered if I am," Horstmann said.

"We're not going to kiss them," said Otto. "It's not as if we'll be unsteady on our feet or anything."

"If they want us to do it without booze they can bloody well come with us," said Eichner.

There was a chorus of agreement.

The Chief rapped on the table.

"Gentlemen, we are going to do everything as we usually do it. The operation's what matters, not their film."

Thank fuck for that. I poured the usual healthy measure of rum into my coffee.

"Don't know how you can do that," said Teuffel. "I've never liked hot alcohol."

"Weren't in the trenches, were you?" Lentzke said with a grin. "Hot anything was a bonus."

"That's for sure," agreed Horstmann.

The film crew did try to come closer, but Fellmann shooed them back to their place. None of us heard what he said, but there was a definite note of steel in his voice.

By the time I'd suited up, I'd completely forgotten about them – but as Schiffer helped me to fasten my harness, I suddenly remembered the Air Service superstition about not having your photograph taken just before a flight.

This is different. It's a film and there's nothing to say they're pointing the camera at you. And superstition's crap, anyway.

Half an hour later I wondered whether it was crap or not. Eichner had spotted a two-seater, which seemed to be directing artillery fire. It looked like a classic set-up, and we approached cautiously – and we were right, but we hadn't reckoned on *two* flights of SE5s. Thank God we were a double Kette, but even so we were outnumbered.

The commander of one of them went straight for me, and I was sure it was me he wanted. And the bastard could fly. I'd never been so thankful for the Triplane's agility, as time and again I turned the tables on him.

But Schulte was a couple of hundred metres below, hard-pressed by another Tommy, and not turning tight enough. No one else was in a position to help him.

I'll have to do it – but breaking off from this fellow won't be easy—

I threw my aircraft onto her other wingtips and rolled into the dive, hoping to get away before he could follow me. For a vital couple of seconds it worked. I turned in behind Schulte's opponent and gave him a good burst.

He broke off, but Schulte was already spinning.

Poor little sod.

Now I had two of them to deal with and they worked me over properly. Whatever I did one of the bastards was turning in behind me, spraying lead.

Any moment they'll hit something vital – like me.

Each time one passed in front of me I shot at him, more for effect than with any hope of result. And then my right gun jammed, and I knew if I got the hammer out they'd see.

And then the left one jammed as well.

Fuck.

Keep bluffing, Franz. Just keep them off your tail.

For a few insane moments I actually enjoyed it – the Triplane was so wonderfully responsive that it was the nearest thing to being a bird that I could imagine. It was the most glorious flying I'd ever done.

It stopped being fun when a third Tommy joined in. *That's that,* I thought with overwhelming finality. *It's all over.*

I'll never see Karl again, never hold him tight against me. Maybe he'll be sad...

Teuffel was on the tail of the newcomer, forcing him to break off, and half a minute later they all broke for home.

I was soaked in sweat, my heart pounding, unable to believe I was still alive. *Jesus. That was bad.*

I got the hammer out and gave each gun in turn the biggest whack I could manage. Neither would clear. I would have to go back.

I moved up alongside Beilke, who was leading the other Kette, pointed to my guns and gave a thumbs-down, then pointed east. He nodded and then pointed to Teuffel, and then to me and eastwards. *Thanks.*

Teuffel sat locked into position on my right wingtip. *Good of Beilke to lend me someone experienced – let's hope we don't meet trouble.*

I shook properly as we flew home. *It's a while since I wrote myself off like that. I'd forgotten what it feels like, to give up on life and cross over completely in your mind.*

As we taxied in I noticed a group of strangers with a movie camera. *What – oh, fucking hell, it's the bloody film-makers! Get a grip, Franz, or the great German public will see a pale, trembling wreck.*

Do them good to see the price of the gongs.

I slid down and leaned nonchalantly against the fuselage. The cameraman was getting closer, and Fellmann wasn't there to keep him away.

I was dying for a fag, but knew I wouldn't be able to light it.

"Schiffer, would you light a cigarette for me?"

"Of course, sir."

I just about managed to get the thing into my mouth without dropping it, and his hand around the flame hid how much the fag was wobbling.

"Thanks – get Schmidt here pronto."

Schmidt had taken over from Ziegler as chief armourer.

"That was a bit hot," Teuffel said as casually as he could. There was a distinct tremor in his voice.

"Yes. Thanks." That was all I could say.

"Not at all."

The film crew were upon us.

Fortunately Schmidt arrived a second later.

"Double jam," I said.

He looked at me, horrified. "Sir – I am so sorry. I'll get it sorted out at once."

"Did you have a problem, sir?" asked the director.

Did I have – what sort of question is that? Teuffel's eyes met mine and we both started laughing.

"Both my guns jammed in the middle of a fight," I replied.

I was almost doubled up with mirth and I could hardly get the words out. Reaction, of course.

"Gentlemen," said Fellmann very firmly. "Oberleutnant von Kralewski-Zentzytzki told you to remain over there."

"Yes, but we're here on the orders of the War Office in Berlin."

"I dare say – but the Oberleutnant is Kaiser here," Fellmann continued, "and he won't be best pleased to see you by the flight line."

The man actually looked as if he were about to argue. Fellmann gave him a commanding stare, and he turned to his crew and said, "We'd better do as we're told."

"Fucking hell," said Teuffel as they retreated. "Brass neck he's got."

"Sorry, chaps," Fellmann said. "I was on the phone when you came back. It never occurred to me that those stupid bastards would disobey the Chief."

"Oh, don't worry," I said. I was starting to feel a fraction steadier.

"What happened?"

I told him.

"You could have done without that," he said quietly. "I'll get a full report from Schmidt as soon as he's finished."

"Poor old Schulte got shot down," I said. "I don't suppose you've heard anything?"

"That was the phone call. He's all right – well, he's got a hole through his right leg, but he managed to land the thing – with your Gotha friends, oddly enough. It'll just need someone to go over and fly it back."

Just then the others arrived back, all together. The second the Chief finished debriefing, the film fellow went up to him.

"Sir, if possible we'd like some footage of you and Leutnant Becker climbing into your aircraft and looking westwards."

"All right – but we're only doing it once each."

Fifteen minutes later I was finally able to go and get out of my damp shirt, by which time I was bloody frozen and trying not to shiver.

When I peeled it off I realised it was Karl's shirt, the one I'd kept after he'd been shot down – and all I wanted was to feel safe in his embrace. My longing for him was so powerful that everything else disappeared.

Remember me, Karl, when the bastards get me at last...

I draped the shirt over the chair we used to put against the door, and put on a dry one of my own.

Horstmann opened the door and I actually jumped.

He grinned. "Scare you, did I?"

"You always fucking scare me – God knows what you do to the Tommies!"

I walked to the mess with a strong feeling of unreality. *I'm alive, and I didn't expect to be – but how do I know I'm alive? Horstmann and I could both be dead, walking across a phantom airfield to a mess full of ghosts.*

But then the film-makers would have to be dead as well, and the bastards are obviously very much alive.

They wanted to film us in the mess.

"You'll have to put your schnapps in your coffee again," Bretti said to Lentzke, who grimaced.

"I'm not in the mood for diluted."

"Neither am I," I said.

"I said they can film for half an hour," said the Chief. "So we'll be playing cards, or reading, or writing letters, and so on. We can do as we damn well please once they've gone."

"Are they staying to dinner?" Beilke asked.

"No. Berlin did want us to put them up but I said we don't have room, so they're staying with the General."

"Thank fuck for that," said Horstmann.

"Oh, I don't know," Bretti said. "It's rather fun being in a film and knowing that lots of people back home are going to see it."

"Going to be a movie star, are you?" teased Reinhard.

"No, he's far too ugly!" said Otto. "Anyway, what's happening about poor old Schulte and his aircraft?"

The Chief looked at me. "Becker, Schmidt says your guns need replacing, so you might as well go and fetch his Albatros. If Fellmann takes me to the hospital we can drop you off on the way. Beilke, Horstmann, you can lead the last patrol. The film crew will be leaving at the same time as the three of us, so you won't have to worry about them."

As if on cue there was a knock at the door, and the director looked in.

"Are you ready now, sir?"

"Yes," replied the Chief. "I suppose you want everyone to behave as if you weren't here?"

"That's it exactly."

Bleif served coffee, and I almost choked. It was very well laced with rum. Otto tasted his and giggled.

"Christ, if they only knew how much we all put away," he muttered as we sat down on the small sofa with the *Berlin Illustrated*.

I drank mine and smoked another fag, wishing the feeling of unreality would go. *Maybe the film crew are all dead as well. Maybe their lorry took a direct hit.*

If this is the afterlife then I don't like it much.

"Gentlemen, your time is up," the Chief said politely but firmly. "And that's it for today."

"We'd like to follow you to the hospital, sir," said the director.

"Well, you can if you like, but I doubt they'll let you in."

"Oh, that doesn't matter, sir. The main thing is to show you going to visit your wounded comrade."

Lentzke snorted and left the room.

"Sentimental crap," Horstmann said.

The director flushed. "We know what our audiences want to see, sir."

"Yes, well maybe they should be shown the truth, such as some unedited film of Verdun and the Somme. The war'd be over if everyone had seen that."

The Chief gave Horstmann a very sharp look and then turned to the film crew. "We'll be leaving in ten minutes, so I suggest you start packing up."

Once they were out of earshot the Chief said, "You are, of course, entitled to your opinions – but keep them to yourselves while our guests are present."

There was a chorus of "Yes, sir."

That told us.

"How much longer do we have to put up with them?" asked Horstmann.

"Only tomorrow morning," the Chief replied, and headed for his office.

As I followed him out of the mess I heard Teuffel say, "I think it's bloody rude, them poking a camera at us all the time."

There was a murmur of agreement, which I felt like joining in.

Fellmann almost managed to lose them on the way to the Gotha base. There was a right old traffic jam at a crossroads, with the military police directing, and we got waved through and they didn't.

"I suppose we'd better wait for them," the Chief said a few minutes later.

There are times when I wish your devotion to duty were a little weaker.

Fellmann sighed audibly. "I really can't stop, sir – we'd be right in the way."

Unfortunately there was a side road a couple of kilometres further on.

"Pull in there," said the boss, and of course Fellmann did.

I was very glad to get out at the Gotha base. Flying Schulte's Albatros home was nice and simple, even if the cockpit did smell of blood.

There was quite a party atmosphere that evening. Schulte wasn't badly injured, and we were all in the mood for a proper piss-up, anyway. The sky had clouded over and a brisk south-westerly had sprung up, which encouraged us considerably.

If I get really pissed then I'll have a bad hangover, and that'll prove I'm alive. Surely a ghost can't have a headache.

By the time Horstmann and I struggled to our room it was raining fairly steadily, and when I woke in the small hours it was rattling on the roof.

So they have rain in Hell, I thought – and then remembered the poor bastards trying to fight and stay alive in the swamp of the Front. *Oh, yes – there's definitely rain in Hell.*

I couldn't get back to sleep. The young Englishman came back, so vividly that I almost thought he was in the room.

When I die they'll all be waiting for me.

That was such a horrifying thought that I abandoned any idea of sleep and sat up smoking instead.

"You awake?" asked a quiet voice.

"You'd better hope I am, or the fucking hut will burn down." *Why the fuck did I mention burning?*

"Mind if I put the light on?"

"Please do." *That might chase the bastards away.*

"I never thought I'd like rain again, after the fucking Somme."

We sat in silence, smoking and waiting for the dawn. In the end we went to breakfast ridiculously early. Beilke and Lentzke were already there.

"My, my," said Fellmann, "two more insomniacs."

"Speak for yourself," Horstmann retorted.

"Oh, I was…"

The Chief walked in, looking far more awake than the rest of us. He went to the window and made a show of looking out.

"Fellmann, I don't think this weather's much use for filming," he said, deadpan. "And we're not likely to fly before lunchtime, so there won't be anything to film, anyway."

"No, sir. Shall I telephone now and put them off?"

"Good idea. We don't want them wasting petrol, after all."

And with that he helped himself to rolls and sat down.

The only man who was disappointed was Beilke.

"I was really hoping to have a good look at their camera and talk to the cameraman," he complained. "I've got a list of questions I wanted to ask him."

"Well, hard luck!" said Bretti.

"Ask Fellmann to get him on the phone for you," I said, and Beilke brightened up instantly.

By three it was obvious that the day was a washout.

Lentzke poured himself another schnapps. "Hair of the dog, anyone?"

"Yes, please," I said, and we settled in for a pleasantly mellow afternoon.

I still had the feeling of unreality, and I was getting very fed up with it.

"Hey, Otto," I said. "How do we know we're alive?"

"What?"

I repeated my question.

"Franz, what the fuck are you on about? Bloody philosophy?"

"What's that about philosophy?" asked Reinhard.

"Know something about it, do you?" Eichner said.

"Well, I was going to study it at university—"

"What's this?" Horstmann asked.

"Franz asked how we know we're alive."

Horstmann looked at me.

"Ah," was all he said. After a short pause he added, "Lentzke, got any ideas?"

"Not bloody likely! It was cadet school, Lichterfelde and barracks in Stettin for me – I can quote you plenty of Clausewitz, though."

"You can stick your Clausewitz up your arse," said Eichner. "I've had enough of continuing diplomacy by other means."

So have I, but there's no end in sight.

The weather broke properly. October was drawing to a close, and I began to have cautious hopes of seeing another Christmas.

Early in November, we were in the middle of lunch when the phone rang. No one paid any attention until Möller came into the mess, went up to the Chief and said something to him very quietly.

"Would you excuse me, gentlemen?" he said, getting up.

We all exchanged glances.

"Must be something important," Bretti said.

The boss discouraged interruptions at mealtimes, as he reckoned we needed to relax and fuel ourselves up.

"Do we carry on eating or wait?" asked Lentzke.

"Carry on," I said. "Let's hope his doesn't get too cold."

The Chief came back after about five minutes, looking stunned. He rapped on the table.

"Gentlemen, I'm very sorry to disturb you, but—" he paused as if unsure what words to use "– there have been two fatal accidents involving wing failure of the Fokker Triplane, one involving Leutnant Gontermann, so that's a good man gone. As a result they've all been grounded pending a full investigation."

We looked at each other in appalled silence. I thought of all the times I'd thrown mine around the sky, and a cold shiver ran down my back. Horstmann and Beilke exchanged glances, obviously thinking something similar.

This is the last thing we fucking well need. Why can't the sodding manufacturers get it right?

"Jesus," said Fellmann quietly. "Gontermann."

Another Pour le Mérite gone.

"What are we going to fly?" asked Lentzke.

"We're getting the latest Albatros, the D.Va. Apparently it's stronger than the D.V, but you still have to be a bit careful with it."

"I don't want to 'have to be careful' when I've got some Camel fellow up my arse," Lentzke said with an edge to his voice.

"So we have a choice between the blasted aircraft breaking up and being shot because we can't manoeuvre." Horstmann sounded as pissed off as I felt.

The Chief sighed.

"When are we getting those parachutes they keep talking about?" I asked.

"Yes," said Otto. "If they can't build strong enough aircraft then at least they should give us a means of escape."

"Believe me, we're putting on as much pressure as we can," the Chief replied.

"I'm sorry, sir, but you're wanted on the phone again," Möller said. "It's Rittmeister von Richthofen."

"He'll be pissed off as well," Eichner said as the boss left the mess.

"Pissed off isn't in it," said Lentzke. "It's almost enough to make me transfer back to the infantry."

"Bleif, would you reheat Herr Oberleutnant's food, please?" I asked.

"Yes, of course, sir."

This time the boss was on the phone for a lot longer. Bleif served him his reheated lunch, with added gravy, and he looked at it and grimaced.

"What did Richthofen say?" asked Fellmann.

"He's been on to a friend in Berlin, and they're moving heaven and earth to get the problem sorted out."

"I should bloody well think so," said Horstmann. "Effectively we've got no decent fighters at all now."

"Exactly," Lentzke agreed.

"We'll just have to hope it keeps raining," said Beilke.

Normally no one would have said that in front of the Chief, but he let it pass without even a look. We knew he'd keep his feelings to himself, but they had to be similar to ours.

"Fellmann," he said, and the two of them headed to his office and, unusually, closed the door.

There was silence for quite a few minutes.

"Fokker, of all companies," Otto said. "I mean, it's a bloody fantastic aircraft to fly, but—"

"Just not fucking strong enough," said Lentzke. He lit another cigarette and gazed out of the window thoughtfully.

"Pfalzes would be better," said Beilke. "At least the wings stay on."

"Does any of it matter?" asked Horstmann.

"You mean the man with the scythe's going to get us anyway?" said Eichner with a half-smile.

"Exactly."

Bretti pulled a face. "I'd just like a chance of getting to 'after the war'."

"I was so enjoying being out of the fucking trenches," Lentzke said. "But if they don't sort this out, then I really will go back."

Horstmann stared at him. "You mean you *want* to be shelled again?"

"Well…"

"Lice," I said. "And filth. And never getting enough sleep."

"And being wet for days on end," added Horstmann. "Though it was always the shelling that got me. It's just so fucking random—" He broke off, his right eyelid twitching.

"At least if the wings come off it's quick," I said. "Better than lying out in No Man's Land for days."

"All the same," said Lentzke. "It's the thought of not being able to trust the aircraft. It just - well—"

"Look," said Bretti. "Every weapon goes wrong sometimes, doesn't it? About the only thing that's foolproof is a club - and that's only any use if you actually get to the enemy."

I looked at him in surprise, then remembered his brother had been an infantry officer.

"My brother had to do Verdun *and* the Somme," said Reinhard, "and he said to me not to join the infantry, whatever else I did. He said it was just slaughter."

"You've forgotten what it's like," said Teuffel. "Why don't you get a pass – go and visit your old regiment, see your friends?"

Lentzke laughed. "Be a bit difficult. Most of them are dead."

"Exactly," said Horstmann. "You're off your fucking head even thinking of going back."

"Next time we fly have a good look at the Front," I said. "And remember what it's like in those shell-holes—"

It was my turn to break off, because I could see Kurt's blood running down into the water.

"The way I see it," said Beilke, "it's not *if*, it's *when and how*. There aren't many good ways to go, but ours are quicker than most, and that's good enough for me."

Nicely put, I thought, amid the general murmur of agreement.

Platzer turned up a couple of days later accompanied by a spotty youth, both in shiny new D.Vas. Lentzke gave them a very dubious look.

"So what's the difference between this and the much-loved D.V?" he asked, with evident sarcasm.

"The gap between the wings is slightly smaller, sir, and as you can see, the aileron cables are routed differently," said the boy, with nauseating self-confidence.

Too young for the Front. Wonder how you got accepted for pilot training?

"That's not what I hoped to hear," Lentzke replied.

Platzer sighed. "Believe me, we're working on it. We do appreciate the situation."

"Yes, we know you do," the Chief said in a conciliatory tone.

"Trouble is, that doesn't help us," said Horstmann.

"What about parachutes?" asked Otto.

Platzer looked uncomfortable. "Sorry – that's not sorted out either."

We all exchanged looks.

"Oh, well, Death's sharpening his scythe again," Bretti said later.

"I'm surprised he's got the energy," said Eichner.

The Tommies had finally called a halt to their offensive. God knows how many men were rotting in the Flanders mud.

That's three big battles over the same bit of festering swamp. It must stink even worse now than when I was there – and that's hard to imagine.

"He must have an army of helpers," Reinhard said.

Otto grinned. "Yes – us!"

"You? You can't hit anything!" Bretti retorted.

I suddenly realised that Otto had probably never killed anyone – he'd been knocked over right at the start at Langemarck, and as a two-seater pilot he hadn't had a gun.

"That Ace of Spades must be ironic!" said Teuffel with a grin.

Otto stuck his tongue out.

Funny – we joined up on the same day, and my hands are dripping with blood and Karl's even more so, and here's Otto still snowy white and with a clear conscience...

"Becker."

"Sorry, Fellmann, I was miles away."

"Didn't look like anywhere nice, either! The boss wants us both."

"Oh, right."

The Chief looked very serious.

"We've been promised four Pfalz D.IIIs," he said, "but they won't be here until next week at the earliest."

"That's something," said Fellmann. "Those and the new Albatri will stand in for the six Triplanes we can't fly."

The Chief sighed. "But of course we're four aircraft down until the Pfalzes get here."

"And somehow we have to make it look as if we're still at full strength," I said.

"Exactly."

"It's going to be obvious that we're not in our usual aircraft," I said. "And the Tommies are bound to notice that there aren't any Triplanes up."

Fellmann gave a slightly rueful laugh. "I'm sure they know all about it by now."

Between us we came up with a flying programme that we thought would be effective. It used the available aircraft far more intensively than usual.

"Will they hold up to it?" asked the boss.

"Hopefully," Fellmann replied. "I'll see if I can get a couple more spare engines."

It would suit me if it rains till Christmas, I thought as we climbed into the afternoon sky.

The Albatros cockpit felt strange after the Triplane, and the contrast between the two was stark. What the Triplane lacked in speed, it more than made up in agility. The Albatros, which had once felt so sleek and fast, was a lumbering beast in comparison. A Camel could run rings round it. And always in the back of my mind was the need to be cautious and limit the speed.

You can't use its one good feature. This is not fun at all.

Judging by the others' faces, they didn't think it was fun either. There was none of the usual banter as we walked to the mess. Everyone just looked relieved to have survived.

That night I had the burning dream again, and woke shaking and sweating. *I think I prefer the young Englishman,* I thought, staring at the ceiling. *If only Karl were here!*

But in spite of my desperate longing for him I was so glad he was safe. I would never see him again, but he would survive the war.

"The first two Pfalzes are available for collection from the aircraft park," Fellmann said over second breakfast.

Good – I might escape the next patrol to go and fetch one.

The dawn flight had been so ghastly that I was forcing my food down and hiding my trembling hands under the table. Lentzke poured a generous measure of schnapps into his coffee, and Horstmann's eyelid was twitching again.

Only Reinhard and Böhle – Ewald's replacement – looked fresh, and that was because they didn't know how close they'd come to being killed. I'd seen Beilke getting a Camel off Böhle's tail before he even knew it was there.

"Oh, good," said the Chief. "Reinhard and Böhle can go and fetch them. Fellmann, could you organise the transport, please?"

"Of course, sir."

Shit. But of course the boss is going to send the children on a safe errand like that.

Teuffel looked at me and shrugged.

"Well, at least we're not flying quite as much with the aircraft shortage," he said after the boss had left the mess.

"And it's clouding over," said Otto.

Lentzke was staring vacantly into space.

"How about Claudette's as soon as it rains?" I asked, trying to lighten the mood.

"I'm in," said Horstmann.

"Me too," Bretti said.

There was a chorus of assent, from everyone except Lentzke.

"Not coming, Lentzke?" Beilke asked him.

He started. "What?"

"Claudette's."

"Oh – yes." He gave a short laugh. "Assuming the obvious."

"Goes without saying," said Bretti.

It didn't rain, and the last flight of the day was even worse than the dawn one. Horstmann and I changed in silence and headed for the mess.

I'm going to get pissed. Really pissed. Then maybe I won't dream.

As we passed the Ops Office door, we heard the Chief asking, "So where are they, then?"

We exchanged glances. *Who?* I almost asked, and then remembered that the two children had gone to fetch the Pfalzes.

"Surely they can't have got lost?" Horstmann muttered to me. "The sugar factory chimney stands out a mile."

But lost they were, and the light was fading fast as the cloud thickened.

"Let's hope they've had the sense to land somewhere," Teuffel said.

"Well, I reckon it's drinking time," said Otto. "I mean, *real* drinking time."

About an hour later it was pitch dark outside, and I was starting to feel a lot better. There was still no sign of Reinhard and Böhle. I suppose I should have been concerned but I wasn't.

It was as if there were two squadrons: the core of men that I knew and who were lasting quite well, and those who came and went. I'd given up trying to get to know the latter group.

The phone rang.

"It's for you, sir," Möller said to the Chief.

We carried on playing the gramophone and singing. The piano still stood in the corner of the room, but no one could really play it. Not like Karl.

"Gentlemen, a bit of quiet, please!" Fellmann's voice cut through the noise and we all fell silent.

"Yes, I see," said the boss heavily into the phone. "And what about you?... Yes, all right, all right. We'll send someone to fetch you... Now where are you?... All right, Böhle, all right... No, no – don't worry about it… Look, put the artillery fellow on the line, would you?"

We looked at each other. *That does not sound good.*

"Thank you, yes, I've got that… Goodbye… Fellmann, would you organise the recovery crew?"

"Right away, sir."

The Chief came into the mess. "Not good news, I'm afraid. Reinhard and Böhle got lost – the wind picked up more than they were expecting. Reinhard crashed trying to land and he's dead. Böhle's aircraft's slightly damaged."

Teuffel swore under his breath. *Yes – that's one new aircraft we're not going to get, and another that already needs repairing.*

"Poor little sod," said Eichner – which was, of course, the appropriate response.

Sometimes I wonder just what I'm turning into.

"He was a nice kid," said Beilke.

Lentzke sighed. "This is no business for nice kids."

"No, quite," I agreed. "I knew a sniper once who was fifteen, but I wouldn't say he was a nice kid."

"Fifteen? Bloody hell!" said Bretti. "Makes me look old."

"You can't be a decent bloke and a sniper," said Teuffel. "The two are mutually exclusive."

"I don't see why," said Horstmann. "Believe me, if you're on the wrong end of a machine gun it's useful to have a chap who can pick off the crew."

"And get rid of their snipers," I added.

"Well, maybe," Teuffel conceded, "but it still seems fucking cold-blooded to me."

"I reckon we should stop talking and get on with drinking," said Lentzke. "There'll be another funeral tomorrow."

It was late before Böhle came into the mess, looking shaken. He obviously didn't want to talk about it to anyone except the Chief, and he ate his dinner in silence and then got stuck into the booze.

We buried Reinhard in the pouring rain. There was an audible splash as the coffin met the water in the bottom of the grave, and a stream of bubbles as it sank.

"Burial at sea," Otto muttered to me as we left, and I had to bite my lip hard to stop myself laughing.

When we got back we had a good look at the surviving Pfalz, and we didn't like what we saw.

"It's got the same skinny lower wing as the Albatros," Lentzke said, his voice full of mistrust.

"But it is much stronger," Fellmann said reassuringly.

We all failed to be reassured.

"Promise me it won't break up," said Teuffel.

Fellmann shrugged. "You know anything will break up if you overload it."

"But where's the point of overload?" asked Beilke.

"I suppose we'll just have to find out," Horstmann said.

"Or rather not," added Bretti.

Mercifully the rain continued, and even when it stopped the ground was so wet that the gravel strip was only useable for the odd day here and there.

The Chief began sending men on leave, starting with Beilke. We got him so pissed that he passed out on the floor of the mess, and we had to almost carry him to the car.

Fellmann was laughing when he got back.

"God knows where he's going to end up," he said. "I had to help him onto the train and he was out of it the second he sat down."

"Wherever it is, it'll be better than here," Lentzke said.

He was about halfway through a bottle of schnapps, and still remarkably coherent.

"Oh, it'll be your turn before long," Otto said.

Lentzke just looked at him and emptied his glass down his throat.

Late in the evening he came and sat next to me.

"Becker, do something for me?" he asked.

"If I can."

"There's a girl… in Stettin."

"There's always a girl," I said flippantly.

"Not like this."

He opened his wallet, and handed me a picture of a round-cheeked woman with a small boy on her knee. The resemblance between him and Lentzke was striking.

"He looks just like you."

He laughed. "Poor little sod! No, Becker, thing is, I haven't done right by them. You see, she's not the right… I couldn't marry her. I send her money, but I haven't given her my name or the boy legitimacy."

He paused and took another long drink. *How in God's name can you speak so clearly when you've put so much away?* I wondered as I refilled our glasses.

"She's a shop assistant," he continued, "works in a jeweller's. I went in to buy my mother a present and there she was. And it was like being struck by lightning. But I'd just been commissioned, and it would have been professional and social death to have a wife – well, you understand. Not of the right standing."

"Yes."

"And now I don't give a shit about any of that. I sent a letter to our lawyer – I want her to have my portion if I'm killed. No – what I really want is to marry her, but there's no chance of that happening."

I thought for a moment. "Why don't you tell the Chief about her and ask for leave? He went home to get married – he won't begrudge you the same."

"Do you think so?"

"I'm certain of it."

"But you're due for leave before me."

"Oh, I'm holding out for Christmas." *Fat bloody chance.*

"When you do get leave," he continued, "will you be going near Berlin?"

"If Karl's home, yes."

"Would you take another letter to the lawyer? The thing is, I don't trust him. He won't want to give her the money, but if you give him the letter he can't pretend he didn't get it."

"Yes, if I can I will."

"Thanks, Becker. You see, the thing is, I love her and I want us to be a proper family. But I had to go to war to find that out."

Oh, fuck. Now he's going to get sentimental. That's the last thing I bloody need.

"And little Fritze, of course. He's a smashing lad… But that was what really got to me. Last time I was on leave, a year ago, I went to see them, and he looked at me and said, 'Mama, is that man coming home with us?' And I thought, Christ, my own son doesn't even know who I am. I should have married her then, but I was such an idiot."

"Go and see the boss in the morning," I said firmly.

He sighed. "Will do. Fancy another?"

Before I could answer, Bretti put a record on and we all started singing. Luckily it wasn't anything soppy.

"Christ, you two looked bloody serious," Horstmann said as we undressed.

"Just as well we don't have the Court of Riotous Behaviour any more," I said, laughing, "or I'd be comatose instead of just pissed!"

Lentzke saw the Chief the next morning and came into the mess smiling.

"What are you so bloody cheerful about?" Teuffel demanded with pretend grumpiness.

"I'm going on leave tomorrow!" Lentzke said happily. "And I'm getting married!"

"Claudette's tonight, then!" said Bretti. "Make the most of your last scrap of freedom!"

The sky had cleared and there was a brisk north-westerly wind. It was right across our strip and the crosswind was far too strong.

"Good drying wind, my mother would say," Otto said, looking out of the window.

"Just need it to go round a bit," said Eichner.

"Should be on for tomorrow," Teuffel agreed.

Lentzke scowled at the sunshine. *So would I in your place. Maybe the boss will keep you on the ground first thing, make sure you get away all right.*

But we were two men light and we had enough aircraft for the rest of us, and HQ wanted a show of strength, so we were all down for dawn. No doubt they wanted to show the Tommies that we did still have fighter squadrons, even if the aircraft weren't fit for purpose.

If they were then maybe I wouldn't feel so fucking scared, I thought as I forced down a roll, and a mug of coffee well laced with schnapps. The flame of my lighter shook as I lit my fag, and I didn't want to look at it. *That's what's waiting for me* – I snapped it shut quickly.

Everyone was pale. Even the Chief looked drawn and thoughtful. It was a relief to get outside into the twilight where there was a chance of hiding my nerves.

I shook so badly that I dropped my flying helmet, and Uhlig, who was back with us, picked it up and helped me put it on.

"Go and get another one for us, sir," he said as he tightened my straps.

Bugger getting another – I just want to come back in one piece.

That's not how Karl would think, is it? Where's your fucking backbone? At the very least you can try to take one with you.

"I'll do my best," I said with a rather fixed grin.

He clapped me on the shoulder as he always did. *It's good to have you back.*

The strip was still a bit greasy, but in no time we were climbing into the rapidly lightening sky, my stomach churning. The sick fear stayed with me until the first fight began, when – thank God – it evaporated.

And I got a two-seater, by sneaking up behind and beneath with Lentzke and Bretti guarding my back.

No sooner was it spinning earthwards than we were attacked by a flight of Camels. Their leader went straight after Lentzke, who was in one of the new D.Vas.

He was turning as tight as he could but the Tommy was gaining on him, and I couldn't break off. Luckily the Chief had seen and was diving down towards them.

Lentzke tried to dive away from the Camel, pulling the turn tighter in desperation – and then rolled out of it very carefully, heedless of the shower of lead.

The Tommy broke off as the Chief gave him a burst, and Lentzke left the fight, heading east.

I could barely spare him a thought. Another flight of bloody Camels turned up and things got far too fucking hot.

The west wind was all that saved us. I'd forgotten about Lentzke completely, and when we joined formation over Houthulst Wood, I wondered for a moment why there were only nine of us – and then I was shaking too much with cold and reaction to care.

When we got back Fellmann came out to the flight line with a very serious face.

"What news?" asked the boss.

"Not good, I'm afraid. He made it back over No Man's Land and tried to land on the first bit of decent ground, but the wing failed as he turned finals. He's on his way to hospital, very bad they said."

"Where?"

"About fifteen kilometres away."

"Do they think he'll make it?"

"Very unlikely, they said."

"What bloody awful timing," said the Chief.

Worse than you realise.

When we reached the main hut I said, "Sir, do you have a moment?"

"Of course."

He raised his eyebrows as I shut the door behind us.

"Sir – this is very awkward. I don't like to break anyone's confidence, but this time I must." I took a deep breath. "How much did Lentzke tell you about his marriage?"

"Just that he was engaged and he'd like to get it done."

"There's a bit more to it than that. He's got a young son, with a girl who's not – well, she's a shop girl."

"Good God. So he wanted to – Jesus. This is going to leave the poor girl in an awful jam."

"Unless she can get here in time to marry him before he dies."

"Assuming he's conscious, of course. Where is she?"

"Stettin."

"Look, you go through his papers, get her name and address. I'll have a word with the doctor, check whether there's any point, and if there is I'll get Möller to send a cable."

"Thank you, sir."

"No – thank you for telling me. Let's hope we can get this sorted out. His family will be livid, but that's their problem."

Lentzke's room was empty – he shared with Schulte, who was still in hospital. I found his girlfriend's letters, and luckily she'd put her address on them. I didn't have her last name, but that wasn't a major problem.

The room was silent and depressing, dust motes swirling in the pale sunlight.

I don't want to have to be careful when I've got a Camel up my arse...

The Chief was in the Ops Office, on the phone.

"Yes, yes, I see… Thank you. I'll be there later today."

He turned to me.

"Ah, Becker. Would you come with me to the hospital? I think it would be better to ask Lentzke what he wants."

"Yes, sir, I agree. I've got the lady's address here."

"Good. I suggest we set off straight after breakfast."

The mood was very subdued. Structural failure had crystallised into a reality which had taken one of us. No one wanted to talk about it, but it stopped us talking about anything else.

Getting out of the mess would have been a relief, if we'd been going somewhere nice.

Horrible fucking places, I thought as we went up the stairs in the hospital. *But then, what's good about a place full of smashed-up blokes?*

And Lentzke was smashed up, all right. The doctor assured us we were at the right bed, otherwise we wouldn't have known. Most of his head was bandaged. Only one eye was visible, swollen almost shut in a face that was one huge bruise. Both arms were splinted and he was barely breathing.

I'd like to get those bastards at the Albatros factory here. It would be bad enough if this were the result of English bullets, but to have a good man like this because of German incompetence is just too much.

"Lentzke," said the Chief.

There was no response and he tried again, louder, but with no result.

"Shall I see if I can find the chaplain?" I asked.

"Yes, good idea."

The Lutheran chaplain was helping someone to write a letter

home, and I waited until they'd finished before approaching him.

His eyes went from my face to my Pour le Mérite and back again.

"Father," I began, and stopped because I wasn't sure what to call him.

He smiled slightly at my confusion. "Can I help you?"

"No, I'm a Catholic," I said. "That is, I'm supposed to be a Catholic." *Oh, for fuck's sake, Franz – try to make sense!* "It's my squadron mate who needs your help."

"I see. Or rather, I might if you were to tell me a bit more!"

"Do you have a few minutes? It would be better if we talked at his bedside – he might have come round."

"Yes, of course." As I led the way back down the corridor he said, "Haven't we met before?"

"No, Father – but you might have seen me on those postcards or something."

"Ah, yes. What's your name?"

"Becker, Franz."

"Doesn't ring a bell."

His expression changed as we reached the door of the dying room, and grew graver still at the sight of Lentzke.

"Ah, yes – Leutnant von Lentzke. I visited him earlier but he was unconscious."

"As he still is," said the Chief, getting up.

The chaplain looked quite astonished. *Yes – you wait years to meet a Pour le Mérite and then two come along at once.*

He did recognise the Chief's name.

"This is quite an honour," he said as they shook hands. "Now, how can I help?"

"Leutnant von Lentzke has a fiancée," said the Chief. "He was due to go on leave today to get married. Would you be prepared to marry them, if she can get here in time?"

"Provided he can understand the ceremony and make his vows," said the chaplain. He gestured towards the door and we followed him.

"You never know how much a man in that condition can hear," he said once we were outside. "As I understand it, he may not last until tomorrow. It would be a shame for the lady to have a wasted journey – and I would have to be certain that he knew what was going on."

"Yes, of course," said the Chief. "Thank you for your time. We'd better be getting back."

"So what do you think?" he asked me on the way back.

"He was very definite when he told me about her, said he didn't give a shit any more about her social position, just wanted them to be a family. The only question is whether he'll be in a fit state for the wedding."

"Indeed… It seems unlikely – but I think we have to give it a chance, for the boy's sake."

"Yes, sir, I agree."

"I'll get Fellmann to make the travel arrangements."

And so cables went to Stettin, to Fräulein Ingeborg Whoever, and to Berlin for permission for her to travel to us.

"She'll need an escort from the border," said Fellmann.

"Well, you can do that," said the Chief. "Unless you've any objection?"

"No, of course not, sir. I just hope the whole thing comes off."

"So do I."

By that time it was quite late. Horstmann and the others were flying, and we went outside when we heard their engines.

There were a few spots of rain in the wind, and the sky was heavy. *It can't rain too heavily or for too long.*

Everyone was back safely, and Horstmann was jubilant because he'd sent one of those Bristols down in flames.

"That tips the day in our favour," said Teuffel. "Two of theirs to one of ours."

"Four to one, really," Bretti said. "It was two two-seaters."

"Good excuse for a party, anyway," said Otto.

By the time we'd finished dinner it was pissing down, and we all got very merry. That Lentzke was dying just made us even keener to have a good time.

It was about eleven when Horstmann and I made it to the mess for breakfast. Fellmann had just sat down with his coffee and cigar when the phone rang.

"Oh, bugger it," he said, but the call was for the Chief.

He came into the mess a few minutes later.

"Change of plan, Fellmann," he said. "I thought it wise for the lady to have an escort for the whole journey – well, from Berlin, anyway. My cousin's at the War Ministry these days – not fit for active service any more – and that was confirmation that he'll bring her here."

"Oh, good," said Fellmann. "Have we heard any more about Lentzke?"

"Not since this morning, no." He turned to us. "The chaplain called me earlier, and said Lentzke was lucid during the night and asked him to get his fiancée there. So we're doing the right thing."

"Or rather, we will be if he lives long enough," Horstmann said. "It'll be a right bastard if he kicks the bucket too soon."

"Or doesn't know what's going on," added Bretti.

"Quite," said the boss. "Anyway, Max is going to let us know when they'll be here."

The weather was utterly filthy – or rather utterly glorious – for the next two days. Lentzke was still critical, and intermittently conscious.

The Chief and I went to see him again, and I wished we hadn't. He recognised us and asked us to be present at his wedding. Of course I said I'd be delighted, when in truth I never wanted to set foot in the bloody hospital again. And I certainly didn't want to have to look at the poor bastard, and be reminded of what could happen to me.

Finally the weather cleared, and we had the dubious prospect of being able to fly once the field had dried a bit. I wish I could say we were keen.

"We'll have a look at it after lunch," said the Chief.

Halfway through the meal the phone rang.

"Excuse me, sir – it's for you," said Möller. "It's Hauptmann Graf Sonnenberg."

Who?

"Oh, good," said the boss.

"Who the fuck's that?" asked Teuffel once he was out of the room.

"Some posh staff officer, I expect," Bretti said with a grin.

"We'll find out in a minute," said Horstmann.

The Chief came back almost at once.

"They're here," he said. "Becker, Fellmann – I'm sorry to interrupt your lunch, but we really should get going. Horstmann, you assess the state of the field and sort out a flying programme if possible."

"Yes, sir."

"I'll bring Beilke's camera," said Fellmann. "The more evidence we have of this wedding, the better."

It took us over an hour to get to the station, through the mud and the traffic. Three people were waiting for us – a tall Hauptmann, leaning heavily on two sticks, and the woman and the boy in Lentzke's photograph.

"Shit," muttered the Chief, "I wasn't expecting her to bring the boy."

"I blame those bloody photographs," I said. "The ones that show a nice, clean hospital and lots of cheerful fellows."

Fellmann stopped the car and we all got out.

"Good to see you, Max!" said the boss. "How are you?"

Sonnenberg shrugged. "Same as usual… This is Fräulein Goldstein."

We bowed over her hand in turn, feeling rather awkward because we'd assumed that she would be Lutheran, like Lentzke, and we'd obviously got it wrong. *What happens now?*

"And this is Fritze," said Fräulein Goldstein. Her eyes were red around the edges but she was composed and dignified.

He looked at us with huge eyes. "Mama said I'm going to see Papa."

The Chief bent down and shook his hand. "Well, your papa's not very well, so we'll have to see."

"Are you famous?" asked the boy.

"A bit," answered the boss, with splendid understatement.

"How is he, sir?" his mother asked. Her voice was more cultured than I'd expected, but still had a bit of a twang.

"Holding on," said the boss, "but I think we should go straight to the hospital… Er – the Lutheran chaplain's expecting us, if – er – if he's the right fellow?"

"That's perfect," she said. "We converted in Frederick the Great's time."

Generations ago. Maybe you should have changed your name as well.

No one quite knew what to say on the way to the hospital. We'd never been confronted with the fiancée of a dying comrade before.

Little Fritze broke the silence. "I've never been in a car till now! And the train was full of soldiers – and they all had guns!"

And on he burbled, asking endless questions and commenting on everything.

Sonnenberg met my eye and grinned. "He's been like that the whole time he's been awake. Reminds me of my older son."

"How is the family?" asked the Chief.

"Growing fast – Willi's five now."

"He can't be!"

"Frightening, isn't it?!"

"And Amalia?"

Sonnenberg sighed. "Not too good."

"I'm sorry – I shouldn't have asked you to leave her."

"Oh, that's all right – her mother's staying. Probably be good to get out of each other's hair for a few days."

When we reached the hospital, Sonnenberg got out of the car with some difficulty, both sticks in one hand. Little Fritze leapt out, almost knocking him over, but he managed to remain upright, and helped Fräulein Goldstein down with perfect courtesy and not a trace of snobbishness.

But it's not your family that she's marrying into…

"My dear," Fellmann said kindly, "you really need to be prepared for what – well—"

"I do realise he – what the situation is."

"He's got a lot of injuries," Fellmann said. "And the fellows around him are all in a bad way too. It would be better not to take the boy in until you've seen for yourself."

She hesitated.

"You could leave him out here with me," said Fellmann. "Just until you decide if you want him to see his father like that."

She looked appalled at the idea of leaving her son with a man like Fellmann.

You're wrong. From what I've heard, Fellmann likes a good shafting, and I'd be astonished if he's interested in small boys.

Fellmann's face held resignation, tinged with sadness.

Humanity really is hopeless. Why do we always find an excuse to hate each other?

"Leutnant Fellmann's right," said Sonnenberg quietly. "I spent rather a long time in one of these hospitals, and they're no place for a child. You don't want the little chap to have nightmares."

"I agree," I said. "It's not like those pictures you've seen."

Fräulein Goldstein hesitated.

"Look, why don't I see if there's a nurse who'll look after him for an hour or so?" said the Chief diplomatically.

"Yes, thank you," she replied.

"Fellmann, shall we go and find the chaplain, make sure he's ready?" I said.

"Yes, good idea. If you'll excuse us, Herr Hauptmann, madam?"

The boss found a nurse who was just going off duty, and her face lit up at his request. *Make a nice change for her.*

Fräulein Goldstein turned pale as we entered the dying room, and she gasped out loud at the sight of Lentzke.

He was conscious, but only just.

"Oh, my love, what have they done to you?" she said, her voice breaking. She sat on the bed and laid her hand carefully on his shoulder.

He looked at her wonderingly. "Inge?"

"Yes, my love, I'm here."

His eye searched around the ward, then focussed on us. "Am I dreaming?"

"No, Friedrich," said the chaplain. "You're awake, and I'm here to marry you, if you want that."

"Yes. *Yes.* More than anything."

"Then let's get started."

"If it's all right I'd like to photograph the ceremony," said the Chief.

The chaplain nodded. "In the circumstances I think that would be very wise."

The man in the next bed started groaning.

"GAS!" he shouted suddenly. "GAS! *Jesus, they're coming!*"

This is hardly the wedding you both imagined. No smart uniform and pretty dress, no garlands of flowers, but a dying man whispering his vows in a room filled with pain and delirium.

I just hope the chaplain can hear him over that poor fellow.

Halfway through the service Lentzke stopped responding. Fräulein Goldstein looked at the chaplain in concern.

"Friedrich," he said, "can you hear me?"

"Darling! *Darling!* Wake up!"

There was no response, even when she shook him gently, and for one awful moment I thought he'd stopped breathing. All we could hear was the other man defending a desperate position, giving order after order.

A minute later Lentzke looked at us and his fiancée in puzzlement, and then he smiled and asked, "Where had we got to?"

The chaplain repeated his last words.

"Oh, yes," said Lentzke. "Let's carry on."

But he was obviously starting to drift off.

"I'll fetch the doctor," said Fellmann. "See if he can give him something."

He returned a couple of minutes later with a bespectacled doctor.

"Is there anything you can do to keep him awake?" asked Sonnenberg. "He's in the middle of getting married."

"Yes, so I'm told... An injection of strychnine should do the trick. Just give me a moment."

"Isn't that poisonous?" asked Fräulein Goldstein.

"Madam, many substances are poisonous in excess but beneficial in smaller doses," he replied, rather condescendingly.

"Oh."

It hardly matters if it shortens his life. He'll probably be dead tomorrow.

"Let's just hope we can get this finished," Fellmann muttered to me.

"And would it be possible to give Oberleutnant Schnorr a shot of morphine?" asked the chaplain. "It would be better for everyone."

"Yes, I should think so… I'll send someone."

"Bloody Army doctors," Sonnenberg said with feeling. He shifted his weight from one stick to the other, obviously uncomfortable. "Er – do excuse my language, madam."

"I have heard it before," she said with a smile. "Why don't you sit on the foot of Fritz's bed?"

"Thanks." He sat down very awkwardly, his face set.

"Let's hope they don't mix up the injections," muttered the Chief.

Fräulein Goldstein looked at him in horror. "They wouldn't do that, surely!"

"No, of course not," Fellmann said quickly.

The remainder of the ceremony was conducted in relative peace, Schnorr being unconscious. Lentzke lost the thread a couple of times, and we all held our breath until the chaplain said, "Those whom God has joined together, let no man put asunder."

Thank fuck for that.

Tears poured down Frau von Lentzke's face as she leaned down to embrace her husband. "You get well, my love, and I'll take you home."

Jesus. She can't really believe that?

"I think we should leave them alone," said the chaplain quietly.

Lentzke had started crying as well, which was more than a bit embarrassing. We congratulated them and made our way outside.

A fine drizzle was falling. None of us minded, Sonnenberg least of all.

"Thank God that's sorted out," he said, breathing out a large cloud of smoke.

"And we've got plenty of evidence," the Chief said. "I suggest we write out a statement to the effect that the ceremony was conducted correctly and all sign it, and I'll ask the chaplain to do the same."

"Two copies and two prints of each of the photographs would be a good idea," Sonnenberg said. "One for her and one for her lawyer."

"Yes," said Fellmann. "I suspect the family will be rather peeved."

The chaplain came out.

"Leutnant von Lentzke would like to speak to you, sir," he said to the Chief.

"Yes, of course."

"We'll wait here, then," said Sonnenberg. He turned to us. "Shall we sit in the car?"

One of his sticks slipped in the mud, and Fellmann caught his arm just in time.

"Thanks – wouldn't be the Western Front without mud, would it?!"

We didn't have to wait long for the Chief.

"He just wanted to say thank you," he said. "I offered his wife our hospitality but she said she'd stay with him."

"What about the boy?" I asked.

"They're going to sort out a billet with the nurses," he replied. "Let's get home."

When we got back we heard that the squadron had been up, but without success or loss.

"So what happened?" asked Horstmann.

"Lentzke's married," replied the Chief.

"Thank Christ for that."

"It was a bit touch and go," said Fellmann. "The doc had to give him strychnine at one point."

"But he knew what was going on?" asked Horstmann.

"Oh, yes. No doubt about that," said the Chief.

"Where's his family?" Bretti asked.

"Want someone your own age to play with, then?" teased Teuffel.

"At the hospital," I said.

"Well, they haven't got much time, have they?" said Horstmann.

"No, quite," Sonnenberg said. He stretched his legs out awkwardly and looked round the mess. "Very civilised set-up you've got here. Far better than you get in the poor bloody infantry!"

"Unless you're a staff officer!" Bretti said.

"Quite."

"What happened, sir?" asked Eichner, gesturing at his legs.

He smiled. "Present from the Frenchies – one of their 7.5 centimetre shells."

"Kind of them! Where?"

"Douaumont – the village, not the fort."

Ah – you're the cousin the boss told me about after we'd visited Karl.

"From what I've heard you were lucky," said Eichner.

Sonnenberg smiled again. "In more ways than one. It was pretty well a direct hit and it was at night."

"Why's that lucky?" asked Böhle.

Horstmann rolled his eyes. "Because you can't be carried back in daylight, you stupid sod."

"Oh."

"Anyone for Claudette's?" asked Otto.

"Count me out, thanks," said Sonnenberg. "Paying for tarts is not something I miss."

"No," said Böhle. "You'll soon be back home with your wife."

A look of profound sadness flitted across Sonnenberg's face, and I wondered what was wrong with her.

"Well," said Horstmann, "you can go home to your girlfriend if you get blown up, too!"

Böhle grinned. "Claudette's tarts have suddenly got a lot more attractive!"

"Be off with you all," said the Chief. "Max and I have a lot of catching up to do."

"And I've got a mountain of paper waiting for me," said Fellmann. "I swear it breeds when I'm not looking."

When we got back, the three of them were sitting together in the mess, most of the way through a bottle of schnapps and clearly very mellow – which was more than we were. Claudette's had been infested with lesser carmine-collared bastards, and we'd been bottom of the heap.

"Honestly," Bretti said as we entered the mess, "I don't know why we need so many of them."

"No," agreed Horstmann. "All they do is fuck things up."

"Who's that?" Sonnenberg asked.

"Bloody staff officers," said Otto. "I mean, why do they all have to go to the house of joy at the same time?"

Sonnenberg smiled. "I see some things never change. Probably just as well I didn't go with you."

"My best friend was at Verdun as well, sir, and he said he'd happily put the Fifth Army staff against the nearest wall," I said.

"Except for Excellency von Lochow," Horstmann added. "Karl reckons he's a decent bloke."

Sonnenberg's smile broadened. "Your friend and I are in complete agreement. Which regiment was he in?"

"The one next to yours, I believe," I said. "He was there at the beginning."

"Good Lord! He must have been in that blasted wood, then. Nasty place, that was – perfect killing ground and we walked straight into it. Where is he now?"

"In hospital in Baden-Baden. Got shot down in July."

"You might have heard of him, sir," Otto said. "Leutnant Karl von Leussow – he's got the Blue Max as well, been on those postcards."

"Sorry, I don't really keep up with aviation – too busy."

"What is it you do, sir?" asked Bretti.

"Ah – can't really say. Sorry."

The evening took the usual turn, and by the end no one was feeling any pain at all. Sonnenberg's presence did stop us playing the usual silly games, for which the mess furniture should have been grateful.

The rain and the chilly night air hit my face with a dizzying blast, but somehow I stayed upright.

Sonnenberg was thoroughly pissed, and his sticks went one way and he the other on the slippery duckboards. Fellmann managed to grab him, Bretti grabbed Fellmann, and for a moment it looked as if they were all going for a swim.

"Cheers," Sonnenberg said.

Fellmann kept a firm grip on him. "It's not far – that's if you don't mind sharing with me."

"Don't be so bloody stupid. Of course I bloody don't." He stopped and turned to face Fellmann. "Look, you don't want to take any notice of people and their stupid bloody prejudices."

Well said – funny how those who want acceptance can be so bad at extending it to others.

"What was all that about?" Horstmann asked in our room.

I told him.

"Oh, for fuck's sake!" he said. "Stupid cow—"

He may have said something else, but I'd fallen onto my bed fully clothed—

All the men I'd killed surrounded me, staring at me with their empty sockets, stinking of death and saying, 'We're waiting for you'.

I woke screaming and shaking.

"You all right?" asked a quiet voice.

"Yes, fine," I managed to say.

"Put the light on if you like."

"Thanks."

Horstmann was sitting up in bed, looking very pale.

"Sorry I woke you." My voice shook embarrassingly.

"You did me a favour – I'd lost my left lower wing and we were just starting to spin."

"Nice."

"You know, I'm more scared of that than of bullets," he added.

"Me too. The bastards have missed so far, after all."

It was still raining when we headed for breakfast. Everyone appeared in dribs and drabs, Fellmann and Sonnenberg arriving together.

"Gentlemen, your hospitality is quite something," said the latter. "The pain in my head is blotting out that from my legs – and that takes some doing!"

"We have had a few compliments," Bretti said modestly.

The phone rang, and a few minutes later the Chief came into the mess. I glanced at his face and knew what he was going to say.

"Gentleman, that was the chaplain at the field hospital," he said quietly. "Lentzke died half an hour ago, in his wife's arms."

We all looked at each other.

"Are we burying him here, or will she be taking him home?" Horstmann asked.

"Good question."

"What does the family prefer?" asked Sonnenberg. "It would be better if she got it right."

"I'll see if there's a note in the next of kin book," said Fellmann.

But there wasn't.

The Chief sighed. "I suppose, Becker, Fellmann, we'd better go to the hospital with Braun and some of the chaps, and ask the lady what she wants to do."

"Yes, sir," I said without enthusiasm.

"Would you like me to come as well?" Sonnenberg offered.

The boss shook his head. "No – you might as well stay here – though on second thoughts she might be pleased to see you. Oh – and we'd better make a third copy of the statement and photographs. I'll send it to his family with the usual letter."

Why oh why can't it be a lovely sunny day with a dry airfield? Then I could go flying instead of to that bloody hospital.

IX

Frau von Lentzke was waiting for us in the hall, with Fritze. She was doing her best to keep her composure, but when she saw us she started crying.

"My dear, I am so very sorry," Sonnenberg said gently.

"Thank you."

"Where's Papa?" asked Fritze. "Mama said we were going to see him."

Sonnenberg bent down as best he could. "Your papa's had to go away, on a very long journey for the Kaiser."

"When's he coming back? And why is Mama crying?"

"Not for a very long time – and it's because she misses him." He straightened up.

"Did you take him to see his father?" he asked.

She shook her head. "You were right. All of you."

That was as close to apologising to Fellmann as she was likely to get.

The Chief took her on one side. She shook her head again and then nodded, and said something we couldn't hear.

"We'll be burying Lentzke in our cemetery," he told us, "in accordance with his wishes."

There was a rather dingy café across the road.

"Shall we go and have a drink?" Sonnenberg said to Lentzke's widow. "Maybe they'll have milk or something for Fritze."

"Thank you."

She took his arm, and I wasn't sure who was supporting who. The thought suddenly struck me that the three of them looked like a family – but that was quite absurd.

I wondered again what was wrong with Sonnenberg's wife.

Lentzke was already in a pine coffin in the mortuary.

Braun frowned. "Won't do at all, sir," he said to the Chief.

"Will it do for taking him to the airfield?"

"Yes, sir – I meant, they haven't – well, I'll have some work to do for his lying in state."

I didn't want to think what that might involve.

"Well, let's get him in the lorry."

Just then the chaplain came in.

"Oh, I'm so pleased to have caught you, Oberleutnant," he said. "That was a very good deed you did – he'd been very upset that he was going to leave his son illegitimate and his lady penniless, but thanks to you gentlemen he died in peace, and – well, it was one of the better passings I've seen."

The Chief looked rather embarrassed. "Er, I'm glad we were able to get things resolved."

The chaplain smiled. "I wish his widow could stay with us," he said quietly. "She got round the doctors properly – tough little thing, she is."

She'll have to be.

Once the coffin was in the lorry, the Chief went to fetch the others from the café.

"You'd better sit in front with the boy, madam," he said.

"Thank you."

The rest of us got in the back. We were all very quiet – no one was used to having a widow present.

"They'd better have the other room in my hut," Fellmann said. "I'm sure Kramer won't mind moving for one night."

"Is the boy coming to the funeral?" the boss asked Sonnenberg.

"I don't know – I'm not sure it's a good idea."

"No… You remember my little sister, when we buried Grannie? Screamed her head off when the coffin went into the tomb, had nightmares for weeks afterwards."

"Yes," Sonnenberg replied, "and who'd told her Grannie was in the box?"

"Oh, shut up!"

We couldn't help laughing – and then had to hope the engine had drowned it out. I had a sudden, vivid picture of Hauptmann Graf Sonnenberg and Oberleutnant von Kralewski-Zentzytzki as a pair of mucky, mischievous small boys.

When we got to the airfield, I thought Fritze would explode with excitement.

"Aeroplanes!" he shouted, and ran towards the hangars.

"Oh, let him go," said Sonnenberg. "He won't come to any harm."

Fellmann and I followed more slowly.

"Who's this, then?" asked Uhlig, crouching down to the boy's level.

"Looks like a new recruit," said Zaffke, his eyes smiling above his fierce moustache. "Want to see the aircraft, young man?"

"*Yes, please!*"

"Right, then – up we go!" Zaffke picked him up and sat him on his shoulders.

"Am I really a young man?" asked Fritze.

"Of course," said Braun. "You're young, and when you grow up you'll be a man, won't you?"

Fritze sat taller on Zaffke's shoulders.

"Right," said Uhlig, "here's the cockpit…"

Fellmann grinned at me. "I'm not sure who's having more fun."

Schiffer heard him. "Well, sir, most of us miss our nippers – and it'll take the poor little fellow's mind off things, won't it?"

"Yes, indeed it will."

Sonnenberg had brought his best uniform and medals, and insisted on taking part in the guard of honour.

The Chief had wisely put him down for only one hour. At the end of it he was as white as a sheet and could hardly move, and as he stepped stiffly away from the coffin he almost fell. Bretti caught him, and helped him outside and along the duckboards.

Horstmann and I followed behind. *Bretti's turning into a tall, strong young man.* He had his arm round Sonnenberg's waist and was holding him up easily. When we got into the mess he lowered him carefully onto the small sofa.

"Thanks," Sonnenberg said with some effort.

Bretti bowed smartly. "My pleasure, sir," he said, and obviously meant it.

You're maturing as well – but then you don't have much option out here.

Horstmann handed Sonnenberg a very large brandy.

"Thanks," he said, and downed it in one.

I hope I never have to find out what that feels like, I thought as I refilled his glass.

To my surprise, he also insisted on joining the procession.

Frau von Lentzke had packed a black dress, and a suit for Fritze.

"Are you sure the boy should come?" Fellmann asked her. "He could stay here with Uhlig or Zaffke – the men who were showing him the aircraft yesterday."

"It wouldn't be right to leave him out," she said.

His eyes opened wide at the sight of all of us in our best uniforms, polished and gleaming in the autumn sunlight, and at the band and the gun carriage with its black horses.

"What's in the big box?"

"Treasure," said Sonnenberg. "Special treasure, that we're going to bury to keep it safe."

Frau von Lentzke stifled a sob.

"Like pirates do?"

"Just like that."

"That's so exciting!"

"Now, you must be a good boy and be quiet and hold Mama's hand," Sonnenberg said. "So the pirate captain" – he indicated the Chief – "will think you're a good crew member."

"Aye aye, sir!"

He was as good as gold. *Oh, the innocence – the wonderful, trusting innocence. I wish I could believe that the coffin contains pieces of eight from some plundered galleon, rather than the shattered remains of a good man.*

Who will be next?

Lentzke's widow kept her composure far better than I'd expected. She cried quietly as the coffin was lowered into the grave and we sang that song, but that was all.

Sonnenberg had a lot of difficulty walking back. The Chief gave him his arm, and the two of them fell gradually behind. As we passed through the village I noticed that they'd stopped.

I headed back towards them, to ask if they'd like me to bring the car. As I approached, the Chief gave me a warning look but not before I heard his cousin say, "I'm at my wits' end, Berti – she can't stand the sight of me."

"Excuse me, gentlemen," I said, "but I was wondering whether to fetch the car."

Sonnenberg looked embarrassed for a second. "Yes, thank you, Becker. I'm sorry to put you to trouble."

"It's no trouble at all, sir. I'm sorry if I intruded."

He sighed. "No, you didn't. I was burdening my poor cousin with my problems."

"Not at all," said the Chief firmly. "You have to talk to someone… There must be a doctor somewhere who can help her."

"I hope we find him soon, before she – well, won't finish that."

I walked back as fast as I could. When I got back with the car they hadn't got much further, and Sonnenberg was sitting on a wall, clearly in pain.

"Haven't walked that far – well, since I got blown up," he said. "Might have done some good."

"Maybe," said the Chief doubtfully.

"Look, Becker," said Sonnenberg, "I don't want you to have the wrong idea about the Countess." He sighed deeply. "She hasn't been right since our youngest was born – everything upsets her. She says the world's a terrible place, not fit for children. Seeing me limping about the place just makes it worse. She's convinced our sons are going to get killed in the next war. I've tried to tell her there'll be lasting peace after this one, but she won't believe me."

Neither do I. There's always a next war.

"The doctors must know more about the mind these days," I said. "After all, a lot of men have lost theirs because of the war."

I stopped suddenly, because I saw poor Widemayer talking to himself and screaming, and because I knew my own nerves were very frayed.

"We just have to hope," he replied.

When we got back Fritze was in the hangars again, and had to be prised out to wash his hands before lunch.

"Grand little lad, he is," said Zaffke. "Just like my Hans was at his age."

"Spitting image of his father," added Uhlig.

"Now what do you say to these nice men?" said his mother.

"Thank you very much!" said Fritze. "I want to be a pilot when I grow up and fly up high into the sky!"

"Pity we're not a two-seater squadron," I said to her. "I could have taken him for a flight."

A look of absolute horror crossed her face. *I hope she doesn't mollycoddle him.*

After lunch the Chief gave her the statements and photographs.

"I can't thank you all enough," she said. "You've all been so kind."

"Madam, there is no need to thank us," said the Chief. "Leutnant von Lentzke was a valued comrade and we were all glad to help."

He and Sonnenberg had a brief, private farewell, and we waved them off with a strong feeling of relief.

"I can do without all that again," said Otto.

"You and me both," Horstmann agreed.

"Made me very uncomfortable, that did," Teuffel said.

"Yes," agreed Bretti. "Not the sort of thing you want to think about, widows, is it?"

"No," said Eichner.

"Fellmann, Becker, let's examine the field," said the Chief.

It was useable, which raised the enticing prospect of going off to fight in outclassed aircraft that could break up.

Maybe Lentzke had a point about going back to the trenches.

"Better crack on," said the Chief. "Not that much daylight left."

I could see that the others felt as I did, and yet everyone got in his aircraft without hesitation.

What makes men go off to fight, when they know what's in store for them?

The western sky was clouding over and the light faded fast on the way home. I was chilled to the bone and I had to concentrate hard on the landing.

Böhle made a dog's breakfast of his, standing his Pfalz on her nose. The Chief sighed and took him to his office. He looked thoroughly pissed off when he emerged five minutes later.

We had a proper wake for Lentzke. Horstmann and I sat on the small sofa in silence, working our way through a bottle of brandy.

Bretti came and joined us. "Got a smoke? I've run out."

Johnny sat down next to Karl and me. "Give us a fag, Bruv."

"Becker. *Becker.*" Horstmann was gazing at me in concern.

"What?"

"Where the fuck had you got to?"

"Sorry – almost nodded off." I could see he didn't believe me. "I was thinking about Johnny."

"Oh," said Bretti. There was a pause and then he said, "That Sonnenberg fellow was a good sort."

"Yes, he was," Horstmann agreed. "You seemed to hit it off well with him."

"He reminded me of my older brother."

That's why you took such care with him.

Otto limped over, cigarette in his mouth, bottle of schnapps in one hand. He pulled up a chair, and the four of us concentrated on getting completely pissed.

November ended in rain and fog, and December brought freezing weather and short days.

I used to find the darkness depressing, but now I'm just glad there are fewer hours in which to get killed. But what's truly depressing is that it's winter again, and my chances of seeing another summer are even worse than they were a year ago.

I don't want to think about the men who were with us then, who are now bones.

Beilke and Schulte were back, and in place of Lentzke and Reinhard we'd acquired Benner and Brockmann – the former poached shamelessly from another Jasta by Fellmann, and the latter straight out of the fighter pilot school at Valenciennes. Benner had three victories, though nothing like Lentzke's experience.

"Well, Brettschneider," said the Chief over lunch, "you can lead Eichner and Becker this afternoon."

Bretti's face lit up. "Thank you, sir!"

"Bloody hell," Eichner said as we suited up, "the boss is really scraping the bottom of the barrel, letting you lead!"

Bretti just grinned at him. "You're on my left wing, Eichner, with Becker on my right."

"Whatever you say," Eichner replied. "I'm just glad Becker will be there!"

About ten minutes after we reached the lines I spotted a flight of Camels, some way north and at about the same altitude, and pointed it out to Bretti.

Now we'll see how much you've learned. At least if you fuck it up, I might be able to sort the mess out.

He didn't fuck it up, but made good use of a bank of cloud to get us into position without being seen.

Nice, Bretti.

It was one hell of a scrap, and it got bigger and bigger as more of ours and more of theirs joined in. *There's no way Bretti will be keeping track of this.*

A Camel flashed past my nose and I don't know how we missed each other – and another was on my tail and I daren't put any more load on my Albatros.

I don't want to have to be careful when I've got a Camel up my arse.

No, Lentzke, neither do I… Either he shoots me or the wings break. With a bit of luck he'll miss—

Eichner got behind him and gave him a good burst, and on it went.

We were down to five hundred metres and the flak was bursting black instead of white.

I just hope our flak gunners are as useless as the Tommies'.

The Camels broke off and we let them go, and the sky cleared. I spotted Bretti and locked onto his right wing, and we headed for the rendezvous.

We had to circle for a few minutes before Eichner joined us. I was suddenly bloody frozen, the frigid air blasting right through to my sweat-soaked shirt.

Bretti led us back up and up, and I got ever colder. Reaction set in and I was shaking so much that I had to move out slightly – and then my stomach turned over as I saw a two-seater with a Camel escort.

Shit. We can't let that go.

For a moment I thought of pretending I hadn't seen it – but I couldn't do that. It meant harm to the fellows in the trenches, and the poor sods needed all the help they could get.

I pointed it out to Bretti, and he pointed to it and then to Eichner.

Let's just hope it's not a set-up. There's so much cloud about that the bastards could be hiding anywhere...

No sooner was Eichner under the two-seater's tail than a flight of Nieuports joined the party, French, from the cockades. *That's unusual round here.*

The minutes that followed were thoroughly unpleasant. We were heavily outnumbered, and Eichner, blast him, took far too long to see the new arrivals. Whatever I did, one of the fuckers was on my tail, spitting lead at me.

I shan't be getting out of this.

I felt a sudden, lunatic exultation. *Yes, I'm going to die – but you bastards are coming with me. If the wings break, they break. It doesn't matter any more.*

The Albatros pivoted on her wingtips, my cheeks sagging. One of the Frenchies passed in front of the nose, and I pulled the turn tighter and got right onto his tail, ignoring his mate who was right on mine.

And I got the fucker. His aircraft reared up and then fell into a spin, trailing smoke and then flame.

His friend broke off as a strange Pfalz turned onto his tail. There were two Kettes of them, and within a couple of minutes the Frenchies all buggered off, with the Pfalzes in hot pursuit.

Must find out which Jasta they were from and send them a case of champagne.

Eichner and I formated on Bretti and – thank God – he took us home. I was almost out of ammunition.

If I'd had reaction after the first fight it was ten times worse after that one. *I need a very large brandy and some dry clothes, and to hug the stove. And a fag or ten.*

The strip was greasy and the breeze was slightly across it, and it took all my concentration to stay straight as we touched down and rolled to walking pace, and then we almost got stuck taxying in.

Uhlig put the chocks in and I shut the engine down, my ears ringing in the silence.

"Any luck, sir?" he asked as I slid down the fuselage.

"One French Nieuport," I managed to say.

His face cracked into a grin. "Well done, sir!"

"Thanks – could you light a fag for me?"

"Of course, sir – shall I do that anyway, now it's winter?"

"Yes, please." *Tactful fellow, Uhlig.*

I drew the smoke into my lungs, wishing I could stop shaking.

Uhlig studied my aircraft, his face suddenly grave. "That's rather a lot of holes, sir."

He wasn't joking, and there was a long rip in the right sleeve of my flying jacket and another in my left boot.

"Well, it was a bit hot… Bretti, Eichner, let's thaw out."

There was a definite atmosphere as we walked towards the mess.

Eichner stopped suddenly and turned to Bretti. "Why the fuck did the Chief let you lead? You bloody near got us all killed!"

"No, he didn't," I said firmly.

"It was fucking obvious that two-seater was a set-up!"

"Then why did you go for it?" I asked him. "And more to the point, why did it take you so long to notice the Frenchies turning up?"

"No, I spotted them right away."

Bretti laughed. "Becker and I engaged them well before you broke off your attack."

Eichner looked at him and then at me.

"Bretti's right," I said. "I was cursing you for a blind idiot."

"Oh."

We carried on. Eichner put a hand on Bretti's shoulder and said, "Sorry, mate. Bit worked up."

"That's all right," said Bretti. "Be surprising if you weren't after that."

"Bleif, can we have some tea with rum?" I asked.

"Right away, sir."

The others weren't back yet, and we sat next to the stove.

"Bretti, I thought you did very well," I said, and went through both fights. "I'll be putting in a good report to the Chief," I finished, just as engine noise announced the return of the others.

They were all back safe, if shaken.

"You collected a lot of holes, Becker," said the Chief when I went to make my report.

"It was rather hot, sir."

"Yes, it was for us as well. That's four aircraft grounded for repairs."

"At least they all stayed together."

"Quite... How did Brettschneider get on?"

"Very well," I said, and gave him the details.

"Good," he said. "If we have a run of decent weather he can get a bit more experience. Oh, by the way, Fellmann and I have finished the leave roster for this month – you've got Christmas, but not New Year, I'm afraid. Eichner's got that."

"Thank you, sir – I really do appreciate it."

"Well, I thought – otherwise this would be your fourth in the field, wouldn't it?"

"Yes, sir."

"So it seems only fair."

I have to stay alive for another three and a bit weeks, and on today's form that's wildly optimistic.

All the same, I started writing to my parents to give them the good news.

"Tempting Fate, aren't you?" said Horstmann.

"Just because you're jealous!"

Otto was standing over me with a bottle of champagne. "Put that pen down, Franz, and start drinking!"

I didn't need to hear that twice, and nor did Benner and Brockmann – the latter had joined the Air Service from the infantry, and his head was cast from concrete.

Horstmann and I wandered to bed under a clear, starry night.

"Be frosty tomorrow," he said.

"Don't care."

"You will at four thousand."

"Be warm once we meet the other lot!"

He laughed. "Not too fucking warm, I hope!"

Why the fuck did you have to say that just before bed? But I was pissed enough to fall straight asleep, and stayed that way until Schiffer brought the shaving water.

Bretti led again on the dawn flight. It was clear that the Chief was thinking of promoting him, and he knew he had to prove himself – and once again he did a surprisingly good job.

Maybe I shouldn't be surprised, I thought on the way home. *I'm used to thinking of Officer Cadet Brettschneider as a frivolous youth, but that seems to be well out of date.*

It had been another hard patrol, and I was still shaking when we sat down to second breakfast. I told myself it was the cold. It had been utterly vicious at altitude, as Horstmann had predicted.

Beilke was facing the window. He started visibly as he glanced out, and said, "Sir, we – er – we seem to have visitors."

Everyone on that side of the table looked up, their jaws dropping, and the Chief turned round.

"Shit," he muttered.

I turned at that, and my jaw dropped as well. A staff car had pulled up outside the main hut, and a general was getting out of it – a real live general, with red stripes down his trousers, red collar patches with gold braid on them, Pour le Mérite glistening in the sun, and polished boots that sank to the ankles in the mud. He was accompanied by an immaculate colonel.

Both of them looked around, the Colonel said something to the driver and the two officers headed for the steps.

Bloody hell. The last time we had a general here it was because Karl's father had died. What's this about?

The Chief got up. "Gentlemen, would you excuse me?"

"Please tell me I'm not seeing things," said Brockmann. "I know I hit the bottle last night, but imagining a general is just a bit—"

Otto grinned at him. "It's all right – there really is a staff car, and a general."

"Thank Christ for that!"

"And I want to speak to everyone who signed that statement," said a voice outside the mess door.

"Yes, of course, Your Excellency. Fellmann, would you show our guests into my office, please?"

The boss came into the mess. "Becker, we have a visit from Generalleutnant von Lentzke. Would you come to my office, please?"

"Right away, sir."

"And Bleif, we'd like coffee for five, please."

The General did not look happy.

"Leutnant Fellmann, Your Excellency," said the Chief, "and Leutnant Becker. Both gentlemen were witnesses at your son's wedding. The chaplain is, I believe, still at the field hospital, and Hauptmann Graf Sonnenberg is in Berlin at the War Ministry."

Lentzke glared at us. "So you're responsible for my son's so-called marriage."

"The ceremony was conducted correctly, Your Excellency," said the Chief, "and at Leutnant von Lentzke's insistence."

"First, I find that hard to believe. Second, how did that woman come to be here?"

"Your Excellency – your son was going on marriage leave the day he crashed. He came to see me the day before to request it. When we heard he was dying, I decided to cable his fiancée to ask her to come here. The chaplain can tell Your Excellency that your son was very upset at the thought of leaving his son illegitimate and the boy's mother destitute – as any decent man would be – and we can all confirm that he was very happy indeed to see her, and that he wanted to marry her, as he said, more than anything."

"Hmph." The General turned to me. "And I suppose you'll back up your CO?"

"Yes, Your Excellency. In fact, I instigated the whole thing."

The General's face was starting to match his collar patches – not that I gave a shit.

"Your son confided in me two days before he died," I went on. "He said he hadn't done the right thing by his family. He was a good soldier and a good comrade, and – whether Your Excellency approves of his choice of wife or not – he was an honourable man."

"What's to say the boy's even his?"

"Oh, there's no doubt about that, Your Excellency," I said. "The resemblance is striking."

"Hmph. Leutnant Fellmann?"

"It was just as Oberleutnant von Kralewski-Zentzytzki and Leutnant Becker say, Your Excellency."

"And how in God's name did she get here?"

"She was escorted from Berlin by Hauptmann Graf Sonnenberg, Your Excellency," replied the Chief.

The General looked at him for a moment. "What's his Christian name?" he asked abruptly.

"Maximilian."

"Which regiment?"

"The 24th."

"Hmph. Not the fellow I'm thinking of."

"That might be Manfred, Your Excellency, Max's brother. Fell at the Somme."

"That's him. My late son's battalion commander – my other late son, that is. Decent fellow, by all accounts."

The General suddenly looked old and tired, and I felt unexpected sympathy for him.

He rubbed his forehead. "So I'm stuck with this trollop as my daughter-in-law."

"Your Excellency hasn't met the lady yet?" asked the Chief. "She couldn't have been more devoted to your son. I wouldn't describe her as a trollop."

"Any woman who goes to bed with a man she isn't married to is a trollop."

The Chief gave him a level stare. "I'm sure Your Excellency did not intend to call my wife a trollop."

The Colonel stiffened and shot the Chief a warning look. Fellmann and I exchanged glances.

"What the devil are you talking about, man?" demanded the General. "I never said anything of the kind!"

"My wife went to bed with me before we were married," said the Chief, ignoring the Colonel completely. "More than once, in fact. On the basis that I might not come home."

"Well, I – er – I certainly – obviously there are exceptions—"

"Indeed, Your Excellency. The younger Frau von Lentzke might not have been born a lady, but she can become one, and she is the mother of Your Excellency's grandson, who will carry on the family name. Might I suggest that Your Excellency meet them both?"

The General sighed. "I shall be speaking to the chaplain, and to Hauptmann Graf Sonnenberg. I bid you gentlemen good day."

He got up, and we all stood and bowed as smartly as we could. As they left the room, the Colonel turned to the Chief and hissed, "I cannot believe your insolence."

The Chief brought his heels together again with a slight inclination of his head, and then gave the Colonel a look that said, very clearly, 'I couldn't give a damn what you believe'.

The Colonel went puce.

"Stegelitz!" came the General's voice from outside. "*Stegelitz!*"

Stegelitz gave the Chief a filthy look and hurried after his master. *Who'd be a general's dogsbody?*

"Thank fuck they've gone," said Fellmann.

"Quite," said the Chief. "That had been festering for a while, but I didn't think he'd actually turn up."

And I'll bet he wishes he hadn't, after you shot him down like that.

"Gentlemen," the Chief added slightly awkwardly, "I know I can trust you both not to repeat what I said about my wife."

"Of course, sir," we said together.

You didn't need to ask.

The others looked up expectantly as we went back into the mess.

"What did they want, sir?" asked Eichner.

"That was Lentzke's father – the General, that is – wanting confirmation that his son's wedding was genuine."

"Well, no doubt you put him straight," said Horstmann.

The Chief smiled slightly. "I did my best. He's off to talk to the chaplain, and Sonnenberg at some point."

"So what really happened?" asked Bretti after the boss had gone back to his office.

I grinned at him. "You think I'm going to repeat any of it?"

He grinned back. "Worth a try!"

"He didn't look any happier when he left," said Benner.

"And that Colonel looked like a pompous wanker," added Böhle.

Everyone laughed.

"He was a bit of a stuffed shirt," I said, "but what do you expect?"

"Quite," agreed Horstmann. "Bloody staff."

"I did feel a bit sorry for the General, though," I said quietly.

The others looked at me.

"He'd already lost one son."

"Bugger that!" Horstmann snorted. "How many blokes has he sent to die? I've got no sympathy at all!"

"You're all heart!" I retorted – *Burkhardt used to say that. It seems so long ago, now, that I held his hand as he died.*

Such a fucking waste, all of it. Why can't the idiot politicians make peace?

"And at least you and the boss got your Pour le Mérites by your own efforts, which I doubt he did," Horstmann added.

The Chief came back in.

"Well, gentlemen, time for briefing…"

And the patrol was another shocker that left me shaking and unable to understand how I was still alive.

I don't know how much more of this I can do, I thought as I peeled off my shirt, which was stuck to my vest with sweat.

"Jesus, I can almost wring this out," Horstmann said as he draped his shirt over the back of a chair. "And my underwear."

"That's called incontinence," I said. "Or fear!"

He inspected his long johns with mock seriousness. "No – not yellow, or brown. Though I shall be soon. Yellow, that is."

"You and me both… How did Bretti do?"

"Rather well – much better than I expected. He'd be perfectly capable of managing on his own, and that's what I told the Chief."

"Be good to see him get his epaulettes," I said.

"Indeed."

As I pulled on a dry shirt I realised it was Karl's old one. The silk settled against my skin, and the memory of his touch sent a shiver down my spine. I turned my back to Horstmann and finished dressing.

"Anyone fancy Claudette's?" I said when we got to the mess.

Beilke shook his head. "Spent all my money back home, buying food on the black market."

"Count me in," said Bretti.

"And me," said Otto and Böhle together.

There was a major with a girl on his knee. Johnny stopped in the doorway, turned to Karl and said, 'Pa's in the salon!'

Why do I have to see the dead everywhere?

"Ah, gentlemen, how lovely to see you!" said Claudette. "I have two new girls…"

The ghosts retreated.

A couple of days later the post came, bringing a parcel from my family and a letter from Karl.

It's always good to hear from you.

'My dear Franz, many congratulations on your latest victory – you'll be ahead of me soon! Yesterday some of us went to the pictures, and there you were, climbing into your Triplane and looking heroically westwards, and taking off to shoot down the accursed Tommies! Seeing your ugly mug quite made me smile – even if I didn't recognise many of the others.'

He chattered on a bit more in the same vein.

"Got a love letter?" asked Otto cheekily.

"No, you stupid bastard – it's from Karl."

"Could have fooled me!" said Schulte. "That's the sort of face Horstmann's got when he hears from the lovely Susanne!"

"Load of cobblers," Horstmann said. "You make me sound like some doughy boy."

"You're just jealous cos you've got no mates," Böhle said to Schulte.

I let them all get on with it. *Otto looks very soppy when he hears from that nurse of his.*

'This is my last letter from Baden-Baden,' Karl went on. 'I'm being discharged tomorrow and I'm going home. I can't begin to tell you what that means to me. By the time you read this I'll be there. Please come and stay when you can get leave – it would be wonderful to see you.'

And you. I'll be there as soon as I can, and we can sit by the fire and talk, and do – whatever we fancy doing. I'll have your arms round me again, and—

Shit. Christmas.

There's no way my parents will accept my spending my Christmas leave with Karl. Not in a thousand years.

I'd been looking forward to a proper Christmas at home with my family, the first since before the war, but there was no contest between that and being with Karl.

How in God's name am I going to get out of going home?

I looked at Bretti, playing cards with Beilke and Schulte, and had an idea.

"Have you got a moment, sir?" I asked at the boss's office door.

"Yes, of course." He looked at his watch. "Briefing's in five minutes."

"That's fine." I closed the door and sat down.

He looked at me expectantly.

"Sir – Bretti's been doing very well. I was wondering how close he is to being commissioned?"

"I wanted to talk to you about that. Everyone's given him a favourable report, but Kramer's senior to him, by quite a long way."

Otto can't lead the way out of a wet paper bag.

"I think there's a good case for passing Kramer over. He doesn't have the same… well, he's slow to see things, and his marksmanship's never been good. Whereas Bretti's got his head screwed on, and I feel I can have confidence in him. And Bretti's would be a Regular commission, and we've definitely got a vacancy."

"My opinions exactly. I'll have a word with Kramer, explain why Brettschneider's getting it and he isn't. Hopefully he won't be too disappointed."

"To be honest, sir, I don't think he'll mind."

"Well, if he does, he does. Was there anything else?"

"Yes, sir, there was. I was thinking – if Bretti gets his epaulettes before Christmas, he could have my Christmas leave. That would be rather nice, for him to go home with those."

He looked at me in astonishment. "You'd give up Christmas at home?"

"Not for Bretti's sake," I said hastily. "I've just heard from Leussow – he should be at home in Brandenburg by now and he's asked me to stay. Christmas would be rather awkward."

"That *is* good news," he said with a smile. "Do give him my best wishes when you write. Well, of course you want to see him – and I see what you mean about Christmas."

"Yes, my family – well, they're expecting me, but I'll think of something."

"I might be able to help you there… This came yesterday."

'This' was a letter from Hoeppner, the Commanding General of the Air Service, stating that there would be fighter aircraft trials the following month at Adlershof airfield, and asking the Chief to attend with another pilot from the squadron.

Adlershof was near Berlin.

"You'd be the best candidate," he said, "so I was rather regretting giving you that Christmas leave. If we move it to January, you can have two weeks – which you certainly deserve – and then go to Adlershof."

Three weeks away from the Front. A few days at home, a few with Karl, and then all sorts of fun testing out new aircraft without anyone trying to kill me – except the aircraft manufacturers, of course.

"Thank you, sir – I'd like that very much."

"Right – I'll get Fellmann to draft the reply. We'd better get going."

There was no time to write to anyone before the patrol, and during it I really thought, yet again, that I wouldn't make it to the end of the flight.

This can't go on, I thought as I walked to the mess on rubber knees. *I'm writing myself off almost every time we fly, and every time I have to get back from the other side. And it's getting harder to do.*

It's as if I keep leaving part of myself there, again and again.

I settled into a chair with a large brandy, feeling my body thawing out, grateful that darkness was falling and that I was safe for the rest of the day.

This is part of the problem. When you're in the trenches the danger's continuous but low level – yes, you could be unlucky and get shelled or caught up in some offensive or other, but otherwise if you keep your head down you stay in one piece. We have extreme danger every time we fly, and then we come back to almost complete safety. It's the contrast – it's too great.

Maybe that's what broke Bruch and Widemayer. I hadn't thought about Bruch for ages, and I didn't want to. *How did they get his brains off the wall?*

"Aren't you going to open your parcel?" Otto asked.

"Oh, God – I'd forgotten all about it."

He shook his head. "Your people really are wasting their time on you."

The parcel contained another shapeless sweater from Johanna, perfect for flying. As I opened it out, a box of condoms fell onto the floor.

Eichner stared at it in amazement. "Your *girlfriend* sent you those?"

I laughed. "No, my sister."

"Your *sister?!* Hey, boys – Becker's sister sends him condoms!"

"Not all the time," I said. "Just once."

"Bloody good idea," said Horstmann.

"Can she send me some, too?" asked Bretti. "My last one split."

"We don't want to know!" Brockmann exclaimed, just as Benner said, "Keep it to yourself!"

"That's the problem," said Bretti. "I didn't!"

"Well, you hardly need worry about Claudette's tarts getting pregnant," said Eichner. "The list of suspects is very long."

"And the girl would try to pin it on the carmine-collared, not some penniless cadet who's about to get killed!" Otto said.

"I'd be more worried about what came in than what went out," I said.

Bretti pulled a face. "Don't."

"So why's your sister sending you condoms?" Eichner asked.

"She wants to be a doctor – gave me quite a lecture on not getting the pox last time I was home."

"A nice girl shouldn't even know about things like that!" he said, obviously shocked.

"Oh, I don't know," said Horstmann. "They need to be aware of the dangers as well."

"That's just what Johanna – my sister – says, that there must be lots of women who've behaved perfectly but caught something nasty from their husbands."

"Mm," agreed Brockmann. "Must be a lot of that, with everyone fucking tarts."

"I still don't think it's right, girls learning about that sort of thing," said Eichner.

"They've made a film about it," Beilke said. "I saw it at the pictures back home."

"Can we change the subject before I go off sex completely?" Böhle said.

"I wish I could go off sex," said Benner. "I'm so sick of paying."

My family's letters had obviously crossed with mine about Christmas leave, as they didn't mention it. *They're not going to like the next letter one bit, but I'd better not put it off.*

Why bother? The next letter they get from here will be the Chief's, telling them you were killed instantly and so on.

I'll write to Karl instead – there's just as little point, but I like writing to him.

'I've got leave next month, so if I'm still here I'll come and see you – I'll let you know the dates nearer the time, and wire you when I know what time I'll be there.'

If I make it...

The weather turned, to my complete joy. *I'll have to write to my parents today,* I thought as the rain bounced off the roof of the main hut and ran down the windows.

I dressed it up as an exciting opportunity to be involved in the choice of new fighter aircraft, and stressed what a compliment the boss was paying me by inviting me to take part. I also made it crystal clear that I'd be going to Brandenburg a few days ahead of the trials, to see Karl.

"Kramer, have you got a minute?" asked the Chief.

Otto got up, looking as if he were about to be executed, and went to the boss's office.

He looked very relieved when he came back, and sat down next to me.

"Phew," he said, "I thought I'd had my chips."

"Why?"

"Oh, come on, Franz – you know I've never managed to shoot anything down, and what are fighter pilots for? I mean, one day the Chief will have had enough, won't he? And I thought it was today."

"Otto, the boss has never said a word to me about chucking you out."

"Well, he wouldn't, would he? I mean, yes, you're his second-in-command, but he knows we're old friends."

"You're a useful fellow, Otto," I said. "Your score may be a nice round number, but you've saved everyone's bacon at some point."

"Oh. Cheers."

"So what did he want?"

"I'm not allowed to say, but I think you know. I'm just relieved that was all it was."

"Ah. Right."

Sure enough, five minutes later the Chief appeared again. "Brettschneider, have you got a minute?"

"Of course, sir."

Bretti came out positively alight with joy.

"What are you looking so pleased about?" asked Brockmann with mock grumpiness.

"I've got Christmas leave!" Bretti said, giving me a huge grin.

"You jammy little bastard!" said Eichner. "How the fuck did you get that?"

A shadow crossed Bretti's face. "Well, it's partly because I've never been home for Christmas since I left in '15, and partly because there's only me now. I had a brother, but – well. The boss thought my parents would like to have me home."

"Yes, I'm sure they will," Horstmann said quietly.

"Was that the brother Sonnenberg reminded you of?" asked Böhle.

"That's right. About the same age, too – on the calendar, anyway."

I knew what he meant. Sonnenberg, like every veteran of Verdun, was far older than a calendar could ever show.

"Christmas at home," Benner said wistfully. "Now that would be something."

"We'll probably have a better one here," I said. "Better food, anyway."

"You're telling me," said Beilke. "Unless you buy on the black market, you starve. I didn't want to give those bastards money, but then I found out Mama had been giving me part of her ration and I couldn't let her do that."

"We'll put together a hamper for you to take home," Schulte said to Bretti.

What a change from Christmas '14.

Two days later Fellmann came into the mess, obviously bursting with excitement.

"Come on," said the Chief, "spill the beans!"

"You're going to like this," Fellmann said, spinning the moment out. "Fokker have sorted out the wing problem, and new wings are on their way to us even as I speak."

"Say that again," said Horstmann. "That's the sort of news I want to hear twice."

Fellmann obliged.

I felt a huge weight sliding off me.

"When will they be here?" asked the boss.

"Well, let's see now…" Fellmann made a show of consulting some papers.

"Fellmann, if you don't spit it out now I'll bloody well squeeze it out of you!" said Horstmann.

Fellmann raised an eyebrow archly. "Promises, promises! You can squeeze it out of me any time you like!"

Horstmann shook his head, laughing. "Sorry, you're not pretty enough!"

"Do stop encouraging him," said the Chief. "Fellmann, the first delivery date, before we all die of suspense!"

"Today."

"WHAT!" exclaimed the Chief.

"You *bastard*!" I said, and there was more of the same from the others.

"Yes," Fellmann said happily, "a consignment of shiny new wings should be here within the next couple of hours – Flanders mud and the traffic permitting, of course."

The wings didn't arrive until after dark, but we all piled out of the mess to watch them being unloaded.

"They don't look any different," said Schulte.

Horstmann rolled his eyes. "Of course they bloody don't – it's all inside, isn't it, Fellmann?"

"Yes – stronger ribs. Braun, how long to fit them?"

"We'll work overnight, sir, have two aircraft ready for dawn."

Fellmann nodded. "The CO's and Leutnant Becker's. We should have the next delivery in a couple of days' time and another in a week or so – and that'll be all our Triplanes airworthy again."

"Thank fuck for that," breathed Beilke.

I went to bed feeling far more hopeful than I had for weeks – and had the fucking burning dream.

That was the end of any positive feelings about the dawn flight. I smoked my way through first breakfast, and the roll I tried to eat turned to sawdust in my mouth. I sank two mugs of strong coffee, well-sugared and with a slug of schnapps in the second one, and struggled to keep even that down.

The cold, sick fear got worse as I suited up, and I remembered Widemayer vomiting. *If I'm sick then I'm sick – just please don't let me shit myself.*

Though I'd hardly be alone in that.

As soon as the first fight began I was calm and focussed, as always – and oh, the joy of being back in my agile little Triplane, and of knowing that I could throw her around as hard as I liked and she wouldn't break.

"Lucky bastard," Horstmann said to me as we changed. "Just break your ankle or something so I can have your aircraft!"

I just laughed.

A week later we had six airworthy Triplanes, with a promise of six more. Bretti had another victory, as did Horstmann and Benner, but for some reason I didn't. It was bloody frustrating, especially as my last one hadn't been confirmed.

Horstmann did get confirmation, which made him an ace. That was the excuse for a real blinder of a party.

The next day it pissed down, and most of us didn't appear until lunchtime.

"Bloody hell, Horstmann, that punch is lethal," said Brockmann.

"Glad you liked it!"

"I don't think it likes me!"

The Chief smiled at our pasty faces and red eyes. He was bright-eyed and cheerful as usual, but then he had more sense than to drink the way we did.

As Bleif was serving coffee the boss said, "Excuse me a moment, gentlemen," and disappeared towards his office.

He came back a minute later and rapped on the table.

"Gentlemen," he said, "I'm sure you will all join me in congratulating Leutnant Brettschneider on his commission."

Everyone cheered and applauded, even more so when the Chief went over to Bretti, pulled a set of bright new silver epaulettes from his pocket and handed them to him.

"Thank you so much, sir," Bretti said, looking as if birthday and Christmas had come at the same time.

"Get Kessler to sew those on for you, and we'll have a party for the whole squadron this evening," said the boss.

"The girls will be all over you," I said.

"Yes," said Horstmann, "quite the dashing young flier!"

Bretti laughed. "My family will be so pleased. Especially with my being home for Christmas – I haven't told them I'm coming, so it'll be a double surprise."

"Congratulations, Herr Leutnant!" said Otto with a grin. "You deserve it."

"Thanks, Kramer – look, I – er – I don't know why the boss put me forward—"

"But I do, and he was right. It should be you – I'm a war volunteer and if I never get commissioned it won't bother me at all. Just so long as someone lends me a coat to go to Claudette's!"

"I'll see if I can get two," Bretti said.

"You'll be lucky, with the shortages," said Beilke.

Bretti left in search of Kessler, and came back looking very fine indeed, with the sergeant's braid removed from his collar and his epaulettes catching the mess lights.

Mine are getting rather tatty, probably because I wear my tunic under my flying jacket. My best uniform still looks smart, though, and tatty says experienced.

"Ah, very smart!" said Beilke. "Now, I want a picture for the squadron album."

He pulled a chair over to the window.

"Sit here – no, hang on, that won't quite do – that's better. That's got the light in the right place."

The party began as soon as he'd finished. The ground crew all shook Bretti's hand and said, "Congratulations, Herr Leutnant!" until I wondered if he was getting sick of hearing it – but of course he wouldn't be.

He must have dreamed of this since he was a boy. One of those fortunate fellows who knows exactly what career he wants.

Otto said as much to me over dinner.

I looked at him in surprise. "But you want to be a lawyer, don't you?"

"Well, yes, but not the same way, if you see what I mean. I mean, Bretti's like Kurt, only ever wanted to be a soldier."

I wished Otto hadn't mentioned Kurt.

"Whereas I don't have any burning desire to be a lawyer – it just seemed like a good idea. And I'll go back to it after the war because I can't think of anything else to do."

'After the war'. Dear old Otto, believing in that.

"What about you?" he asked.

I've killed too many men, I wanted to say. *How could I become a lawyer after that – even if I were still alive?*

"Oh, I'm not making any plans," I said. "Apart from seeing Karl."

That set him off chattering about Heidelberg, while I stared into my glass and tried not to think.

"Christ, you were looking solemn over dinner," Horstmann said to me later.

"Otto was talking about university."

"Oh. Not something I ever – well, it was cadet school for me, as you know… I suppose your whole class joined up."

"That's about the size of it. Not many left now."

"Nor of my classmates, either." He refilled our glasses. "Only one thing to do!"

Brockmann sat down at the piano and we had a good sing-song. He couldn't play like Karl, of course, but well enough for us to sing.

Patschke used to ask for marching songs.

"Any requests?" asked Brockmann.

Otto grinned at Horstmann. "How about 'I stand in Darkest Midnight'?"

Everyone laughed.

"I'd like that, too," said the Chief.

"Right," said Brockmann. "Here we go – for every man with a sweetheart at home, and for Fellmann!"

"How do you know Fellmann doesn't have a sweetheart?" said Eichner. "They come in all shapes and sizes, after all!"

Fellmann suddenly looked completely miserable, and turned away on pretence of lighting his cigar. *You must miss Johnny terribly.*

"She loves me still—" *How Patschke used to take the piss out of Horstmann!*

I got wrecked, with no thought as to the morning. *There's no point watching how much I drink. The outcome will be exactly the same. I'll be joining the others soon enough.*

Teuffel came back from leave, and gave Bretti a very suspicious look.

"You'll get court-martialled for that," he said.

"For what?" asked Bretti.

"Impersonating an officer!" said Teuffel, and then clapped him on the back. "Well done, Bretti, very well deserved."

"Shut up, for fuck's sake!" said Horstmann. "Or the little bastard's head won't fit through the mess door!"

The winter solstice was almost upon us, and we waved Bretti off on leave with his haversack crammed with cheese, tinned food and even some real coffee.

"Bloody hell, this is heavy!" he said as he picked it up.

Horstmann and I laughed.

"Not compared to what you'd have been carrying in the infantry," Horstmann said. "Even as an officer!"

"Thank you all so much – my parents will be really pleased."

"Now bugger off and give our love to the homeland," said Benner.

"And to as many lovely German girls as possible," said Otto.

"I shall do my best!"

"Lucky bastard," said Brockmann. "Christmas at home!"

"We'll have a bloody good one here," I said. "You'll see."

Just like last year, but with so many different faces…

We had a Christmas Eve party for the whole squadron, and this time I handed Zaffke his present.

"This is from Leutnant von Leussow as well as from me," I said.

"Thank you, sir – and I'll write to thank him as well."

"He'd like that," I said.

All I could think as we sang carols round the tree was that this was my last Christmas. *Well, at least I'm spending it with good blokes.*

Everyone looked wistful in the candlelight, remembering families and sweethearts so far away…

We had a very lazy Christmas morning and sat down to a late lunch.

The food wasn't quite as good as the year before, but then Fellmann, the Chief, Otto and I were the only men who could remember that.

I looked round the table. *This time last year Karl was here, and Johnny – no, hang on, Johnny went to their pa at General von Grimnitz's HQ – and poor old Widemayer. Then there was the Prof, Geschke had Christmas leave, and – I've left someone out. Oh, yes – Buchholz, but he was in hospital.*

And there was someone who crashed just before Christmas, but I can't remember his name.

Three of those men are dead, and most of those who've come here since. The Prof's the only one who's unscathed, in his laboratory. Widemayer's probably locked up somewhere.

Karl's having Christmas by himself. That'll be fun, in that big house with memories for company.

"Bloody hell, Becker, that's a long face," said Otto. "You'd better be grateful we don't have the Court of Riotous Behaviour any more."

"I was thinking about last Christmas, and about Karl."

"At least he's safe now."

"Yes… be good to see him next month."

The Chief was rapping on the table. "Gentlemen—"

There was a sudden noise of aircraft engines, and then an almighty explosion right outside the mess. The windows blew in as we hit the floor.

"What the blazes—" Horstmann began, but the rest of the sentence was drowned out by the next detonation.

"Fucking bastards!" exclaimed Otto.

There were two more loud bangs and then the engines retreated. Just as we raised our heads they started getting louder again.

Then we heard machine-gun fire. Our two ground-based guns, and one – no, two sets of aircraft guns.

And then they were gone.

We picked ourselves up off the mess floor and surveyed the wreckage. Everything was covered in broken glass, including the table.

Fucking bastards. It's Christmas Day, for God's sake.

Quite a contrast to 1914.

"At least we'd finished eating," said Böhle.

Horstmann shook his head. "Typical – thinking only of your stomach!"

"I'll go and check on the ground crew, sir," said Fellmann.

"I'll make sure Bleif and co are all right and then I'll be right with you," the Chief said.

The rest of us went outside with Fellmann. There were four craters in the field, one right by the main hut. Luckily none of the bombs had fallen on the hangars or on our gravel strip.

The ground crew were emerging, looking rather shocked, and Braun and Zaffke were walking towards us from the machine-gun pit.

"Everyone all right?" asked the Chief.

"Yes, sir," said Schiffer. "Their aim was bloody awful."

"We missed the fuckers as well, sir," Zaffke said with obvious disgust.

"What were they?"

"Camels, sir," Braun replied. "Two of them."

"Well done, both of you," the boss said. "You took quite a chance going out there."

"We couldn't let them get away with that, sir," said Zaffke. "Not without fighting back."

Definitely better to be on the same side as the Brandenburg Corps. Right bunch of gung-ho, aggressive bastards.

The Chief looked at his watch. "It's 3pm our time, so 2pm Tommy-side."

He looked round. Fellmann was just coming out of Hangar Two.

"Fellmann, what's the situation?"

"Minor damage to Horstmann's Triplane and Brockmann's Pfalz, sir, but that's all. Except that the oil store took a couple of hits, so we'll need a fresh delivery."

"How much have we got left?"

"Enough for two days' flying."

"Right." He turned to us. "The Tommies have their presents on Christmas Day. Anyone up for making them a gift of lead?"

"Yes, sir!" said nine voices in unison.

"Is mine airworthy?" asked Horstmann.

Fellmann shook his head. "And neither is yours, Brockmann. Sorry."

"Not as sorry as we are," said Horstmann.

Half an hour later we were climbing into the afternoon sky. *I wish I hadn't had quite so much to eat. It's rather disagreeing with me. And I don't usually have that much to drink before I fly – though I feel stone-cold fucking sober now.*

The Chief led us low over the lines, and I had a glimpse of astonished faces turned up towards us. No Man's Land was a filthy, cratered swamp – and then the figures below wore khaki, but we'd passed before they could reach for their rifles.

We didn't know which base the Camels had come from, and we didn't care. We just headed for the nearest one and shot it up properly, hangars, huts and aircraft, and then climbed as rapidly as we could and set off home.

The flak gunners opened up but missed as usual, and a couple of enterprising Tommies had a pop at us – and we were back home in no time.

"That was the shortest patrol I've ever been on," Benner remarked.

"I wish I knew how much damage we did," said Eichner.

"I don't think that matters, sir," said Braun.

"Quite," said the Chief. "Great shame that things have sunk to this level."

"Yes," I said. "Not like the first Christmas."

"Did you have a truce where you were?" asked Böhle.

"Yes, we did. It was quite extraordinary – the war just stopped for a day. But then no one thought it would go on, did they?"

X

We headed for the mess.

"It's going to be bloody unpleasant without windows," said Horstmann.

"At least our quarters are undamaged," said Schulte. "That would be far worse."

"Oh, you'd manage," I said. "It's amazing what you get used to."

Bleif and co had almost finished sweeping up the glass.

"Well done, chaps," said the Chief.

"Don't sit down, sir!" Bleif called out hurriedly. "We need to check all the chairs first."

"You fellows carry on," said the boss. "We'll take some bottles to the Ops Office."

That and his office were on the other side of the hut, and still had windows.

Möller looked up expectantly. "Did the Tommies like their Christmas present, sir?"

The Chief gave a rather grim smile. "Probably about as much as we did. Where's Leutnant Fellmann?"

"Gone to the village with Aircraftman Zaffke, sir, looking for windows."

"Thank God for Zaffke," said Horstmann.

"Indeed," agreed the Chief.

They arrived back at about seven, with three complete windows. By that time we were back in the mess, wearing our flying kit against the cold – though we were all too full of booze to feel it.

"These were the closest to the right size that we could find," Fellmann said. "Zaffke reckons he can get them to fit."

"I'm sorry, sir, but I won't be able to fit them all this evening," said Zaffke. "I could probably manage one, and board up the other two until the morning."

"Zaffke, you may do whatever you judge necessary," replied the Chief.

"It'll be a bit noisy, sir," Zaffke said doubtfully.

"Let's all go to my room," said Fellmann. "I'll just have to trust you all not to wreck it!"

"I'll bring the gramophone," said Böhle.

"And I'll bring the records," said Schulte.

"I suppose the rest of us can bring the booze, then!" I said, and we traipsed along the duckboards.

Some time later Zaffke knocked to say he'd finished.

"I'm not sure I can be bothered to get up," said Teuffel, who was on the floor reclining against the side of Fellmann's bed.

"Well, I'm off to bed," said the Chief.

"Back to the mess, then," I said. "Thank you for an excellent Christmas, sir – even if it did take an unexpected turn!"

The boss laughed. "We wouldn't want to be bored, would we?!"

The mess looked almost normal, and frankly we were too pissed to care.

"Bloody good blokes we've got," said Horstmann.

Bleif brought in champagne and snacks, and looked quite astonished as we cheered him loudly.

"We should send some out to the ground crew," said Brockmann. "Their Christmas got messed up as well."

Fellmann smiled. "I did that earlier. They should be very mellow by now!"

"Strange Christmas this turned out to be," Otto said in my ear.

I started laughing and couldn't stop. "Bretti missed all the fun! He's probably having a really dull time at home, with church and the family, when he could have been shooting up the Tommies' airfield with us!"

My hangover the next day was truly impressive. Horstmann and I dragged ourselves to the mess mid-morning.

"Something doesn't look right," Horstmann said, peering at the room rather blearily.

"No. But I don't know what."

After a few minutes we gave up scratching our heads and sat down to rolls – which I couldn't really face – and coffee and cigarettes, which I desperately needed.

"Neat job Zaffke did," Eichner commented.

I looked at the table, and the chairs. They didn't seem to have any fresh repairs, but then Zaffke's work tended not to show.

Eichner started laughing. "Your faces! Do you really not know what's different?"

Teuffel gave us a very serious look. "You know booze has really got out of hand when it messes up your memory."

"There's nothing wrong with my memory," said Horstmann, somewhat testily. "I'm perfectly aware that we had an altercation with the Tommies yesterday, and that all the windows – ah! That's what's different!"

In place of our old, plain windows we had more ornate ones, clearly from three different houses. None of them quite matched the apertures, and Zaffke had tailored the frames to fit. The result was rather picturesque.

"Very neat job," I said.

"We should get Zaffke an extra present," said Brockmann.

"Yes," agreed Eichner. "The question is what?"

"I'll ask Braun," I said. "He might have an idea."

After breakfast I set off for the hangars. I wanted to talk to Zaffke as well, about something Sonnenberg had said.

Uhlig was sanding the propeller of my Triplane.

"It's the gravel, sir," he explained. "Bounces up and nicks the blades. You'll need a new one in a month or so."

No, I won't. In a month I'll either be dead or in Germany.

"Do you know where I can find Braun or Zaffke?"

"I think they're in Hangar Two, sir."

"Thanks."

I found Zaffke first.

"Zaffke," I said, "there's something I want to ask you… You remember Hauptmann Graf Sonnenberg, who came here with Frau von Lentzke?"

"Yes, sir."

"Did you know he was in the 24th?"

Zaffke's face cracked into a grin. "Was he, now, sir? I thought there was something about him."

"He mentioned a wood, at the beginning at Verdun." Zaffke's face clouded instantly and I regretted having raised the subject, but I could hardly stop at that point. "Said it was a nasty place. Was that the Caillette Wood?"

"No, sir – that was our second time in," he said slowly. "The first wood was where I got hit. We lost half the company there. What was it Herr Leutnant wanted to know?"

"Just that it was the same place, that's all." I hadn't the heart to pry any further. "And I wanted to thank you for the excellent job you did on the mess windows – you were wasted in the infantry, that's for sure."

"Thank you, sir."

Braun was at the back of the hangar.

"Braun, do you have a minute?"

"Of course, sir."

"Let's walk out to the front of the hangar, get some fresh air."

Schwarte was patching holes in Eichner's aircraft, and the smell of dope was powerful.

Once we were outside I said, "Zaffke's done a superb job on the mess windows, and we certainly keep him busy mending the furniture."

There was a hint of a smile, which Braun was far too well-disciplined to allow to develop.

"And neither of those tasks is within his proper duties," I went on. "So we'd all like to give him a token of our appreciation, but we don't know what."

Braun thought for a moment. "Well, sir – this wouldn't exactly be for him, but he's got two sons, and he said they've got pictures of all the aces on their bedroom wall, cut out from the papers. So a signed photograph of the Oberleutnant would make him very happy."

"Thanks, Braun – that's perfect, and very easy to arrange."

I went to the boss's office. "Sir, we want to get a present for Zaffke, to thank him for sorting out the mess windows – and the furniture, now and then."

The Chief smiled. "That's an excellent idea. What did you have in mind?"

"I've just been talking to Braun, and he said Zaffke's sons would love a signed picture of you."

"Is that all? It seems a bit thin, but if that's what he wants... Hold on, though – there are three Pour le Mérites in the squadron. How about one of each of us? We can give him yours and mine here, and you can get Leussow to sign one of him and send it straight to Zaffke's home."

"We'll have to get Fellmann to present them." *It would look awfully big-headed doing it ourselves.*

"Yes, definitely – not the sort of thing we can do ourselves, after all." He paused, and then added, "It might be better to make it private. We don't want to sow discord, or for any of the others to think he's been currying favour."

"No, sir, I see what you mean. We could just hand them to him in the mess, next time he mends something for us, and then roll them up into one of those cardboard tubes to send home."

"Good idea. Let's sign them now and give them to Fellmann."

He didn't need to say why we had to sign them right then. The weather was clearing, and there was just time for a patrol before it got dark.

Needless to say the Tommies had not been impressed with their Christmas present, and they were out for blood.

You started it, I thought as the Jasta engaged two flights of Camels – but as with all quarrels, the origin was no longer relevant.

The Chief got one, which gave us another excuse for a party, and Eichner sent another out of the fight with petrol streaming from his fuel tank, but of course that didn't count.

And that was it for the year. On New Year's Eve everyone assembled in the mess, and the boss made exactly the same speech as the year before. Those who remembered pretended not to notice, and we all applauded at the end of it.

Horstmann's lethal punch got the party off to a good start. At some point in the early hours of the morning I was sitting on the small sofa, glass in one hand and fag in the other.

So many men have died. I can't possibly list all those who I knew who've fallen. If I just stick to my friends, there are Anton, Kurt, Burkhardt… I don't even want to think about all those we lost in the regiment. Just out of the snipers there was Spots, Dietz – and then if I start going through my old squadron…

"Becker. *Becker.*" I looked up. Teuffel was standing over me with a bottle of schnapps in his hand.

"Stop staring into space and have another drink!"

Böhle and Schulze had the gramophone going. Eichner was dancing with Benner, Brockmann and Fellmann were having a 'sabre' fight with chair legs, which got really silly as Otto and Beilke joined in.

How could I not have noticed all that row?

Teuffel sat next to me.

"You look like a man who's *thinking*," he said gravely. "And you really don't want to do that!"

"No, you're right!"

"Come and dance!" Horstmann pulled me to my feet.

Things went downhill from there. The table objected to five of us jumping up and down on it, and threw us off in a tangled heap.

I crawled back to the sofa, my head swimming.

Absent friends, the Chief said after we drank to the Kaiser and to victory. God, that sounded hollow. Every bloody New Year we've drunk to victory.

But this time it just might happen. The Russians are out of the war now.

Absent friends. Since last New Year we've lost: Geschke, Buchholz, Johnny, Lensch, Lentzke—

Otto grabbed me and dragged me to the middle of the room. "We used to have – have a trad – tradish – wha's word?"

"You're pissed," I said.

"And you're being serious at a party."

Horstmann had a dangerous glint in his eye.

"Schulte, put the Liesl song on," I said desperately.

And bless him, he did, and by the end of the first verse all danger of the Court seemed over.

Leichardt – no, he went before Christmas '16, so he's one of that year's dead. Come on, Franz – you can't just forget them all.

Patschke, Westermann, of course – how could I have forgotten him? – Reinhold – the names went round and round in my head.

The song had finished.

Lensch, Leichardt, Patschke – who have I forgotten? Poor little Hauschke, bleeding to death with Karl, of all men, holding his hand, Schaff…

I left the others to their games, and went to bed and stared at the ceiling in the darkness. *No 'fireworks' this year – there's no Johnny.*

That's it, then. Won't see next New Year.

The thought was still there in the morning, and I couldn't get rid of it.

Zaffke came in to repair the furniture, and we took the opportunity to give him the signed portraits.

His face lit up. "Thank you so much, sir – my boys will love these."

"There's one more to come," said the Chief. "Leutnant Becker will be going on leave soon, and he's going to visit Leutnant von Leussow, so your boys will have one of him as well."

He looked even happier at that, understandably given the history they shared.

"We'll send it to your home from his house," I said.

"Thank you, sir – and do give him my very best wishes."

I only have to survive four more days, I thought as we suited up. *Then I'll have three weeks of guaranteed life.*

I put that idea out of my head.

The day was bitterly, appallingly cold – even with grease on my face and a scarf wrapped round it, and two thick sweaters between my uniform and my flying suit, I was chilled to the bone in no time. *It'll be even worse after a fight or two, when I'm soaked through.* I wiggled my toes to try to get some blood flowing through them.

We were flying as two Kettes and a four, in loose formation – close enough to see and support each other, but far enough apart to have room to manoeuvre.

It was Böhle who saw them – a pair of those Bristol two-seaters, over our side. Horstmann's four peeled off to deal with them.

So where are the fighters? They'll be here somewhere.

The afternoon sky was bright, a layer of cirrus diffusing the sunlight. I scanned the pale expanse until my eyes hurt, my nerves winding up almost unbearably. *I'm sure it never used to be this bad—*

SHIT! My stomach turned over with a sharp jolt as I saw two flights of Camels, higher than us and just rolling into their dive. We scattered and turned to meet them.

The leader of one flight went straight for me. *Yes, it's Franz Becker, with the white knight on his fuselage and the Blue Max round his neck. Wouldn't you love to have me on your victory list?*

But you're going to have to do better than that. As am I if I want you...

Neither of us could quite get on the other's tail – and then one of his mates joined in, and I saw two of the others attacking the boss.

Schulte flashed in front of my nose, pursued by a Camel, with Benner after that and another after him, and I pulled up sharply. The onset of the buffet was sudden in the thin air, and I had to relax the back pressure and ease the bank – and that let one of the bastards close in behind me.

His first burst went wide, but the second whined round my ears and one even pinged off the edge of the windscreen – and then to my utter horror there was a sharp stink of petrol.

The tank was holed. Vapour was pouring out in a white trail which I saw only too clearly as I turned my head.

Shit – I'm going to burn. Fuel's spraying out, the engine's nice and hot, I'm under fire, and I've got phosphorus tracer rounds in the belts.

I shut the engine down instantly, fired all my remaining ammunition into space, and dived out of the fight as hard as

I could, sick terror churning in my guts. The Tommy followed and gave me another burst.

One spark and the vapour will ignite, then the fabric will catch, followed by the wood and my clothes and me. I'll be a screaming mass of flame and then a shrivelled, charred lump like Johnny and the others.

When it catches it'll go in no time. I fumbled to unfasten my harness, my hands shaking. *I have to get out in time, not like Johnny. How long will it take me to fall to earth?*

At least that won't hurt.

Fear was replaced by absolute finality. *I'll never see Karl again*, I thought with profound, overwhelming sadness. *I was so looking forward to it—*

The Camel broke off and climbed back towards the others.

I was clear of the fight, and as I checked my tail I saw that the vapour trail was no more.

The fuel had all gone.

Nausea rose in my throat, and I ripped my scarf and stocking off and vomited over the side, and then sagged, shaking, in my seat.

Fucking hell…

Get a grip, Franz. Strap yourself in and find somewhere to land. And for fuck's sake don't wreck the bus and break your neck. That would be just too stupid.

At least we were over our side, and we'd been good and high when it happened, so I wasn't faced with trying to land in the maze of rear and comms trenches.

The water in the fields gleamed in the afternoon sun. *Why does Flanders have to be such a fucking great swamp? There must be a dry bit somewhere.*

But there wasn't, and I had to decide.

There was a howitzer battery, and the ground around it didn't look too bad, apart from a nasty rutted area where they must have moved the guns in.

I got the nose a bit higher than usual for the landing so the tailskid would touch first, and for a moment I thought we'd got away with it. Then the mud gripped the wheels harder, and my poor Triplane stood on her nose and stuck there.

Three artillerymen were running towards me, and one had a fag in his hand.

"*Stop there!!*" My voice came out cracked and hoarse.

They faltered.

"HALT, DAMN IT!!"

They halted. I unstrapped myself, climbed awkwardly onto the rim of the cockpit, and jumped clear of the wings. My feet slipped, and I landed on my arse with a splash.

The three men looked at each other, clearly wondering what to do.

"Are you hurt, sir?" one of them called out, cautiously promoting me to Hauptmann.

"No, I'm fine. And it's Leutnant." I clambered to my feet, slipping and sliding.

"Can we help you, sir?" asked the man with the cigarette.

"Not with that in your hand," I said. "There's fuel all over the place. Can you fetch whoever's in command?"

"Of course, sir."

I started walking away from the aircraft, and realised that the smell of petrol was accompanying me. My jacket and flying suit were soaked with it.

Fucking hell.

I need to get out of these.

My shaking hands fumbled desperately with the buttons, and I managed to get the jacket off just as their Leutnant approached.

"Here, let me give you a hand," he said, and pulled the flying suit off my shoulders.

"Thanks," I said, struggling out of it and my heavy boots.

"Christ, you blokes wear a lot of kit," he said as I rolled up the petrol-soaked clothes and stuffed them into the cockpit. Fortunately my sweaters were dry – the sun was sinking, and the temperature was falling fast under the clear sky.

"It's bloody cold up there," I replied. "Becker."

"Birkmayer. What happened?"

"The fuel tank got—" I couldn't say another word.

He handed me his hip flask, and I took a hefty swig of spirit.

"Cheers," I croaked.

"You must be bloody frozen," he said loudly, and then added more quietly, "Come to our command post and thaw out – it's not much but it's home."

"Don't worry – I was in the trenches."

"Oh, Christ – it's not as bad as that!"

No, I'll bet it isn't, all the way back here – but then you get the crap shelled out of you as well.

He led the way towards a cottage which bore the scars of the Tommies' attentions. An officer cadet and a Sergeant were standing outside it, looking at me with curiosity.

"This is Leutnant Becker," said Birkmayer, and introduced the other two as Woitzik and Schrempp respectively.

"That looked interesting, sir," said Woitzik.

I needed a crap, and badly. Very badly. And my underwear was wet and heavy with sweat, and I hoped that was all it was.

"Where's your latrine?"

"Oh, we do better than that! We've got a proper earth closet, with seats," said Birkmayer with a grin. "That door there."

"Thanks."

There was a proper roll of lavatory paper as well. *Beats the hell out of doing it on a spade and chucking it out of the shell-hole, or perching on a beam over a pit and hoping the shells don't land too close.* And – thank God – I hadn't shit myself. Which I would have been fully entitled to do.

Birkmayer was waiting by the cottage door.

"I'll need to phone my squadron," I said.

"Yes, of course. Do you want to do that first – or rather second?!"

I laughed. "Yes, please."

The cottage was more like a hovel, with one large room on the ground floor partitioned into two. One part held the map table and the telephone, and Schrempp stood up as we entered.

He got the squadron on the line for me. Möller answered.

"Möller, it's Becker. Could I speak to Leutnant Fellmann?"

"Yes, of course, sir. One moment."

"What have you wrecked now?" Fellmann asked with feigned weariness.

"Oh, not much – just a hole in the fuel tank, and she's standing on her nose in the mud. Don't worry, your precious engine should be all right, it wasn't under power."

"I'd guessed that, being as you'd lost the fuel. Honestly, Becker, we give you a perfectly good Triplane and you wreck the poor thing! Where are you, anyway?"

"Visiting the howitzers. Hang on, I'll put Leutnant Birkmayer on – he can tell you."

"What – you've found an artilleryman who knows where he is? All right, put him on."

A couple of minutes later Birkmayer hung up and turned to me.

"They'll be about two hours," he said. "Might as well get warm and have a drink!"

The other part of the room was comfortably furnished with scavenged odds and ends. Most of the windows were boarded up, giving it a rather dingy air, but a fire was blazing cheerfully in the grate.

I glanced at it and turned my back quickly.

"Smoke?" offered Birkmayer.

"Thanks."

I forced myself to look at the flame of his lighter. *I have to face down my fear, or it'll start to take me over.*

I peeled off my sweaters. Birkmayer stared at me open-mouthed, and for a moment I wondered why.

Then I remembered my Blue Max. I wasn't showing off by wearing it – the regulations stated that it was to be worn at all times when in uniform.

"Er – what did you say your name was?"

"Becker, Franz."

"Bloody hell! My Oberleutnant will be so pissed off when he gets back from leave. He's itching to join the Air Service and he reads everything he can get his hands on about fliers. He'd have given his eye teeth to meet you."

"Oh," I said, very embarrassed. It had never occurred to me that anyone fighting on the ground would be interested in our exploits.

Just as well I didn't shit myself. That would have been too good a story.

"Has he applied?" I asked.

"Several times. Passed the medical for pilot training, but the Colonel won't release him – you'll appreciate we've been rather busy."

"It certainly looked that way."

Woitzik put his head through the door, gave me a look of blank astonishment and left quickly.

Oh, fuck – he's probably gone to tell everyone he can find.

Sure enough, a couple of minutes later he came back with a Hauptmann, two Leutnants, and two more cadets.

"It would give the chaps a real morale boost if you came and spoke to them," said the Hauptmann.

My scepticism must have shown, because he went on, "We got seven colours of shit knocked out of us during the Tommies' big offensive – and we often saw your chaps shooting down their spotter aircraft. To be honest we could have done with a bit more of that, but we saw their fighters having a go at you as well."

"Well, sir, of course I will, if you think they'd like it—"

But won't they think I'm some posing prat who has a nice easy life?

"That's settled, then. Come on."

I reached for my sweaters.

"They'll want to see the gong," he said.

It was bloody freezing outside, but my blushes kept me warm as I was taken from gun to gun. I'd never been so embarrassed in my life. I shook hands with everyone, and tried to deflect their questions by asking about their service and their families. The last thing I wanted to do was talk about myself.

By the time we'd finished it was dark, and I was chilled to the bone and starving. I'd lost my lunch, after all.

"Thank you," said the Hauptmann, whose name I'd forgotten. "I'd better let you thaw out – and your people should be here soon."

As the words left his mouth there was loud hooting, and the squadron lorry drew up.

Fellmann climbed down, setting his feet carefully into the mud.

"All right, Becker, where's your wreck?!"

The Hauptmann bristled slightly.

"I do apologise, sir – I didn't see you," Fellmann said, saluting smartly. "It is a bit dark."

"So it is – can we offer you gentlemen a drink?"

"We'd love one, thank you," I said just as Fellmann answered, "Yes, thank you – but I should look at the aircraft first."

"I'd better be getting back to my guns," said the Hauptmann. He turned to me. "Thank you so much – I could see the men really appreciated your taking the trouble."

"My pleasure, sir."

Birkmayer looked very pleased with himself, as did Woitzik, and I realised their stock had probably risen.

"Been the centre of attention, have you?" Fellmann asked with a grin as we made our way to my Triplane.

"Oh, shut up!"

"Braun, can you move the truck so the headlights point this way?" Fellmann called out.

Braun, Zaffke and Uhlig joined us. The stink of petrol was very apparent, and I started shaking again as I realised how soaked everything had got.

There was a spatter of vomit down the side of the fuselage and on the tailplane.

No point trying to pretend I wasn't scared.

"Better not smoke anywhere near this," Braun said quietly.

"It's my flying suit and jacket as well," I said. "They're rolled up in the cockpit."

All four of them looked at me, and then at each other. They all looked as if they wanted to say something, but didn't know what.

Fellmann's face was heavily shadowed, his eyes full of sorrow.

Losing Johnny's really hit you hard.

"Let's get this disassembled and in the lorry," he said, "and then we can get home."

"Would you like to warm up again?" asked Birkmayer. "You must be frozen, but we really did appreciate it. And you'd be very welcome as well," he added, turning to Fellmann.

"Thank you," we both said. The ground crew didn't need our help and we'd only be in their way.

This time there was tea with rum, and cheese rolls. The smell of petrol had taken my appetite away, but I forced myself to eat one.

I have to keep a grip. I can't start feeling sick and scared at the smell of fuel, or at the sight of a tame fire. I stared at the flames in the grate. *They won't hurt you – and you were going to jump, anyway.*

Suppose I get hit and can't get out? What happens then?
No point thinking about it.

Fellmann and Birkmayer were chattering away, and I suddenly realised I was ignoring Woitzik.

"Sorry," I said to him. "Miles away."

"That's all right," he said. There was a pause and then he added, "We took a direct hit back in the summer, before they moved us here, and I was buried for hours."

That's a nice way of saying you understand.

"You know, that always used to bother me in the trenches," I said.

"Yes," he went on, "it was pitch-dark, and one of the fellows was trapped with me, but he – well, he died before they got to us."

He stared into space for a moment.

"Where were you?" he asked.

"Not too far from here," I replied, and we got talking properly. In no time Braun was knocking to tell us that they were ready to leave.

Fellmann and I sat in the front with Zaffke, who was driving.

"We'll get you a new flying suit and jacket," said Fellmann.

"No, don't – I'd rather keep those. Most of it will wash out."

"If you're sure," he said doubtfully.

"Yes, I am."

I wasn't superstitious – at least I tried not to be – but I'd scored all my victories in that kit, and so far I'd remained unscathed. Physically, anyway.

I was overcome by weariness, and I closed my eyes for a moment – and woke with a yell as my clothes caught fire.

"Sorry."

"Don't worry," said Fellmann.

"No trouble, sir," said Zaffke kindly.

You must have yours after Verdun.

"Where are we?"

"Nearly there, sir."

A few minutes later we turned in through the airfield gates, and I remembered that I'd thrown up all down the side of my Triplane.

Oh shit, everyone's going to see that. It's almost as bad as being sick in front of them all.

I forced myself to look as the fuselage was wheeled into Hangar One. To my relief the left-hand side was rather muddy, but with no trace of vomit. I checked the other side, just to be sure, and it was the same.

"Thanks," I said to Braun.

"No need, sir. We'll wash the petrol off, put her back together, fit a new propeller and do the engine runs, and she'll be ready for first thing. We could clean your flying kit at the same time."

The night sky was starry, with the promise of a fine dawn. *Best to get straight back on the horse, Franz.*

"Thanks, Braun – much appreciated."

"The wanderer returns!" Otto called out as I entered the mess.

"Cheers, mate, buggering off and leaving us!" said Benner.

"I love you too," I replied. "Not much I could do with fuel pouring out everywhere."

They exchanged eloquent glances.

"Collect one through the tank?" asked Horstmann, with a poor attempt at nonchalance.

"That's right. Sprayed everywhere," I said in the same sort of tone. "I'd better make my report."

I left them sitting in silence, and went to the boss's office.

"Ah, Becker – welcome home! I saw you leaving the fight – what happened?"

I knew he would have been told, and that he just wanted my account.

"Got one through the fuel tank, sir. The stuff was going everywhere."

The Chief was one of the calmest and most self-controlled men I've ever met. Nothing seemed to bother him – but in that moment I saw fear flicker in his eyes.

"So I shut the engine down and fired off all the ammunition, and ended up with the howitzer crew."

"Well done. Will she be ready for dawn?"

"Braun reckons so, sir – and they're going to get the petrol out of my kit as well."

I actually managed to get the last words out in a reasonably level tone. God knows how, because I was starting to shake.

"Good. Well, I'm very pleased there's no severe damage."

Not as pleased as I am. "The howitzer crews were very interested in flying, sir. It got a bit embarrassing."

He smiled. "I know just what you mean."

"So I thought, being as they were so hospitable, maybe we should send them one of those signed photos of you."

"It should be you, not me – and I think that's a very good idea. Have a word with Fellmann. And get yourself a stiff drink or two."

I felt very awkward asking Fellmann to send the photograph.

"It's a really good idea," he said. "Look, Becker, I know it feels like self-promotion, but I've seen how much people appreciate those pictures – and don't forget, they're negotiable currency!"

I laughed. "Maybe it'll be some use to them, then!"

The gramophone was going and the atmosphere in the mess was quite jolly. Everyone knew that Death was standing at our shoulders, and that the only questions were *how* and *when*.

I felt as if I'd been given a warning, and let off until another day. That made it party time – and besides, the boss had ordered me to have a drink or two…

Three more days, I thought as I fell onto my bed.

To my surprise I didn't have any nightmares – I woke in the early hours with a profoundly disturbed feeling, and lay awake for what felt like hours, but that was all.

But I shook as I was shaving and cut myself twice, and appeared in the mess with two scraps of paper stuck to my face.

I tried to eat a roll but it turned to sawdust in my mouth, and I gave up and stuck to fortified coffee.

It can't get much worse than yesterday. I suddenly felt more optimistic. *That's almost as close as I can get to buying it without it actually happening.*

My kit still smelled faintly of petrol.

"Am I safe to smoke?" I asked Uhlig with a grin.

"I reckon so, sir!" he replied and lit my cigarette.

Böhle and Brockmann took a step away from me.

"Chicken!" I teased.

Both flying suit and jacket were still damp, and there was frost on the ground. *This is going to be fun.*

By the time we got to three thousand I was longing to meet the Tommies, just so I could warm up a bit.

I wasn't disappointed, on that flight or on the other that day. And on that second patrol I got a two-seater.

That's for the artillery boys.

It was amazing how much better I felt in the evening. *I can still do it. I had the fright of my life yesterday, but today I'm back in business.*

Two more days.

Just two more days.

Bretti came back the next day, looking rather unhappy. *Can't say I blame you for that.*

"Good leave?" asked Otto.

"Yes and no – I mean, it was bloody good to be home for Christmas and to see my parents, but everything's so bloody grim. There's nothing to eat, everyone's so thin, so many people are wearing black."

"No fun, then?" Böhle asked with a grin.

"Oh, well, yes – plenty of girls feeling lonely—"

"So you let them feel you instead!"

Bretti looked a bit more cheerful. "I didn't go without," he said modestly.

"It's those nice new epaulettes," said Benner very seriously.

"Bollocks!" retorted Brockmann. "I've been wearing them for two years now and they haven't done me much good."

"That's because you're so ugly!" said Teuffel.

"Anyway, my parents said to thank you all very much for the food," said Bretti.

We had a party to welcome him back, of course, but any relief at being back to full strength was short-lived – the day before I left we lost Böhle, down in flames over No Man's Land.

I got completely pissed at the wake, because I wasn't flying the next day and I knew I would live another three weeks.

And that night, just when I wasn't expecting it, I had the fucking burning dream again and woke screaming.

"I reckon a fellow's entitled to have bad dreams after getting – after your interesting experience the other day," said Horstmann.

"At least you've got three weeks of peace and quiet now," I said.

He snorted. "I should be so lucky! You'll probably have a new room-mate when you get back. Berlin, you jammy fucking bastard. Women. German women. I bet Leussow takes you to meet those dancers again."

"Who knows?" I could hardly tell him what I had in mind for my week with Karl. "He might not be well enough."

"There is that... Look, I'm going to try to get a bit more sleep."

I turned my bedside light off reluctantly and lay staring at the ceiling, afraid to close my eyes. *No one's going to try to kill you for three whole weeks – just be happy with that.*

And I'm going to see Karl.

Fellmann took me to the station, loaded up with supplies as Bretti had been.

"Fellmann, can you really keep doing this?"

"As long as you keep shooting down Tommies and signing photographs! We just need Horstmann to get a few more, and Beilke."

"But won't that reduce the value of the currency?"

"Maybe – but we'd have more of it!"

As I got out of the car he said, "Give Leussow my best wishes, won't you?"

"Of course I will."

It was dark before I got to Germany. I had to change at Cologne, and as before, the station was full of soldiers. I stared, shocked, at the recruits on their way to the Front. They were skinny, half-grown boys, dressed up as men and weighed down by men's equipment.

That's the result of three and a bit years of war and privation. I'll bet the Tommies and the Frenchies don't look like that, never mind the Americans, who must be on their way across the Atlantic. They'll all be strapping great fellows – and how are those boys going to fight them?

They won't stand a hope in Hell.

Mixed in with the children were veterans, some with pinched, peaky faces. One Sergeant was leaning on a cane, and seemed to need it. *You should be in a training camp, not on your way back to the war.*

The proud pre-war Army was gone, all the best regiments decimated. I had the horrible feeling that our chance of victory had gone with it.

The station was freezing, the waiting room and café unheated, and there was next to nothing to eat. I ordered coffee and bread and margarine, and wondered what everything was made of. It all tasted peculiar, and I was hungry again the second I'd finished.

The civilians were just as Bretti had described – thin and miserable, worn down by lack of food, and hollow-eyed with worry.

This is a long way from the nation that went to war.

I bought a bottle of schnapps, and settled myself into a compartment on the train south. I was joined by a Grenadier Leutnant and a Jäger Oberleutnant, and we passed a few convivial hours playing skat, passing the bottle round, and smoking until we could hardly see each other.

Outside it was snowing steadily, and the compartment was freezing.

"Bloody hell, it's almost as cold in here as it was in my dugout," said the Grenadier.

"Warmer than at three thousand metres, though," I said.

"Wouldn't get me up there," the Jäger said. "Fucking well bonkers, the lot of you."

I glanced out of the window, and the swirling white curtain gave me a brief glimpse of the Rhine.

We marched down the dirt road, the unfamiliar weight of my pack digging into my shoulders, my boots still not quite broken in.

'Fast stands and true the Watch, the Watch on the Rhine,' we sang, our young voices ringing out into the autumn air.

I'll never be able to see the river again without that in my head. And how many of those men are still alive?

'And if my heart should break in death—' *How we'd belted that out, because of course it couldn't happen to us...*

"Becker. *Becker.*" I started and the compartment came back into focus. "Pass the bloody bottle, would you?" said the Grenadier.

"Sorry."

The Jäger was also looking out of the window. "Long time since I've been home."

"Stop thinking, you two," said the Grenadier. "We've got to empty this before my station."

The Jäger and I shook hands in Stuttgart. I wished him a broken neck and legs, and he wished me shots in the neck and stomach.

Not the only resemblance between war and the theatre.

Eventually I got to my home town, and regretted not wiring my family with my arrival time. Two fellows got off the train ahead of me and took the only two cabs.

Won't do me any harm to walk, and it might clear my head a bit. I certainly wasn't drunk, but I was aware that I'd had a drink.

My boots crunched through the fresh snow, and the weight of all the provisions from the Jasta increased with every few steps. *God, I'm so out of condition – when I was in the infantry I carried a lot more than this, kilometre after kilometre.*

There was the turning into my street... and there was our house. *Home. Home that I thought I'd never see again. My family will be waiting for me—*

But there were no bright welcoming lights. The curtains were all closed tight against the January cold.

I hope they're at home.

I rang the bell, and after a couple of minutes I heard footsteps. Klara opened the door and stared at me for a moment as if unable to speak or move. Then she smiled.

"Come in, sir – and welcome home."

"Thank you."

She moved to help me off with my haversack and coat, but I stopped her.

"Who is it?" asked Papa.

He appeared in the hall, and it was his turn to stand mute and rooted to the spot.

Then he recovered himself. "Franz, my boy, my dear boy—"

He took hold of my shoulders, turned me towards the hall light, and studied my face.

I had the feeling that there was something he didn't like, but that he didn't want to spoil the moment.

"Who is it?" Mama called out rather impatiently.

Papa laid his finger on his lips, and I followed him to the drawing room door.

He opened it wide.

Mama dropped her knitting, stood up and ran towards me. A second later I was in her arms.

No one's held me since Karl was shot down. I wrapped my arms round her, and for one absurd moment I felt as if I were a child again, as if the war had been a bad dream.

She, too, studied my face, and again I had the feeling that something wasn't quite right.

"Where's Johanna?"

"At a friend's house. She should be home soon," said Mama. "Take your coat off – we managed to get some coal."

The stove was giving off a bit of heat, which barely reached across the room.

This is what it's like in a well-off household. God help the poor.

Papa helped me off with my haversack.

"What on earth have you got in here? It weighs a ton!"

"Unpack it and see," I said.

He pulled out a small bag of coffee. My parents gazed at it in disbelief.

"Where on earth did you get that?" Mama asked.

"Fellmann – our technical officer – can get hold of just about anything."

Their eyes opened wide as Papa pulled out the tinned food and two loaves of good bread.

Mama started crying.

"Aren't you pleased to see me?" I teased.

"Of course – but we haven't seen things like this – except when your father…"

Buys on the black market, but no one admits to that.

"Do take your coat off," Papa said.

I could see the pride in their faces.

"Well done, my boy," he said, shaking my hand. "That looks very fine."

"Yes," said Mama. "Let me have a closer look."

I took my Pour le Mérite off and handed it to her.

"It's beautiful," she said. "To think the Kaiser gave you this!"

"The letter from our King was even better," said Papa. "We had it framed. You've done so well. We're both very proud of you."

Once again I had the feeling that something wasn't quite right.

I jumped as the front door banged. Seconds later, the drawing room door burst open and Johanna flew in with a gust of cold air.

"FRANZ!" she squealed, and threw herself at me.

I caught her and swung her round. "Hello, Sis!"

"God, you do smell of booze and fags!" she exclaimed.

Ah – maybe that's what the parents didn't like.

"Oh, I shared a compartment with a couple of other fellows, and we did have a few of both."

"Johanna, I've told you before about your language," said Mama.

Language? Better watch what I say, then.

"Why don't you both go and wash before dinner," Mama continued. "I'll take these things through to the kitchen – Klara will be so pleased."

"Make sure she gets a share, won't you," I said.

"Must look after the troops, eh?" Papa said jovially.

And you a Socialist.

Johanna and I went upstairs.

"Thanks for the condoms, Sis," I said quietly. "Much appreciated, I can tell you!"

"They were quite hard to get hold of," she said, and then started giggling. "But then I suppose that's the idea!"

"Christ, don't let the parents hear you! How's it going, anyway? Has Mama relented about the nursing?"

She pulled a face. "I'll tell you all about it tomorrow, out of the house... Where's your Blue Max? I really want to see it."

"I took it off to show Mama. Look, Sis, I'll see you downstairs – I want to change."

My bedroom was bloody cold and I changed quickly, and then looked in the mirror over the washstand to brush my hair – and had the most peculiar feeling, because I almost didn't recognise myself.

I've worn nothing but uniform since last June. And now I'm in civvies, and my face doesn't go with my clothes. Even if I survive the war, I'll never be a civilian again.

I'll ask Johanna about Maria tomorrow, I thought as I went downstairs. *I'd like to be sure their going away had nothing to do with me. Though it'll all be academic in a few weeks' time. Maybe I won't bother...*

"Sorry about the five o'clock shadow," I said. "I didn't get the chance to shave on the journey."

"Don't worry," said Johanna. "You look just like a disreputable tramp!"

"It's so nice to come home to a warm welcome!"

"I did think we'd have one of my better bottles with dinner," Papa said, "but I think you've had quite enough already."

You what? "Do I seem drunk?"

"Well, no, but you must have had a lot to smell of it like that."

Christ – you should see us on a party night.

"Let's have wine, Josef," said Mama. "I'm sure Franz knows when he's had enough."

The wine was beautiful, a fine, delicate Riesling. I looked at the label.

"Oh – I've been past here on the train, several times."

"After the war we'll take a tour along the Rhine," said Mama. "It always looks so beautiful in pictures."

"Oh, it is."

"And I'd love to go to Koblenz and see that big fortress – what's it called?"

"Ehrenbreitstein," said Papa.

'Fast stands and true the Watch, the Watch on the Rhine…' we sang as our boots beat the rhythm on the road.

'Christ, this pack's getting heavier by the minute,' said Anton.

'Bloody softies, you students!' Kempff retorted.

"Franz." Mama was looking at me with concern.

"What? Oh, sorry, miles away."

She and Papa exchanged glances.

"You must have been," she said with forced levity. "That was the third time I'd called you… We were so proud to see you in that film."

"Has that made it here?"

"Oh, yes," said Johanna. "All my friends want to meet you."

Do they really?

"I'm not sure that's a good idea," Papa said. "There have been quite a few scandals in the town – girls getting into – er, trouble. We don't want that in our family."

"Honestly, Papa," said Johanna. "We'd all be in one big group – there wouldn't be any chance of hanky-panky."

I suddenly saw what a lovely young woman my sister had become. *If anyone's giving it to her I'll bloody well kill him.*

"You shouldn't be thinking about things like that," Mama said sternly. "It's all those unsuitable books you keep reading."

"Make your mind up, Mama – you want me to work in the maternity hospital, and then you say I shouldn't think about how the babies got there."

"Don't speak to your mother like that!"

"Josef, she didn't mean to be rude. It's Franz's first evening – let's not fall out."

I nudged Johanna's foot under the table, and gave her a glance that was supposed to say 'shut up' as sympathetically as possible. She stuck her tongue out at me.

"And don't pull faces!" said Mama. "Franz is only here for a short time. It's a shame he can only spare us a week."

There was a definite edge to her voice.

"We'll talk about that after dinner," said Papa.

Dinner was over only too quickly. I was still hungry when Papa got up from the table, and I realised to my dismay that there wasn't any more.

I looked at my parents more closely, saw how thin and tired they looked. Papa was noticeably grey, and Mama's face was lined.

"Franz, let's talk about your leave in my study," Papa said.

It was bloody freezing in there. I swear I could see my breath clouding.

"I think it would be considerate of you to change your plans," he said.

No chance.

"I want to see Karl – I haven't seen him for months."

"You haven't seen us for months, either. Won't he be at Adlershof? Surely they'll want his opinion."

"I don't know if he'll be well enough."

"But he was shot down in July."

"Yes, and he only came out of hospital last month."

I didn't want to talk about how bad Karl had been.

"Can't you fly in the daytime and see him in the evenings?"

"No – it's too far. Anyway, I promised."

I knew he had no answer to that. I sighed quietly, wishing I hadn't had to mention the hospital. *I've seen far too much of those places, and I never want to find myself lying in one.*

"Franz, you're not listening!"

"Sorry, Papa. Look—"

I wanted to say that when you fought beside someone and trusted each other with your lives, that the bond between you was one of the strongest there is, but the words wouldn't come out and he had no way of understanding.

"You should be grateful to Karl. He's saved my life more than once."

"If your life was saved then you should thank God. And I don't see why I should feel grateful to that Prussian lout with the morals of an alley cat."

"He's not a lout – his family have owned their land for nearly three hundred years."

"That doesn't stop him being a lout, as you should know. I'd say the aristocracy – and especially the Junkers – produce more louts than the rest of society put together."

Oh, God, here we go – another Socialist diatribe. I used to believe in this, just as I used to believe in God. But it's all just words, and I've no time for priests or politicians.

I half-listened, because I didn't want to remember Karl's grey face twisting in agony, or the deep despair that had filled me as I sat on his bed.

He's alive and safe, and next week you'll be with him again.

"... cultureless barbarian boneheads, whose sole education consists of learning to tell one end of a gun from the other—"

"Let's go back to the drawing room," I interrupted. "It's rather cold in here."

And I could do with a brandy, but I doubt I'll get one.

He opened his mouth to say something else, and I just looked at him. Suddenly his expression changed and he got up abruptly.

"Any chance of a brandy?" I asked in the drawing room.

"I don't think you need one," Papa said.

"Of course I don't need one – only alcoholics *need* a drink," I replied. "But it is a nice way to finish a meal."

"Josef, give him a brandy, please," said Mama.

"Thanks."

Papa looked at me with disquiet. *Oh, for fuck's sake, it's only a bloody brandy, and a small one at that* – and then I realised the problem wasn't the drink. It was me.

I lit a cigarette, not wanting to meet his eyes. I knew what he'd seen, because I saw it in the mirror: the look every soldier had after a few months of war.

Everything I've had to do is written in my face.

"What would you like to do tomorrow?" asked Mama.

"As little as possible!"

"We could go to my club for lunch," said Papa. "And it would be rather nice to have a proper portrait of you, with all your medals. The one you sent is very nice, but it's a bit small."

Oh, shit. I really want to sit in some bloody photographer's studio like a stuffed dummy.

"Beilke – one of the other pilots – takes the pictures, but he can't print anything bigger."

"And we could go for a walk in the afternoon," said Johanna.

"Yes, I'd like that."

"I do hope you won't be bored," said Mama. "There's not much to do here."

"Peace and quiet will suit me just fine," I said with a smile.

But when I went to bed I wondered whether it would. I was dog-tired from the journey, but my nerves were too keyed up for sleep.

Suddenly a voice said, 'Murderer.'

I started violently.

'Murderer,' it repeated, then added, 'We're waiting for you', and there they all were, shuffling towards me, stinking, black flesh hanging from their skulls and I was screaming—

There was a series of loud, flat detonations, and I hit the ground.

"Franz! FRANZ! Are you all right?" shouted Papa.

"What? Yes, fine." The bedroom door started to open. "Don't come in!"

"Are you sure?"

"Yes. Please go back to bed. Sorry I disturbed you."

The door closed, and I heard his footsteps going away.

I sat up in bed, shaking and sweating, turned on the bedside light and lit a cigarette, feeling utterly sick.

If only Karl were here!

I pulled the curtains back so I'd see the dawn come up, and stayed awake the rest of the night.

I felt bloody dreadful in the morning. My room was so cold that I shivered and cut myself shaving. I put on two sweaters and that still wasn't enough.

No one is going to kill me today, and I don't have to kill anyone else either.

I ran that thought through my head a couple of times. It felt very strange.

Better not get used to it.

"How are you feeling?" Papa asked over breakfast – what there was of it. God knows what the bread was made of.

"Fine, thanks. Sorry about the shouting."

"That's quite all right," said Mama. "We do understand."

No, you bloody don't, and you never will.

Johanna looked at me and then at the ceiling.

"I'll call the photographer as soon as they open," Papa said.

Maybe they'll be fully booked... but of course they weren't. I agreed to meet Papa at the studio, and off he went to work.

"Franz, you'd better give Klara your uniform," Mama said. "It could do with a sponge over."

"It needs more than that," Johanna said, laughing. "It's got fag ash ground into it and booze stains!"

"No it hasn't," I retorted. "That's my flying uniform. I came home in my best one." *The one I wear for funerals*, I just stopped myself saying.

"There were some articles about you in the local paper," said Mama. "We've put them all in a scrapbook. Would you like to read them?"

I laughed. "No, thanks! I doubt I'd recognise myself!"

"You wouldn't," said Johanna, "and it would give you a swollen head, anyway!"

I got quite a shock as I walked to the studio. A middle-aged couple started staring at me. The man turned to the woman and said something, and she stared even harder. Then they pointed me out to a third person, a rather older man.

By that time I was quite close to them, and they were still gazing at me. *I'm sure I shaved and put my clothes on.*

"Good morning," I said politely.

"Good morning," they replied, and then the first man said, "Excuse me, but you look rather like Leutnant Franz Becker."

What? "Well, er – that's because I am Franz Becker."

"Would you be very kind and give me your autograph?" he asked.

"And could you open your coat collar?" asked the older man. "We'd love to see your Pour le Mérite."

"Yes, of course... What would you like me to sign?"

The man pulled his diary from his coat pocket. "By today's date, please."

"Of course – do you have a pen?"

As I was handing it back to him, another voice said, "Could I have your autograph as well, please?"

I turned round, and saw to my astonishment that about a dozen people had gathered, all holding something for me to sign.

Bloody hell. I could feel myself going scarlet. I never expected this—

I was late for the photographer.

"Where on earth did you get to?" Papa demanded.

"I'm really sorry," I said, "but I got a bit held up. I'll tell you about it later."

I took my coat off, and he looked at me with dismay.

"I thought you were going to wear your medals."

Of course – you want something really splendid to display.

"They're at the squadron – we usually only wear them for—" I broke off. *It won't do them any harm to hear the truth.* "For funerals."

They looked at each other.

"So I'm afraid it's the ribbons – apart from these two, of course."

Four ribbons plus the Blue Max and the Iron Cross First Class still look pretty good, I thought as I assumed a suitable expression for the portrait. *It's all bloody daft, anyway – I've only just matched Karl's score, and yet I've got more bits of tin than he has, courtesy of the King of Württemberg.*

And all I've done is my duty. I don't really deserve any of them.

My feet stuck in the mud and I stumbled over the furrows. The English fire intensified, and suddenly Schürmann wasn't beside me any more. I turned round and saw him on his knees—

Rescuing a wounded officer under fire, they called that, and gave me the Iron Cross Second Class. I could hardly leave him in the lurch, could I?

"Franz."

I suddenly realised that the photographer and my father were giving me a strange look.

"Oh – have you finished?"

"Yes," said the photographer.

"Right, time for lunch," said Papa as we left.

"Can we take a taxi?" I asked.

"Why on earth do you want a taxi? It's no distance, and it would do you good to walk. You're not looking well at all – I'm sure you don't get enough exercise, and you drink too much."

Jesus.

I tried to laugh. "We used to have a kickabout most evenings, but the airfield's like a swamp now – we'd just lose the ball. And I don't drink any more than the others."

"I had no idea we were being defended by drunks."

This time my laughter was real – at the thought of anyone going off to war without drink.

"Oh, we're always sober enough to fight," I said. "And the Tommies and the Frenchies are just the same – it's whisky for one and red wine for the other. And the Russkis probably drink vodka all day."

"We'll walk," he said.

XI

We hadn't gone fifty metres before someone stopped and stared at me. It took half an hour to walk less than a kilometre, and I signed my name over and over, and even had to pose for a photograph with someone.

Papa was visibly swollen with pride.

"Is that why you wanted a taxi?" he asked as we finally entered his club.

"Yes – and why I was late to the studio."

The cloakroom attendant stared as I took off my coat. *I'm not going out in uniform again.*

There was more nonsense to come. All the rich, smug businessmen shook my hand and congratulated me, and came out with shit about heroes and 'iron youth'.

What a load of bollocks.

"So tell me, young Becker," said Herr Weber, in that pompous manner of his, "what do you think about as you're taking off? I'll bet you can't wait to send another Englishman down in flames!"

I hope I'm going to come back in one piece, but no one wants to hear that.

"I concentrate on doing my job," I said, and tried to change the subject.

"And have you met Rittmeister von Richthofen?" asked Herr Zabel.

"No – he's not based anywhere near us."

The disappointment was palpable.

On they went. I felt like arranging them all in a semi-circle and telling them exactly what it was like – but what was the point? I couldn't have got the words out, and they wouldn't have understood, and it wouldn't have put them off their lavish lunch, all imported from Switzerland on the black market.

Apparently Papa's Socialist principles enabled him to forget the pale, pinched, hungry people outside and enjoy his meal.

Is this what we're fighting for, to keep rich men in illegal plenty while the poor starve?

Just enjoy the time off. It'll be over in a flash.

Herr Reddemann came in.

"How's Stefan?" I asked.

"Much better, thank you. The operation in Berlin was successful, and he can walk with a stick – and, thank God, that means they can't send him back to the front line."

Honesty from someone, at last.

"Is he at home?" I was hoping for an evening out. I'd cabled Chris Sevening's home, but he was at the Front.

He shook his head. "No – he's an instructor at a training camp, teaching – oh, God, what's the technical name for it? Something to do with assault troops."

"Wish him all the best from me, won't you?"

"Yes, of course."

At least the old bastards kept me well supplied with champagne and schnapps. I could see Papa frowning, but so what? By the time he was ready to leave, I was nicely mellow.

"We're taking a taxi home," he said firmly.

"Had enough attention for one day?" I asked with a grin.

"I don't want everyone seeing you half-cut."

I laughed. "Dear Papa, I assure you I'm not even a quarter-cut!"

It was a relief to get home and hang my uniform in the wardrobe. *I'm not putting that on again until I leave.*

I fell asleep in my chair, and was rather roughly woken by Johanna.

"You must have had a good lunch," she said. "I've been calling you for about five minutes!"

"Bad night as well."

"Yes, I heard. Come on, let's go for a walk."

"No way, Sis. Tomorrow."

"You promised."

"Shouldn't you be at school?"

She rolled her eyes. "I've finished for today, stupid. We've just got time to get to the park before it gets dark."

"All right, then."

"Oh, God," she said as soon as we were out of the gate, "I can't tell you how good it is to have you home."

"Trouble with the parents?"

"I nearly did run away to Berlin – it was only your letter that stopped me. They're driving me mad. All I want is to get some nursing experience to help with my studies later, and Mama just won't have it, unless it's bloody maternity."

"Language, Sis!" I said, laughing.

"It's better than yours!"

"I'm a soldier. You're a nicely brought-up young lady." I stopped and lit a fag.

"Can I have one?"

"No, you damn well can't!" This time I really was shocked. "The only women I've ever seen smoking are tarts."

"You're still—"

"Yes, of course I am," I interrupted quickly. I didn't want to hear her choice of phrase for that. "And my squadron mates were most impressed with the condoms."

"You *told* them?!"

"The box fell out of the sweater in front of everyone."

"Oh." She laughed. "You stink of booze and fags again!"

"Oh, shut up!"

"No, but you do drink a lot."

"Sis, if you start on about that I'm going home. I've had it up to here from Papa."

"Now you know how I feel. I just want to get away. As soon as the war's over I'm off to medical school in Berlin, whether they like it or not. I can stay with your friend, can't I?"

Alfred.

"I haven't heard from Alfred for weeks. I don't know if he's even alive. He's a storm troop officer, for God's sake. He's got as much chance of seeing the end of the war as I have."

Suddenly I realised what I'd said. I ground my cigarette into the dirt, wishing I could take the words back.

She squeezed my arm. "It's all right – I'm not stupid. You don't have to pretend."

Yes, I do. I have to pretend all the bloody time. Pretend I'm brave and don't give a fig for my likely fate, pretend I'm not starting to fall apart. My hands started trembling and I hid them behind my back.

"Sis, about the nursing – you don't realise what a state some of the fellows are in. You'd be dealing with horrible injuries all the time, and death."

"Yes, I know. I've got a penfriend – she's a nurse in a field hospital. She invited me to go and help out – she said they always need more hands."

I'll bet they do.

"Reading about things isn't the same as real life," I said slowly. "I've been in those places, visiting people, and they're really horrible. If you want experience then get it in one of the hospitals here."

"How's Karl?"

I sighed. "I don't really know – please don't ask for the details. He nearly died, that's all you need to know."

"Will he be going back?"

"I can't see it."

But he was brought up in that Prussian cult of death for the Fatherland – he'll want to go back...

"Then I could stay with him!"

"No way! Sis, last night Papa said he has the morals of an alley cat. Frankly, that was insulting to alley cats."

She laughed. "You don't trust him with me."

"When it comes to women, I trust Karl as far as I could throw him – and you've seen the size of him."

"Well, I just might marry him."

That sent a real pang through me. *Yes – I'll get killed and you'll share his bed.*

Why in God's name should that get to me?

"I was only joking," she said. "There's no need to pull a face like that."

"Let's get back – it's bloody freezing out here."

If I'd thought my uniform would stay in the wardrobe, I was mistaken.

The next morning Papa said, "Oh, Franz – Bergmann asked me if you'd give a talk at the school."

Bergmann was headmaster of the Gymnasium I'd attended.

"Me? Why?"

Papa looked at me in disbelief. "Don't you understand? This is a small town. You're a fighter ace, you've got the Pour le Mérite and both classes of the Friedrich Order and of the Iron Cross – and that Hohenzollern decoration. Your picture is on postcards and you've been in a film. You can't walk down the street without being asked for your autograph. Think of the effect a talk from you would have on the senior boys."

"Oh – you mean it would encourage them to join up. They'll be conscripted soon enough."

"Franz, we need more men at the Front. You must realise that."

You are telling me that we need more men. Where do you imagine I've been?

"We need to make a final big push before the Americans arrive," he continued.

"Yes, I know." I sighed.

The last thing I want to do is talk to a room full of starry-eyed boys, and inspire them to get killed sooner than they have to.

Quite apart from the tremor in my hands – God knows what they'll make of that.

I'd thought it was pre-combat nerves, or reaction, or the cold. Then I'd thought that I really had been drinking too much. But none of those applied now, and I realised with a shock that it was becoming permanent.

"Yes, all right. When would he like me to do it?"

"This afternoon."

"That really gives me time to prepare, doesn't it? Why do you have to spring things on me?"

"All he wants you to do is talk about your job. It can't be that difficult."

"No, I suppose not."

"Just make sure you don't stink of booze and fags!" said Johanna.

"I love you too, Sis!"

I set off later with my coat fastened up to the neck and my cap pulled right down, in the hope of not being recognised. It didn't work. Too many people had told their friends and neighbours that I was home, and I was stopped twice within the first five minutes.

After that I gave up trying to be inconspicuous.

I never wanted any of this, I thought as I signed yet another autograph. *I just wanted an adventure, a quick campaign with a bit of action and excitement, and – of course – to take part in another glorious victory like 1870.*

I looked at the thin, lined faces, at the gaunt hands holding out postcards and bits of paper for me to sign, and suddenly realised that a scrap of reflected glory made things just a bit less dismal for them. That was a very sobering thought, and one that stayed with me to the school.

Bergmann greeted me with open arms.

"Becker – welcome back! You always were one of my better students, and now look at you – a real hero! I'm very glad you could find the time – the boys are so excited about your visit."

"I hope they won't be disappointed."

"No danger of that, I can assure you."

I entered the classroom, and stopped dead. The walls were decorated with pictures of German and Allied aircraft, and of all the top aces.

There was Richthofen, and the Chief – and Karl, gazing at me with his calm, pale eyes. *Just a few days, now.*

The boys stood up and applauded, and I blushed.

Bergmann motioned with his hand, and they stopped clapping and sat down.

"Leutnant Franz Becker needs no introduction from me, so I'll let him get on with his talk."

The rows of expectant faces looked at me, just as starry-eyed as I'd feared. *This needs a bit of humour.*

"Before anyone asks, no, I haven't met the Red Baron! Sorry for any disappointment."

There was a polite smile from some of the boys.

"My CO – that's Oberleutnant von Kralewski-Zentzytzki, whose picture I see opposite – has spoken to him several times."

They all looked awed, and I realised what heroes both men must be to them. *Jesus, I hope they don't think of me the same way...*

I gave them a brief account of my service, and then described life at the squadron – some of it, anyway. Obviously I left out the boozing and the tarts and the gambling. I kept looking at Karl's picture, and it was almost as if he smiled at me.

Next week he really will. My heart lifted in the most stupid way, and the tremor in my hands eased.

It returned as I talked about flying and meeting the Tommies – suddenly there was a strong, sharp smell of petrol, and I had to make a huge effort to keep the room in focus and continue speaking.

I want a fag, and a drink. The tremor was threatening to spread from my hands to the rest of me.

"Any questions?" I finished with relief.

There was a long pause. No one wanted to be the first to ask, and I thought I was going to get away with it.

A boy in the third row put his hand up. "I can't see colours. Does that stop me flying?"

"I don't know – you'll have to apply, and ask the doctor when you have your medical."

Another asked, "Will the war be over before we get there?"

I looked at him, and the most unnerving, horrible thing happened. The flesh disappeared from his face, and all I saw was a skull staring at me.

"No," I said quietly. "At least, I don't think so."

Not for you, anyway – because you're going to be killed. My hands were shaking properly, and I clasped them together behind my back.

I couldn't get out of there fast enough. Fortunately there were only a few more questions, and I finished by saying, "You are all potential officers. Remember: learn to obey that you may learn to command, and never forget what life is like at the bottom."

They gave me a standing ovation, which had me completely scarlet.

"Thank you so much," said Bergmann.

"Not at all," I replied, and headed home.

Please, no one ask for my autograph, because I don't think I can sign my name. I've never heard of having a premonition for someone else.

Is that what happens to people with second sight, like Karl's grannie? Or was it just some ghastly hallucination from one of my nightmares?

I never want to see that again.

I did get stopped, of course, and blamed my wobbly signature on being frozen through. The afternoon was bitter, and it was snowing again.

The house was stone cold. At first I thought no one was at home, but the drawing room door was slightly ajar and I heard voices, Johanna's and another girl's.

"We've got opportunities no women before us have ever had," my sister said. "And I'm going to take every advantage I can of them. I'm going to be an orthopaedic surgeon, and maybe one day even a professor of medicine. We're every bit as good as men – look at all the things we've shown them we can do. You're crazy if you don't make the most of it, absolutely crazy!"

"I don't know if I want a career," said her friend. "I mean, how do you look after your children if you work?"

"You pay someone else to do it, of course. Or you don't have any."

I'm eavesdropping, but none of the other rooms are heated.

"And there won't be enough men to go round, anyway, or to do all the jobs—" Johanna broke off as I entered the room. "Oh, Franz – you weren't meant to hear that."

"No problem. You're right. There won't."

The other girl gave me a look that was not exactly friendly.

"Sorry to interrupt," I said.

"Don't be stupid," said Johanna. "Sit down. You remember Liese, don't you?"

"Yes, of course," I lied.

"I was just saying that—" Johanna broke off again.

"I heard. And you're right – about the opportunities, that is. Not about being as good as men, though – that depends what at, doesn't it?"

"What do you mean?" asked Liese, rather sharply.

"Well, I can't see you down a coal mine, wielding a pick like a man, or in the front line—"

"We've got far too much sense to go to war," said Johanna. "If women ruled the world there wouldn't be any wars. We'd solve everything by talking."

"That's for sure!" I said, and she stuck out her tongue at me.

"I need to get home," said Liese. "My parents don't like me being out after dark."

"Shall I walk you home?" I offered.

"No, thank you," she said stiffly.

Johanna went to the front door with her and then came back.

"What's wrong with her?" I asked. "I only offered to take her home."

She gave me a very serious look. "I think it's to do with Maria Hertel."

I felt a shiver run down my spine.

"What about her?" I tried to sound casual.

"Well, they all went away—"

"Yes, you told me."

"– and it was all a bit strange. They didn't say where they were going, or when they're coming back. No one could talk about anything else for weeks."

I'll bet, I thought, imagining all the small-town gossiping tongues.

"Well, Liese's Maria's best friend, and she knows something. At least, I think she does, but I can't get it out of her."

"What has she said?" I didn't sound casual at all.

"Nothing. That's the really irritating part. You know, 'don't tell anyone' always means 'tell just one close friend', but she won't even do that. But every time I mention your name, she stiffens up."

Oh, shit.

She must be pregnant. I'll have to marry her, and I hardly know her. It's not like Lentzke and his wife – they really loved each other, you could see that. Maria's a nice girl, but—

And yet, the thought that I might have created life instead of destroying it was rather strange. *One life, to set in the balance against how many?*

Maybe her parents just want to keep her away from me. No doubt they found out about the hotel, and I'm the vile seducer. She won't have admitted that she leapt into bed with me.

"So what's your conclusion, Sis?"

I lit a cigarette and had to snap my lighter shut, because the flame set my heart pounding.

"You did see quite a bit of her in June," Johanna said. "And she did have a postcard with your picture on it – though there were about four other pilots there. And she did say you'd written to her."

Trust a girl to not keep her mouth shut. "What else did she say?"

"That was it, really. And then there was all that business about the food making her mother ill – just like all the rest of us – and then they went away. But she'd have had to be really stupid to go to bed with you."

Thank fuck for that.

"But then she is really stupid," Johanna added. "And I really hope you didn't go to bed with her, because I don't want her as a sister-in-law."

"Why not?"

"Because she's stupid, and because of the politics."

"What politics?"

"Her parents joined the Fatherland Party."

I laughed. "Further right than Genghis Khan – that's what Johnny said, anyway." *Or was that the Pan-German League? Same thing.*

"Who's Johnny?"

"Was. Karl's brother, who flew with us. You probably saw his picture in the papers as well."

"Oh, yes, that's right – Karl's better-looking, though. What happened to Johnny?"

"Got shot down."

The flames were spreading right back to the Red Eagle. Johnny jumped out and fell blazing through the sky, like some ghastly meteorite—

"FRANZ! God, where were you?"

"Sorry, Sis. Lost the thread."

I linked my fingers together and pressed hard, trying to stop them shaking.

She gave me a very penetrating look. "That happens a lot, doesn't it? And your hands."

"I don't know what you mean." I changed the subject pointedly. "And are you still a good Socialist, Sis?"

She pulled a face. "About as good a lefty as I am a Catholic! But the Fatherland Party's just where Johnny said, and we don't want that in our family. Papa would go berserk, anyway."

That won't matter if I've made Maria pregnant.

I started laughing. There was absolutely no chance of my having to marry Maria. She was God knows where, and I wasn't coming home ever again.

I looked at Johanna, and the laughter came very close to turning to tears. *This is the last few days I'll ever spend here. After Adlershof I'll go back to the squadron, and then I'll be dead.*

"I'll go and change," I said quietly.

"Yes, do," she said. "Then we can pretend there isn't a war – and I'll bet you wish you could."

"You're not wrong there."

But of course it didn't matter what I wore. I was just the same on the inside.

I stayed in for the next two days. All I wanted was peace and quiet.

You don't deserve them, I thought, as I lay sweating and staring at the ceiling after another ghastly nightmare. *Not after what you've done and will do again, given half a chance.*

On the Sunday my family went to Mass, and I stayed in bed. I called out through the bedroom door that I wasn't feeling well – which was true, though not in the way that they took it.

I'll never feel well again – but I won't have to put up with it for much longer, so it really doesn't matter.

I pulled the quilt round my ears and curled up, and imagined I was lying in Karl's arms, warm and safe.

Someone knocked on the door. I started violently.

"Come in!"

Mama put her head round the door. "Are you feeling better now? It's lunchtime."

"Oh – I must have gone back to sleep. I'll be down in a minute."

No need to bother shaving, I thought, and threw my clothes on. I was ravenous.

"Franz, really!" said my father. "You could have shaved – it is Sunday."

"You look like a tramp again!" Johanna said.

"But at least I don't stink of booze and fags!"

"Yet!"

Lunch was, to my astonishment, pretty good. *This must have cost a small fortune.*

"Can I contribute?" I asked. "I get extra pay for flying, and there's not much to spend it on."

"Only drink, I suppose," Papa said.

And tarts.

"No," said Mama. "Thank you for offering, Franz, but it's our treat for you. We – we can't understand what it's like for you, but we do want to – not say thank you, but – all of you are—" She broke off.

"Thank you, Mama," I said. "I really do appreciate it. And just being home."

Papa gave me a look that said plainly, 'Why aren't you staying longer, if you like it so much?'

Instead he said, "I saw the Mayor at church, and he asked if you'd give a talk tomorrow evening, in the meeting rooms."

"He wants *what?!* But it's my last evening! What did you say?"

"I said I'd ask you."

"*No.* I'm supposed to be on leave, relaxing. The Chief's been on tours round the country, talking all over the place, and I've always been very thankful I didn't have to do that."

"It would make people happier. They've got a very heavy burden."

They should try climbing out of a trench under fire, or burying yet another boy who's barely old enough to shave, or getting soaked in petrol... But then that's my job.

There was that sharp stink of fuel again. My lunch rose in my throat and I swallowed hard.

"Please think about it," Papa said.

I couldn't reply.

"Franz, are you feeling ill again?" asked Mama.

I shook my head, swallowed hard again and lied, "No. I'm fine."

All I wanted to do that afternoon was get pissed.

"Let's go for a walk," said Papa. "You could do with some fresh air – you've been cooped up in here too long."

I really didn't want to, but I made the effort for their sake.

I tried on my suit, but it was tight across the chest and shoulders, and a bit short in the leg.

What was it Alfred wrote? Men don't reach full size until about twenty-five, wasn't it?

We're all adolescents, killing each other before we're even fully grown. How fucking depressing is that.

So I had to wear uniform, and the result was as expected. We went to the park and, in spite of the snow and the bitter wind, it was full of people out for a stroll. Older men, women, children – *you can tell there's a war, even without the occasional fellow minus a leg or arm.* And of course people noticed me and wanted my autograph.

"I'm really looking forward to your talk tomorrow evening," said one woman as I handed the postcard back to her.

"Oh. Well, I hope it'll be interesting."

I did my best to keep my voice friendly, but it was rather difficult. I was so angry I could have thrown Papa right into the vegetable beds that had replaced the roses.

I kept my self-control until we got home – and I tried hard to continue keeping it. The last thing I wanted was a major row.

"Papa," I said, "you told me—"

"Yes, Franz, I know. But he didn't even wait for an answer, just assumed you'd do it. And I knew you wouldn't disappoint everyone."

"Why couldn't you just have been honest with me?"

"I do wish you wouldn't look at me like that."

"Like what?"

"I don't know how to describe it, and I don't think I want to."

Oh. My anger died abruptly.

"Of course I'll do it," I said quietly.

Papa smiled.

I met my eyes in my bedroom mirror. *At least I don't look as hard as Karl,* I thought, and wondered whether he still had that look, or whether time away from the Front had softened it.

I'll see him the day after tomorrow. Suddenly nothing else mattered.

The talk went quite well, and to my relief I didn't have any disturbing hallucinations. My hands starting shaking a couple of times, but I hid them behind my back. I was glad to get it over with, and go home for what remained of the evening.

This is the last time I'll ever sit down to dinner with my family. I looked round the table, and sadness almost overwhelmed me.

Papa produced an excellent bottle of wine, and then his best brandy and a good cigar each.

"I wish you could stay a few more days," Mama said.

"Karl's all alone in that house," I said. "His brothers have both been killed, his parents are dead, he was very badly injured, and it must be very depressing for him."

Her face filled with sympathy. "I didn't realise. He must be looking forward to your visit."

"He's safe now, isn't he?" asked Johanna.

"I hope so. I can't see him flying again."

"When are they going to give you parachutes?" Papa asked.

"God knows. After the war, I expect!"

"It really surprises me that they haven't done that yet," he went on.

One spark and the vapour will catch— "Can we talk about something else?"

"Yes, of course. I thought you spoke very well."

"Thank you."

Some time later I went to the lavatory, and when I came out Johanna was waiting.

"All yours, Sis."

She took hold of my arm. "Franz, please say something about my going to medical school."

"I don't want to cause an argument on my last evening."

"That's just it. They won't want one, either."

"All right."

I sat down and lit another cigarette.

"You know, Johanna's really got her heart set on becoming a doctor," I said, "and I think she'd make a very good one."

There was instant tension in the room.

"It's not a suitable occupation for a young lady," said Mama.

I looked at my hands.

"There won't be enough husbands," I said. "Women are going to have to look after themselves. Just look at all the jobs they're doing now."

"Yes, but that's just until the war's over," Papa said. "When the men come home, the women will go back into the house."

"An awful lot of men aren't coming home. You know that." I changed my approach. "She'll be a good doctor because she's passionate about it – remember why you became a lawyer? You told me you wanted people to have justice. Well, she's just as determined to mend their bodies."

Papa sighed. "Berlin's a long way away – and the city has a terrible reputation."

"I've got a friend who was a medical student before the war – his family lives there, and I'm sure she'd be able to lodge with them."

"Under the same roof as a strange young man?" Mama sounded quite shocked.

"Oh, I wouldn't worry – I don't think he's interested in women."

My parents looked at me in horror.

"You mean he's a *pervert*?" Papa asked, appalled. "And he's your *friend*?"

"Not like that!" I laughed. "I can assure you I prefer women."

That's true – I do. Karl's an exception, and I'll never understand why I'm attracted to him.

"Well, that's something. How do you know this – this fellow?" Papa's disgust was obvious.

God, you'd be horrified if you knew about Karl and me! I almost laughed again.

"We were in the same regiment and we've kept in touch. He's a storm troop officer now, brave as a lion and – well, the sort of fellow you'd rather have on the same side."

Johanna came back into the room and looked at us all expectantly.

"All right," Papa said with a sigh. "But after the war. I don't want you going away when things are so uncertain."

She squealed so loudly that my ears rang. "THANK YOU, PAPA!!"

"But you're not nursing men," Mama said firmly. "Becoming a doctor is one thing, but washing strange men is quite another matter."

Johanna pulled a face and I gave her a look. *Be happy with what you've got, Sis.*

That night I couldn't get to sleep, and when I did I wished I hadn't. The young Englishman died in my arms as I lifted him out of his aircraft, and suddenly he turned into Karl, and it was Karl's lifeless body that I was holding, and Karl's blood all over me, and I gave such a loud howl of misery that I woke myself up.

That can't happen. Karl's out of the war now. It'll be me that gets killed.

I put the light on and sat up in bed smoking. Eventually I got up and went downstairs.

Mama was in the drawing room, tidying up.

"Sorry if I woke you," I said.

She crossed the room, and put her arms round me and held me tight. I bent down and rested my head against her hair.

"It doesn't matter," she said quietly. "I just wish I could – well, I can't, so there it is."

"I wish I could change things too," I said.

I had to leave straight after an early breakfast to be sure of making my train, but at least that meant I didn't have to sit around waiting.

My family came to the station with me, and the walk took every one of the extra minutes I'd allowed.

"You'll be happy to get back to the Front to get away from this," Johanna muttered in my ear.

"That's going a bit far!" But there was some truth in what she'd said.

"Thank you," she added.

"No need."

The train was pulling in as we reached the platform.

"Look after yourself, son," said Papa. "What's the phrase you airmen use?"

"Break your neck and legs."

"Well, that, then!"

"Come home safely," Mama said, tears in her eyes.

"And stinking of booze and fags!" said Johanna. "Or it just won't be you!"

"Cheers, Sis – you say the nicest things!"

I waved out of the window until they disappeared from sight, sat down, lit a cigarette and took a swig of brandy. To my astonishment Papa had filled my hip flask as a parting gift. I don't think he'd expected me to start on it quite so early, though.

That's that, then. I shan't see them again. I hope Papa keeps his promise to Johanna, when I'm not there to remind him.

I stared out of the window at the white landscape, thoroughly depressed – and then the thought that I was on my way to Karl's house lifted my spirits.

He won't ask me stupid questions about the war, or comment on my nightmares or the look in my eyes, or ask me to sign postcards or give talks. I'll be able to relax properly.

It was snowing again. I gave up trying to look out of the window, and leafed absently through the newspaper I'd bought in Stuttgart while I waited for the express.

What a load of shit. Why did I spend good money on this?

"Anything interesting in that?" asked the Bavarian Leutnant opposite, looking thoroughly pissed off.

"Load of bollocks. You can have it."

"Thanks. Smoke?" he offered.

"Thanks."

"Got a light? Mine's out of fuel."

"Yes, of course."

I lit our fags, took a deep drag and almost choked.

"Bit strong?" he asked with a grin.

"Just a bit." *Rough is more the word.* "Where did you get those?"

"From the Russkis – we took a whole load prisoner, and they wanted to stay on good terms with us."

He was on his way to Döberitz.

"Last place I want to bloody go, I can tell you. I've had it up to here with those bloody Prussian pigs. Verdun was the last straw – they sent our blokes in again and again, till there was bugger all left of them. Three of my mates got killed at Fleury – I was just bloody lucky I missed it, got clobbered in December '15…"

Finally he paused for breath. I tried to point out that the Prussians had been slaughtered as well, but he wasn't having that.

"I can't think why you want to stick up for the bastards. Where are you headed, anyway?"

"Wilds of Brandenburg."

"Why the fuck are you going there? It's crawling with the bastards!"

I grinned. "I'm going to stay with my best mate – he got shot down last July and he's on convalescent leave."

"Oh – right – well, I suppose someone has to be friends with them! Hang on – did you say shot down?"

"Yes."

"You a flier as well?"

I had my coat done right up – the train was freezing, and I didn't want any more attention.

"Yes."

"You're off your fucking head."

I laughed. "I'm not about to argue!"

We were joined by a pair of Hussar officers, who were on leave and planning a riotous time in Berlin. They were already well lubricated and very cheerful.

I'd forgotten just how long a journey it was. It was mid-afternoon by the time we got to Berlin, and then I got a cab to the Stettiner Station for my train north.

I only just made it – there was a hold-up and a lot of police on the streets.

"What's going on?" I asked the driver.

"Bleedin' munitions workers, out on bleedin' strike again. They gets too much bleedin' money anyway, 'fyou ask me."

"They should be grateful they're here and not in the trenches."

"Too bleedin' right. Makes me sick, the wages they gets…"

On he went, while I tried not to fret about missing the train.

"'Ere we are, then."

I paid him, ran into the station, and leapt on the train just as it was starting to pull out.

It was still snowing and the light was fading, and I could see almost nothing out of the window. The train was bloody cold, and I pulled my collar up and my cap down, and smoked to try to keep warm. I'd finished the brandy, which was probably just as well – not that Karl would mind me smelling of booze and fags.

I hope he's at home in the warm and not standing on a freezing station platform. He can't be well yet, not after that.

My mind shied away from the memory. Seeing Karl like that had shaken me far more than I wanted to recognise. *I've always been far more afraid of being badly injured than of being killed. Dead is dead, but mutilated is quite another matter.*

I really don't need to sit here thinking about what could happen to me – but there was nothing else to do, and my hands started shaking again. I lit another cigarette, trying not to look at the flame of my lighter.

The train stopped.

Where the fuck is this? I couldn't see the station name, and I opened the window and stuck my head out into a blast of snowflakes.

Eberswalde. Just a few more stops.

We crawled the next few kilometres so slowly, stopping and starting, that I lost count of the stations.

Where are we now?

This is it, you stupid bastard!

I grabbed my haversack and leapt out – and there was Karl, and everything else disappeared.

He was leaning against the wall, wearing a fur coat and hat. When he saw me he straightened up, and we closed the small distance between us.

I expected him to lift me off my feet and squeeze me half to death, but he just stood and looked at me, as if unable to believe that I was really there.

"Franz." He smiled, his eyes suddenly soft.

I wanted to throw my arms round him, but he made no move to embrace me.

Maybe it's too public – but that's never bothered him before… Maybe it would hurt. Better leave it to him.

"Karl, it's so good to see you."

"And you." His voice was warm, his smile lighting his face.

I realised how sharply his cheekbones were standing out. "How are you?"

He shrugged. "Better than the last time you saw me, that's for sure… Let's get home – it's going to take a while, I'm afraid. Just the one horsepower."

He led the way out of the station, and I was shocked by how slowly I had to walk to stay behind him.

There was a pony and trap tied up in the dark, deserted street, both well covered in snow. The animal's head was hanging and it looked thoroughly dejected.

"Behold my elegant carriage!" he said, with a wave of his hand.

The pony looked up and shook its head impatiently.

"There's a blanket under the tarpaulin," he said.

And, thank God, it was warm and dry.

He untied the pony, got in beside me, and sat for a moment, out of breath. *We've walked no distance,* I thought with dismay.

"Karl, you should be at home, not out here in this cold."

He sighed and picked up the reins. "I couldn't send Henning. He's an old man and it's bloody freezing."

He's probably in better shape than you.

"Did you find somewhere warm to wait?"

"I went into the pub and had a beer. I don't think I was very welcome – no one said a word the whole time I was in there."

That surprised me – I'd always thought Karl's family was well respected.

"There was a lot of unrest in Berlin," I said. "I nearly missed the train because of the munitions workers out on strike."

"Fucking jammy bastards don't know how lucky they are."

"No, they don't... How is it out here?"

"Hard to say – I've not been back long."

The warmth from our bodies was starting to thaw me out.

"This is almost like sharing a blanket in the barns," I said.

He turned to me and his smile was just visible. "Yes."

That wasn't what you wanted to say.

I put my arm round his shoulders, and he moved closer to me. We sat in silence for a while, the lantern picking out the snow-covered road.

"I'm sorry it's such a slow journey," he said. "I can't get petrol now."

"It doesn't matter." *I've missed you,* I wanted to say, but it would have sounded soppy. "I'm just glad you're home and in one piece."

He gave a short laugh. "You might revise that opinion!"

"And that I'm here."

"Are you really?"

"Of course I am, you stupid bastard. I wouldn't have come otherwise, would I?"

"No, I suppose not... I'm bloody glad you did, though."

I squeezed his shoulder, and realised with a shock that I could feel bone under the fur coat. I'd never felt Karl's bones before – they'd always been well hidden by those beautiful muscles.

Jesus, you must be thin.

Neither of us spoke after that. Nothing I wanted to say felt appropriate, and I didn't want to talk about trivia – and there was no need to talk, anyway. Sitting beside him gave me a quite ridiculous feeling of happy contentment.

Eventually the big iron gates appeared, standing open as always, and the pony turned of its own accord and trotted through them. After a couple of turns the house came into view, a faint glow from one of the ground floor windows gleaming on the fresh snow.

Karl stopped outside the door.

"You go in," he said, "and I'll deal with Thomas."

"I'll give you a hand – it'll be quicker with two."

"If you're sure?"

"Don't be daft – I've come to see you, not to sit by the fire while you work in the stables!"

Halfway through rubbing the pony down, I was very glad I was there. Karl was working more and more slowly, and there was something awkward about his movements. It took me a moment to realise that he was using his left hand, while his right stayed in his coat pocket.

Apart from the pony and an old draught horse, the stable block was empty and echoing. The beautiful horses Karl's father had bred before the war had all gone to the Army.

They're probably dead by now, I thought sadly.

He picked up my haversack with his left hand as we turned to leave, and looked at it for a moment as if wondering how best to carry it.

"I'll take that," I said.

"Franz—"

I took it from him.

"You carry the lantern," I said, and we linked arms and walked slowly towards the house.

It was about two hundred metres to the front door and I wanted to hurry through the burning cold, but Karl was breathing fast.

"Shall we pause?" I asked gently.

He shook his head, and we carried on.

At the bottom of the steps up to the front door he stopped, and stood with one hand resting on the stone coping. He glanced up and then down again, and as the light from the house caught his face I saw the weariness on it.

He put a foot on the first step and started to drag himself up. *Jesus – last time we were here you leapt up these and left me trailing.*

After three steps he paused as if gathering his strength. I put my arm round his waist.

"How do I do this without hurting you?"

"I can do it."

"All right – I just don't want you to fall."

By the time we reached the top he was horribly out of breath, and leaning on me more than he would have wanted to acknowledge.

"Thanks."

"No need."

Jesus – I knew you wouldn't be well, but I never expected you to be as bad as this.

Our boots rang on the hall floor, and Henning appeared. He was just as I remembered him, straight and tall despite the years, still with his full head of white hair.

"It's good to see you again, sir," he said as he took my haversack and coat, and I had the feeling that he meant it.

"It's good to be here."

"Dinner will be in half an hour, sir," he said to Karl.

Oh, good, I'm starving – don't expect much, Franz. You know how things are.

The house was even colder than ours, and the silence was oppressive. As before, I had the eerie feeling of being watched, and I almost turned to see who was there.

Karl led the way past two closed doors and I had a strong desire to open them, in case the watchers were behind them.

It's all in your mind – Karl opened one of the tall wooden doors, and we were met by light and warmth, and the haunted feeling disappeared.

"Ah, that's better!" he said. "Brandy?"

"Thanks."

He gestured at the chairs either side of the fire. "Have a seat."

The fire was blazing properly, and the tiled stove in the corner was belching out heat.

"This is the first time I've been warm since I left the squadron."

He handed me my drink and sat down. "So how is everyone?"

"The Chief's fine – sends you his regards – and so's Zaffke – oh, and Otto's back. Horstmann's still with us, Bretti is now Leutnant Brettschneider—"

"Good – I'd like to see him with his epaulettes."

"Poor Lentzke got married on his deathbed—"

"Who?"

I realised that Lentzke was after Karl's time. So many men had joined and left us in those months.

"Lost track, haven't you?" he asked with a grin. "Suppose I ask you. Beilke."

"Still with us."

"Kühn."

"Dead – shot down while you were in hospital."

"Patschke."

"Also dead. The Tommies raided the field – he crashed on take-off."

"Ah. Eichner."

"Still with us."

He nodded. "Good. I didn't see the casualty lists for a long time, as you'll realise, and to be honest I don't want to look at them in case – well, you know."

"Oh, they don't want me in either place. And the Chief would write to you, anyway."

He raised his eyebrows slightly. "So tell me about the Fokker Triplane."

That wasn't what you wanted to say.

There was a slight barrier between us, and I couldn't work out why. *Maybe it's just that we haven't seen each other for six months* – but that didn't make sense. *I hope you're not regretting our previous intimacy* – but that didn't make sense, either.

"Well, it turns on a sixpence and it climbs well, but it's slow – and they had to ground them due to structural problems…"

A minute or so later he fell asleep, his head in the corner of the wing chair.

Now I can have a proper look at you.

His cheekbones and jaw stood out sharply, just as they had in hospital, and there was a hint of grey in his complexion. *You don't look well at all. In fact you look quite ill.* His hands were resting on his thighs, and I could see the bones and sinews clearly.

I could hear him breathing, rather fast for someone sitting in a chair.

This is what happens when you get badly hit. It fucks you up for months, maybe even for good. At the same time I was relieved, because there was no way he was fit to return to the Front and he probably never would be.

I looked round the room. The walls were lined with books, and old, faded curtains shut out the cold night. There was a table between the windows, covered in papers, and a rather shabby Persian carpet was spread over the floorboards.

This chair's seen better days too. The padding's quite thin. I smiled to myself, at the gap between people's idea of a nobleman's house and the reality.

It's nice and cosy, though, a good refuge for the winter, and he only has to heat one room.

There was a knock, and the door opened.

"Dinner is served, gentlemen," Henning announced, and left.

Karl hadn't stirred.

"Karl. *Karl.*"

I shook his shoulder gently, and he gave a loud yell and started violently.

"Sorry. Dinner's ready."

"What?" He looked at me in complete bemusement. "Franz?"

"I've come to stay, you stupid bastard." I ruffled his hair. "It's dinnertime."

"God, I must have nodded off. Sorry – awful manners."

"When in God's name would you need manners with me?"

He smiled up at me, his eyes alight with warmth. My hand still rested on his hair, and he laid his left hand on mine, and our fingers intertwined.

"Come on, you," I said softly, and pulled him gently to his feet.

The dining room was chilly and horribly empty. Karl sat at the head of the table with me on his right, and eight vacant chairs surrounded us.

Just a few years ago they would all have been occupied: Karl's uncle, his parents, the four children, guests… And now they're nearly all dead.

Ilse brought in plates of stew, plain but solid and filling. It was proper food, and it actually tasted as food should.

I was ravenous, and it was a while before I noticed that Karl was hardly eating anything. He picked out a few bits and moved the rest around his plate. *No wonder you're so thin.*

"Would you like the rest of this, Franz? Frau Henning's given me too much again."

I hesitated. I was still hungry but I wanted him to eat.

"No, thanks – I'm full."

"Bollocks," he said. "I can't eat it so you might as well."

"But you need it."

"Don't nag."

Nag? I've barely said anything. "Sorry – didn't intend to."

There wasn't a second course, but then I hadn't been expecting one.

"I'm sorry I can't offer you coffee," he said, "but all we can get is that disgusting acorn muck, and I won't have it in the house… There's plenty of good brandy, though!"

Once again he poured me a generous measure and himself a small one, then sat down and poked the fire.

It flared up in a great crackling blaze. Fear jolted through me, ran cold down my spine and turned my stomach over. For one nasty moment I thought I was going to lose my dinner.

"Mind if I smoke?" I managed to say.

"No – go ahead. I can't these days," he said ruefully.

My brandy glass clattered as I put it down. I fumbled with my cigarette case and lighter, dropped both, and finally got my fag lit, the tremor in my hands obvious.

I took a deep, shaking drag, forcing myself to look at the fire. I could feel Karl's eyes resting on me, and I didn't want to meet them. It would have felt like being stripped bare.

Please don't ask if I'm all right.

He raised his glass to me. "At last I can congratulate you in person."

Congratulate? Oh – my Pour le Mérite. "Thanks – but as you know, it's just a case of getting to the right number."

He smiled warmly. "As we both know, it's not that easy – or everyone would have one!"

I started to relax, just a little.

"How's your family?"

"All right, I suppose – Papa tried to put me off coming here, though, and he wasn't very complimentary about you. 'That Prussian lout with the morals of an alley cat', he called you."

"And what did you say to that?"

"That you're not a lout!"

He burst out laughing. "Well, the rest of it's fair description – though maybe a trifle rude to alley cats!"

I laughed too, and suddenly felt much better. "And he let me in for giving talks at my old school and at the meeting rooms."

"Oh, Christ! That must have been fun!"

Suddenly I remembered the horrible hallucination I'd had at the school, and my hands started shaking again. He noticed, of course, and I saw the concern in his eyes.

"I'm just so glad to be here," I said. "I couldn't go out without being recognised – you know how it is."

"Yes, I do – remember how it was in Berlin, after we left Kempinski's?"

"Yes… And the shortages are dreadful – that was the best meal I've had since I left the squadron."

He nodded. "Henning's son lives in Berlin and we send them food every week, and people from the towns come out here scavenging. 'Hamster trips', they call them. Trouble is, we haven't got much ourselves… And what about that girl of yours?"

"It's really strange… She'd been writing to me about getting married, which made my hair stand on end, I can tell you – I mean, I wanted someone to write to me, and to have a nice time with on leave, but I didn't want anything serious, and I hardly know her.

"Then a couple of months after you got shot down, she stopped writing and I thought, she must have gone off me or found someone else, and either way I'm off the hook. But then Johanna told me they'd gone away. And when I was home just now, Maria's best friend was dead off with me and Johanna said it was something to do with Maria."

He looked at me. "Franz, I don't want to say this – but do you think she's pregnant?"

"I don't even want to think about it."

"It would make sense. Did they say why they were going away?"

I shook my head. "Some nonsense about the food disagreeing with her mother – as Johanna says, it disagrees with everyone."

"Hm."

"I hope to Christ she isn't pregnant, because then I'll have to marry her. Assuming I make it to the end of the war, or to my next leave."

He smiled. "You'll make it to the end, Franz."

"I suppose your grannie told you that!" I thought again about the boy's face turning into a skull, and shuddered.

Concern showed through the smile. *Don't ask about me, Karl* – but what he said was, "I don't see that you'd have to marry her."

"But if she's got my child—"

"You can provide for them both without ruining your life."

"Is that what you'd do?" I was more than a bit shocked.

"I wouldn't get married unless I was certain I wanted to. You said you hardly know her."

"No – I mean, our parents have always been friends, but I never really took any notice of her until last summer. But I can't leave the child illegitimate. That's what Lentzke was worried about – though he'd been with his girlfriend for years."

"Come on – tell me about Lentzke!"

He loved the part about the Chief shooting the General down in flames.

"Oh, God – I wish I'd been there to see that! But Franz, that's a completely different situation. Look, if I were you – which of course I'm not – I'd get to know the girl, after the war, and then decide whether or not to marry her. One bastard more won't make any difference – there must be thousands. And that's assuming there is a child, and—"

He broke off. *And that it's yours*, he'd been going to say.

"I never thought I'd hear you say things like that."

But the nobility have always been practical about these things. The odd bastard here and there is expected.

He sighed and looked at me. "All I'm saying is, do what will make you happy – and don't be told what to do by a load of civilians who have no idea what you've had to deal with. Refill?"

"Thanks."

I tried not to notice the effort he had to make to get up and fill my glass.

"Aren't you having another?" I asked.

"I'll be comatose if I do – this is about all I can manage these days."

"I don't know – can't smoke, can't drink – what hope is there for you?"

"None! How's Fellmann?"

"Missing Johnny."

His eyes filled with profound sadness.

"So do I," he said quietly. "He was so full of life."

"Yes."

Neither of us spoke for a while, and the silence was broken only by the crackling of the fire. Karl gazed into the flames as if he were looking into another world, and there was something else in his eyes that I couldn't quite name.

It must be unbearably lonely here, knowing they're dead.

He shook himself slightly, looked at me and smiled. "I'll bet you want a bath."

A bath? A real bath, with hot water? "You've still got hot water?"

"The boiler's wood-burning. I'll get Ilse to run it for you."

"Shall I give you a hand up the stairs?"

"No, no – you go up and have your bath. I can manage. Oh – I forgot to tell you – I've given you Johnny's room, opposite mine. I thought you might feel a bit isolated in the guest rooms."

"Thanks – you're right."

Of course you have to give me a room, for appearance. I hope that's all it is – you haven't even put your arms round me.

He must be feeling really bad, Franz. Just give him time.

Johnny's room was plain and simply furnished, like all the rooms in the Leussow house, and there was a good fire in the grate. It was wonderful to feel warm as I undressed and put on the silk brocade dressing gown that lay on the bed.

Ilse knocked. "Your bath's ready, sir."

"Thank you."

Something about Ilse made me think I'd seen her before – the cast of her features, maybe, or the shape of her eyes?

Too complicated.

The bath was bloody lovely. I actually felt myself starting to relax, as if the Front were seeping out of my pores.

As I walked along the cold corridor to my room, the feeling of being watched came back powerfully and I turned round – but of course no one was there.

I shut the bedroom door, and the feeling disappeared. I got into bed, less tense than I'd felt for a long time.

I was with the old group from Heidelberg. We were running across No Man's Land to recapture a trench from the English. They were throwing everything they had at us, and the air sang with flying metal.

Anton went down, and then something hit my right knee hard and my leg crumpled, throwing me to the ground. Kurt helped me into a shell-hole and then went on with the others.

There was something odd about him, and after he'd gone I realised there was no flesh on his face. *Of course – he was killed last year.*

I was sharing the shell-hole with a stinking corpse and two other wounded Germans. As we lay there the sun rose higher, burning hot. My leg hurt horribly and I was parched with thirst. The terrific din of the battle continued overhead, and I knew I was going to be stuck there all day.

Suddenly a huge Tommy appeared in the shell-hole. A dreadful scream cut right through the noise and I realised he'd killed the fellow furthest from me. To my utter horror he began to decay at once, literally rotting before my eyes. I was cold with shock, shaking, and I dragged my eyes away. There was another scream, right beside me. I daren't look, I couldn't, I was paralysed with terror. I wanted to run but I couldn't move.

Then the Tommy was standing over me and there was no flesh on his face, either, it was just a death's-head, and the bayonet was coming down towards me, dripping blood, and I screamed—

I woke with a jolt, trembling and drenched in sweat. In the darkness I could see nothing and I started to panic. The screams rang in my ears and I had no idea where I was. *Does it matter, Franz? It was a dream.*

Thank God – but someone really is screaming. My hair stood on end, and after a moment of paralysis I managed to reach for the light switch.

To my infinite relief I wasn't in a shell-hole full of bodies, but in a strange bedroom. *Karl's house, the room opposite his* – I leapt out of bed, pulled on my dressing gown, ran into his room and switched on the light.

He was thrashing about and yelling.

"Karl, wake up!"

He sat bolt upright and lashed out. I caught hold of his shoulders and shook him.

"*Wake up!*"

He was running with sweat and shaking, staring straight through me, his eyes wide with terror. Then they focussed on me and he sagged.

"Franz, thank God! I thought – I thought – oh, God, that was horrible!"

He shuddered and covered his face with his hands. I sat on his bed and put my arms round him, and we clung to each other like a pair of frightened children.

I realised with a shock that I could feel his ribs and vertebrae, and that his shoulder blades were almost sharp, as if my nightmare had come to life.

You always held me so tight in those strong arms of yours, and now you feel unbearably fragile. No wonder you didn't hug me at the station.

I loosened my hold slightly, afraid of hurting him, and he released me and leaned back against the headboard, his face white.

The quilt had fallen down, leaving his upper body bare, and I stared at the scar between his breastbone and his right nipple. It was four to five centimetres across, ridged and discoloured. Beneath it a length of rib was missing, and the flesh sank inward.

No wonder you were in such agony, I thought, aghast. *How did you survive that?*

He opened his eyes, saw where I was looking and gave a humourless smile. "Pretty, isn't it?"

It wasn't. It was hideous.

"Sorry – I didn't mean to stare."

"Oh, don't worry – I stared enough myself the first time I saw it, when it was still... before it had healed."

He paused, looking down at his hands.

"I didn't look for the first few weeks, didn't really want to know. And the only times I could have seen it were during the – when it was uncovered, and I usually had my eyes shut."

I'll bet you did. I don't envy you one bit. You might be out of the war but the price is far too high for me.

"I don't know about you," I said, "but I need a drink."

"You and me both. I'll fetch the brandy."

"No, you stay here. I'll go."

XII

The house was in darkness, and I had to switch on the lights as I went. I wondered what the servants thought of the racket we'd made.

No doubt they're used to Karl having nightmares.

I shivered as I walked along the icy corridor and down the broad wooden staircase. Eyes watched me from the portraits on the walls, fleshless ghouls lurked in the corners – *oh, for God's sake, Franz, get a grip!*

I fetched the brandy and glasses from the library, and was glad to re-enter the bright warmth of Karl's room. All the way up the stairs I'd felt as if I were being followed, and the feeling didn't go away until I closed his bedroom door behind me.

He was sitting up in bed, the quilt pulled up, that ghastly scar no longer visible.

"Get in," he said. "You'll freeze."

"Thanks." I handed him a brandy.

"Christ, don't give me that much!"

"Oh, you can manage it."

I left the dressing gown on a chair and got into bed beside him.

"Thanks for waking me," he said.

"You woke me, and you did me a favour – I was dreaming about a skeletal Tommy bayonetting injured blokes in No Man's Land, and it was about to be my turn!"

He laughed. "Well, we've seen Death wearing khaki often enough."

"That's for sure… What was yours?"

"Oh… they'd all come back – you know, the Frenchies and the Tommies, wanting a word…"

"I get that one too."

"Most of the time I just can't sleep – it all goes round and round in my head. I've tried reading but I can't concentrate."

"It should get better now you're out of the war."

He laughed. "You really think I'm out of the war? Franz, I could live to be a thousand and I wouldn't be out of the fucking war – or rather, it wouldn't be out of me. Some nights I'd give anything to be able to stop thinking."

"You just need to drink more!"

"I did try, but it just made it worse."

There was a long pause. I wanted to hold him again, because I wanted his bare skin against mine, but also because I knew his embrace would make my demons retreat.

"I'm glad you're safe," I said. "No one can hurt you now."

I refilled both our glasses. He looked at his uncertainly.

"If the ghosts come back I'll wake you up," I said.

"All right – but don't say I didn't warn you!"

A few minutes later I noticed the glass tilting in his hand, and managed to catch it before the brandy spilled onto the bedclothes.

He stirred as I took it from him. "Mm?"

"Why don't you lie down, being as you're nodding off?"

"Was I?" He gave me a very sleepy smile and settled down on his left side, facing me. "Good night, then – and remember, you're on sentry go!"

"Don't worry," I said solemnly. "If I see a spook I'll shoot it."

He fell asleep in no time, and I put the bedside light out and finished my brandy in the darkness. I felt so much more relaxed with him beside me, and I lay down as well, feeling that the spectres were just a bit further away.

When I woke, light was coming through the chinks in the curtains. For a moment I wondered where the hell I was.

Karl was fast asleep in my arms, and I didn't want to wake him. Sleep was precious, and God knows he needed it.

After a while he woke and blinked at me.

"Morning," I said.

He smiled. "Morning," he said sleepily. "Lovely surprise."

He stretched lazily, then rolled onto his side, facing me, and put his arm around me. I laid mine across his ribs, very aware of how fragile he felt, cautious of embracing him in case I hurt him.

We looked into each other's eyes, and the distance between us disappeared.

This is more like it, I thought a while later. *Now I really feel we're together again.*

I remembered how afraid I'd once been to touch him, in case he rejected me, and had to laugh at myself.

"What's so funny?" he asked with amusement.

I told him and he laughed.

"Well, you weren't to know and I wasn't about to tell you – I didn't know how you'd react. So I decided to take advantage of the dancers being there. It would have been another bit of fooling around, and if you'd pushed me away I'd have laughed it off, and I hoped you would too."

"So, er, when did you first...?

"Lose my virginity? Franz, I went to boarding school. What do you think goes on, all those boys cooped up together? I can barely remember being a virgin... It was boys at school and girls in the holidays."

"And if you had to choose?"

"What – restrict myself to half the population? Perish the thought!"

"You are such a tart."

"Guilty as charged! You hungry?"

"Starving."

"Suppose we'd better get up, then." As he got out of bed he caught sight of himself in the mirror and scowled. "Bloody bag of bones."

"You're lucky to be here at all," I said quietly.

"Am I? Look at me. What you mean is I *was* such a tart. Who in God's name will want me now?"

So that was it. You thought I wouldn't want you any more.

"Cast your mind back a few minutes."

He looked at me, his eyes suddenly softer than I'd ever seen them, but then he turned away abruptly and picked up his dressing gown.

"Would you like the bathroom first?" he asked, his voice far warmer than the words.

"Yes, thanks."

"See you downstairs – oh, and borrow my clothes if you like."

"Thanks – I will. Be good to get out of uniform."

The house felt almost normal, apart from a strange, slightly chilly feeling on the staircase. *It was only my imagination last night – probably my nerves.*

The library was bright and cheerful with the curtains open and daylight pouring in. The snow had stopped falling, and the sun shone from a clear blue sky.

Beautiful flying weather, I thought, and wondered what was happening at the squadron.

I had to wait ages for Karl to come down, and with nothing to do and no one to talk to I started feeling shaky again. I lit a cigarette and wandered round the room, trying to calm myself down.

The papers on the table all related to the estate, and I was careful not to look at them. Even the account books lay open, next to a pile of bills. Beside them was a large, leather-bound book. That was open as well, the pages filled with the Major's neat, precise handwriting. *That must be his journal. Didn't he have an office in one of the outbuildings?*

There were a few family photographs in silver frames, including one of a parade on the Tempelhof Fields in Berlin, the Kaiser saluting as the Foot Guards marched past.

Karl showed me that the first time I stayed here, when I mentioned to Friedrich that I'd seen the film of the big review two years earlier.

I picked it up for a closer look.

Where's Friedrich? Oh, yes – there—

The door opened, and Karl came in before I had time to put the picture down. I knew how much he loved his oldest brother.

"He was a fine man, Karl," I said. "And a good soldier."

He took the photograph from me and stood looking at it. "Yes, he was."

He put it down carefully.

"They were such a contrast, those two," he said. "They couldn't have been more different."

"That's for sure!"

Friedrich was a professional soldier to his core. I wonder what he'd have made of Johnny's tangled relationships, and his selling his cartoons under his pen name.

"You're more like Friedrich," I said.

"Don't know where you get that idea – last thing I ever wanted to be was an officer!"

"No escaping your fate."

"Quite. Shall we eat?"

Over breakfast he said, "There's not much to do here – I do hope you won't be bored."

I can think of plenty to do, I would have replied if Ilse hadn't been there.

"I've had more than enough excitement for my whole life – peace and quiet will do fine."

Once again he ate hardly anything, and when he suggested a walk I agreed, hoping it might give him an appetite for lunch.

The bitter cold hit us as Karl opened the French window from the music room onto the terrace. We stepped out, our boots crunching. The lake was frozen over and covered in snow, its edge marked by the reeds. Everything was white and almost too bright to look at.

"It's a shame to mess it up," I said, looking back at our footprints. Obviously no one had expected us to come out this way, and the terrace and steps hadn't been swept.

I linked arms with Karl, and kept a firm grip on him as we went down the steps and onto the path. We strolled slowly along the avenue of limes towards the rose garden, our breath clouding in the frigid air.

His hand found mine. It didn't feel quite the same with gloves on, but I didn't care. I was with Karl and nothing else mattered.

Except—

"Can we be seen from the house?" I asked.

"Do you care?"

I thought for a moment. "No."

"They won't be looking – and even if they are, I promise you Henning will never say a word to anyone."

"I don't give a shit what anyone thinks, anyway."

He squeezed my hand and we carried on, but I realised he was getting out of breath.

"Let's sit down for a moment," I said.

"Are you sure? We'll freeze."

"Yes."

We brushed the snow off one of the stone benches between the trees, and sat turned towards each other.

"It's so beautiful here," I said. "And so peaceful. You could almost forget there's a war."

He didn't answer.

That was really stupid, Franz. He's been to the edge of the grave, he's lost both his brothers and he's haunted by Verdun – and you imagine he could forget the war.

"Sorry," I said.

He smiled. "Don't be daft. I know what you meant... Let's get back."

We'd gone almost no distance, and I realised how much the previous day had taken out of him. When we got to the foot of the steps I put my arm round his waist.

"I can manage."

"You mean you don't want my arm round you?" *Argue with that.*

"Oh, all right then!"

The house stood on a slope. There were more steps up to the terrace than to the front door, and they were steeper. He was soon leaning on me heavily, and breathing hard.

I stopped, and when his breathing eased took him slowly up five more, and then stopped again.

"Go on," he said.

"I'm enjoying the view."

"Bollocks."

I tried to stop again after another five steps, but he pressed on. By the time we reached the top he was barely able to stay upright.

We had to stop then, and he leaned on the stone coping, bent over, trying to catch his breath. Then he started coughing, and I could feel that it was hurting him.

The cold was burning into my face. *I need to get you inside, but we'll have to stay here until you can move.*

After a couple of minutes he straightened up, his face grey and drawn, a tinge of blue in his lips. *That was too much for you. If I'd realised how bad you are, I'd never have done this.*

"Let's get inside," I said.

The music room was cold, but several degrees warmer than outside. The piano stood waiting, its lid closed.

"Will you play for me later?" I asked as we took our coats off.

He shrugged. "Maybe – I'm so out of practice."

"Well – you've got plenty of time now. How much leave have they given you?"

"I have to go before a board in March."

Three months? Do they usually hand out convalescent leave in lumps like that? Maybe it's a formality before they give you a medical discharge.

The fire was blazing in the library. I glanced at the flames, and started shaking as fear ran cold down my back and curdled in my stomach.

"We don't have to have the fire," he said quietly. "The stove does a pretty good job."

"I'm all right," I replied, my voice sounding harsh.

"And I'm all right too."

I sat beside the fire and forced myself to look at it, then lit a cigarette and made myself look at the flame of the lighter.

There. That wasn't so bad, was it?

Karl was looking at me with concern.

"Fancy the paper?" was all he said.

"Which one is it?"

He laughed. "Well, it certainly isn't *Vorwärts!*"

No, you wouldn't read the socialist paper.

"It's the *Kreuzzeitung!*" he said, waving it at me.

"Karl, how can you read that right-wing rubbish? It makes Attila the Hun look like Lenin."

"I can't – but I can't read any of the others, either. They're all shit. Pa always had this one, so I've just carried on with it."

"All right, then – it might be worth a laugh."

It was complete crap.

"Listen to this," I said, and read out a ridiculous opinion piece about the reparations and land that we should demand from the defeated Russians. At least, I tried to read it out. We were both laughing so hard that I could only manage a few words at a time.

"It's not funny, really," he said. "Not when you think – well, what if we lose? What will the Allies demand from us?"

They'll crush us...

Lunch rescued us from that conversation.

It was the same as breakfast – rye bread with a few thin slices of cheese and ham.

"I'm sorry I don't have more to offer you," Karl said.

"Don't be daft – this is real bread, and you won't see ham or cheese in the towns."

He ate quite a bit more, and I didn't comment.

We settled ourselves back in the library. The sun had moved round and was starting to come through the western windows.

I wish I could stay longer...

"Penny for them, Franz?"

"I was just thinking that I wish I could stay longer."

He smiled, his eyes warm. "So do I. Come back when it's all over and stay as long as you like."

When it's all over...

"I'll be in Valhalla," I said.

"No, you won't."

"Karl, you can't possibly—"

The horrible illusion I'd had at the school came back, and I shook so badly that he must have seen. I fought to steady myself, and then I said, "Can I ask you something?"

"Yes, of course."

"Do you – this is going to sound really stupid, but do you see things that are going to happen to people?"

He looked at me sharply. "Why do you ask?"

"When I gave the talk at the school, one of the boys was worried that the war would be over before he got to it – and it was – I saw his skull and I had a strong feeling that he's going to be killed. It was really disturbing, I can tell you."

"Mm." He nodded. "Sometimes, yes. I told you about my East Prussian grannie, didn't I?"

"Yes."

"I think there's a lot we don't understand. Kurt had a premonition, and I've known that happen to other fellows as well, and yes, I've known someone was going to get killed. And you must have had that instinct that tells you to change shell-holes, and then the one you were in gets a direct hit."

"And you put it down to chance the first couple of times."

"Exactly… On the other hand, it could be that you hear something in the way the shells are falling, or that the other fellow's a reckless idiot who had it coming."

"And premonitions are self-fulfilling."

"Quite."

There was another question I wanted to ask him – whether he felt that presence on the stairs as well.

I'm not sure I want to know. Yes and no would be equally disturbing.

I was trying to make my mind up when I saw that he'd fallen asleep.

I picked up the paper and tried in vain to concentrate on it.

It's months since I actually read anything. At the squadron all I do is leaf through the papers – someone always interrupts, or puts the gramophone on, or it's time to go flying again – and now I get to the end of the sentence and have to read the beginning again.

My life is running out. I've only got a few days here, then it's Adlershof, and then the Front and the end of me – whatever Karl might think.

The sun crept round, sinking ever lower, until it was setting across the frozen lake in a blaze of colour.

How beautiful it was last year, sitting on the terrace watching the light fade. Karl will be here in the summer, gazing at the sunset on the water, and I'll be bones under a wooden cross.

The sun had gone, and the twilight lingered. Ilse came in with a basket of logs and fed the stove.

She was as quiet as possible, but Karl stirred and then woke with a start. He looked round for a moment, completely disorientated, and then looked at me.

"Franz, I am so sorry – I've done it again."

"Doesn't matter."

Ilse knelt in front of the fire to feed that as well. *That's a very shapely arse. I wouldn't mind getting behind that.*

My eyes met Karl's. He raised an eyebrow and shifted his position slightly. *You're thinking just the same as me, aren't you?*

She left, closing the door.

I let a couple of moments pass and said, "Where did you find her?"

He grinned. "Fancy her, do you?"

"You can talk!"

"I think – only think, mind you – that she's my half-sister."

Ah. "That's why I keep thinking I've seen her somewhere before."

"Probably. I've got my suspicions about quite a few people round here. Pa was a randy bastard, as you know – fucked every woman who'd have him."

"At least it was only women!" I retorted.

"Fair comment! Anyway, Ilse's off the menu as far as I'm concerned."

"It was only a passing thought. There'll be plenty in Berlin."

"Ah, yes – Adlershof."

"Fancy coming with me?"

He shook his head. "No. I don't really want to face everyone yet – and on the form to date, I wouldn't stay awake!" He paused, and then added, "Mind you, someone I know should be court-martialled."

I looked at him.

"Falling asleep on sentry duty – you were supposed to be scaring the spooks away, remember?!"

I laughed. "Damn – I thought I'd got away with that!"

The room was filled with the last of the evening colour.

"Beautiful, isn't it?" he said. "And tomorrow we'll see it again. That's been almost hard to get used to – knowing I'll still be alive this time tomorrow."

I daren't get used to it, I thought, envying him – and then I put what he'd suffered on the other side of the scales.

"And I have paid for the privilege," he said, echoing my thoughts. "Franz, what happened when I was shot down? All I know is I was trying to get that two-seater and then I got hit – my own damn fault for not watching my tail."

"That's about the size of it – it was one of those new Sopwith fighters."

"The one they call the Camel? I saw pictures in the *Berlin Illustrated*."

I nodded.

"What's it like?"

"Fucking horrible," I replied. "Turns on a sixpence. Even if you'd kept your stupid eyes open you'd have been pushed to get away in an Albatros. Anyway, I saw him going for you, but I got there too late and you were spinning."

"Mm. Did his guns jam? It was beautiful, accurate shooting and I should have been riddled."

"Yes. You were bloody lucky."

"Was I?" He poked the fire, sending up a flurry of sparks. After a moment he said slowly, "It's all a bit vague after that…"

"Tell me what you remember and I'll try to fill in the gaps."

"Well... she started to spin as I passed out, and then I came round to find myself in a spiral dive, and then I made a right dog's breakfast of the landing – I was really fading by then. I tried to get out but I couldn't, but there were soldiers all around and they got me out and shouted for the medics. Then a bit later you were there, and another fellow with you—"

"Fellmann."

"Ah, that's who it was. Another question – had they put me with the hopeless cases?"

I hesitated.

"Franz, I know I was in the dying room later."

I sighed. I really didn't want to think about any of it, but he had a right to know.

"Yes. You were in a field outside the hospital, and they'd left you... How did you know?"

"It was early morning when I was shot down, but the sun was high when you were there so it had to be hours later. And then you came to the hospital, and I probably talked complete nonsense."

That was said with a failed attempt at light-heartedness.

You're worried what you might have said.

"Pretty well – look, no one expects sense from someone in that sort of state. One of the orderlies said, 'They say all sorts of things and no one takes any notice'. So – the first time, you thought you were in the trenches. The second time, the Chief came with me and you were talking about Verdun, and you said 'du' to him—"

"I said 'du' to the Chief?! I'll bet he liked that!"

"Actually he held your hand and said 'du' back."

He looked at me in disbelief.

"Yes, I know – I thought I was hearing things. And the third time you said something about sitting in the sun, but I didn't hear the rest of it."

Is it my imagination or did your face clear slightly?

"Franz, you came three times?"

"Four, but the last time you weren't there. It gave me a hell of a fright. I thought – well, that you were dead. Then they told me you were in the hospital train."

"You came three times and sat in that—"

He broke off, got up with some effort and went to the table to pour me a brandy, keeping his back turned for a minute or so.

"I don't know how you could stand it," he said quietly as he handed me the glass, "but it meant a lot to me, knowing you were there."

"I'm glad I helped. I – it – I wanted so much to – this is going to sound stupid, but I wanted to do something, to help you. And of course I couldn't – though the Chief did persuade them to give you morphine."

A brief grimace crossed his face. "Then I wish he'd been there for the next few weeks… What was that about the hospital train?"

"They said you were on your way to Germany – but we found out later that they'd taken you to Brussels. I thought I might get there to see you, but the Chief went off to get married and left me in command."

"You wouldn't have enjoyed it, believe me… So, old Adalbert's married! That must have caused tears all over Germany."

I laughed. "He still gets propositions by the sackful – they don't give a shit about his wife!"

"And I'll bet you get them as well."

"I can't believe those women are so stupid. Do they really think I'm going to jump into bed with them?"

"Worth a try, isn't it?! So are any of them in Berlin?"

"I don't bloody know! The only women I know in Berlin are Helena and Marion, and the women I met at the free love club – and I don't have any of their addresses."

Henning announced dinner. *Oh, God, that's one day gone already...*

Don't count, Franz. For God's sake don't count. But I knew I would.

Karl ate about half his food and gave the rest to me. I tried to protest, but he said, "You have to fight when you get back – I'm just sitting here, doing fuck all."

"You've earned a rest," I said. "You fought for nearly three years, in some of the worst places, and you've been hit twice and damn near killed."

"I got what was coming," he said with a shrug. "I'd dished it out enough."

That was a thoroughly unpleasant thought. Once we were back in the library I said, "I don't see that you deserved it – it was your duty, and what choice did you have? It's us or them, after all."

"I was a sniper, Franz. I had a choice."

"It's still us or them. Each fellow you shot was one less to stick a bayonet in me the next day. And there was that Tommy sniper you got rid of."

"Oh, I don't mind about him – he was playing the same game, and I was just lucky I got him first... But there are a couple I'd like to forget – that staff officer for a start."

"He was up to no good, going up to the front line."

"Yes, and it had to be done – but he had a family... And the other—" he paused and stared at his hands a moment before continuing, very slowly, "he appeared in the gap in their parapet, and either I fucked up the deflection or the wind, or he slowed down – and he didn't drop, just staggered against the parados and turned towards me, and his eyes, both of them – I'd blinded him. And that was not what I intended, and I don't know which is worse... I've seen him in my dreams ever since."

"Karl, Taschner wouldn't have given a shit about either of them."

He gave a short laugh. "That's for sure – he told me once he'd shot a captain who was helping one of his fellows back to their trenches. He said he could see they were both injured. I told him straight out that I thought that was shit, and he said, 'Everyone knows you're part English' – as if that had anything to do with it... But perhaps he was right, and I'm wrong."

"No, you're not. I think we have to keep as much decency as we can. What you said when we volunteered was dead right. It's a filthy business."

"I can't say being right gives me any pleasure... Life's easier for bastards like Taschner. He enjoyed it, and he couldn't see anything wrong in that. My problem is... That job took a lot of skill, and you know how it is. When you do something difficult and you do it well, you feel proud of yourself – and then afterwards you think what you actually did, and you ask yourself whether you enjoyed doing it, and you don't want to face the truth, don't want to look in the mirror."

It was my turn to stare at my hands.

"The Taschners of this world are much better off," he continued. "They know they enjoyed it and they don't care. I don't suppose he has the sort of nightmares we have. Sometimes I feel I really am the murdering bastard you all thought I was."

I looked up. "Karl, I—"

"You too, Franz. Even you gave me that look."

"It was Wolter. It made me really angry, him being shot when he was just rebuilding the parapet, and I suddenly thought about you and I couldn't get it out of my head. Then I thought about it a bit more, and realised I couldn't judge you. And don't forget, you put your life on the line every time you went out."

"True..."

"So are you saying I've got it coming too?" I asked reluctantly.

"You know the proverb: live by the sword, die by the sword. Or in our case the bullet."

I laughed, rather uneasily. "If I'd known you were going to come out with crap like that I'd have stayed at home!"

He smiled. "God knows I don't want anything to happen to you. I just feel it's my turn to suffer what I inflicted on others."

"That's crap, Karl! Total crap. You've spent too much time thinking. You did your duty, like any soldier, and there's no point feeling guilty about it."

"*They* don't think that, do they – or they wouldn't keep coming back."

I had no answer to that.

"I just wish I knew what it's all for," he said quietly.

I had no answer to that, either. "So do I."

"When I think of my regiment just before Verdun, all the bloody good blokes we had—" he broke off and poked the fire "– and all the other men we knew… I just wish someone could tell me why they died, and what benefit it's brought."

"And now we have to keep going, because otherwise the enemy will be in Germany."

"Can we really win? We've got half the world against us and we're running out of everything."

I stared into the fire, not wanting to answer that. "Let's talk about something else."

"Good idea. Tell me about the Fokker Triplane again – I fell asleep last time."

So I did, and he fell asleep again. *I'll tell you the rest of it tomorrow.* I lit another cigarette.

I picked up the paper and tried to read, but gave up in disgust after a couple of attempts. *Karl won't mind my having another brandy.* I went quietly to the table.

He snored loudly and woke himself up.

"Franz, I can't believe I've done that again! Next time please wake me up."

"You need the sleep – it'll help you get better."

"If I sleep now I'll lie awake half the night."

"Shall I pour you a brandy?"

"Please. Do help yourself to anything you want, won't you?"

I put the brandy on the small table beside him.

"Thanks," he said – then he caught hold of my hand and kissed my palm. It tingled right down my spine.

He leaned back in his chair and looked up at me, his eyes bright. "Come to my bed in the morning, if you like."

"*To* your bed, or *in* it?"

He laughed. "Both, I hope!"

"How about this evening?"

There was a sudden shadow in his eyes. "Not after I've climbed the bloody stairs."

"No, of course not," I said quietly. Stupid of me – I'd seen how exhausted the steps up to the terrace left him.

Once again I went up first, and he followed some time later. *You don't want me to see what dragging yourself up to the first floor does to you, and I can't blame you for that.*

I had a bad night – I must have slept a bit, but it felt as if I'd spent the whole time staring at the ceiling in the darkness. It was one of those nights you just want to end.

Finally it began to get light. *In half an hour I can go to Karl's room...*

"Come in!" he called out when I knocked.

I locked the door behind me, discarded my dressing gown and turned to face him.

"Come here," he said, his voice thick, his eyes intense, and I crossed the room and slipped into his bed.

A while later I said, "Karl, I – well, I don't want to go any further."

"You don't want to do that again?"

"Oh, I do, for sure – I meant, I don't want to – I don't want to fuck. That's going a bit too far."

"I never thought you would."

He propped himself on his left elbow and looked down at me, his eyes gazing into mine. He stroked my eyebrow gently with one finger.

"Franz, I will never, *ever*, do anything you don't enjoy."

He lowered his head and kissed me very softly.

I put my hand behind his head and prolonged the kiss. He closed his eyes, just too late to hide the deep tenderness in them. It was the last thing I'd imagined his eyes could hold.

I thought of the Corporal and his lover at the station in Berlin, and for a moment I wondered just what Karl's feelings for me were.

That's stupid. We're a couple of very good friends enjoying a bit of fun. That's all.

He was starting to tremble from the effort of supporting his weight. I released him and he lay beside me, somewhat out of breath. *They really have wrecked you*, I thought, holding him as close as I dared.

"Mind you, I don't think I could fuck anyone now," he said after a couple of minutes. "I get knackered so quickly – just can't get my breath."

"You need some girl to sit on you," I said. "That would do the trick."

"That's a good idea – maybe I'll order a tart from Berlin. Or you can choose one and send her to me!"

I don't want to leave here. I don't want to go to Adlershof, and I certainly don't want to go back to the Front. I just want to stay with you.

Yes, Franz, very practical – you have to go to Adlershof and so on. You're a Pour le Mérite now and you have to set an example.

You can hardly skive when you have so many decorations. Just think of this as a beautiful interlude, a memory to keep. And Karl will still be here after the war, you can come back...

'After the war'?

I didn't want to think about the bloody war – but how could I avoid it when I could feel Karl's bones?

My stomach rumbled loudly.

He raised an eyebrow. "Breakfast?"

"Good idea."

He rolled away from me and started to get out of bed, then stopped suddenly.

"*Fuck!*" It came out in an agonised gasp.

I knew any concern on my part would only irritate him.

"Thought we agreed we wouldn't," I said flippantly.

He eased himself very carefully back onto the pillows, trying not to move his right arm, then lay still, his eyes closed, his face grey and lined.

That hurt a lot. I wonder which movement caused it.

Bugger your pride. "Is there anything I can get you? I mean, do you have any pills or anything?"

He shook his head.

"I'd be taking them every bloody day if I did," he said, his voice strained. "It's pretty well constant – not usually as bad as that, though."

"What happened?"

"Tried to push myself up with my right arm – forgot I can't do that, would you believe. Bloody idiot."

"What was it that Schmidt fellow called you – you know, when you were a sniper and about to take the Express Ticket? 'Stupid cunt', wasn't it?"

"Cheers, bastard!"

We both laughed, and I said, "At least you're not pissed off that I saw."

He looked at me and smiled. "After what we've just done?" There was a pause and then he added, "And you saw me in a far worse state in hospital, after all."

"That's for sure. That time you were screaming – it just went right through me."

His face changed, and I wished I hadn't spoken.

"Oh – I didn't realise you were there – I remember you being there after the injection, but I didn't realise... At least I think you were there. It all turned into a rather strange dream – I thought we were here, in the rose garden."

"Oh, that's what you meant about sitting in the sun. It was the morphine, Karl – they'd given you rather a lot. And the fever made you hallucinate as well. We all thought you were going to die."

"So did I. And later, the pain was so bad that I wished I were dead..."

"What – worse than when you were screaming?"

"In a way – because they couldn't leave me like that. But later, when it was just really bad – they couldn't give us what they didn't have... We were all left in pain for hour after hour. I thought I'd go mad."

If I get hit then it'll be me lying there like that. Unless I crash to my death, of course.

"Anyway, that's quite enough of that subject," he said. "You don't need to listen to that sort of thing."

I got up first, so he could get out of my side of the bed and use his left arm.

If I were living here with you, I'd learn what you can and can't do, then I could—

I stopped myself. I would not be living there with Karl. My leave was running out fast, and my life with it.

As he turned away from me, I saw the small, neat scar of the entry wound, between his spine and his right shoulder blade.

That's all it takes – one piece of metal...

He suggested a walk again after breakfast. It was another glorious day, and I did want to get some air and stretch my legs, but I didn't want him to have to struggle up the steps again.

My uncertainty must have shown in my face.

"It'll do me good," he said, "a bit of fresh air and exercise – and I'll feel less like a bloody invalid."

"Can we come back in the front door?"

He smiled. "If we do that then I shall feel exactly like a bloody invalid. It's bad enough not being able to make it to the rose garden. I have tried, you know."

"You need to rest."

"Franz, I've done fuck all except rest for months. I am fucking sick of bloody resting. I'm going for a walk, and you can come with me or not as you choose."

I ignored the rather tetchy tone. "Of course I'm coming with you, you stupid bastard."

He put his arm round my shoulders. I turned towards him and we embraced – and once more he closed his eyes as if to hide them.

And even though he was so painfully thin, I felt safe in his arms.

We walked hand in hand under the limes, the low sun striking diamonds from the snow. I had never been so deeply content and I wished time could stand still.

I wish I could choose life with you over death at the Front – but duty is duty and I have no choice. And if I could make that choice, then you would lose all respect for me, and so would I.

We managed one bench further than the day before.

"Sorry, Franz – I'm so fucking slow."

"I'm not in a hurry," I said with a smile. "I've got all day, after all."

I took him back up the steps very slowly, pausing after every three. *You're going to behave yourself while I'm here.*

"You go into the library, Franz," he said. "I need a pee."

I sat by the fire and realised again how worn my chair was. *I'll bet yours is the same,* I thought – and it was. *This must be so uncomfortable with your bones sticking out.*

I looked round the room in search of a cushion, and something caught my eye, hidden in the corner between the fireplace and the wall.

A walking stick.

Karl, for God's sake – why the fuck do you have to pretend with me? If you need a stick then for fuck's sake use it.

I was back in my own chair when he came in.

"Oh, the *Military Weekly*'s come," he said. "Fancy a read?"

"Thanks – after lunch."

"What would you like to do this afternoon?"

"Sit here and watch the sun set – and enjoy not having to do anything."

He smiled. "There is one thing we could do – my neighbours to the east – their son's just finished his pilot training and he's off to the fighter pilot school next week. And of course the poor little sod's got no idea what's waiting for him. They asked me to talk to him, and I did, but – well, they wanted me to go in uniform, and all he saw was the glamour. If you can call it that."

"Yes, I know what you mean," I said cautiously. The Pour le Mérite was enough to dazzle any youth.

"And I've been away from the Front for months. Would you have a word with him, tell him what to expect?"

I sighed. *The last thing I want to do is talk to another starry-eyed boy about the war. He won't last five minutes. It's too fucking depressing.*

"If you'd rather not then it doesn't matter," he said. "They don't know you're here. I didn't tell anyone."

"Thanks – can I think about it?"

"Of course."

We had a lovely lazy afternoon sitting by the fire. I leafed idly through the *Military Weekly*, just in case there was news of anyone I knew.

And bugger me, there was.

"Alfred's got another gong," I said.

"Good for him – what is it?"

"The Austro-Hungarian Medal for Bravery, in Bronze."

"What for?"

"Disabled an Italian machine-gun nest under heavy fire, accompanied by three of his men: stormed the position, killed the crew, captured the gun."

He laughed. "That sounds like Alfred. Mad bastard."

"And of course he got whacked."

"Not badly, I hope?"

"No – couple of bullets in his leg."

"Italians can't shoot straight, then!"

"I'll probably get another letter from him soon," I said. "He usually writes when he's been hit. Probably gives him something to do in hospital."

"It does get a bit dull once you can think straight. Tell the bastard to write to me, won't you?"

"I'm sure he'll be happy to – especially being as you saw him last year."

"Yes... I never told you the full story about that. Things happened so fast I never got round to it."

"Go on, then."

"Well," he said, "I think I just said I saw him... I'd been to see the lawyer, had to sign a load of papers, and I was dying for a beer. So when I got back to the Adlon I went into the bar, and there was Leutnant Alfred Friedemann looking very smart with an assortment of ribbons, both black and white and coloured.

He bought me a beer in celebration of my Blue Max, and we were sitting there having a good old natter when in walked old Fessler."

"What – Fessler from the training camp, who wanted you to be his batman?"

"The very same. Anyway, he looked rather put out at seeing me there, and he excused himself and went upstairs. So I said to Alfred, 'Where are you staying?' and he answered, 'Here,' and I said, 'Together?' and he went bright red and looked as if the sky were falling in. So I said, 'Don't worry, I won't tell anyone.' Of course *you* don't count."

"Alfred's queer, then?"

He burst out laughing. "Franz, you need to ask?!"

"Well, he's not camp like Fellmann, or one of the orderlies when you were in hospital."

"Neither was Great-uncle Heinrich. And I doubt Frederick the Great was, either, or Julius Caesar – though he was like me, by all accounts. But yes, Alfred's queer all right."

"I did think he must be – that's one reason I'm happy for him to help Johanna get into medical school, because I'm sure he doesn't want to get into her knickers – but I've never had it confirmed before."

"I reckon she's safe with him – though you can never be completely certain... It was good to see him again, especially after the previous meeting."

"What previous meeting?"

"Ah... that was at Verdun. We – what was left of us – were on our way out, and he was heading up with his storm troops. And a finer bunch of thugs you wouldn't want to bump into – just the sort of fellows you want beside you."

"Pity you were going in opposite directions."

"Yes. We only had time for a few words... It'd be really good to meet up if he gets convalescent leave."

"I'll tell him to write."

"Thanks." He smiled warmly.

Beautiful eyes you have, I thought, and remembered them gazing at me from the portrait on the classroom wall.

The portrait— "Shit! I almost forgot!"

"Forgot what?"

"To ask you to sign your photo for Zaffke."

"Of course – I'd be glad to, but I don't have one to sign."

"Ah, but I do – I'll go up and get it before I forget."

I fetched the cardboard tube from my room. The sun had set and the staircase and corridors were in gloom, and once again there was a chill and a feeling of being watched.

Of course it feels cold, you idiot – it is fucking cold. Remember what Karl said in the trenches – 'You've never been in our house in the winter?' Well, now you know what he meant.

The library was almost hot in comparison. Karl was staring into the fire and he jumped half out of his skin when I closed the door.

"Sorry."

"What? Oh – I must have nodded off again."

No, you were wide awake, just a long way away. There was that look in his eyes again that I couldn't quite name.

"Come and sign the picture."

I unrolled it on the table.

"Bloody hell, old Beilke's got a talent for this!" he said. "I don't believe I ever looked that good. Why am I doing this now?"

"It's to say thanks for mending the furniture every other day. That's what he said he wanted, signed pictures of the squadron's Blue Max holders for his boys."

"Was that all? Well, I'm more than happy to oblige, for obvious reasons."

He wrote, 'To Zaffke, my esteemed comrade, with very best wishes', and signed it.

"I'll write a covering letter tomorrow," he said, "and Henning can get it posted."

"Thanks," I said. "That'll complete the set."

"There is absolutely no need to thank me – I'd do almost anything for the fellows who were at Verdun with me."

He didn't say any more. *One day you might be able to talk about Verdun, but clearly not yet.*

Maybe that wasn't a good subject to touch on before dinner – but to my surprise he did eat rather more.

I'll see if you can manage a longer walk tomorrow, or maybe two shorter ones.

When we got back to the library he poured us a brandy each, and then ferreted in the papers on the table.

"Ah, here it is," he said. "This might amuse you, Franz."

He handed me what I thought was a photograph album – but it was full of Johnny's drawings.

"I've tried to get them into chronological order," he said. "You remember how he was always sketching, and chucked half of them away."

"The ones he couldn't sell, you mean!"

"After he was killed, when I was sorting out his things, I found a folder full of them, and when I came back here I found a whole lot more in a drawer. It's given me something to do, putting the album together."

It started with sketches of life on the estate: there was the Major about to go hunting, the harvest, with everyone working – everyone except Johnny, who had drawn himself sketching.

His father was walking towards him with a face like thunder, and I could almost hear him shouting, 'Put that bloody pen down and do some bloody work, you idle young bugger!'

A draught horse pulled a plough, the straight furrow behind it neatly parallel to the others. The ploughman looked familiar.

"Is this you?" I asked.

"Yes – I've always enjoyed ploughing. It's very satisfying."

Next came university. Johnny's corps brothers sat round a table groaning with beer glasses. The air was thick with smoke, and the students sagged in their chairs, blearily drunk. On the opposite page two of them fought a duel, and I could almost hear the ring of the sabres.

Superb. He'd had the knack of suggesting movement or an expression with a few lines, and his figures sprang alive from the paper.

Johnny himself was on the next page, raising his glass to me. He was exactly as I remembered him, his expression cheerfully impudent, his face seamed with scars.

"That's him to the life," I said, turning the album towards Karl.

"Yes, isn't it!"

He'd captured the army perfectly. An NCO bellowed at a line of recruits, men marched down a road with their rifles and packs and spiked helmets. There was a trench half full of mud and water, soldiers bailing it out in the pouring rain. Men swam in a canal, splashing and laughing.

The scenes changed to aviation. The different types he'd flown, caricatures of his instructors, a party in the mess, the table collapsing and glasses flying. There were sketches of all his squadron mates, Karl and me included.

"Look, he's got both of us! And there's Otto – and he's caught that look the Chief has when someone's annoyed him… These are superb, Karl, they really are."

There was the Christmas party at the General's HQ, the staff officers in their best uniforms looking like a row of stuffed dummies, and an enigmatic half-smile on the Major's face. *Probably knowing Johnny expected a grilling about his two fiancées, and enjoying not obliging…*

I turned the page and froze.

There were two photographs, facing each other: on the left was Johnny's funeral procession, led by Karl, his father immediately behind him and the squadron grouped around the gun carriage. The other photograph was of the grave, Johnny's name and the dates of his birth and death carved on the broken propeller blades.

All I could see was Johnny falling on fire through the sky, and I nearly lost my dinner. I had to change the subject.

"He was a bloody good artist," I managed to say, my voice trembling. "I'll never forget those drawings you had in your room at university."

"Oh, the rude ones! Yes. I've still got them, on my bedroom wall. Henning doesn't approve. Oh, he won't say anything, but he looks at them as if they smell."

"I'm surprised I didn't notice."

"Well, you had other things on your mind!"

"That's for sure... I've always meant to ask you – it is you, isn't it?"

He laughed. "What do you think, Franz? Do you think Johnny sat there drawing me fucking?"

"Yes, I do! You put on quite a show for me, after all."

"Glad you liked it."

"You know I liked it – and everything after it. I couldn't help but. So – are you going to answer my question?"

"He could have been drawing from imagination, you know." He was laughing again. "But you know perfectly well it's me. Johnny and I had a couple of weekends like the one we had, and I took Friedrich to meet them as well, after he'd lost his eye. I thought he needed cheering up."

"Are you telling me those two girls have been to bed with all the Leussow brothers?"

"Not both girls. Friedrich's not an exhibitionist like me – he likes to keep it private."

He suddenly realised he'd used the present tense. His eyes widened slightly, and the sparkle in them died, replaced by a look of deep hurt. It was the look of someone who'd suffered too much, who'd been pushed to breaking point or perhaps beyond it, and I wished I could undo everything that had happened.

How often do you slip like that, and then remember that they're all dead?

"Do you still manage to write to Elisabeth?" I asked.

"Yes, not often, but we keep in touch. She knows what's happened."

"How's her husband?" I wasn't sure if I should ask.

"All right, last thing I heard – but that's weeks ago. He's somewhere on the Western Front, but she couldn't tell me where, of course. He's a lieutenant colonel now – if he's still alive. It's a real bastard having family on the other side, I can tell you."

"If you ever meet the Kaiser you can compare notes on that one."

"He's never had to wonder if he'd recognise his brother-in-law before pulling the trigger. And I've always liked Henry – he's a good sort. I was going to spend part of summer '14 with them… and now I haven't seen them for over four years." He sighed. "The boys must be getting quite big now. The older one will be… Good God, he'll be seven!"

"Does she have trouble because of the war?"

"I don't know. I hope not. Her English is very good – she sounds like a native speaker, to me, anyway. She's got that English intonation which I can never quite manage."

"Your English is excellent."

"Thanks. Mama made sure we all spoke it, from the beginning."

He stared at his hands for a moment.

"I'm glad she didn't have to see her parents' countries at war – it would have really upset her. We were all so close, used to visit each other every year – it was like having another home, though rather grander than this one." He laughed. "I used to come home and wonder why we lived in such a small, plain house, why we didn't have a house in Berlin as well."

Small house – this? Jesus, the Bartletts must be loaded.

"I said that to Pa once and he gave me a thorough beating, told me to be bloody grateful for what I had… Everyone was so pleased when Henry and Elisabeth got married – no one could guess what was coming."

He poked the fire and the logs blazed back to life. I forced myself to look at them.

"Elisabeth's stuck now and it must be so hard… There've been such strange reports about people in England hanging dachshunds, and accusing people of spying and so on – I just hope nothing nasty happens. We always write in English, so no one gets the wrong idea."

"Her husband's family will protect her, though, surely?"

"No doubt…"

"Do you think the boys get stick on your account?"

"Uncle Karl being a German ace?" he said with a note of self-mockery. "I'll bet they keep quiet about it."

It's not only Elisabeth who's stranded. Karl's on his own now, in this lonely, brooding house. Once I've gone, there'll be no one to talk to except the ghosts…

I didn't want to think about ghosts, not before bed.

My bad nights were catching up with me and I was struggling to keep my eyes open, but I was afraid to go to sleep. I'd have sat there half the night, needing to sleep yet not wanting to, but I realised Karl was flagging.

"Can I have another bath?" I asked.

"Of course – you can have as many as you like! Make the most of it."

There was a big jar of bath salts on the shelf, and I added a generous handful to the water. There was a wonderful smell of herbs, like being in a walled garden, and I relaxed as the warmth soaked into my body.

I wonder whose they are. Can't imagine Karl using bath salts, but they're very soothing.

I wrapped myself in the quilt, hoping the war would leave me in peace for just a few hours.

XIII

Of course the war did not leave me in peace. I must have fallen asleep straight off, but not long after I woke with a jolt – and that was that. I lay wide awake, with my head so full of the trenches that at times I was almost hallucinating.

I wonder whether Karl's awake. I really could do with some company. This is getting beyond a joke.

My bedroom door opened and I jumped half off the bed, terrified that one of my demons had materialised.

To my enormous relief, a familiar voice asked quietly, "Franz, are you awake?"

"Yes. Come in." I moved to the left side of my bed and waited.

He closed the door softly, and after a moment I felt his weight settle beside me.

"I hope you don't mind," he said. "I was having an awful night."

"So was I. I'm glad you're here."

He rolled into my arms, rested his head on my shoulder and laid his right arm across my body.

"Is that all right, your arm lying there?" I asked.

"Fine for now, thanks."

We lay in companionable silence for a while, and then he said, "Franz, I don't want you to feel – I mean, you don't have to do anything just because we're in bed."

I held him a bit tighter.

"I've never felt I had to do anything," I said quietly. "I've really enjoyed everything we've done – that's obvious, surely?"

"Give me a fellow with a hard cock and I can be almost certain to make him come."

"Karl, you could make Michelangelo's David come."

"Gravel."

"What?"

"Gravel – David's spunk would be gravel, don't you think? In a little pile on the floor of the museum!"

"Never mind where else it could get to!"

We couldn't stop laughing. Suddenly I felt so much more relaxed.

"I'm going to have to move," he said after a minute or so, and shifted onto his back. I rolled onto my side, my body close against his.

"Going back to what I was saying before we got completely silly," he said, "what I meant was that even if the fellow didn't really want me to touch him, he might well let me. A lot of men are a bit curious as to how it would feel – probably most men, if they're honest with themselves."

"It's not like that," I said. "When you touched me the first time I – well, as I said, I'd never thought of doing that – but you – no one's ever made it feel like that. I'll always want more."

"I don't want you to think you have to do anything in return."

"I don't. I enjoy that too…"

We lay in each other's arms in the afterglow, his head resting against mine. I held him close and stroked the silken skin of his back, the warm embrace and the scent of our bodies filling me with deep contentment. My lips met his in a soft, lingering kiss, and although I was satisfied, I had no desire to break the contact and roll away from him.

I should have realised, then, that we loved each other, but I was almost wilfully blind.

At some point I fell into a deep, dreamless sleep. When I opened my eyes it was broad daylight, and we were facing each other. For a moment Karl's eyes were softer than I would ever have believed, and then he smiled as he hid that expression and replaced it with a more neutral one.

There was a quiet knock at the door. Karl got slowly out of bed and retrieved his dressing gown from the floor. I noticed that he put his right arm into the sleeve first and pulled it up onto his shoulder, and then bent his left arm back into the other sleeve.

You can't move your right arm back, can you? That must be really awkward.

There was a second knock and I called out, "Come in!"

It was Henning, looking rather ill at ease.

"Good morning, gentlemen," he said, and turned slightly towards Karl. "I'm very sorry to disturb you, sir, but there's a Leutnant Sakowski of the Home Defence downstairs with an NCO and five men. He says he has to see you. I told him you're indisposed but he said it's important."

Karl sighed. "I suppose he wouldn't say what it was about?"

"No, sir. I did suggest that he come back later, but he insists on seeing you now."

"Oh, all right. Show him into the library, take the rest of them into the kitchen and see what you can give them. Tell the Leutnant I'll be with him as soon as possible."

"Very good, sir." He closed the door behind him.

Karl turned to me, somewhat puzzled.

"God knows what this is about," he said. "Show of strength, I think, Franz."

I nodded.

"How quickly can you get dressed and downstairs?" he asked.

"Five minutes or so."

"Can you keep the fellow company, give him my apologies for keeping him waiting and say whatever you think appropriate? I'll be down as soon as I can."

I shaved and washed as quickly as I could, put my uniform on and went down to the library.

The Leutnant was looking at the bookshelves, clearly rather fed up. *A bit young for Home Defence* – then he turned towards me, and I saw the empty right sleeve and the bruised look in his eyes.

Those eyes went straight to my Pour le Mérite.

"Leutnant von Leussow? Sakowski, Home Defence. I have here the order of—"

"No, no," I said. "I'm not Leutnant von Leussow. He'll be down shortly. I'm a guest here. Becker, Air Service."

We shook hands awkwardly.

"Leutnant von Leussow sends his apologies. He'll be down as soon as he can."

"The butler said he wasn't well."

"No. He was shot down over Ypres last July and he came out of hospital last month." I could see the implication of the dates sinking in. "Cigarette?"

"Thanks."

I lit it for him. "Where did you lose your arm?"

"Verdun." The shadow in his eyes deepened.

"Ah, yes… I escaped that one. I left the infantry at the beginning of '16, so when it began I was learning to fly. Then I was posted to the East."

"You were well off out of it," he said.

"Yes, so Karl – Leutnant von Leussow – told me. I gather it was pretty nasty."

"Yes, it was." He paused. "I'm sure I've heard his name before. Which regiment was he in?"

The door opened and Karl came in. He'd always cut a good figure in uniform, but now his tunic hung loose on him and the belt gathered it in at the waist. The grey fabric made him look even paler, seemed somehow to deepen the lines in his face.

He introduced himself courteously, very much the dignified head of an old, proud family. I felt a degree of sympathy for Sakowski, who was looking awkwardly from one of us to the other. He was well aware that he was intruding and, while he'd known he was going to be at a social disadvantage, he clearly hadn't expected to be confronted by two Pour le Mérites.

"I do apologise for keeping you waiting," Karl said. "I'm a bit slow at present."

"That's quite all right. I do understand." There was a pause. Sakowski clearly didn't want to launch straight into official business. "Leutnant Becker tells me you were at Verdun."

Karl smiled and dropped a little of his reserve. "Yes, I was. I have to say I'd had enough after the first couple of weeks. I'd been thinking about a transfer to the Air Service for some time and that convinced me. By the time the transfer came through we were back there, and I remember thinking I probably wouldn't live to get it."

"I wish I'd thought of that. I got this at the end of May and I was glad to be out of it, and I don't mind admitting it."

"So was I."

They were both silent for a moment, then Sakowski asked shyly, "May I ask which regiment you were in then?" His face brightened at the answer. "Good God! So was I!"

"Well, I'll be damned!" Karl said warmly. He changed suddenly, from a nobleman faced with an unwelcome official matter to the man I'd always known. "I thought I'd heard your name before. Which company?"

"The Tenth. I was an officer cadet when it began."

"I was in the Seventh… Were you there on the first day?" Karl asked.

"Yes, I was."

"I've never been able to hear that since without remembering…" His voice thickened and he stared at his hands.

"No, neither have I," Sakowski said. "It always brings it – that is, all the fellows…" he broke off, gazing at the floor, then blew his nose and cleared his throat loudly.

I studied the library shelves, feeling I'd seen something I shouldn't.

After a moment Karl said quietly, "What can I do for you? Henning said it couldn't wait."

Sakowski had recovered his composure. "I'm very sorry about this, especially in the circumstances. We have orders to search all farmsteads. The authorities are concerned that food isn't reaching the towns."

"That I can believe. Search all you like. You'll find four pigs, a cow, a few chickens, a draught horse, and a pony. In the barn you'll find some hay and straw, and in the storerooms there are a few kilos of potatoes and turnips and some sacks of rye. The larder's not much better. There's nothing in the distillery – it's been shut down for two years. The place has gone to rack and ruin since the war began, and there's bugger all here."

"Thank you. I'll come and report back to you before I go."

Karl and I had breakfast and went back into the library, and he stood gazing out of the window into space, his fingers drumming on the glass. The rhythm was starting to sound familiar…

He started humming to himself, very quietly.

"'The Glory of Prussia,'" I said.

"You did well to get that from the rhythm."

"You were humming."

"Oh, didn't realise… We went in singing it on the first day at Verdun."

That's why it upset you so much in Brussels. That's why Sakowski was almost in tears just now.

I heard the singing, heard the French fire. The song faded as the men fell…

Just like Langemarck. Just like bloody Langemarck. Only this time they were soldiers, not students. A Brandenburg regiment, with its glorious history, advancing to that magnificent tune – my hair stood on end.

"We weren't the main assault," he continued. "God knows why, but they just sent patrols in at five, then we followed at six when it was nearly bloody dark. And the rest of the Brandenburg Corps went in the next day. I've no idea what happened in the other Army Corps, but I presume it was the same. Why they didn't send us in at dawn, mob-handed, I've never understood. And someone told me they had the bands playing for the main assault. Bloody unbelievable."

"And I can guess what they played."

"Of course. It was like saying to the French, 'We smashed you in 1870 and we're going to smash you now.'"

But it's not the nineteenth century any more. With the bands playing. Dear God.

He sighed. "It was supposed to be a walkover. The bombardment was unbelievable. I was afraid I'd go deaf. God knows what it must have been like for the French. They were all supposed to be dead, but there were plenty left and they fought like tigers. After the first couple of days we were down to half-strength. We cleared the wood, but the price was so high – and on it went, more of the same.

"You should have seen the place after a few weeks of that. The stink was unbelievable. You could smell it when you were coming back up, long before you got there…"

"Like Ypres."

"Worse. I know that's hard to believe, but it's true. Sometimes you could hardly breathe for it."

It's the same every time. Every new offensive gets bogged down in slaughter and no one knows when to put a stop to it.

Karl had never been able to talk about it before, not consciously, anyway. I hoped Sakowski wouldn't come back, not just yet.

"Was that the wood Sonnenberg described as a perfect killing ground?"

"I expect so." He gave a short laugh. "You had to admire what the Frenchies had done there – you couldn't move without being shot at and you couldn't make out where they were, and then you realised there were blockhouses built into the terrain, and the artillery hadn't destroyed them, not at first, anyway. We had to take them one by one."

That must have been fun.

"When the Chief and I visited you in hospital, you said something about a village and your company being down to forty men," I prompted.

For a moment I thought he wasn't going to answer. He walked slowly to his chair and sat down.

"It was in the bottom of a valley and the Frenchies held most of the high ground. They just threw whatever they liked at us, and all the cellars were reinforced and full of machine-guns. It was completely fucking impossible – I thought we were all going to die there."

How did they get the wounded back, out of a mess like that? Probably better not thought about – it was probably impossible.

"They had to pull us out after that – the Corps was fuck all use any more. There were so few of us left and we were all exhausted… They sent us to Alsace, but after only five weeks we were back at fucking Verdun again and it was even worse, because the Frenchies had got their act together—" He broke off. "Franz, I'm sorry. You're on leave, you shouldn't have to listen to shit about Verdun."

"No problem. I wanted to hear it."

"You did? Why?"

"Because of Brussels."

"Oh. I see… " He shook his head. "That village was only part of it… By the time my transfer came through, most of the men who'd been there on the first day were gone. And that day in Brussels the music brought it all back, so vividly, and I could see it all again, and all the men who are dead – bloody good blokes they were too…"

And you'll think of them every time you hear it.

"When I met Alfred—"

There was a knock at the door and Sakowski came in.

"It's just as you said, Leussow, and I'll be reporting to that effect. I don't think you'll be troubled again – not for several months, anyway. I'm very sorry for the intrusion."

"Don't mention it," said Karl. "It's not your fault. Would you like to stay to lunch? It won't be lavish, as you've seen, but the conversation might make up for the table."

"I'd love to, but I'm not allowed to accept hospitality."

"No, I see. Well, the invitation stands, if you find yourself in a position to accept it. Just turn up – I'll be here for another couple of months."

"Thank you," he said, and took his leave of us.

"Poor sod," said Karl. "That's a hell of a job they've given him."

"You were going to give him a hard time until you found out you'd been in the soup together."

He grinned. There wasn't really anything he could say to that.

"What were you saying about Alfred?"

"Oh, just that you could see that they were on their way up for the first time by how fresh they were. No one looked like that after a week or so."

I'll bet they didn't.

"The worst thing was when you were in the line you didn't sleep – there was almost no pause in the fighting and the shelling was constant. Half the time the rations didn't get through, we were desperate for water, taking bottles from the dead and hoping there was still some left. Sometimes we had to drink out of shell-holes – you can guess what that was like. It was forbidden and it gave you the shits, but we were so bloody parched... After a week of that we were all completely wrecked."

Quite apart from the carnage.

"And that's enough about that ghastly place – I've said far more than I intended."

"I'm glad you did – I've always been – I'm going to sound like one of those Freudian fellows – but it's always bothered me that you couldn't talk about it."

He smiled. "There's a post-war career for you – become an alienist!"

"Not bloody likely! I've got enough crap of my own – I don't want to listen to other people's." Suddenly I realised what I'd said. "Present company excepted, of course."

"Goes without saying... I think I'll go and get changed. Frederick the Great used to call his uniform his shroud, and I reckon he was right."

"It's been that for a lot of men."

I wanted to go and change as well, so I could pretend there wasn't a war, but I knew Karl wouldn't want me to see him on the stairs.

Instead I went in search of a cushion for his chair. There were none in the library, and I tried to remember where the drawing room was.

Next to the music room?

Right first time. The room was elegant and spacious, with three French windows onto the terrace. The sun was just coming round and casting diamonds of light on the floor, but it did little to raise the temperature.

The first time I stayed, we sat in here before dinner, with the evening sun streaming in. It feels so different now with the furniture under dust sheets, so empty in the silence—

Someone was standing close behind me – I turned swiftly but there was no one there. I shivered. *It's broad fucking daylight, for God's sake. That sort of thing's only supposed to happen at night, isn't it?*

In happier times this room would have been full of people – Uncle Heinrich in his wheelchair, Karl's mother and sister reading or sewing, maybe Friedrich home from cadet school…

And all the generations who lived and loved and quarrelled and died here.

'Yes – it's ours and you're intruding. So be a good chap and bugger off…'

I took a couple of cushions from a sofa, and left the room to the dead.

I put the cushions on Karl's chair and tried them out. *That's much better. Now if you had a footstool and a blanket, you could sleep when you needed to, in comfort.*

Something told me not to push it.

Karl came in, and looked at the cushions with suspicion.

"Franz, what are those doing there?"

I grinned at him. "Just try it."

This time the suspicious look was directed at me.

"Just for me. Go on."

"All right – but I'm only doing it to please you!"

"I'm going to change," I said. "If you don't want them then put them on my chair instead!"

He laughed. "Didn't realise you were uncomfortable!"

Getting changed took me a fraction of the time it had taken him. *It's not just the stairs, is it? Everything must be hard work for you.*

The cushions were still on the chair, under Karl's bottom and behind his back.

"So how is that?"

He pulled a face of pretend protest. "Oh – I'll force myself to endure it to keep you happy! Fancy a walk?"

"Yes, good idea." As we got to the door I said, "Haven't you forgotten your stick?"

His face fell for a second, and then he recovered himself.

"My dear Franz," he said, "you are bigger, stronger, and less likely to slip in the snow – and a bloody sight better-looking!"

He put his arms round me.

"And I'd far rather hold on to you than some bit of wood," he murmured in my ear.

"No need to turn on the charm," I said. "I am impervious to your flattery."

"Of course." He held me tighter, and we kissed.

"At this rate we won't be going anywhere," I said thickly. "And downstairs is far too dangerous."

He released me. "Lean back against the door."

But it's far too dangerous – we might be seen – oh, so what...

That was fucking stupid. "We mustn't do that again – not down here, that is."

"I suppose you're right," he said with a smile. "Now are we going for that walk?"

A path had been swept on the terrace and the steps. *This wasn't here yesterday.*

"Someone's swept the terrace," I said as casually as I could.

"Yes – must have been first thing this morning, when we were still in bed."

I hope to Christ no one saw us just now.

"Don't worry, Franz – look round at the library windows. There's no way you can see the door from here."

I turned, and he was right. All I could see was the dazzling white of the snow reflected in the windows, almost too bright to look at.

"And I wouldn't have been so bloody stupid as to do that if there'd been anyone out here."

"No, of course not."

All the same I was careful not to hold his hand until we were some way from the house. Putting my arm round him to help him up the steps was just sensible.

After lunch we went back into the library. Karl settled himself comfortably into the cushions, and I said nothing. *I'll sort out the footstool tomorrow, and see if Henning or Ilse can find a blanket.*

I wish I could stay here with you...

"Penny for them, Franz?"

"I was just thinking I'd like to stay here."

He smiled warmly. "I wish you could. When I – when they moved me, once I knew what was happening, all I could think was that – well, that I wouldn't see you again."

"I was so worried that you – the Chief tried to get you moved, but the doctor said you weren't strong enough, and then they did move you…"

There was a pause, which stretched itself out as if there were something that should be said, but which hung unspoken in the air.

Why didn't I understand then?

After quite a few minutes of friendly silence he said, "Now what were you telling me about the Triplane and structural problems? I promise to stay awake this time!"

That was quite a change of subject.

I told him about the weakness in the top wing, and the aircraft being grounded.

"Why can't they get it right?" he asked.

"God knows. And we need something to beat that infernal bloody Camel as well – the Triplane can just about manage in the right hands, but nothing else can cope with it. The only consolation is that the Tommies keep crashing them."

"So what's on offer at Adlershof, or don't you know yet?"

"No idea. I'd like something strong and fast, with a good rate of climb and a nice high ceiling, and that I can dive and turn as hard as I like – and that has room for a parachute."

He laughed. "That's quite a shopping list! I suppose you'd like guns that never jam as well!"

"Of course!"

What I really want is never to have to fly over the Front again... Be careful what you pray for, Franz. The price for that is ending up like Platzer, or suffering like Karl.

"If we had parachutes then none of the rest of it would matter," he said, and of course I noticed the 'we'.

You're out of it, Karl. There's no way you'll be fit for the Front again. Just accept that, for God's sake.

"No," I said. "God knows how many men have died for lack of those."

"Including Johnny."

I don't want to think about Johnny falling—

My hands started to shake. I was desperate for a fag but knew I wouldn't be able to light it – and I didn't want to have to look at the flame of the lighter.

I forced myself to look at the fire.

"There's something I've been wanting to ask you," I said, "but it's a bit personal."

He looked at me and raised an amused eyebrow. "Franz, you can ask me anything. Whether I'll answer might be another matter."

"At Johnny's funeral and at your father's, we sang 'Now thank we all our God', and I wondered why we were singing a hymn of thanksgiving. Is it family tradition?"

He smiled. "Yes, it is – going back to Leuthen."

Ah – Leuthen. The great Prussian victory of 1757 over the Austrians and their allies – including Württemberg.

"You do know about Leuthen, surely?" he asked, misunderstanding my expression.

"You can't go through an officers' course at Döberitz without them banging on about the great Frederick's masterstroke, as you well know! As I recall, your lot managed to slaughter our lot, even though we were in a much better position on top of the hill and outnumbered you massively. I blame the Austrians – they must have fucked up as usual."

He laughed. "Sorry – I'd forgotten your people were on the other side! I don't think our lot expected to win – I think they expected to be slaughtered. Anyway, there were two Leussows there – August, who was thirty-five and a major, and who'd fought in all the campaigns since 1740, and Karl, his youngest brother, who was seventeen and had just joined the regiment.

"After the battle August realised Karl was missing, and found him lying in the snow, bleeding badly and beyond help. Someone began to sing that hymn, and everyone who could joined in – probably couldn't believe they were still alive, never mind victorious. Karl died in August's arms during the singing – and we've sung it at our funerals ever since, in his memory."

There was a pause and then he added, "That's the sort of thing I was brought up on. I used to think that because I was called Karl, I would die young in battle as well. Once I got past seventeen I reckoned I was safe." He laughed. "And two years later, look what happened!"

I laughed as well. "But the man with the scythe kept missing, didn't he – and now he'll have to wait until you die of old age!"

He gave me a rather straight look. "The war's not over yet."

"You're named after August as well, and he made it to thirty-five – it'd have to go on a hell of a long time to get you then! What happened to him, anyway?"

"Fell two years later at Kunersdorf, when our lot really did get slaughtered. At least we presume he fell there – he was missing and never turned up."

"And you're descended from him?"

"No, from Wilhelm, his next younger brother. August only had daughters – don't suppose he was too pleased about that."

"And what about Wilhelm?"

"Lost a leg at Roßbach, the poor bastard, and died some time later. Never saw his son – that was another Friedrich. He made it to general, got killed at Jena making a heroic stand against Napoleon's cavalry."

All such a fucking waste.

"Glory doesn't come for free," he said wryly.

That's for sure.

The last scrap of sunlight disappeared. *Another day over, another day closer to settling my own bill.*

He stretched. "I should sort out the family archive some time – we've got some interesting stuff, and I suppose someone should write the family history, before it's too late."

"It would give you something to do."

"While I'm convalescing, yes – don't know if I'll have time to finish it, but I can make a start."

"Karl—"

"After all, I'll be going back."

"Do you really think so?" I asked. I didn't want to spell out that he'd never be fit to fight again.

"Of course."

"You know," I said slowly, "the war can't go on much longer. There could well be peace before you get passed fit."

"There's a fine pair of suppositions."

"Why don't you get a job in Berlin, say with the Technical and Testing Commission, like that friend of Fellmann's?"

He gave me a very suspicious look. "Don't you start."

"What do you mean?"

"Have you forgotten? They tried to get me to take that job in Berlin last summer, to keep the name from dying out?"

"Oh – yes, I had. Completely."

It's hardly relevant now – your right lung must be fucked, and there's no way you can fly and fight at altitude. You'd pass out.

"And I am nowhere near as fucked up as Fellmann's friend. He's a right wreck."

There's more than one way of being fucked up...

Dinner didn't touch the sides – mine, that is. Karl managed about half his food, and seemed to have to force that down. It was very disturbing to see – he'd always had a good appetite.

You need to build yourself up again – but if I say anything I'm only going to make things worse. There's been too much about Verdun today, with Sakowski turning up like that, and talking about meeting Alfred there.

On the way back to the library I remembered him saying his chest hurt constantly, and wondered whether that was making him feel unwell.

"You know, Franz, I hate to admit it, but this chair is a lot more comfortable with your 'modification.'"

"Well, if you put some weight on, it would be better still!"

He sighed. "Please don't start on that. I eat as much as I can."

"Can they do anything about the pain?"

"Discomfort," he corrected firmly. "They said to give it time."

"And what about your leg?"

He looked at me in surprise. "How do you know about that?"

"You told Westermann – you remember, his had been broken and he hurt them getting out of the aircraft."

"Oh yes – I'd forgotten. It's a while ago now."

I shouldn't have mentioned Westermann. The flames in the grate leered at me menacingly.

"The poor bastard," Karl said, gazing into the fire. "I saw far too much of that sort of thing at Verdun... They used flamethrowers to clear the blockhouses, but—"

Why did I hope you'd tell me more about bloody Verdun?

"– the Frenchies learned very quickly to shoot the operators." His voice was very quiet and I wished it were completely inaudible. "Some of our fellows were stuck in the brambles, couldn't get loose, and the flame hit them and the whole lot burned..."

Karl, for fuck's sake shut up!

The stink of petrol filled my nostrils. The Tommy turned in behind me, firing again. *One spark and I'll fry—*

I was sitting by the fire in Karl's house, shaking from head to foot. I'd spilled brandy on my trousers, and the glass fell over as I tried to put it on the table. I fumbled for a cigarette and dropped my case and lighter on the floor.

"Franz, I'm so sorry. I had no idea," Karl said with gentle concern.

"I'm all right," I answered roughly, and bent down to retrieve my fags and lighter. I couldn't manage to get hold of them.

Karl picked them up from the carpet, and put one of my cigarettes in his mouth and lit it. He took a cautious drag and coughed.

"Horrible hot smoke!" he said, handing it to me. "How you manage without a holder I'll never understand!"

"Thanks." I took it from him with trembling fingers.

He pulled himself up with the aid of my chair, and refilled my glass.

"Sorry – I spilled it," I said.

"Doesn't matter," he replied with a smile.

"Johanna said I stank of booze and fags." I tried to sound light-hearted but failed completely.

"You wouldn't be a soldier if you didn't... Have you got just the two weeks' leave?"

"Three."

"Is that including Adlershof? Then it's only two. Adlershof isn't leave." He paused. "Franz, please don't take this the wrong way, but you need a proper rest."

"I'm all right."

He looked at me, very directly. "Just now, I called you several times but you didn't hear me, and then suddenly you were back. How often does that happen?"

I didn't want to meet his eyes. "Now and again."

"Last year, when Widemayer cracked up, all I could think was that I'd be next. I couldn't sleep, I had episodes like yours just now when I thought I was somewhere else... I was lucky – I got that bullet through me and so I had to stop. It all builds up so gradually that you don't realise how bad you're getting – it wasn't until I was in hospital in Baden-Baden that I knew just how far down I'd gone."

"Karl, I haven't had anything like the war you had, I'm absolutely fine and *I'm not going to end up like bloody Widemayer!*" My voice rose shrilly on the last words, and I grabbed my brandy glass and threw a generous slug down my throat.

"No – but you do need a break from the Front. You'd be surprised how much difference it would make. When you see the Chief, tell him you'd like six months at one of the fighter pilot schools."

I stared at him. "You're off your head. That's completely impossible."

I wouldn't be able to go back at all after a break like that.

He smiled, in spite of my tone. "I knew you'd say that."

"You wouldn't take that job in Berlin."

"Mostly because of the reason."

"And because, like me, you'd feel like a skiving coward if you left the Front. When I was home last week, people kept stopping me in the street and asking for my autograph. They all seemed to think I was some kind of hero – and what would I be if I stopped fighting?"

"Do you care what they think?"

"No – but I have to be able to look in the mirror. I wish, more than anything, that I could just stay here with you, but I can't. Duty is duty, as you well know."

"Indeed I do – and in your place I'd say the same."

"I tried to get you posted away last summer," I said. "The Chief asked me how you really were, after your father died. I said that I thought it was very hard to lose a brother and a father in such a short time, and that you'd had a bad war, and then I let slip about the job in Berlin – it just slipped out, and I said that maybe you should be ordered to take it."

"You said *what*? For fuck's sake, Franz – what possessed you?!"

"Sorry – but it was the same thing. I could see you needed to stop, and I knew you wouldn't listen."

His anger evaporated. "You're right. Fine pair we make – but please think about it."

"All right – I will. Think about it, that is." *For all of half a second, as you'll realise.*

He's just trying to keep me safe, just as I want him to be safe. If only this shitty business would come to an end.

It would be stupid to fall out over wanting to protect each other.

"I stole some of your bath salts last night," I said, changing the subject.

"You rotten thief!"

"Well, they were just sitting there and I didn't realise they were yours – it was just now that I put two and two together. Do they help?"

"A bit – they're some herbal thing… You realise you'll have to pay a forfeit for that!"

I gave a mock shudder. "I suppose I pay in the morning?"

"That's right – you've got all night to ponder your terrible fate!"

When I went upstairs I looked more closely at the Frederician portraits. The uniforms looked like fancy dress to me, and those curls! *And each had his long plait hanging down his back. Wigs – they must have been wigs. All the same, how the hell could they be bothered?*

The blood and death were the same, though. No high explosive or rifle bullets in those days – they got hacked to death with swords, or mutilated by cannon or musket balls.

Wilhelm gazed at me with exactly the same eyes as Karl and Friedrich.

Horrible way to die, especially back then when medicine was so primitive. Having your leg cut off without anaesthetic doesn't bear thinking about.

The next portrait was August's. I looked at him closely, and suddenly I was standing on the battlefield littered with dead and wounded.

A rough chorus of thousands began to sing, 'Now thank we all our God, With hearts and hands and voices—'

August sat in the bloodied, trampled snow, holding his dying brother, tears pouring down his face—

A shiver went through me and the spell was abruptly broken. I was left thinking of Anton dying after Langemarck, and Kurt in the mud, in the pouring rain, everything grey except his blood as it ran down into the muddy water…

I turned away from the portraits and went to my room.

The fire was burning down, but its flicker still lit the room after I turned out the light. I forced myself to look at it.

You've already faced the worst. And if you're hit and can't get out, then roll the aircraft inverted and you'll drop.

I wished I hadn't thought about Anton and Kurt. I couldn't get either of them out of my mind.

'Don't forget us, Franz,' they said. *Forget you? I wish I could...*

I must have slept, but it was hard to tell the difference between dreams and thoughts. Once or twice I started awake with a feeling of doom, but unable to remember why.

Dawn cannot come soon enough, I thought in the small hours. *And then I can go to Karl and pay my forfeit.*

Once again I enjoyed the appreciation in his eyes when I shed my dressing gown.

He threw the quilt back.

"Very nice," I said.

Later we settled into each other's arms, and it was broad daylight when I woke.

"Karl, what time is it?"

"Does it matter?" he asked softly.

"No. Not at all..." I relaxed against him.

If it weren't for the servants I'd suggest we just stay in bed.

My stomach gave a loud rumble.

"Hungry?" he asked with a smile.

"And I'm dying for a pee. Suppose I'll have to get up – though it would be lovely to stay here all day."

He wrapped both arms round me and squeezed gently. *You used to squeeze the breath out of me,* I thought sadly.

"Yes, it would," he replied. After a moment he added, "I thought you might not want me any more – now I'm like this."

"Stupid bastard." *I'll always want you,* I thought but couldn't say. "You'd better let me go or you'll have a very wet bed."

He laughed and released me. I got out of bed reluctantly and picked up my dressing gown.

"See you downstairs," I said.

Time to finish my 'modifications' to your chair. I went into the drawing room.

'Oh, it's you again, is it?'

I won't trouble you for long, and I'm trying to look after one of yours... Now what would serve as a footstool?

After a couple of minutes I found an ottoman which I thought would do very well. It was on castors so I wheeled it to the library and put it by Karl's chair. *That's perfect – you'll be able to move it easily.*

Now all I need is a blanket. I remembered seeing a large box in the hall, and sure enough it contained a couple of travel rugs.

I sat in Karl's chair, and put my feet on the ottoman with the blanket round me. *Very cosy, especially with the stove and the fire, and the sun coming in. Let's hope he takes it the right way.*

When I heard his footsteps on the stairs I went out into the hall. *He can see that after breakfast. And besides, I'm fucking starving.*

The look on his face when we went into the library was quite something.

"Franz, what the fuck are those doing there?"

"Try it."

He looked at me. "I am not a fucking invalid."

Yes, you are. That is exactly what you are.

"Just for me."

"Yesterday it was cushions. Now it's this – and all 'just for you'. What the fuck am I going to find tomorrow? A bloody daybed? A nurse?"

I laughed. "Shut up and sit down, you ungrateful bastard!"

"Oh, for fuck's sake." His eyes suddenly softened. "All right – but only for you."

"It's just so you can have a kip in comfort, after a bad night. That's all."

He put his feet up and wrapped himself in the rug, gave a loud pretend snore, then yawned and rubbed his eyes.

"Now, how does that feel?"

"Tell you later, when I've tried it for real. Walk?"

"Why not."

It was another glorious day, except that a brisk east wind had sprung up.

"Bloody hell – that feels like it's come straight from Siberia," I said.

"Probably has – nothing to stop it, after all."

We'd better not stay out long. It's far too cold for him.

"Hope they haven't got this at the Front," I added. "It'd be a right bastard getting back."

"Yes," was all he said. I could hear how fast he was breathing.

"Let's sit down."

"Not yet."

We passed the last bench we'd sat on before. *This is getting silly. You have to get back.*

Do I say anything?

"Karl—"

He shook his head, and carried on slowly but determinedly past the next bench. His hand was starting to tremble in mine.

"You don't have to prove anything to me," I said. "We're stopping here."

I detached my hand from his and put my arm round him.

"Use what passes for a brain in your thick Junker skull." I led him firmly to the nearest bench.

He was horribly out of breath, and then he started coughing and couldn't stop. He pulled his handkerchief from his pocket and clamped it over his mouth.

Jesus. Now I have to get you back to the house, and I really don't fancy carrying you. I suppose I'll have to go and get Henning—

Finally he stopped coughing, and as he moved the handkerchief I saw the bright red stain on the white cloth.

I caught hold of his wrist. "Karl – that's blood!"

He struggled but couldn't break my grip. "*Let go!*"

There was such rage and frustration in his voice that I released him immediately. He stuffed the handkerchief into his pocket.

"Why did you – *oh, Jesus Christ!*"

"I'm sorry."

And I am, truly sorry, because all I've done is remind you how weak you are. You used to have a grip of iron, and I held your wrist, so easily.

I put my arm round him.

"It was the blood," I said quietly. "It gave me a fright."

He didn't answer, and I could feel how drawn into himself he was. *You need to get indoors, but I don't know how long you need to recover.*

"It's not what you think," he said after a couple of minutes. "It's not consumption – I've had tests."

"It's the injury, then?"

"Yes – it happens now and again. They said to give it time. Like every other bloody thing."

That must hurt. "Are you ready to head back? It's bloody freezing."

"All right."

We got up and started back, very slowly. I wanted to suggest that we go in the front door, but I didn't want to put my foot in it any more than I had already.

I didn't think we were going to make it up the steps. *We are not doing this tomorrow. It's too much for you.*

"Let's have a brandy," I said once we were in the library.

"Just a very small one, or I'll fall asleep."

"Would it matter if you did?" I held out the glass. "Even if you just rinse your mouth, get rid of the taste."

He stared blankly into space.

"Karl."

You're doing what I do, aren't you? I put the glass on the table and shook him gently.

He started violently.

"Are you back with me?" I asked quietly.

"Yes. Thank God."

"Where were you?"

He paused, and then said slowly, "When they carried me away from the aircraft, blood was pouring out of my mouth, and after they put me down someone gave me water, but he said not to swallow it, just to rinse my mouth and spit it out."

"And my saying something similar sent you back."

He nodded. "Yes – that's usually what does it. Something someone says."

Yes, you said that at the squadron.

"What does it to you?" he asked.

I had to think about that. "I don't really know. Sometimes it's that, but other times it just seems to be random. It's really frightening."

That was the first time I'd said that to anyone.

"Yes, I know." He took hold of my hand and I sat on the footstool. "Embarrassing, sometimes, too – like that day Patschke said what he did and I was back at Verdun, and then I realised it had happened in front of everyone."

"Don't worry about that," I said. "My guess is it happens to everyone after a while. It almost happened to me when I was talking at the school, though."

"I wonder what they'd have made of that."

I didn't want to talk about it any more. "Would you like the paper?"

"No – you have that, and I'll look at the *Military Weekly*."

I'd no sooner handed it to him than Henning announced lunch.

"Don't nag me, Franz, please," Karl said.

"All right."

The dining room faced east, and the light was much cooler

than in the library. Karl looked even more grey and drawn, and I realised that the lines around his mouth and eyes were probably due to pain, or rather 'discomfort'.

After lunch he fell asleep over the *Military Weekly*, and I sat smoking and trying to concentrate on the paper.

I was failing dismally until I turned the page.

'Schönwald court-martial,' said the headline. *Well, bugger me*, I thought as I read the article. *I'm surprised my family didn't mention this.*

When Karl woke up I said, "You remember Gräfin Schönwald?"

"The blonde woman at the dance in Villingen – the one you were pissed off with me for fucking?"

"That's the one. Well, you had a lucky escape. Her husband's an artillery officer, and he went home on leave, didn't tell her he was coming, wanted to surprise her. He was the one who got the surprise – she was in bed with another fellow."

Karl started laughing. "Some other unsuspecting chap she'd seduced! So what happened?"

"Schönwald drew his pistol and shot the fellow dead. Right there in the bed."

"Jesus. What about her?"

"He left her alone – just walked out and handed himself in at the police station."

"So what's happened to him?"

"He's been court-martialled and they've reduced him to the ranks."

"Bloody lucky he's not going to be shot."

"Quite…"

"Someone had some sense," he went on. "I mean, you get used to shooting people, don't you? It becomes normal."

"And that transition from the Front to the homeland isn't easy."

"No – though what I don't understand is why he shot the lover and not his wife. She was the one who'd betrayed him, after all."

"So you do think of it as betrayal, then?"

"I do have some morality, Franz – if you make vows and break them, that's definitely betrayal."

"But you went to bed with her – and with that baroness when we were at Heidelberg."

"In both cases the lady decided her vows weren't worth anything, for whatever reason. If you ask me, the whole business of marriage is fatally flawed. How can anyone keep a promise never to go to bed with anyone else for the rest of their life? It's ridiculous."

"Well, you would think so!"

"All right, Franz – suppose you married your girl, and then you came here to see me. Would you stay out of my bed?"

"Well…"

"And suppose you'd married her on your last leave. Would you stay away from Claudette's?"

"Well…"

"You'd fall down on both counts, and you know it."

"So if you made vows to someone, would you keep them?" I asked.

"At some point, after the war, I'll have to find a suitable wife, preferably one with some money – but it'll be on the understanding that, once we have the heir and spare, neither of us is bound to the other."

"Very modern."

"Very old-fashioned, if you think about it! That's how it's always been done."

"Except that it's usually gone one way," I said. "I wouldn't be happy about my wife having lovers."

"You can't complain if you've got them yourself, can you?"

"But does it count if it's just physical, like Claudette's or the free love club?"

"I don't think so," he answered. "And anyway, you'll be marrying for love, which makes it rather different. For me it'll just be a practical arrangement."

"You never know," I said. "You might really fall for someone."

He smiled, rather sadly. "Who knows?"

Time to change the subject. "Will you play for me?"

He sighed. "I don't know... I'm so out of practice. Maybe tomorrow – we'll have to get the stove lit in the music room."

I tried not to notice that the sun had set. *I wonder how long I'll last when I get back to the Front...*

"Mind you," he said slowly, "I can't help wondering whether having children is a good idea. I've got to, because of the entail, but I'll just be producing more officers to die for Prussia."

"Sonnenberg – the Chief's cousin who brought Lentzke's fiancée to the hospital – said his wife is convinced their sons will be killed in the next war."

"She's probably right... There'll be another war – there always is. Someone will want revenge for this one."

"You'd hope that we'd learn."

"What good would that do? I had learned, Franz – I grew up watching poor Uncle Heinrich wheeling himself about and drinking himself to death, and I didn't want to die on some ghastly field of slaughter like my ancestors, but I volunteered all the same. And our sons will do just what we did. Especially *our* sons."

"Why?" I asked uncomfortably.

"Why do you think? Look at all your gongs. Your sons will look at them and think, that's what I have to do. And you won't try to stop them, will you?"

"Not if Germany's in danger, no."

"And how in God's name will you know that? Do you believe one word of what we were told? It was Austria's quarrel and we should have stayed out of it. Bismarck was right about not getting tied to them, and about keeping out of the Balkans."

Dinner interrupted us. The dining room felt very unfriendly, as if the ghosts were sitting round the table.

I'm not surprised Karl can't eat. He'd be much better off with a tray in the library – but I'd better not suggest that yet.

It was a relief to get back in there. Karl poured us each a brandy.

"Now where did I put them?... Ah, here they are." He handed me a box of cigars. "These are all yours, Franz – I think I'd choke if I tried to smoke one!"

"It won't bother you if I do?"

"No – go ahead."

He sat down and looked at the ottoman with a mixture of suspicion and temptation.

"Just for you – because it would be a shame to waste your efforts!" he said, and put his feet on it.

"This is a bloody good cigar," I said appreciatively.

"Pa did know a bit about them – you might as well take those with you, and I've got another couple of boxes you can all have."

"Thanks."

"Going back to what we were saying," he said, "history will always repeat itself, if only because no one can pass on his experiences. Young men will always want to fight, and they have to find out for themselves what it's really like. There's no way of making them feel what it's like to cross No Man's Land under heavy fire, or to see your friends killed – or to kill, come to that."

"Maybe we have to try."

"Franz, we can't even talk to each other about it – that's one of the reasons we feel so easy in each other's company, because we both know the other won't ask stupid questions."

"I could write about it – if I survive, that is." *If.*

"Yes. I think you should – but remember, no one who wasn't in the war will understand what you're talking about."

"Why don't you write down everything that's happened to you?" I said. "For the family archive."

"I've never thought of myself as a writer."

"You wouldn't have to be. It wouldn't be for publication, after all – just for your children."

"I'm not sure I'd want them to know everything I did," he said slowly.

"If we don't tell people, it'll all be lost. We're part of history, aren't we? When they write books, in the future, you and I will be in them."

He gave a wry smile. "I'd rather have stayed obscure!"

"Would you? Really?"

"Yes – but I can't change it, can I, so there's no point thinking about it."

Ilse brought in more logs, and once again we both looked at her curves. *It'll be good to get my leg over in Berlin. There are bound to be opportunities.*

"I know what you were thinking!" he said after she left the room.

"Don't pretend you weren't!" I retorted.

Would you and I still want women if we lived together? I realised I knew the answer. I could easily imagine a future in which we were both married but still enjoyed being in bed together.

Now supposing we married women who liked sharing each other's beds as well...

"Penny for them, Franz?"

I told him, and he laughed. "That sounds like a bloody good set-up!"

"Though it would be in that mythical place called 'after the war.'"

"You'll get there, as I keep telling you."

"You're the one who'll make it," I said, and he just smiled.

A while later I realised he'd fallen asleep. I got up and went over to him quietly, unfolded the blanket and laid it over him.

He looked so vulnerable, so pale and thin. *I wish I could stay here and look after you and help you recover. That's the only thing I really want to do.*

If I'd got there quicker that day I could have stopped this happening – but that's stupid. He'd have been shot down another day, and probably killed.

I picked up the *Military Weekly* and tried not to think.

After an hour or so Karl gave a loud shout and woke up, staring about himself.

"It's all right," I said. "You're at home and I'm here."

"Oh, God—"

"Where were you?"

"Bloody Verdun. I wish that fucking place would leave me alone."

I do not want to talk about Verdun.

"Franz, do help yourself to brandy and anything else you want – you bastard! I'm wrapped up like some doddery old wreck!"

"And it's so uncomfortable that you've been asleep for an hour!"

"Oh, shut up!"

We talked for a while, and then I said, "Can I have another bath?"

"Only if you stop trying to mollycoddle me!"

"What's the price for stealing more bath salts? Same forfeit?"

He put on a thoughtful look. "I might have to think of something different… On the other hand, it was bloody good – so yes, same forfeit!"

I whispered in his ear in graphic detail.

"I'll leave you with that idea, then," I said. "Good night!"

XIV

I tightened the turn, my cheeks sagging, the engine roaring at full throttle. I was gaining on him, he was nearly in my sights – bullets cracked past my head and I heard the rattle behind me. I pulled the turn tighter still, hot and cold with terror.

Too late, engine over-revving, sweating, buffet beginning, ease the back pressure, glance behind – *Oh, Christ, so close* – gasping for breath in the thin air, heart pounding, hammer blow to my right knee, windscreen shattering, flames – *flames!*

Oh, God, I'm going to burn! Get out, Franz – GET OUT! Can't move my leg – thick smoke, flames almost reaching the cockpit, smoke choking, heat increasing, searing, scorching, hands face clothes on fire, white-hot incandescent screaming screaming—

Heavy shaking and buffeting, someone calling my name, half-heard through the mad screaming agony—

"*Franz!*"

"FRANZ! WAKE UP!"

Karl's voice, his hands on my shoulders, shaking me, his face, no fire, bedroom.

My stomach heaved. I pushed him aside, leapt up and ran to the bathroom. I just made it. I was violently sick, and as if that wasn't enough I had to use the lavatory for its other purposes as well. I sat there shivering with reaction and with cold. Finally I found the strength to get up.

I splashed cold water on my face and left the bathroom. The light in the corridor was on, and the portraits looked at me with mocking eyes.

'Fine hero, aren't you?' they said.

I never wanted to be a fucking hero.

My bedroom door was open and Karl was sitting up in my bed. I closed the door and joined him.

"Shall I turn the light off?" he asked.

"No. Not yet."

He lay down.

"Come here," he said gently, and wrapped his arms round me. "God, you're frozen!"

"It's your bloody bathroom."

"I know – I'm surprised the pipes don't freeze."

"Aren't I making you cold?"

"Don't worry about it." He stroked my back and I buried my face against him. "You're safe now."

"I bloody won't be," I mumbled.

"Want to tell me what it was about?"

"I was being shot down – like – like Westermann."

"Oh."

"And I couldn't get out because my knee was smashed… It's the same every time. Every bloody detail." My voice cracked and I shut up.

"You're not going to burn."

"I nearly did, before I came on leave." I told him what had happened.

"Shit," was all he said, but he held me tighter and kissed the top of my head.

"And then afterwards I thought I'd faced the worst – but in the dream I can't get out."

"If that happens, you can roll inverted and fall out."

"That's what I tell myself – but what if I can't?"

"Carry your pistol, then you can shoot yourself."

"I have thought about that… It's always the bloody same, that dream. That's what really shakes me."

"Yes… I know what you mean. I have a horrible one about Friedrich – that's always the same as well. He's been shot in the stomach three times – it's always three times – and he's lying in No Man's Land screaming and I'm just standing there, and I want to go and help him but my feet are fixed to the ground and I can't move. And every time when I wake up I wonder if that's what happened."

"You didn't find out any more?"

"No. There was a Guards officer in the hospital in Baden-Baden, but he was in a different regiment. I just wish I knew the truth – but I wrote so many lies at Verdun…"

"Karl, you're not being punished for everything you did, you know."

"Maybe I should be… Are you starting to warm up?"

"Yes, thanks. I don't want to go back to sleep, though."

"No, of course not."

But you need to sleep. "Put the light out, if you like – there's no need for you to stay awake as well."

"You're sure?"

"Yes. I'll be fine with you here. Do you need to move?"

"Mm. Sorry."

"Don't be daft. Hang on – let me light a fag while I can still see."

Then he put the light out, and I felt him settle down beside me.

I sat smoking and staring into the darkness.

I've got two more days here, then there's Adlershof, and then I have to go back and fly over the Front again. And I have absolutely no idea how I'm going to do that. Each time takes just a bit more courage, and each time it gets just a bit harder to find.

It's only a matter of time before I run out completely. I just have to hope the war's over before that happens – or that I march off to join the Great Army.

Good phrase, that – I wonder if I'll be with the men I knew. Be a bit tricky, with some of them being pilots and others in the infantry…

My head jerked, and I realised I'd almost dropped my cigarette onto the quilt.

For fuck's sake, Franz – if you do that the bloody burning dream will come true without the help of the Tommies, and you'll burn the place down along with everyone in it.

I had a sudden vision of the house as a blackened ruin, and I stubbed out the fag very thoroughly in the glass ashtray.

Might as well lie down – though I really don't want to go back to sleep…

Next thing I knew it was morning. I was facing Karl and he was propped up on his left elbow, looking at me.

You can't have been doing that for long.

He smiled, his eyes blue and warm. "Good morning, Sleeping Beauty."

"Does that make you the handsome prince, then?"

"I live in hope!"

"If I kiss you, will you turn into a frog?"

"Probably," he said. "Let's find out – and then there's that promise you made last night…"

As usual I went downstairs first.

I wish I could stop time, I thought as I wandered idly round the library. *Maybe they'll make peace before I get back…*

I had to laugh at that idea. *If they were going to make peace they'd have done it by now. I wonder whether the Russians going out balances the Americans coming in.*

That wasn't worth thinking about.

I looked again at the photographs on the table. There was one of Elisabeth's wedding – the family of the bride, looking awkward in her gown. Lives for the stables and preferably in the stables, Karl had told me once. Her parents stood either side of her, and Uncle Heinrich glowered from his wheelchair, probably having difficulty focussing. Friedrich was next to his uncle, immaculate in his cadet's uniform, and Johnny and Karl were beside their mother, both in suits.

How little it took to destroy this family – and it must be the same all over Europe.

For fuck's sake don't get caught holding this picture. It must go through Karl like a knife.

There was a studio portrait of his mother, gazing at the camera with eyes almost exactly like Johnny's. *Sad that such a beautiful woman should have been dead at what – forty-five? I couldn't imagine what it would be like to lose Mama and I didn't want to think about it.*

No wonder this house is full of ghosts.

The door opened and I jumped, but of course it was Karl.

"Would you like to go and talk to Hans today?" he asked over breakfast.

"To be perfectly honest, no. Nothing I say will make any difference."

"I think it just might, you know. He's got no idea what to expect."

"Would listening to me help? He might be better off keeping his ignorant enthusiasm."

He laughed. "You do have a point."

"How long would it take to get there, anyway?"

"About an hour."

That means you sitting in the cold for two hours minimum. That is not a good idea.

"Why can't he come here? He could ride over."

"True – but we're not on the phone, as you know, so someone would have to go over and invite him. I just feel I have to try to help him stay alive – his mother was very kind to us all when Mama was ill."

I sighed. "All right, then. When shall we go?"

"Thanks, Franz – I really appreciate it. Straight after lunch, I think – then we should get back before dark... Fancy a walk?"

"No. We're going to be out in the cold long enough. I'd rather stay warm."

That was the only way of putting it that he couldn't argue with.

"Fair enough."

We sat in the library reading – or trying to read in my case.

Hans will be bright-eyed and confident, and all the other things that have been burned out of me. I hope I can talk about it without starting to shake, because if he sees that then he'll think I'm a coward.

I'll be happy when this afternoon's over – and that's a bloody irritating thought. The last thing I wanted to do was wish away any of my time with Karl. Oh, well – it's only an hour or so and we'll be in the same room.

"Better get Thomas harnessed up," he said after lunch.

"I'll give you a hand."

"Thanks."

The cold was even more biting than the day before.

"Hope it warms up a bit before Adlershof," Karl said, "or you'll freeze your bollocks off."

I realised all my heavy flying kit was at the Front. "I'm sure they'll have kit we can wear."

We paused on the way to the stables. Karl tried to press on, but our arms were linked and I made him stop, because I could hear how fast he was breathing.

"I'm all right, Franz."

"And so am I."

Brandenburg was an enchanted land of snow and ice, the lakes frozen, the softly rolling hills blinding under the afternoon sun. The bare trees lining the road were all coated with snow, their shadows bluish on the white lane.

We sat close together under two thick rugs, Karl in his fur coat and hat, and me in Friedrich's. Our breath clouded, and the frigid air put enough colour in Karl's cheeks to give the illusion of health.

"Beautiful, isn't it?" he said.

"Yes. I'm glad you made me do this."

I shall remember this when I'm back in bloody Flanders. I tried to soak as much of the peace and tranquillity into myself as I could. *Pity I can't bottle it, then I could have just a bit every evening…*

"What are these people like?" I asked, suddenly imagining what Papa called 'cultureless barbarian boneheads'.

He laughed. "Worried you're about to meet some cliché of a dyed-in-the-wool backwoods Junker and his family, and that the only talk will be about grain prices and hunting?"

"Something like that."

"No, they're city people. Mahlke's got an armaments factory – it was probably his workers on the street in Berlin. You won't meet him. His family moved to the country at the start of the war and he stayed in the city. They're absolutely loaded – new money, and I don't care for him much, but she's a sweetie, as you'll see."

"So is she one of you?"

"Good God, no. Sorry, that sounded awful. I meant she's far too sophisticated, far too city to be one of us – and I doubt any of us would have married him."

"You're like the Jews – marrying in!" I teased.

"It's the best way – you've seen how hard we have to work."

"Isn't their land just as sandy as yours?"

"Yes – but their estate's for status, so they don't care whether it pays or not."

"And they probably have comfortable chairs, and proper heating, and all the luxuries that you lot forswear because they'd make you soft, and not good officer material!"

He laughed. "Now you've been to war, maybe you see the truth in that!"

"I hate to admit it, but you do have a point. You tolerated the conditions in the trenches better than I did."

The Mahlkes' house was larger and more ornate than Karl's. His was a traditional baroque manor house, almost austere in its simplicity, but theirs had fancy stucco work and even a couple of turrets, and there were statues on the circle of grass in front of the house. The inside matched the outside. It was all in excellent taste, but it reminded me of a stage set.

The drawing room was decorated in pale green and gold, and there was a thick carpet on the floor. The stove poured out heat, although the afternoon sun streamed in.

This is what it's like if you're seriously rich – and all this wealth is founded on death.

I suppressed a shiver as Frau Mahlke greeted us. She was about the same age as my mother but far more elegantly dressed, with greying hair piled on her head.

What would you think if you had to look at the results of your husband's work, if you could see the shattered bodies and hear the cries of agony?

"Oh, it is so kind of you to come all this way in this cold," she said when Karl introduced me. "This is Hans, and my daughter Clara."

Clara was a pretty little thing, probably about sixteen. She gave Karl an adoring look, which he didn't seem to notice.

Hans was just as I'd feared – too young to shave, and full of innocence.

Jesus, things are really getting desperate. Here's another child off to war, like the skinny, half-grown recruits at the station. God help us.

"Clara, dear, ring for coffee." Frau Mahlke turned to me. "Are you spending all your leave here?"

"No – I've just come up from the South, from my parents' house. We live near Stuttgart."

"Oh, I do think the South is so beautiful. We've got a little holiday place in Villingen – but that's down near Freiburg. We haven't managed to get there yet this winter, but Clara and I will go once dear Hans has gone. My husband can't get away."

I wondered what she called 'a little holiday place', then I remembered the villa Karl and I had borrowed two years before. It was bigger than my parents' house.

"Your mother must have been very glad to have you at home," she said.

"Yes, she was. It's hard just sitting at home waiting. At least we have something to do."

I daren't look at Karl after saying that. It was all I could do to keep my face straight.

"Oh, yes, it is going to be hard. But we must be brave, mustn't we, Clara?"

Oh, spare me. She'll be going on about 'our brave boys' in a moment.

"How long have you two known each other?" she asked.

"Since university," Karl said. "God knows how the poor fellow's put up with me for so long!"

"I was sane before I met you!"

That didn't go down well. Better keep the gallows humour under control.

The maid brought the coffee.

She looks an awful lot like Ilse. Randy sod, Karl's pa...

"Now you two have important things to talk about, so you sit by the fire," said Frau Mahlke. "Karl, come and sit in the sun with Clara and me. You're so pale, you need some sun."

She took his arm and led him towards the window, chattering on. "How are you? Are you feeling any better? It's such a pity you're not in uniform. It suits you so well, especially with your medals…"

Karl submitted meekly to her fussing. She placed his chair so the sun wouldn't be in his eyes, and plumped up the cushions for him. *If anyone else behaved like that, you'd tell them to go to hell.*

The coffee was real.

Bloody hell, what did this cost? But then everything here is top quality, and the children are just as well dressed as their mother.

Karl was wearing worn corduroy trousers and a sweater that was almost through at the elbows, and the clothes I'd borrowed weren't much better. The difference was that I noticed and he didn't.

I was well aware that I was supposed to be talking to Hans, but his mother's chatter was distracting and I wasn't sure where to start.

You should be at school, not going off to get killed. You're far too young for our filthy business. You've no idea what it's like – you can't imagine the sheer brutality, because no one can until he's in the middle of it. In a way our business is less vicious than the infantry's – we don't usually get covered in the other fellow's blood and brains – but he ends up just as dead.

Looking at Hans was far too bloody depressing – and yet there was something unusual about him. His eyes were pale green like his mother's and almost cat-like, and I couldn't tell what he was thinking. For a moment I thought he might have recognised me, but I couldn't be sure. He sat there studying me, with a look of amusement.

Self-possessed young bugger, aren't you? If you survive the first month, you just might be very good. I was beginning to find him irritating, and then I realised that he was amused not by me, but by his mother.

"When do you leave for the Front?" I asked.

"Tomorrow," he said in a low voice. "But don't tell Mama. She thinks it's the day after. I'm going to creep out of the house in the middle of the night. I wouldn't be able to stand the fuss."

Fair enough. If she fusses over Karl, what would she be like with her only son?

I saw Frau Mahlke weeping her heart out in black, and the cross of broken propeller blades.

I hope you don't burn—

Get a grip, Franz. I was beginning to tremble, and I hoped he wouldn't speak to me. *Don't ask me anything, give me a moment...*

Karl started coughing. *I hope that's not blood again.*

"Clara, give Karl a glass of brandy!" said Frau Mahlke. "You're no better, are you?"

His fingers met Clara's on the glass, and she blushed. He looked at her, his blue eyes full of mischief, and she blushed even more, giggled, and lowered her eyes. I didn't catch what he said, but I heard the teasing tone.

You can't help flirting, can you? And you think no one will want you because you're thin and scarred.

I could imagine how he must have looked to her a couple of weeks earlier: a hero, back from the war with Prussia's highest decoration round his neck, and so obviously damaged and in need of care. *Enough to turn a girl's head, that.*

I'll get killed and you'll be here with her. You said you wanted a bride with money...

Stop thinking crap and talk to Hans.

"I don't know what Karl said to you," I began, "but it won't hurt you to hear it all twice. Who's your CO going to be?"

"Behrend."

"Don't know him. Some have a better reputation for looking after newcomers than others. He'll probably tell you to try to stay out of trouble at first. Do as he says. The first thing you have to learn is how to stay alive. It doesn't matter how well you can fly or shoot if you don't live to do either."

He was looking at me very intently with those almost luminous eyes, his gaze disconcerting.

"Keep your head turning and your eyes open the whole time. Remember, there are three dimensions and an attack can come from anywhere. You'll find it difficult to spot other aircraft at first, and you'll wonder what the others have seen. It'll come suddenly. Then you have to learn to recognise the different types. That takes practice. I recognise aircraft by the way they sit in the air as much as anything. That may sound odd now, but you'll see what I mean.

"Once you've found the dear old Allies and it's broken up into a free-for-all, for God's sake don't fly straight and level – ever. If you get jumped, turn to meet the attack. What are you going to fly?"

"Fokker Triplanes, I think."

"Good aircraft. We've got them. They turn good and tight – but really tight turns take a lot of practice, or you'll spin."

"Do they come out all right?"

"Yes, if you've got enough height. One thing you have to watch with the Triplane – and all aircraft for that matter – don't dive too hard. It's easy to say, sitting here, but things get a bit heated and it's easy to forget the airspeed. Structural failure's killed a lot of men. Don't manoeuvre violently at high speed – it puts a lot of strain on the airframe."

My train of thought was broken by a burst of incongruous feminine laughter.

"But I don't suppose I'm telling you anything you haven't heard before."

"Do you meet Sopwith Camels often?"

"Yes, pretty frequently."

If you come up against an experienced Camel pilot you'll never know what hit you, I thought but couldn't say. I wanted him to be aware enough of the dangers to make him keep his wits about him, but I didn't want to petrify him.

"It's got a rotary engine, like the Fokker," I said, "but it turns very, very tight indeed. It's to be respected. You're going out at a good time – it's been relatively quiet for the past few weeks. Remember, you've got a lot to learn and there are plenty like Karl and me on the other side. Watch your tail all the time – it's very easy to focus on hammering your victim, and forget to look behind. That's a good way to get the wooden cross, as Karl nearly did."

"Yes, he said that was what happened."

"And make sure there aren't several of you going for the same opponent, or you'll meet in the middle. If it happened to Boelcke it can happen to any of us. It doesn't matter how many pretty baubles they give you to hang on yourself – they don't stop you making mistakes."

I was sick of the sound of my own voice. All the talk in the world wouldn't save him. It depended more on how he behaved and on luck.

"You'll wonder what the hell's going on the first few times – there'll be aircraft going everywhere. If you keep your head you'll be all right."

The hell you will.

"When you attack, use the sun as much as you can and get in close and shoot accurately. Aim for the man not the machine. You'll be surprised how many bullets you can put in a machine without having any effect. Forget any crap you may have heard about chivalry. It's nice if you meet it, but war's about killing the other fellow before he gets the chance to kill you."

That's enough. More than enough.

Hans was looking slightly shocked. "May I ask you something?"

If you must. "Yes, of course."

"How many have you shot down?"

"Twenty-three."

His eyes went as wide as saucers. *I was right to go in civvies. If I'd been in uniform you wouldn't have heard a word.*

"But remember, you have to survive first. The sky over the Western Front's a very unforgiving place."

Suddenly he looked at me quite differently. "Leutnant Becker! I should have realised! How stupid of me!"

"Don't worry. I'm glad you didn't."

Clara giggled again. I glanced across, and saw calculating approval in her mother's eyes.

Yes, that match would suit you, wouldn't it – and why do I find that unwelcome?

Too complicated.

The sun was well on its way down.

I want to get Karl home, before it gets dark and the temperature plummets.

"I suppose we'd better be off, or we won't be able to see where we're going," I said casually. "Good luck, Mahlke. I'm sure you'll do well."

"Thank you, sir. And thank you for talking to me."

"That's all right. I hope it'll be useful."

Enough of the pleasantries. Let's get going.

Fortunately Karl didn't argue, but got to his feet with an effort. Frau Mahlke noticed, and I saw the concern in her face.

Clara gave him a look of mingled adoration and sympathy, which went straight past him. She blushed again as he bowed over her hand during our leave-taking.

You won't be in a hurry to wash that hand, will you?

They all stood on the steps in their indoor clothes to see us off.

"Nice people," I said as we passed through the gates into the lane.

"Yes – don't care for the father, though. Doesn't treat his workers well – there was unrest in his factories before the war. Henning's son's one of his foremen and a union leader, and when the present strikes started Mahlke tried to get me to put pressure on him via Henning."

"That's a bit cheeky."

"That's what I thought. I told him his industrial relations are none of my business."

"But for them to be out on strike when we need all the munitions we can get—"

"Quite. And of course the union leaders are all Reds."

"Henning's son's a Communist?" I couldn't help laughing.

"Oh, yes. Has been for years. And I can understand why."

"You *what*?"

It was his turn to laugh. "And you a Socialist! You should understand better than a bone-headed Junker!"

"I'm not sure I've ever really been a Socialist," I said slowly. "I mean, I don't see how someone from a background like mine can really understand what life's like for the poor and the workers. And aren't we just being patronising if we claim that we do?"

"You can decide that for yourself! What I meant was that the factory owners have screwed their workers for decades, and if I had to work God knows how many hours a day and go home to some wretched tenement, I'd be a bloody Red. Have you seen how the poor sods live?"

"But what about your labourers?"

He sighed. "Yes, they work bloody hard – or rather they did when we had some – but in the fresh air, and they have decent accommodation and good food. We've always made sure of that. Yes, there's massive inequality, but you have to try to be decent."

"So are you going to give them the land they work?" I said naughtily.

I got an instant rise.

"That's just fucking ridiculous! They'd starve – each one would get a few miserable hectares of sand, and you can't make a living from that. It only works if you've got a lot of it and you have a distillery or a brick works or something – that's where the money really comes from."

"And do you agree with equal voting rights for all – in Prussia, that is?"

"On balance, yes – but for Christ's sake don't tell my neighbours!"

I laughed. "I'm not likely to."

The shadows were very long, and the sun, just above the horizon, gave little warmth.

"How much further is it?" I asked.

"About another fifteen minutes. Cold?"

"A bit."

Oh, God, there's only one more day... I could almost see Death leering at me.

Karl put his left arm round my shoulders. "'Fraid I don't give off much heat these days."

"Oh, you'll do."

Finally the gates appeared in the twilight, but of course we had to see to Thomas and it was fucking cold in the stables. The old draught horse pricked up his ears, and whinnied softly as we led the pony to the next stall.

I wonder if they miss the other horses. I just stopped myself saying it.

Karl seemed worse. We had to stop twice on the way to the house, and I don't think he'd have got up the steps without my help.

You're staying indoors tomorrow. You got far too cold today.

"Brandy?" he offered as we entered the library.

"I'll get them if you like," I said. "You sit down."

To my surprise he just said, "Thanks," and went to his chair.

And then he put his feet on the ottoman and wrapped himself in the blanket.

Bugger me – you must be feeling rough.

"I'm only doing this for you," he said with an impish look. "I wouldn't want you to feel your efforts were wasted!"

"It's good to get warm. I'm fucking glad I'm not in the trenches."

"You and me both... Thank you so much for talking to Hans."

"I just hope he listened."

I lit a cigarette and took a deep drag. I didn't want to think about him.

"You know, I couldn't work out why you were so keen to go over there until I saw you flirting with Clara!" I said.

"What on earth do you mean?" he asked with blank astonishment. "She's just a schoolgirl – I wasn't flirting with her."

"Oh yes, you were – it's automatic, isn't it? See pretty girl, start flirting!"

"Utter bollocks! I do believe you're jealous!"

Jealous? I laughed. "Now who's talking bollocks! But seriously, she's quite smitten with you. Didn't you see the looks she gave you?"

"Franz, your imagination's running away! What girl would want someone in the state I'm in?"

"That's the whole point. Look at yourself through her eyes—"

"Skin and bone and can't climb the stairs?"

"No, you stupid bastard – famous, decorated, wounded hero, who needs someone to look after him and restore him to health."

He burst out laughing. "What sort of fairy stories do you read?"

"Wrong question. What sort of stories do young girls read?"

"How the fuck should I know?"

"Romances," I replied. "That's what my sister used to read, anyway. Didn't yours?"

"Horse care and management, more like. Mama had hell's own job to get her into a dress."

I was shocked. "What – she wears *trousers*?!"

"Riding breeches. Yes, I know, nice ladies ride side-saddle – but Elisabeth maintains that astride's safer and Pa agreed with her. Especially the way she rides, bloody flat out. I think she only married Henry so she could ride to hounds every winter. Some of the fences I saw her take in England – Jesus."

"Your father let her wear breeches?" I was still having difficulty with the idea.

"Oh, Pa adored her… and we all took advantage of that, I can tell you."

"But going back to Clara—"

"You're talking complete rot!"

"– you did say you'd want a wife with money."

His jaw dropped. "I can't possibly marry Clara."

"Not good enough?" I said with a grin.

"It's not that. You can't ask a girl raised in luxury to live the way we do."

I looked round the comfortably shabby room, thought of the almost bare simplicity of the bedrooms.

"You know," I said, "the first time I came here, I was really surprised at how plain everything is. But the second time, after being at the Front, I felt right at home."

"Quite. This is all we need. No doubt at some point I shall have to marry, but it'll be to one of my own kind. That way everyone knows what to expect."

"Does Frau Mahlke know that?"

"What?"

"She looked very pleased when you and Clara were flirting – sorry, *talking*. It would be perfect from her point of view, wouldn't it? Their money and your name, and your land next to theirs?"

"Christ, you've got a point. I'd better avoid them for a while – though they'll be off south in a couple of days."

"That was their villa we borrowed?"

"Yes… You should see their house in Berlin, and they've got another on the coast that they go to in the summer. It's another world, that kind of wealth."

"I can't imagine having that much money. I'm not sure I'd want it, either – not when it's built on death."

"Or on a significant contribution to the war effort, which is no doubt how Mahlke sees it."

"What does he make?"

"Everything from shells to small arms ammunition – we've probably fired off a fair bit of his stuff, and seen it passing overhead."

"Well then, I hope they keep churning it out!" I paused. "What I really hope is that they don't have to."

He sighed heavily. "I wish with all my soul that it had never bloody started."

"So do I…"

I stared into the fire, trying to picture how things would have been if the Archduke hadn't been assassinated, and if, and if…

Would there have been war anyway at some point, or would we have continued to live in peace?

I got quite lost in reverie, and when Henning came in to announce dinner I jumped half out of my skin – and then I saw that Karl was fast asleep.

I caught Henning's eye.

"I'll wake him," I said softly.

"Very good, sir," he murmured and left without a sound. I saw a much younger Henning on patrol, creeping stealthily past the French...

"Karl," I said. "KARL."

He started. "What?"

"Dinner's ready."

"Oh. Is it?" he said without enthusiasm.

You should be ravenous. "Why not have something on a tray in here?"

"No, no. We'll go through."

He got up slowly and I put my arm round him.

"You don't have to," I said. "Why not keep warm?"

"I'll tell you later. Come on."

To be fair he did try to eat a bit more, but it was with an obvious effort.

I'd much prefer to eat in the library. The dining room's starting to get to me.

"Fancy some music?" he said once we were back beside the fire.

"Won't it be cold in the music room?"

"Sorry – on the gramophone."

"Yes, good idea – didn't realise you had one."

"It's under the table. Would you mind getting it out? And the records are in that box."

I set up the gramophone beside my chair, and lugged the heavy box across the room.

"What shall we have?" I asked, starting to look through the records.

"Well, I don't have the Liesl song," he said very seriously. "How about some Chopin?"

"No, not right now. It's beautiful music but too full of shadows... Schubert's songs?"

"Yes. You choose."

He had all the usual ones: 'The Erl King', 'To Sylvia', and so on, sung by a mezzo soprano with a lovely voice. *It's years since I heard these – before the war, in fact.*

Before the war, when I was an innocent youth with his head full of girls and ideals…

I put the next song on without looking at the sleeve.

'Rest in peace, all souls…'

It was the 'Litany for All Souls' Day', the melody sweetly piercing. *I wish they did all rest in peace instead of haunting my dreams.*

'To see God face to face, In the pure light of Heaven…'

The music ended and the record spun down.

Karl was staring into the fire.

I shouldn't have played that. Neither of us needs to think about Death any more than he has to.

"Do you believe that?" he asked quietly.

"No. I don't believe anything any more. What about you?"

He shook his head. "Obviously I wish I could, because of my brothers especially, but… if I could think that I'd sent them all to a better place…"

"To peace. Rest."

"Yes."

He poked the fire, and I looked away from the burst of flame.

"But then that's justification for murder, isn't it?" he added.

"I suppose so… and mine certainly don't rest in peace."

"Nor mine, as you know. But maybe that's just us feeling guilty."

"So do you think it's just extinction?" I asked.

"No. I've had too many strange experiences…"

There's that odd feeling in the drawing room and on the stairs, for a start.

"When I was in hospital – the one in Brussels – I – this is going to sound weird – well, it was weird."

He looked at me, as if wondering whether I would want to hear it.

"Go on."

"I was standing in the ward, at the foot of one of the beds, looking at the fellow lying in it. He looked dreadful, really grey-faced, and there was a nurse on one side and a doctor on the other, and they were trying to stop him bleeding. And then I realised it was me."

"Jesus."

"Yes, it was quite a shock. And the really strange thing was that the doctor pressed down harder and my body groaned, but I couldn't feel anything. And it made me wonder whether we do carry on after death."

"Maybe – but your body was still alive, wasn't it?"

"There is that."

What was it Johnny said back in the summer? Wasn't it that Karl would hang round the house with all the others if he were killed?

"Karl, talking of strange experiences—" I stopped. The old thing of not talking about the Devil, I suppose.

He smiled. "This is an old house, Franz. They're just my relatives."

"It was August," I said. "I was looking at his portrait and suddenly I was there – at Leuthen, with the men singing and his brother dying."

He didn't react. "And you feel you're being watched on the stairs."

"Yes."

"It's always been like that. There's nothing nasty about it, though."

Good opportunity to suggest eating in the library.

"Karl, would you mind if we had dinner in here tomorrow? It's just I'd feel more comfortable."

"Yes, of course. I know the dining room's depressing, but I can't give in to that. Making you happy is another matter."

You do, I wanted to say. *No one has ever made me as happy as you do. All I want is to live here with you, and let everything else go to Hell.*

"Put another on," he said.

'Singing on the Water'... in the swaying boat, gliding through the water with the sunset colours reflecting all around, the rippling piano accompaniment like the gentle lapping of the waves.

"Next summer we'll take the boat out in the evening," he said, "and it'll be just like that... After I left Verdun I had a couple of days before my pilot's course started, and I came here and went out on the lake in the sunset. It was so beautiful, so peaceful, and I could hardly believe I was still alive."

"It's the contrast, isn't it?" I said. "It's hard to imagine the war's still going on. It feels like a bad dream."

"Let's not talk about bad dreams before bed."

A couple of hours later I wished we hadn't. I dreamed about Langemarck, in horrible detail – only it wasn't quite right, because when we advanced I knew exactly what was going to happen.

I woke with a jolt and lay in bed sweating. All I could think about was that day, and poor Anton screaming all afternoon and dying with his guts spilling onto the ground.

I didn't want to go back to sleep. I got up and put Johnny's dressing gown on, and crossed the corridor to Karl's room.

I don't want to disturb him if he's sleeping. I put my ear to the door and was sure I could hear him snoring softly.

Damn. I went back into my room, pulled a chair close to the window, and opened the curtains. The stars were huge and bright in a black sky, and I lit a cigarette and sat gazing at infinity.

We are so trivial, so unimportant, less than grains of sand. Why in God's name are we destroying each other on this tiny planet of ours? Why can't we have more sense?

Slowly a small, inadequate measure of peace crept into me.

'You don't deserve peace after what you've done,' said a voice in the darkness. 'You're nothing but a murderer. And don't give me that shit about having no choice – you could have volunteered for the medical service, couldn't you? But you wanted to fight. Didn't you stop to think what that meant?'

The cold was seeping into me. *Have a pee and get back into bed. I won't sleep but at least I'll stay warm.*

I was on my way back from the bathroom when Karl's bedroom door opened, and I jumped half out of my skin.

Idiot. It's this bloody house.

"Oh!" he said. "I wondered why the light was on."

"Bad dream."

"Me too. Get into my bed if you like."

"Thanks."

I got into the warm place left by his body, and then realised how selfish that was. *I'll stay here until he comes back. That'll keep it really warm for him.*

I felt so much better lying in his arms, and I did get back to sleep – and then I had the joy of waking and finding him beside me.

I'll really miss this when I get back. I'll wake up alone – apart from good old Horstmann lying in the other bed – and Schiffer will have brought the shaving water, and it'll be time to go and face the fucking Tommies again—

Stop there.

And I'll only have my hand for company, except when we go to Claudette's and I pay for some girl to pretend she actually wants me – but there'll be no warm embrace afterwards.

Stop, Franz. You can't do anything about it.

"I don't want to go back." I'd said it out loud.

"No."

Please don't mention the fighter pilot school again.

"It can't go on much longer," he said.

"I wish it hadn't started as well... I dreamed about Langemarck."

"Oh, God."

"Yes, in detail, from dawn that day to poor Anton dying."

"The poor bastard," he said quietly.

"That was the first time – I mean, I saw my grandmother laid out, but she was old and I wasn't there – I didn't see her die."

"I'd never seen anyone die before, either – I was at school when Mama died, came home for the funeral. Same with Uncle Heinrich – though he died long after he wanted to, not like Anton or the others. They should have had a future."

"Nineteen's no age."

"No... and they'll never be any older. Not like us."

"We're only twenty-two." *But I don't feel it.*

He gave a short laugh. "On the calendar, maybe, but I feel about a thousand – in my soul, that is."

"I said something like that to Johnny when he was getting pissed off about your score – that you might be his younger brother in years, but in experience you were a good deal older."

"That's for sure."

"I feel much the same these days." *I'll never be young again.*

"Going back to Langemarck," he went on, "you know, the worst thing is that we were shafted properly, and by those we trusted. Yes, we got shafted at Verdun, but there at least we were soldiers rather than students dressed up in uniform."

"And we didn't even realise that was all we were – at least most of us didn't. You did."

"Much good that did me."

"You know, one thing that sometimes pisses me off about Otto is that he's never understood how bad it was. He believes all that crap about young heroes storming the enemy positions."

"Well, he got knocked over right at the beginning, didn't he?" Karl said. "So when we were up to our eyeballs in muck and bullets, he was in some nice hospital with pretty nurses!"

"And a leg that took months to heal."

"Months in which he'd have been killed otherwise."

"True… though it's probably just delayed the inevitable. It's good to have him around, though."

He laughed. "Do you remember when we went to the whorehouse, the night before we went to Belgium? Anton's turn came last, and we were all waiting for him, and we were worried that we wouldn't get back to barracks before tattoo."

"At least he had a fuck before he died – though it was a grim dive."

"Ah, yes – the joy of being commissioned and having decent tarts."

"Isn't that an oxymoron?"

"Oh, I don't know… some of Claudette's girls are quite presentable, and Anton's mother's a very high-class act."

"I'd forgotten all about her! Is she still in business?"

"She was last summer – I saw her in Berlin. At the Adlon, that is, in the restaurant, dining with some captain of industry or other, looking very professional."

"I suppose she has to – her customers won't be interested in her private life."

"No… Sorry, but I need to move."

"No problem." I released him. "I suppose we could get up."

"Hungry?"

"Does the sun rise in the East?"

"Before you get up—"

He wrapped his arms round me and pulled me close.

"I know what you want!" I said.

"Mm – but not just yet. I'm not the fellow I used to be."

"What matters is that you're alive."

"You may be right… I'd better let you get up – can't have you starving!"

I wish you were hungry, I thought as he picked at his breakfast. *You must still be losing weight, and that's the last thing you need.*

It's probably because you're so disturbed – and then there's the guilt: at what you've done, and at still being alive when so many men are dead. God knows I've got enough of both.

We just did what every soldier has to do, and none of it was outside the rules of war. But it is a vile business, and I shall be very happy when I don't have to kill again…

It's my last day here, and how I wish it weren't.

We settled ourselves into the library with the newspaper and the *Berlin Illustrated*. It was another lovely day, but while I was waiting for Karl I'd felt the cold seeping through the windows.

To my surprise he didn't suggest a walk, but seemed content to sit with his feet up and the blanket wrapped round him. And to my complete astonishment, Ilse came in at about eleven and said, "The music room's quite warm now, sir."

"Thank you, Ilse… Franz, shall we?"

"Yes!"

"I warn you it won't be good."

"I don't care – I haven't heard you for so long."

"Yesterday evening you said no Chopin—"

"I just wasn't in the mood. Play whatever you like."

I haven't heard this for so long, I thought as he played the Nocturne in E Flat major.

Waltzes, some more nocturnes, then Brahms, bittersweet and aching, love and loss. My fingernails were digging into my palms.

Your technique might have slipped a bit, but you've never played so expressively.

A march in a minor key, getting louder and louder like an approaching army – and then a wistful melody in the major, and I was sitting with the others around a fire in a muddy field, thinking of home and wondering what my family were doing – and then the march resumed, and we all trudged off again…

I'd heard it before but couldn't remember what it was.

"Rachmaninov, Prelude in G minor," he replied when I asked. "Makes you think of tramping along, doesn't it, and then falling out and daydreaming."

"Exactly."

"Probably shouldn't be playing Russian music at present, but here's some more."

Tchaikovsky, and more Rachmaninov.

And back to Chopin, the waltz he'd played that evening in November '15, when we'd found a piano in a ruined house. The music floated out into the night… *Most of those men must be dead by now.*

Karl, play something that doesn't make me think of the war.

Deep bass notes reverberated softly around the room, dark and brooding, the tempo slow like a funeral march. The music built slowly in intensity, shading through the major and then back into the minor in a torrent of raw emotion. It was like someone taking hold of my shoulders and shaking me. My hair stood on end and my hands gripped the arms of my chair.

You played this after the fighting ended at Verdun, as a requiem for the men whose lives were thrown away for nothing.

If we lose the war then everyone will have died for nothing.

The music ended as softly as it had begun. I wanted to say something, but I couldn't speak.

"Remind me what that is," I managed to croak.

"Chopin, Nocturne in C minor… right mess I made of it, too."

"You are joking."

"No – so many wrong notes."

"Karl, if I could play with feeling like that I wouldn't care about the mistakes. Play something a bit happier."

"Of course."

There was a pause and then he started to play the slow movement of Beethoven's Emperor Concerto. The years vanished and I was sitting in the concert hall. Karl sat on the platform, his hair bright under the stage lights, and that beautiful, tender music filled the hall.

But this time it spoke directly to me, flowed into my heart and pierced my soul.

He stumbled, swore and broke off, and the spell shattered. I realised that I'd barely been breathing.

"I can't play that at all now," he said dully. "I've lost so much ground."

"You've got plenty of time to practise now."

"What's the point? I'm stuck here… It was all so simple once – Friedrich would inherit, Johnny would do whatever suited him, and I would swan around the world, stunning audiences everywhere with my breathtaking virtuosity." His voice was full of bitterness and self-mockery. "It was all shit, anyway. I was never that good."

You're wrong, utterly wrong. "Yes, you were, and you will be again. How many pupils does Anton Blum take?"

"He doesn't, as a rule."

"But he took you – and told everyone he had. And he arranged that concert."

"I suppose so."

"Do you really think he would have linked his name with someone mediocre?"

"No, I suppose not." He picked up his signet ring from the table and put it on. "Funny, isn't it? I can't play with this on – feels like a ball and chain."

That's exactly what it is.

"Karl, why don't you sell up? Then after the war you could go to the Paris Conservatoire or the Royal Academy."

He sighed. "It's not that simple. This belongs to the family. I can't get rid of it. And I've met people who've sold their land and live in a nice villa in Grunewald or wherever, and they all have the same – the same sort of rootlessness about them... You know, when I was young I couldn't wait to get away, and now I'm happy just to be here in the peace and quiet. I don't want to lose my home, on top of everything else."

I hadn't thought of it like that. "Then why not engage a manager?"

"And have no money left? No, I just have to accept things as they are."

"Landowners are ten a penny, Karl – talent like yours is something else again."

He smiled. "It's no use, Franz. What I want hasn't mattered since August '14."

There was no point saying any more. I knew how stubborn he was. *You might change your mind once you feel better, and once the boredom of running the estate sinks in.*

"Well, you can enjoy practising, anyway," I said.

"And without Pa carping – you know, he really objected to my having lessons, and the irony is that he had the most beautiful voice."

"Yes, I heard him singing counterpoint at Johnny's funeral – wondered who it was at first... Maybe that's why he—" *hated you*, I almost said, "– objected, because his own talent had been frustrated."

"Hardly matters now, does it?"

It'll always matter. Being hated by your own father can't be easy to deal with.

"I think it was my 'proclivities' that really got to him. The signs were probably there at an early age... You're going to laugh, but Frederick the Great was my hero, not because of anything he did as King or General, but because his father beat seven colours of shit out of him, and I used to think that if he could stick it then so could I."

I didn't laugh. I could imagine, only too well, a frightened child gritting his teeth as his father laid into him, clinging to the thought that another boy had become a great man in spite of the beatings.

"I suppose I'll have to let your Old Fritz off being on the other side to us, then!" I said as light-heartedly as I could.

"No, no – *you* were on the other side to *him*. Do get it right!"

"Depends on your point of view! Thanks for playing for me. It was really beautiful."

"Fooled you, then," he said, and got up and put his arms round me.

I want to stay here. I don't want to go back to the war.

I started trembling. He felt it, of course, and held me tighter and rested his head against mine.

There was a knock at the door, and we released each other reluctantly.

"Lunch is served in the library, sir," Henning said.

He must have his suspicions about us, but he's far too professional to let them show.

It doesn't matter, anyway. I'm leaving tomorrow and I'll never come back.

That's a stupid way to think, Franz – you know what happens to men who believe they're going to die.

The library was as warm and cheerful as ever, and to my surprise Karl managed to eat quite a bit more.

Just please keep doing this after I've gone. I knew better than to say it.

"Fancy a walk?" he said.

"Oh, I don't know – it's so bloody cold out there, and I'm going to freeze my bollocks off in a couple of days' time."

"Well, I'd like to stretch my legs and get some air."

"Then I'll come with you – but can we use the front door?"

He smiled. "Franz, you know what I said about that. I'm not a bloody invalid."

"Tell me something," I said as we stepped out onto the terrace. "Do you feel better for getting out?"

"Yes – I feel I'm doing something instead of just sitting on my arse. And it's so beautiful – it gives me a bit of a lift."

We strolled hand in hand beneath the limes. *This is the last time I'll walk here with you – stop it, Franz. You have to believe you'll survive.*

Just soak up as much of the atmosphere as you can. It might delay the time when your nerves fail...

We sat down, still holding hands. He turned towards me.

"Franz," he began, and then broke off.

I waited for him to go on, but he didn't.

"Go on," I prompted quietly.

He gave me a smile tinged with sadness. "Wasn't worth hearing."

"You can say anything to me. You know that."

"Not quite anything. No one can – there's always something the other might not want to hear."

I squeezed his hand. "I can't think of anything you'd say that I wouldn't want to hear."

"That doesn't mean there isn't anything... Would you do something for me?"

"Of course."

"Would you go and look at the roses? I'll wait here."

It was only another hundred metres or so to the rose garden. I opened the gate and let myself in.

The last time I was here the roses were in full bloom and their scent hung heavy in the air, so powerful that I almost felt drunk.

Now their bare branches are covered in snow – oh. They've been neatly pruned. I wonder who did that.

There was no need to linger, and I was aware that Karl was sitting in the cold. I hurried back, and reached him in no time.

"Well?"

"Very neatly pruned."

"Oh, good. Old Springer said he'd do it, but I wanted to be sure before I paid him."

"They'll be lovely in the summer."

He took hold of my hand. "Come back and see them."

"If I can, I will. Come on, you're getting cold."

I helped him to his feet and we set off back towards the house. The slow pace was in sudden, stark contrast to how briskly I'd walked back from the rose garden, and it brought home to me just how frail he was.

He leaned heavily on me as we climbed the steps. We had to stop three times, and there was a long pause at the top while he got his breath back.

Sickening that a young man should be so ruined – and some of my victims must be dragging themselves around in much the same way.

That was a very uncomfortable thought, and I put it out of my mind.

XIX

He fell asleep in his chair in the library, wrapped in the blanket. *I'm glad I sorted that out for you. You need all the rest you can get – but please don't get well before the end of the war. I need to know you're safe.*

I sat smoking and trying to read the paper, while the sun moved round and sank. My last day of peace and quiet, my last day with Karl, was almost over, and my execution had stepped closer.

Shame I didn't slip on the snow-covered steps and break my leg – I'd have to stay here then. What I really need is a nice Heimatschuss, just enough of an injury to get me sent home – what do the Tommies call that again? It's something strange. I'll ask Karl when he wakes up.

Be careful what you wish for, Franz – there've been plenty of men who've wished for one of those and ended up mutilated. And look at the state Karl's in.

Just a broken leg, then, so I can have a couple of months off.

Maybe Karl was right about the fighter pilot school. The problem is, I can't ask. I'd have to be sent there.

I got up quietly and poured myself a brandy. My hands shook and the stopper jingled as I put it back in the decanter.

"GAS!" Karl shouted. "*Eichler!* Get your bloody mask on, man!"

He started violently, tried to leap to his feet and got tangled up. I caught hold of his shoulders and shook him.

"*What?!* Oh." He sagged suddenly, leaned back in his chair and looked at me. "What the hell are you doing here? *I told you not to come here, you stupid bastard!*"

"You're at home and I'm staying with you."

He gazed at me in puzzlement and then his eyes wandered round the room.

"Oh, Christ... What a relief. I was well away there. I was sure I heard a gas alarm."

"Sorry. It was me, being clumsy. I was trying to be quiet and the stopper rattled in the brandy decanter – it must have got into your dream and sounded like a bell."

"Yes, it did... Did you say brandy?"

I laughed. "Two secs."

As I handed him the glass I said, "I thought you'd like a stiff one."

He smiled. "You know me too well!" He looked at the glass and added, "Christ, if I drink all this I'll be comatose!"

"You don't have to drink it all at once, you daft sod."

It had got dark. Ilse came in to shut the curtains and replenish the log basket, and once again we exchanged glances as she knelt on the hearth rug.

"Are you sure you don't want to come to Berlin?" I asked after she'd gone. "Obviously you don't want to stand round in the cold at Adlershof, but you could spend a night or two at the Adlon or wherever. There'll be girls."

He shook his head. "I do want to go to Berlin some time, but there's no point going anywhere near girls until I can do them – and myself – justice."

"No, of course not. I just thought some pretty creature sitting on you would be – well, would do you good."

"I hope, with all my heart, that you never find out how this feels."

"So do I... You know, earlier I was thinking that I'd like a

Heimatschuss, and then I told myself to be careful what I pray for."

He smiled. "Quite."

"What did that Tommy call it?" I asked. "You know, the one we picked up in No Man's Land?"

"The fellow who was thoroughly miffed at being found by us?"

"That's him. He said he thought he'd got a nice – whatever the word was – but it was us and so he was off to prison instead. What was it he said?"

"'A nice Blighty'. And I must have looked completely blank because then he said, 'one that gets you sent home'."

"That's it. I was trying to remember."

"He was bloody lucky he'd been picked up at all," he said, "never mind being fussy about who it was… We found one poor bugger at Verdun – he'd been out there four days, and his arm was full of maggots and he was half off his head."

"Couldn't he have got back?"

"He'd got it in the leg as well – and that was full of maggots too, but he couldn't see them. He was raving about the ones in his arm. Big and fat they were, too."

"Poor bastard," I said. "That's partly why I became a pilot – I was really afraid of lying out there dying for days on end."

"It used to cross my mind when I was a sniper, believe me. That was one of the reasons I started that book, so if someone didn't come back in we knew where to find him."

Of course it could still happen if I crashed in No Man's Land, as neither of us wanted to say. *Then I'd be listed as 'missing', and my family would be among the thousands who had no idea whether their man was alive or dead.*

"You just hope it's over quickly," I said.

"Yes… There's something I've been meaning to ask you."

I wasn't sorry to have a change of subject. "What's that?"

"You said if anything happened to you the Chief would let me know – and back in the summer you said you thought he'd guessed about us."

"He's never said anything – you were right about that – but he was very kind to me when you were in hospital, and then he changed my leave so I could come here. I had Christmas, you see, and I'd have had to spend all of that with my family."

"You gave up Christmas with your family to come here?"

"It's not – I wanted to see you, and this was the only chance I was going to get."

He stared at his hands, seemingly lost for words, and then he looked at me, his eyes very soft. "I appreciate it more than I can ever say."

"There's no need. I wasn't going to tell you, but it slipped out. Going back to the Chief, I'd say he knows but has never minded."

"Good – you never know how someone's going to take something like that… Maybe he's heard about the ancient Greek regiment that was made up of pairs of lovers."

I laughed. "I've heard everything now!"

"No, it's true – makes sense if you think about it. No one wants his lover to think he's a coward, and no one's going to leave his lover in the lurch, is he?"

"We're not lovers, though." *Doesn't that depend on the definition?*

He smiled. "Maybe not – but it was always good to be in the same scrap, and to know I was there to help you out."

"And when it was my turn to help you I was too bloody late."

"If I'd kept a proper lookout it wouldn't have happened."

"You shouldn't have been at the Front at all. I think the Chief was going to post you away for a while after your father's accident."

"No point going over that, is there?"

"No." I got up to get myself another brandy, and had a thought. *We're not lovers, but—*

I sat down on the edge of his footstool. "As it's my last night, shall we spend it together?"

Maybe I shouldn't have said that. His expression was very mixed. There was dismay at the reminder that I was leaving in the morning, followed by longing, and what remained was a mixture of desire and doubt. He opened his mouth to speak.

I laid a finger on his lips. "I know the stairs knacker you up, so I thought – suppose you go up first, then I'll go to my room for about an hour, and then come to you. Will that give you enough time?"

He kissed my finger and held my hand. "Franz, nothing would make me happier, but you have to understand – I really don't want to have to say this—"

"You don't have to say anything."

He sighed. "I'm not the fellow you shared the dancers with. What I mean is, my appetite isn't what it was."

"Of course it's not. It doesn't matter."

"No, I suppose not."

I freed my hand and stroked his cheek with my finger. "We've spent halves of night together, haven't we?"

"Yes…"

I leaned forward and kissed him. He put his hand behind my head and the kiss lingered.

When I sat back I saw that his eyes were closed. After a moment he opened them, and once again I had the impression that he hadn't wanted me to see what he really felt.

"All right," he said with a smile. "Your wish is my command!"

I wish I didn't have to go in the morning…

The realisation that my leave was virtually over hit me with full force. Cold fear ran down my back and settled, curdling, in my stomach. My hands shook as I lit my cigarette, and I took a good slug of brandy.

I knew Karl had seen. We both knew there was nothing he could say that would make any difference.

Fortunately the worst of it had worn off by dinnertime. *I'm glad we're eating in here, though. That dining room would be a bit much for me tonight.*

Karl had cleared part of the table by the windows, and we sat there to eat. It wasn't quite as warm as our chairs by the fire – the bitter cold outside was seeping through the windows and the curtains – but it was still quite cosy.

He actually ate more than half his food and I was very careful not to comment. *If only you would keep doing this after I leave – but I doubt you will.*

After dinner I smoked one of the late Major's rich, smooth cigars. *I'm not sure how many of these will actually make it to the squadron – maybe I should smoke them all while I can.*

We sat in companionable silence, neither of us needing to say anything. After a couple of hours he stretched.

"I think I'll have a nice long soak in the tub before you come up," he said, and rang the bell.

When Ilse returned to say that his bath was ready, I said, "Don't pull the plug when you get out – I'll top it up and have a soak myself. Might as well make the most of the opportunity."

"I'll give you a shout when I get out, then."

That was sooner than I expected, but then Karl had never been one to linger in the tub. The water was still quite warm and fragrant with the bath salts, and very pleasant indeed once I'd got it nice and hot.

I shall really miss this – stop there, Franz. There's no point thinking.

I went to my room, put a dent in the pillow and disturbed the quilt. It looked perfectly convincing, and I put Johnny's dressing gown on and went to Karl's room.

I didn't bother knocking, just opened the door and went in. The light was on, and he was sitting up in bed waiting for me.

"Leave the light on," he said. "I want to look at you."

We lay facing each other, and he studied my face as if committing it to memory. 'I shan't see you for a long time,' his eyes said.

Never, I thought, and was almost overcome by sadness. *This is the last time we'll be in bed together.*

I moved closer and our lips met.

Some time later he laid his head on my shoulder and sighed. I leaned my head against his, and felt his breathing change and his body relax more deeply against mine as he sank into sleep.

I stayed awake as long as I could. This was the most precious time there was, and I didn't want to waste it.

The rotting, half-skeletal remains of the men I'd killed surrounded me. 'You didn't think we'd leave you alone, did you?'

I jolted awake, running with sweat and trembling.

"Wake up, Franz!" Karl was shaking me.

"What?" I was completely disorientated, my heart jumping out of my chest, the stench of death still clogging my throat.

"You were dreaming."

"Oh, Jesus – that – that was a b-bad one." I was shaking so badly I could hardly speak.

He held me tight. "Yes, I know… It's all right now. It's over. You're safe, with me."

Slowly I stopped trembling, and started to feel a little calmer.

"Sorry." My voice still sounded shaky.

"What for? You've woken me often enough."

"Yes, but it was my idea to sleep in your bed."

He turned my face gently towards his own.

"And I'm glad you're here, and that I woke you before it got any worse. I'd been lying awake for some time, with it all going round in my head – you know what I mean."

"Yes."

"And usually I'm alone with it. Just having you here – well, it's nothing like as bad."

Sweat was trickling off me, and I realised I'd soaked his bed with it.

"Karl, I'm dripping wet."

"Doesn't matter. Let's move a bit this way, then you'll have a dry bit."

"Thanks."

"Come here – no, closer."

"You don't want to hold me – I'm all clammy."

"Do you care when I'm sweaty?"

"No, of course not."

His arms tightened round me again, his warmth comforting, and the tension started to leave me. He stroked my hair with his left hand, slightly awkwardly, and it took me a while to realise that it would have been more natural to move his right arm up from my stomach.

You didn't do that because it would hurt.

"How bad is it really?" I asked.

"What?"

"Your chest."

I felt him shrug.

"You've seen the scar," he said. "Have a good look if you like – just please don't touch it. That makes my skin crawl."

"Yes, I can believe."

I propped myself on my elbow and took a long look. The first time I'd seen it, I'd been so struck by the missing bone that I hadn't really noticed how much damage had been done to his chest muscles.

That looks bad, and God knows what your lung must be like. I'm not surprised it hurts all the time, or that you can't use your arm much. It'll be a very long time before you're fit to fight again – if you ever are.

I settled back against him with a feeling of great relief. Karl would not be going back to the Front for many months, and there was a good chance that the war would be over by then. He was safe.

We lay for some time, talking quietly, and then he turned his face towards mine and our lips met again.

"That was a night to remember," he said as the light came through the curtains. "Just please be sure to come back and give me another."

"I'll never forget it, either. I'll be back if I can."

There was a long pause, and then I said, "Karl, I haven't wanted to say this—"

"Say what?" He looked at me, half amused and half concerned at my serious tone.

"Please don't try to get yourself sent back to the Front. Just answer their questions truthfully when you go for your medical."

"Franz—"

"No, listen." I sat up and looked at him. "You've done your duty. You fought for nearly three years, in some of the worst places, you were given a chance to get out and you didn't take it. You nearly got killed last July – we all thought you'd had it. And I look at those scars and I don't know how you're alive at all. Please just accept that you're out of it now. Stay here and wait for me."

"I wish it were that simple."

"But it is—"

"Not. Oh, it's simple all right, just not in the way you mean. Franz, when we leave this room, look at the portraits. That's what we do, what we've always done. That's what we're for – to put on a uniform and bleed and die for our beloved Prussia." His voice was bitter. "My ancestors, my brothers – it's the same thing, over and over. I had hoped to do something different – but it seems there's no escaping what I am."

"You've done enough," I said. "No one could reproach you… When you were at Verdun, you wrote to me and said, 'Please, for my sake, don't even think of coming here'. Do you remember?"

"Yes. The thought of you being there made my blood run cold."

"Well, now I'm saying, please, for my sake, accept that your war is over, so I know you're safe. Stick with bleeding for Prussia and leave out dying."

He smiled. "You're asking for something I can't give. The war's not over yet, and if I get passed fit I'll be going back. There's nothing else I can do. You'd do the same."

"No, I wouldn't. If I'd been injured as badly as you were, I'd take my pension and thank my lucky stars I didn't have to fight any more."

"You wouldn't, you know. We both have to look in the mirror."

There was no more to say. I lay down again and he rolled into my arms. *You won't get passed fit, anyway,* I thought as I stroked his back. *Not unless you make a miraculous recovery. I don't have to worry about you coming back.*

It was broad daylight.

At some point I'm going to have to get out of this bed, and there will never be a right time.

"I'd better get up," I said reluctantly.

"Yes."

As I swung my legs out of bed, I saw the hare on the bedside table. It was in mid-leap, beautifully carved, so vital and alive that it looked as if it would jump onto the floor and spring away.

Why didn't I see it before? I wondered. *Too focussed on Karl, I expect.*

"That hare is lovely," I said.

"Yes – Spots made it for me. You remember, he was always carving, and one day we were talking in the dugout about animals, and the next day he gave me that."

"Such a fucking waste. When you think he was only just sixteen…"

"Sixteen and highly accomplished in our black art – God knows how many men he'd shot. How's that for corruption of innocent youth?"

There was no answer to that. As I picked up Johnny's dressing gown, I noticed his drawings on the wall.

Karl, Marion and Helena, all lovingly drawn in happier times.

"After the war, we'll have another weekend with those two," I said.

He smiled. "Dreams are free."

I washed and shaved, and put my uniform on. Nothing could have made it clearer that my leave was over.

I did look at the portraits. *This sort of tradition gets a momentum of its own, sons following fathers and grandfathers into the Army...*

'Well, goodbye,' said the eyes – and then, chillingly, 'we shan't be seeing you again.' I shivered and went down the stairs, and into the library for the last time. *The last time this visit*, I thought determinedly. *I shall come back, whatever the ancestors might think.*

When Karl came into the library, he struggled for a moment to hide his dismay.

"You look bloody good," he said.

"Thanks."

He leaned towards me and added quietly, "But you look even better with no clothes on!"

I laughed.

"What time do you have to leave?" He almost made it sound matter-of-fact.

"Eleven should do it." And so did I – almost.

I didn't really have to leave as early as that – all I had to do was check in to my hotel, and go to a reception in the evening. The trouble is that I hate hanging around, and I knew that if

I lingered, my nerves would wind themselves up to screaming point.

I knew too that Karl wouldn't want a protracted farewell, that he would want it over with.

The little time that remained passed all too quickly.

"Karl, why not let Henning take me to the station? Then I won't have to worry about you being out in the cold."

He hesitated. *You're feeling bad.*

"I'd rather think of you sitting here by the fire."

"All right," he said with a warm smile, and rang the bell.

Ten minutes later Henning knocked again. "The trap is ready, sir," he said to me.

"Thank you."

He closed the door behind him, leaving Karl and me alone. *He must know.*

"Franz, thank you so much for coming – I can't begin to tell you, so I shan't try."

I held him close. "Thank you, Karl – it's been – well—"

How useless words are. *The happiest days of my life*, I wanted to say, but that was impossible.

Our lips met, very softly, and again, and then he released me.

"Break your neck and legs, you bastard!" he said. "And all I want to hear is news of your victories."

"Get well slowly," I replied, and stepped away from him and walked to the door. I turned to look at him before I closed it behind me. He was standing in the middle of the room, gazing at me, and I felt a physical wrench as my eyes left his.

Henning was waiting by the front door, and he helped me into my coat and carried my haversack to the trap. As we drove away I turned in my seat, and looked back at the house.

I will come back, in the summer when the trees are in leaf and the roses are flowering. The war will have ended and Karl will be well, and we'll swim in the lake and sit on the terrace as the light fades, and then we'll go to bed...

But all I could see before me were death and destruction, and the harsh demands of duty.

It's over. There is no way back for me.

We turned through the gates into the lane. Brandenburg sparkled white and peaceful in the low sun, and I wished with all my soul that I could stay.

When we reached the station I said, "Henning, perhaps you could serve Leutnant von Leussow's meals in the library until he gives a different instruction."

"If Herr Leutnant permits," he said.

But we know how difficult he can be, went unspoken.

"I know you'll look after him as well as he allows."

He carried my haversack onto the platform, and when the train to Berlin drew up he stowed it above my seat.

"Thank you, Henning."

"My pleasure, Herr Leutnant – and if I may say so, I hope that we shall welcome Herr Leutnant again in happier times."

"So do I."

He left me alone with my thoughts, and a few seconds later the train puffed its way out of the station.

A horrible feeling of black doom settled on me. *I shall never come this way again. What's left will be under a cross in the cemetery – if I'm lucky – and the Chief will write to Karl, and maybe there'll be an obituary in the papers. And in a few decades no one will remember me, or any of us.*

If you think like that, you'll be killed. Think what a lovely time you've just had, and hold on to the dream that there's more to come.

The countryside gave way slowly to houses and the city, and finally the train pulled into the Stettiner Station. It was thronged with soldiers.

You can tell whose leave is starting and whose is ending, and no doubt everyone can see which way I'm going.

I took a cab to the hotel. The horse was so pathetically thin I thought it would collapse, and the driver wasn't any better. The streets were filled with tired, hollow-eyed people, and in an alley I saw a group of black-clad women scavenging in a rubbish heap while their ragged, scrawny children played listlessly.

This can't go on. People can't live like that.

The hotel lobby was plush and prosperous, and many of the clientele had no idea what hunger was. I looked at their well-fed faces with disgust. They all stared at me – or rather at my Blue Max – as I passed, and the feeling intensified to contempt.

We risk our lives while you get fat on the black market, and I don't suppose any of you gives a shit about the poor sods outside.

I stared straight ahead as I made my way to the reception desk.

The receptionist was very pretty, with thick dark hair put up on her head and lovely green eyes.

Nice. Very nice indeed.

She became more and more coquettish, and for a couple of minutes I thought she was actually attracted to me.

Yes, there was a reservation for me, for six nights.

"Could I have a room with a private bathroom, please?"

I couldn't believe I'd last the whole week without the burning dream. *I need my own bathroom. I don't want to be running down the corridor, needing to be sick and trying to find the lavatory. I really hope that won't happen again – the dream's bad enough without throwing up as a finale.*

"All you airmen seem to want your own bathroom," she said. "You're the fourth one today."

"We like lying in the bath. Especially with a pretty girl."

She giggled. "We don't have many rooms like that and I think they're all booked."

There was a pause as if she expected me to say something. I looked at her and the silence continued.

"Perhaps you could check for me," I said, and lit a cigarette.

"Oh, real tobacco!" she said sweetly.

I sighed. *You didn't really think you'd get anything for free, did you, Franz? I wonder how many packets she wants—*

"Is everything all right?" asked a voice at my elbow.

A middle-aged fellow in a smart suit was standing beside me.

"Not really," I said. "I would very much like a private bathroom" – the receptionist started blushing – "but there seems to be a problem."

He turned to her. "Give Herr Leutnant what he wants and charge the extra to Albatros." He turned back to me. "Siebmann, Albatros Works."

"Becker. Thank you."

"My pleasure, Herr Leutnant."

I was well aware that I was allowing him to pick up part of the tab, but I didn't care.

I shall take everything all of you have to offer – and if you imagine it's going to make the tiniest difference you're wrong. We're here to choose the aircraft in which we're going to fight for our lives. All the champagne, pretty girls and favours in the world won't sway me one way or the other.

The room was very pleasant. I unpacked and sat on the bed. *A trifle soft*, I thought, bouncing gently, *but at least it doesn't creak. I'm not leaving Berlin without putting this to its proper use.*

It was half past two. The empty afternoon stretched ahead of me, and I started to feel shaky. *Maybe I should have stayed with Karl – we could have had another night together and I could have left early in the morning.*

It wouldn't have been any easier. I knew that.

Do something, Franz. Don't just sit here.

I'll go for a walk, see a bit of the capital. Last time I was here I saw rather a lot of a hotel room and two lovely girls. I should have asked Karl to contact them for me, given myself a good send-off.

I walked out into the cold street. Many of the people I passed were wearing black armbands, and most of them couldn't remember their last good meal. The war had turned the gap between rich and poor into a chasm – the poor couldn't buy on the black market and they were starving.

The sky had clouded over, and the city felt flat and grey. I went to the Reichstag and looked at the inscription *To the German People* with a profound feeling of cynicism. *This should be the heart of a democratic Germany, but instead we have Hindenburg and Ludendorff.*

Maybe a dictatorship is what we need when our survival is at stake – but how can the generals govern when they can't even do their own jobs?

The gilded statue on top of the Victory Column mocked the exhausted, war-weary people below her. *All we can do is endure and fight on, for as long as we have the strength.*

I walked through the Brandenburg Gate, across Pariser Platz and along Unter den Linden. The street was bleak and sombre, the limes bare against the grey sky. It was busy and I lost count of the number of times I had to salute, but everyone looked grim and worn down.

I couldn't think of a way to stop feeling shaky except to keep walking until I'd had enough, and then have a drink somewhere.

Frederick the Great gazed down from his horse, and I stopped and looked up at his proud, lined face.

You suffered too, in those years of war when you didn't know if you or your country would survive. Did you wonder if your nerve would hold, as I do?

I crossed the road to the Opera House. *He built this and the rest of the buildings around the square. And he was a musician. He must have felt at times that he was on the rack.*

I paused on the bridge and stood staring down at the river. The water looked grey, oily and uninviting.

"'Ere, don't jump! Might never 'appen!"

I laughed in spite of myself and turned round. A couple of urchins grinned at me.

"How do you know?" I said, and they ran off without another word.

I walked past the royal palace out of curiosity, but there was nothing to see – the Kaiser had left Berlin long ago. The gardens opposite had been converted into vegetable patches, and the outlines of the beds showed through the thinning snow. The city was monochrome, the grey sky and the snow draining it of colour.

On impulse I crossed the road again, and went into the cathedral. I'd never been in a Protestant cathedral and I wanted to see what it was like.

It's all nonsense. All my life I've been told that these people are heretics who will burn in Hell, but this place feels just like any Catholic church – peaceful and hushed. It's probably the same in a mosque or a temple.

I wish I could believe in something…

And what about Karl's experience of leaving his body? Fever and morphine, I decided. That's all.

I went back out into the bitterly cold afternoon and looked up at the clouds. *We're all going to freeze during the trials…*

The sky made me shiver anyway. Kurt's face came into my mind and I pushed it away quickly. *If I think about him I'll end up thinking about the others and there's no sense in that.*

I want to talk to someone.

So, bizarrely, I decided to go to St Hedwig's and go to

confession. Not with any hope of absolution, but because it might get some of the weight off my mind.

St Hedwig's was quiet. I lit a candle for my friends and wandered round, unsure whether to go through with it or not.

Why not? It can't do any harm.

The darkness of the confessional was almost comforting, but even so I could hardly get the words out.

"I have – I have… taken life."

There was a pause. "Are you a soldier, my son?"

"Yes, Father."

"And whom did you kill?" The word I hadn't been able to use.

"Soldiers, airmen…" My voice died away. All I could see was the young Englishman.

"You were doing your duty, my son."

"Yes, but – I still feel – it—"

There was a further pause, then the old, slightly tremulous voice continued, "My son, if a man attacked you with a knife, and you killed him in defending yourself, would that be murder?"

"No, Father."

"The men you killed would have killed you and your comrades, if you had been too slow to stop them."

"Yes, but some of them – I'm a fighter pilot. We – it's – most of them never knew I was there."

"But if they had seen you first, they would have killed you." The voice was patient, kind. *He must have had this conversation more times than he can count.* "That is not murder, my son. It is survival."

"Jesus said we should turn the other cheek."

"If you do nothing, my son, your friends will die."

He was right.

"There's something else," I said. "I'm – I'm scared, Father. Really scared. It's getting worse. I have nightmares. I don't know how much longer I can keep going."

I was sweating and I could hear my voice shaking.

"My son, to go to war is to be afraid. The brave man is not the man who feels no fear, but the man who conquers his fear and does his duty."

I've said that to myself a thousand times. He must have served as well. This is Prussia, after all.

"Were you a soldier, Father?"

"1866 and 1870," came the reply. "Königgrätz, Gravelotte, Sedan. I entered the seminary after I left the army."

"And you've made peace with your conscience?"

"My son, a soldier must kill to defend his country, his comrades and himself. He has no alternative."

"It's gone on for so long," I said. "In the beginning I... but now..."

"Nothing of this world lasts for ever. One day the war will end, or you will be killed or wounded. You have only to last until then, day by day. One day it will be over."

He gave me a penance for fornication, to which I had not confessed, and I swear there was a smile in his voice. He obviously reckoned nothing had changed in fifty years.

Talking to him had helped. *Nothing lasts for ever. One day it will be over. I just have to endure until then.*

Evening was falling. I walked back towards the Brandenburg Gate, black against the twilight, then turned and went to the Adlon in the hope of meeting someone I knew.

A pretty young woman directed me to the hospitality of the Pfalz Company. I smiled to myself. *They're all hell-bent on bribery. Much good it'll do them.*

As I entered the room, a voice called out, "Hey, Becker!"

"Good God! Strauss! Still alive, then?"

"Yes – long time since flying school, isn't it?" He raised his glass to me. "Congratulations. You've done bloody well."

"You're not doing too badly yourself."

He was wearing the ribbon of the Knight's Cross with Swords of the Royal Hohenzollern House Order, so he had a respectable score, if not enough for the Pour le Mérite.

"Being alive's enough cause for celebration," he said. "What'll you have?"

"Brandy, please."

He ordered three. "Scheich'll be back in a moment, fellow from my squadron. Should be an interesting few days."

"Yes, indeed. I take it we don't pay for anything here?"

"You're right. All laid on. Saves trying to find something to eat in this bloody town."

When Scheich came back the three of us talked shop for a couple of hours, and then enjoyed the lavish buffet.

I looked at the food, and thought of the pale, thin people outside, remembered the women scavenging in the rubbish heap, and was appalled.

There'll be a price for this. There has to be. They know we're having all this while they're going hungry. If this goes on, Henning's son will get his revolution.

"Where are you staying?" Strauss asked me. I told him and he said, "So are we. Let's finish the evening there. We can drink in the bar and stagger upstairs, or take a bottle up to your room, or mine."

"Good idea."

"Have you noticed," said Scheich as we left, "that the whole country's run by women these days?"

"Well, we know where all the bloody men are, don't we?" answered Strauss.

Don't we just. "Good luck to the girls," was all I said.

"It's going to be devilish difficult to get them all back in the kitchen after the war," Scheich said. "They'll have all sorts of stupid ideas."

"None of us will have to worry about that," Strauss said.

"At least the shortage of men means a better chance for us!" I said.

And it did: we went into the bar at our hotel and ordered some drinks, and two seconds later were joined by three very acceptable tarts.

I'm not wasting time drinking with these two fellows when I could be trying out that bed.

"Coming upstairs?" I said softly to the girl next to me.

She smiled, very professionally. "Yes. Of course."

"Good night, chaps. See you tomorrow." And I left them to it.

"How much?" I asked as I locked the door.

She told me and I handed over the money. *That's the sordid bit over – I'll never get used to paying.*

The bed didn't creak. Afterwards I was very close to falling asleep, but I was careful to get her out of the room first. I had no intention of waking up minus my wallet.

I got back into bed on my own, feeling lonely and empty. Yes, I'd had a fuck, but how I longed for Karl's embrace. *Better to have what we do, and the warmth that goes with it, than cold, commercial sex.*

Karl will be in bed alone as well, and he's in that house by himself, with only the dead for company. We should be together.

'After the war'…

I can forget that, but at least I've got a few more days of life.

The airfield was an amazing sight the next morning. Twenty-eight new aircraft were lined up, attended by their ground crews and the manufacturers' representatives. And there was quite a crowd: the evaluation pilots – all of us from the Front – and men from the Technical Commission of the Air Service, and half of Berlin society.

And there's Richthofen, talking to the Chief. I was dying to meet him, of course, but I didn't want to be pushy.

But the Chief waved me over, and a moment later I was shaking hands with the master, the man who with sixty-three victories was the most successful fighter pilot of the war, on either side.

He was smaller and slighter than I'd expected, and turned out to be modest and rather shy. *I don't suppose you like being fussed over, either.*

We exchanged a few words, then one of the men from the Technical Commission took him away.

"Did you have a good leave, Becker?" asked the Chief.

"Mostly, sir," I answered truthfully.

Go on, said a voice in my head, *ask him if it could be extended, or for a posting as an instructor. Go on…* but I couldn't.

"How's Leussow? I thought he might be here."

I sighed. "Not well at all."

"He was very lucky to survive."

"Yes."

"Do you think he'll be coming back?"

I shook my head. "I can't see it. I don't think his right lung's much use."

"Ah… So is someone looking after him?"

"No. I did what I could while I was there."

"Yes, of course." His tone was very kind, and I saw concern in his eyes. *You do know.* "Where is his place?"

"About eighty kilometres from Berlin, roughly north. I'll show you on the map, if you like."

"Yes, do. I've got a couple of days spare after the trials. I might drive out there and see him." He saw my expression and hesitated. "Or isn't that a good idea?"

"I'd send a cable first, sir. He—" I paused, wondering how much to say. "Well, to be honest, he's rather frail."

"Oh, Lord. Poor fellow. I'd better leave him in peace, then."

The sound of engines cut into our conversation as the flying programme began.

"Let's hope they've got something good for us," said the boss.

"Yes, indeed."

It'll be wonderful to fly knowing that no one's going to try to kill me. I could still crash, but that's different. I'd made up my mind to enjoy myself, and I was determined to fly every one of the twenty-eight aircraft if I could.

It was the most fun I'd had in a long time. All the machines had to be tested for rate of climb and manoeuvrability, giving us a wonderful excuse for aerobatics, and we flew them against each other in mock dogfights, which were followed by merciless banter. Of course the purpose was serious, but we didn't often get the chance to fly for its own sake.

Once I found myself 'fighting' Richthofen, and was surprised that his flying ability was similar to mine.

It's the marksmanship. That's what makes the difference. Karl doesn't fly any better than I do, but he always placed the bullets more effectively.

And the Fokker V11's probably flattering my performance, anyway.

It was by far the best of the types I tested. It had its faults – the controls were very sensitive, and the top wing was a bit too high and hid too much of the sky – but it was superbly manoeuvrable even at altitude, and had a good rate of climb.

The Chief agreed with me, and we weren't alone in our opinion.

"Richthofen said the same as us," he said, which I found rather flattering. "I put at the end of my report that it'll be an excellent fighter once the problems are solved, and that we want to be re-equipped with them as soon as possible."

"That's pretty well what I wrote, sir," I said.

I hope they'll be available before long – I'd feel a lot more confident confronting Camels and SE5s in one of those.

The days sped past. I don't know which was more hectic, the flying or the socialising. One day I found myself having lunch with four other Pour le Mérites and wondered what the collective noun should be. *A glitter, perhaps? Or a mortality?*

To my astonishment, the society ladies were very keen to invite me to sit in their cars and talk to them. I couldn't work out why – and then I realised that the more ribbons a fellow had, the more attention he was getting, and that those with a pretty blue cross were getting the most of all.

They just want a sort of toy – a decorated, preferably handsome young officer to act as escort, and no doubt to provide services in the bedroom as well.

Karl would have had a different one every night, but I didn't feel like being ticked off their lists. And I couldn't think what they saw in me apart from the gongs. All I saw when I looked in the mirror was an ordinary-looking fellow with dark hair, brown eyes, and a face that was rather lined, especially around the eyes. I looked at least forty.

The aircraft manufacturers gave us unlimited food and drink, and pretty girls. Nothing was too much trouble. There were gifts as well, including a silver cigarette case I still use. That was from Rumpler, and a right waste of their money.

Every night I took a tart up to my room and put the bed to good use – and then lay staring at the ceiling, missing Karl unbearably.

I hope you're looking after yourself, or rather allowing Henning to look after you…

I shouldn't have put the Chief off going to visit him – if he sees how bad Karl is he won't have him back, no matter what Karl says to the doctors.

That's if the Chief is still alive.

The boss brought his wife to one of the receptions. I kissed her hand and looked into her eyes, and my blood practically clotted with desire.

You lucky bastard. Where did you find her?

She wasn't particularly beautiful – there was just something in her face, in the way she moved. Then her eyes met his, and her face lit with love and joy, and I understood.

I was suddenly afraid for her, and I turned away with a brief, appalling vision of how she would be when the inevitable happened.

Which is better, to love someone so deeply and then lose them, or never to love at all?

I was talking to Ruthke, one of the Technical Commission fellows, when they came to say good night.

"Elise needs to rest," the Chief said, giving her an adoring look. "Her condition."

"Don't fuss, Berti," she said gently, and gave him the most beautiful smile.

Will any woman ever smile at me like that?

"Congratulations," I said.

"Thank you," they replied in unison.

Ruthke rolled his eyes as they left. "Bloody hell. They were a bit soppy."

"He's my CO – tough as they come at the Front. It's quite an eye-opener to see a more human side of him."

"Well, I suppose a fellow's entitled to be happy with a sprog on the way – might be hope for us yet!"

I laughed, slightly uneasily. *I might be a father soon. Let's see, June, nine months – bloody hell, that's March.*

I'll be dead by then, and I don't know whether Maria really is pregnant. I'll worry about all that when I have to.

I went to get more food.

"Hello, Franz."

"Marion! What a lovely surprise! How are you? And how's Helena?"

"We're both all right. She's here as well. We have to eat."

She looked pale and tired, like everyone. Everyone except the rich businessmen and their wives, that is. Wives who would probably despise the girls at these receptions, probably call them immoral, loose, whores.

"So have you eaten?" I asked.

"No, not yet."

"Come on then."

"Is Karl here?" she asked.

"No."

She stared at me, her eyes wide.

I thought he was just a fuck, just a source of nice presents. I didn't realise you care about him.

"He's at home," I said. "I stayed with him last week."

She sighed. "Thank God. I thought you meant – but it would have been in the paper, wouldn't it? He's quite famous now, isn't he, like you. He came to see us last summer, when he was here, after his father died. And then we saw in the paper that he'd been wounded. We thought he'd be here."

"Marion, he's not well enough…"

"Was he very badly wounded?" she asked quietly. "My cousin – his face—"

"It's nothing like that," I said quickly. "He's not disfigured. He's scarred, of course, but not where it shows. He was shot through the chest and he came out of hospital last month."

"And he's at home by himself."

"Yes. Apart from the servants."

"He needs someone to look after him," she said. "And I wouldn't get past the butler."

I could imagine Henning's face if Marion turned up on the doorstep. More to the point, I didn't think Karl would want to see her.

"He's still got those drawings Johnny did," I said.

"Oh, what they were like, those two!" She started laughing.

"I couldn't believe it when he started drawing – and Karl just carried on with me! But you know what he's like."

It was my turn to laugh. "Yes, I do!"

We'd finished eating.

"Would you like another glass of champagne," I said, "or would you like to come to my hotel?"

"I'd love to. I'll just find Helena."

"I don't want both of you. I'm not like Karl."

She smiled. "We tell each other where we're going. It's safer."

I hadn't thought of that. I had guessed what she'd just confirmed to me: that they'd slipped from accepting presents to outright prostitution – but what could they do? As she'd said, they had to eat, and I'd seen what a challenge that presented.

I hope I've got enough money. I haven't had time to go to the bank.

She came back. "Let's get our coats."

"Marion," I said very quietly, "please forgive me if I've got this wrong – but how – what do you find acceptable these days?"

"I won't take money from you, Franz."

"Then I shall start feeling guilty."

"Why?"

"Because while you're with me, you could be…"

"Earning money from someone else?"

"I didn't want to put it like that."

"Of course, you've never been paid – at least I don't suppose you have. I'm having an evening off and it started half an hour ago, when I saw you."

I kissed her in the cab, again and again. I'd almost forgotten what kissing a woman felt like – the last one had been Maria. The tarts never let you kiss them.

I ordered champagne from room service, and it arrived compliments of the Albatros Works.

This is beginning to feel like a feast for the condemned. They can't do too much for us, and at the end we'll all go back and get killed.

I didn't want to think about that. I didn't want to think about anything. I was in a comfortable bedroom with a lovely woman – and one who actually wanted me. That was the only thing that mattered.

She felt wonderful in my arms, her bare skin soft against mine. I blotted out all thought, drowned it in sensation.

Afterwards she lay curled in my arms, her head on my chest, and I realised she was crying.

"What's the matter?" I asked. "Was I that awful?"

"No, of course not! It's just everything. The war. The way we have to live now. I hate it. I hate being a – being paid. It's horrible. I'd forgotten what it was like to do it just because I wanted to. And there's nothing to eat, not usually, and it's so dark and cold at home. And everyone's dead, all the young men we knew…"

"We're not all dead, Marion. I'm still alive, and so's Karl."

"Yes, but—" she broke off.

"But I might not be for much longer? Oh, I'm well aware of that. Karl should be safe, anyway."

"Won't he go back?"

"I don't think so. I hope not, anyway."

"I'll go and see him. The butler will have to let me in if he wants to see me."

I didn't quite know how to put it. "Marion, don't just go there. Send him a cable first."

"Won't he want to see me?"

"He's not himself at present… He's got your address. Wait for him to contact you."

She sighed. "When's it going to end?"

"I wish I knew."

We lay in silence for a long time. I wanted her again, but I wasn't sure if she would feel the same.

Nothing ventured. The worst she can do is walk out.

I slid my hand from her shoulder to her breast, and to my surprise she responded, her lips searching for mine in the darkness.

Some time later she said, "Would you like me to stay all night?"

"Won't Helena worry?"

"No – she knows I'm with you."

I hesitated. The thought of her warmth next to me, and of finding her there when I woke up, was very appealing. But I was overdue for the burning dream, and I didn't want her to see me like that.

"I suppose I'm warmer to sleep with than Helena." I made my voice as warm as I could. I didn't want her to feel rejected.

"How did you know?"

"That show you put on for Karl and me. You were obviously enjoying yourselves. We were – not exactly superfluous, but… extra."

"We've been together ten years," she said. "Since we were eighteen. I've led her a bit of a dance, really. She's not that bothered about men. I think she'd be happier without any of you, but you have the money. I can't decide which I prefer. I just like both. I need both."

"Where's Helena spending the night?"

"In the flat."

"By herself?"

"Yes. You'd rather I left, wouldn't you? Because of her?"

"If I'd been bothered about that I wouldn't have asked you here in the first place. It's better for me if I sleep alone."

Or with Karl, but he's not here…

"You think you're the only man who has nightmares? You all have them. I'm used to it."

"I'd rather have them in private. It's been a lovely evening. I know you don't want money, but Mr Fokker, or Mr AEG, or someone, gave me a rather nice watch—"

"No. It would spoil it."

You must mean that. A watch would be very useful on the black market.

As she was getting dressed, I asked, "Do you know Alfred Friedemann?"

She stiffened. "Why?" Her voice was slightly defensive.

"Just wondered. Say hello from me when you see him."

She looked at me. "So are you one of us, then? I mean, what you and Karl did doesn't always mean – you could just have been experimenting. And you didn't…"

Fuck, I guessed she meant.

"So Alfred is?"

She blushed. "I'll pass on your message if I see him."

After she'd gone I had a long soak in the tub, feeling very sleepy. *Nothing like a good fuck to send a fellow off to sleep,* I thought as I curled up in bed.

It sent me to sleep all right. I had the burning dream and woke screaming and running with sweat. I managed not to be sick, but I was too afraid to go back to sleep. I put the light on, and sat smoking and staring at the walls.

Why is it always exactly the fucking same? Is that what's waiting for me?

Don't be so bloody stupid.

I wish I were with Karl. He'd hold me close and the horrors would retreat, and I'd sleep again, and then we'd wake up together…

'So are you one of us, then?'

Quite a question. Karl's the only man I've ever had sexual thoughts about, but women are so bloody lovely and soft and desirable and I think about them all the bloody time.

Not really 'one of us', then – but doesn't that depend on the definition? And what's Karl? A randy bastard who'll fuck anyone who'll have him, male or female? Or is there more to it?

And there's that connection between us, that deep understanding that I've never had with anyone else.

It was too fucking complicated, and my head was starting to ache from trying to work it out.

Just be happy that you share something extra with your best friend.

The next day it rained in torrents, and most of the flying programme was cancelled.

"Good opportunity for you to go to the photographer," said the Chief.

"I was hoping everyone had forgotten," I said.

"I'm afraid there's no escape. I'll get one of the Technical Commission fellows to take you there."

Bugger it. The last thing I want to do is sit in front of the camera like some bloody stuffed dummy.

We went to Dühren's studio, and although they were very professional it still felt horribly like showing off. The government certainly got the maximum propaganda value out of us all.

I was about to leave when I had a thought. "Did you photograph Leutnant Karl von Leussow last year?"

"I think so. I'll just check... Yes, we did."

"Do you still have the plates?"

"Of course."

"Would it be possible for me to have a print of one of them? He's a good friend of mine and I've got some pictures taken at the airfield, but I'd like a portrait of him as well."

The photographer brought me the plates. *These are bloody good*, I thought as I looked through them.

Karl's calm, self-possessed strength showed in all the pictures, and his eyes looked directly into mine in that way I knew so well.

Difficult to decide... Come on, Franz, make your bloody mind up.

"Could you post it to my parents' home, please? And could you send them a print of one of the ones you've taken of me? I don't mind which. You choose."

"Certainly."

I left feeling that at least I'd got something out of the day. I'd wanted a picture like that for some time, and I knew what Karl would have said if I'd asked him for one.

It was still raining – cold, miserable rain that bounced off the pavements and ran down my neck. I turned my collar up, and tried not to think about Kurt.

"Where to now?" asked Ruthke. He'd waited patiently in the studio, leafing through some old magazines. *Rather dull for you, and you seem to be a decent sort of fellow.*

"Would you like a drink?" I said.

"You bet I would. I hate this fucking weather. Makes my bones ache."

"Let's go to my hotel and have some of Mr Aircraft Builder's free booze."

We sat by the window of the bar, drinking brandy, watching the rain run down the glass. It was starting to get dark, and I was beginning to feel depressed and shaky.

Don't think, Franz.

"What were you doing before this?" I asked. He was wearing a pilot's badge, and his limp was worse than Otto's.

"Same as you. I was an infantry officer before the war. In the middle of '15 I decided that was a mug's game and moved to aviation. Last May I got shot down and had a hell of a crash – it would be quicker to tell you what I *didn't* break – so here I am."

"Do you enjoy it?"

He shrugged. "The technical side's interesting, but I get a bit bored."

"I have a friend who was shot down a couple of months after

you. He's still convalescent and – well, he wants to go back to the Front, but I think he'd be better off with you fellows."

"It doesn't suit everyone—"

We were interrupted by Strauss and Scheich. We all had dinner together, courtesy of Albatros, and finished the evening in my room with a couple of bottles of brandy. I could hear the rain battering on the window, and I turned my back to it and kept on drinking steadily, determined not to think about Kurt, or Anton, or Johnny, or any of the rest of them. I had a bad feeling, and wanted to drown the ghosts.

I succeeded, but the price was waking at five in the morning with a splitting head, a mouth like a piece of dirty carpet, and a feeling of black nausea. I moved my head and the room turned.

Oh, God, I hate flying with a hangover… and tomorrow I have to go back. Shit. Shit, shit, shit.

I'd hoped to bump into Marion or Helena again on my last evening, as I really didn't want to have to pay, but I was unlucky. The tart was quite attractive, and the last German woman I was ever likely to fuck, but I had that empty feeling afterwards.

The trials had three more days to run, but I knew I was needed at the Front.

"Would you like to fly back?" asked the Chief. "LVG have given us a two-seater as a sort of runabout."

"Thank you, sir, I would – but how will you get back?"

"Oh, I'll see if I can pick up a machine for delivery – I've got another five days in Berlin, anyway… I'll be interested to hear how Horstmann's doing as acting CO."

"I'll let you know, sir – I hope I've been useful here."

"You certainly have – how many of them did you fly?"

"Twenty."

"Well done – not bad for six days' work! I'll see you in Flanders, then."

I said goodbye to Ruthke, Strauss and Scheich and loaded my bags into the observer's seat of the LVG. A few minutes later I was airborne, flying west through the freezing air, back to the war and whatever might be waiting for me.

For exclusive discounts on Matador titles,
sign up to our occasional newsletter at
troubador.co.uk/bookshop